FREAKY REAPERS

A MYSTIC CARAVAN MYSTERY BOOK EIGHT

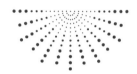

AMANDA M. LEE

WINCHESTERSHAW PUBLICATIONS

PROLOGUE

12 YEARS AGO

*I*t was the end of the world. Or, at least, the end of an era.

That's what I told myself as I stared at the body hanging from one of the antiquated Cass Corridor overpasses. It swayed back and forth in the biting wind. Its open eyes stared back at me. They saw nothing.

I recognized him, of course. *Noble*. That probably wasn't his real name, but it was his street name. He was homeless, like the rest of us, flitting from one part of town to the other. At night, we always ended up here unless there was an ongoing raid or turf war between the rival gangs. It was better to sleep with a group.

Noble was older than us – and a little crazy, if you want to know the truth – but he was a good guy. He was shell-shocked. That's what one of the others said. I think it was Hazy, but he was known for having his head in the clouds so I didn't take what he said to heart. I went to the library once after a shower and a change of clothes. Unlike the others, I always wanted to look my best. I researched certain mental ailments. One of the women behind the help desk happily pitched in.

I didn't need to read her mind to know what she was thinking. She was afraid for me. She didn't know me, didn't know my name was Poet Parker and that I was completely on my own. She didn't know my parents were dead and that I'd fled a foster home that had turned sideways. She did know I was on the street. She recognized that.

1

She wanted to help. She wasn't some do-gooder who got off on helping those less fortunate and then blabbing to everyone who would listen. She sensed something in me. She didn't know that she was sensing it. She believed she simply had strong intuition. It was more than that. She was special. I recognized it in her because I was special, too.

Of course, I was still on the street. A fat lot of good my "specialness" had done for me so far. I planned to turn my ability – I didn't know what else to call it – into a money-making endeavor. I was still trying to figure out how.

Anyway, the woman at the library wanted to help. She offered to buy me lunch and even call someone from the children's services department to get me into a halfway house. I thanked her politely, said I was fine, and didn't take her up on her offer of lunch. The information she provided, however, was illuminating.

PTSD. Post-Traumatic Stress Disorder. After reading only one page on the entry I was certain that's what Noble had. He'd served overseas. He talked about it constantly. He'd left the military before the Gulf War, but thought he should go back for one more tour to serve his country. That turned out to be his mistake.

He was indeed shell-shocked. There was a diagnostic name for what he suffered. He needed help – medication even – but we couldn't provide it, and he wouldn't listen to our recommendations.

So he self-medicated. We always knew where to find him. In the hottest days of summer, he liked to sleep on the beach at Belle Isle. When it wasn't quite as warm, like now, he preferred bunking down in the Corridor. It wasn't as chilly here because the wind was often blunted by the buildings.

It didn't matter now. He was clearly dead. The question was: How did he end up hanging from the overpass?

"What is this?" I demanded, striding forward.

The others were already gathered around the scene, some in awe and others in sadness. I understood their reactions. Seeing Noble hanging from the bridge was surreal … and then some.

"What happened?" I stopped next to Hazy, who seemed lost in his own little world as he stared at the body. His eyes were red-rimmed and I knew he was high. He'd earned his nickname, after all. He was a little older than me – I put his age around twenty – and he'd been on the streets for at least two years. That's all I knew about him other than the fact that he was relatively amiable but pretty much kept to himself.

"Noble is dead," Hazy replied, shaking his head. "I think he killed himself."

I thought of the troubled war veteran and the nights he spent screaming as nightmares chased him. I'd often wondered if he would eventually take his own life. Of course, he also swore he was going to get better and convince his family to take him back. He had hope ... and most people with hope don't commit suicide.

"Are you sure?" I pressed. "He was fine when I saw him earlier. Er ... I guess it was last night. He was fine."

"He's not fine now, is he?" Hazy took a long toke on his homemade pipe. "That is just messed up."

That pretty much summed up the situation. "We need to get him down from there." I started in the direction of the overpass embankment, a wild notion of climbing the hill and somehow finding the strength to cut Noble down flying through my head. A hand shot out of the darkness and grabbed my arm before I could make much headway. "What the ... ?"

I lashed out with my fist out of instinct. It's always wise to punch first and ask questions later. Luckily for me, the man trying to get my attention through the sea of onlookers was used to me throwing punches, and he easily sidestepped my fist.

"Shadow," I muttered, letting out a shaky breath when I saw him. "What are you doing lurking like that?"

Instead of being offended, Shadow looked amused. "Lurking? I see you're still going down to the library once a week and learning everything you can."

The statement wasn't derisive, but it rankled all the same. That library thing was a secret. Only a few people knew. "So what if I am?"

He held his hands up in a placating manner. "I didn't say there was anything wrong with it. I think it's good."

Shadow was a biker who spent most of his time hanging at a bar around the corner. He occasionally came to the area to check on us. He only bothered because we patched him up after a particularly brutal fight outside the bar last year. Someone dumped him in our alley and we decided to see if we could save him. When he came to, he was confused. He was also sore.

He stayed with us for more than a week. That's how long he was in pain. Once he was on his feet again, he made sure to bring us decent food as often as he could manage and he checked on us at least once a day when he was in town. His attitude was vigilant – he constantly warned us if he'd heard rumors about bad dudes hitting the area – and I often thought of him as our knight in shining armor. It didn't hurt that he looked like a model more than a biker. I mean ... he was ridiculously hot. I pegged his age in the twenties, but it was hard to tell.

"I have to get him down." I was adamant as I caught Shadow's heavy gaze. "He can't stay like that. It's not right."

"It's not," Shadow agreed. "But you can't cut him down. The cops will handle it."

I hated the notion of the police being the ones to help Noble. "He belongs to us."

Shadow sighed. "Kid, you're not going to make it out here if you're not careful. You can't spend all your time worrying about others. You have to think about yourself first. You can't help him."

"But ... ."

"No." Shadow was firm as he shook his head. "If you touch the body and the cops decide it's foul play, they might look at you as a suspect. They'll arrest you ... and Poet, you won't do well in prison. You're too soft."

I was positive there was an insult buried under that remark. "I'm not soft."

"You are." His smile turned rueful. "You don't belong out here, kid. You never have."

It wasn't the first time he'd said that to me. I knew it wouldn't be the last. "Well, this is my home. Noble wasn't exactly my friend because he said he hated all of us on a regular basis, but he was still one of us. It's not right to leave him up there. Knowing the cops, it could take them days to get down here."

"I very much doubt it will take that long." Shadow sounded sure of himself. "As for you and your little buddies, get out of here and spend the night some-place else."

"Why should we do that?"

"Because the cops will question you otherwise, and I guarantee Hazy is holding. Groove over there, he's got at least two weapons on him."

I followed his gaze and frowned at the gang leader holding court at the end of the narrow alley. Groove was known for saying little and his ruthless-ness. People claimed he'd killed fifty people. I had no idea if that was true. It was certainly possible. I'd never seen him kill anyone, and he conducted busi-ness in this alley all the time. He let us stay because he said we were harmless and provided a natural cover and alarm should the cops come snooping. Nothing made for a better alert than the homeless scattering at the first hint of a patrol car. But even Groove wasn't ballsy enough to hang around if the cops were going to flood the alley.

"He already looks like he's packing up," I noted.

"That's because he's smart," Shadow said. "You're smart, too. At least most of the time. You need to pack up Hazy and Creek and head out. Maybe go over to Hart Plaza for the night. If you sleep behind those trees to the east you should be out of the elements and away from any cops in the morning."

"I see you've given this some thought," I said dryly.

"Not really. But I think you should get out of here. The cops might try to pin a murder on one of you guys. You know how they are if you're rootless and don't have anyone to stand up for you."

I did indeed know how that often went down. "I don't know where Creek is," I admitted after a beat, chewing my chapped bottom lip as I looked around the alley uncertainly. "She's supposed to meet me here, but she was doing something with Tawny."

Shadow jerked up his head and I didn't miss the expression of fury that momentarily overtook his features. "What is she doing with Tawny?"

A prostitute, Tawny worked the alley most days and made enough to rent a horrific flop two blocks away. It was so bad I thought sleeping on the street was preferable. Tawny always held it over our heads that she had a home, though. It wasn't a great home and she didn't own it, but it was a roof all the same.

Most of us hadn't had a roof over our heads in at least a year.

I shrugged and shrank back at his dark tone. "I don't know," I replied, making a face. "It's not my day to watch her. They said they had business."

"It better not be the business I think it is," Shadow growled. "Creek is too young to start tricking. You tell her I said that."

Creek was my best friend. We were about the same age. She was a few months older, but we had a lot in common. I'd fled a potentially-abusive foster home. She'd fled her home because her mother's boyfriend was starting to look at her in a certain way ... and touch her in an even more inappropriate way. She was tough as iron, but she had a delicate streak. That didn't mean she was opposed to doing what needed to be done.

"I don't think that's her plan – for now," I offered, frowning when my eyes fell on a familiar face. Junk, a local addict, quit using every morning and started again every evening. I gave him credit for his determination. He simply didn't have the wherewithal to go through with it.

Junk stood in the shadow of Noble's body and gazed with slack-jawed awe. "He looks like an angel."

"Oh, geez." Shadow pinched the bridge of his nose and shook his head. "This can't be happening. You guys need to get out of here." He was firm, no-nonsense. "Go over to Hart Plaza. Find Creek, and take Junk and Hazy with you. Get some sleep. By the time you come back tomorrow, Noble will be gone. The police will take care of him."

That sounded unlikely given my dealings with the police. They were hardly ever helpful. "Shouldn't we find a way to get in touch with his family?"

Shadow shook his head. "The police will do that."

"The police won't even try," I countered. "They'll put him in a pauper's grave and forget all about him."

"That sucks, but … it is what it is. There's nothing you can do for him."

"I just can't believe he killed himself." I felt sick to my stomach. "He was fine last night."

"I'm not sure he did kill himself."

Shadow's statement caught me off guard. "W-what?"

"I think it's possible he got in the way of one of Groove's henchmen or something," he replied. "It's also possible he got his hands on some bad heroin or something harder. I can't be sure. I didn't see him. But I don't think he killed himself. The last time I saw him, he was feeling pretty good about things."

That's how I felt. "Do you really think someone killed him?" That was worse than him committing suicide by a long shot. "If someone killed him, the cops won't even look for a murderer, will they?"

Shadow opened his mouth but didn't immediately respond. I could practically see the gears in his mind churning. "Probably not," he acknowledged finally. "There's nothing you can do about that. You can't stay here. You need to find another place to hunker down for the night."

He was adamant about it, so I guess he had reason. "Okay." I jammed my hands in my pockets. "I'll find Creek and take Junk and Hazy with me. This is all kinds of messed up."

"It is," Shadow agreed without hesitation. "You guys need to keep yourselves safe. Stay together … and don't let Creek turn tricks until I have a chance to talk to her. There has to be another way for her to make money."

"She doesn't exactly have a very good skills set," I reminded him. "She didn't even make it through ninth grade. Who's going to hire her?"

"We'll figure it out." Shadow didn't back down, instead making little shooing motions with his hands. "Be careful out there, Poet. Keep your friends close. Things are about to get crazy for a bit. It would be best if you didn't get involved in what's to come. Just … stay clear of it."

"I'll try," I yelled out to Junk and Hazy to get their attention. It wasn't easy because they were both high and easily distracted, but eventually they trudged in the direction I indicated. I glanced back at Shadow when I hit the next street, frowning when I realized his eyes were on Noble. His expression was unreadable.

I was so lost in thought I didn't watch where I was going and barreled into a middle-aged man with salt-and-pepper hair and a curious smile. Out of habit, my hand automatically went for his wallet. I thought it would be an easy lift. If I was lucky, we would be able to get a room at a crappy hotel for the night instead of hunkering down behind Hart Plaza.

Today wasn't my lucky day.

The man's hand shot out and grabbed my wrist before I could escape with his wallet. My eyes went wide as his stern orbs locked with them. I had an excuse on the tip of my tongue, but he didn't allow me to unleash it.

"I see you have sticky fingers, my dear."

The fact that he'd caught me was a small miracle. Almost nobody caught me because I messed with their minds as I was doing the lift, made them think everything was okay despite the theft. This guy obviously hadn't fallen for it, so I redoubled my efforts.

"Magic?" the man noted, his lips twitching. "That's … interesting. What are you?"

I had no idea how to answer the question. "What are you?" I shot back.

"That's a story for the ages." His eyes twinkled. "Are you hungry?"

"I don't turn tricks for food. If that's what you're looking for, you need to search someplace else."

He looked appalled at the suggestion. "I don't want anything from you. I simply want to talk to you."

"Why? You don't know me."

"I don't," he agreed, firmly reclaiming his wallet and returning it to his pocket. "I have a feeling about you. It's quite strong."

"A feeling?" That was the most ridiculous come-on I'd ever heard. "How … awesome."

He ignored the sarcasm. "My name is Maxwell Anderson. Eventually, if I like you, I'll allow you to call me Max. You're not there yet. But you might get there."

"Oh, yeah? Neat-o." I needed to get away from this guy something fierce. He was weird.

"I own Mystic Caravan Circus," he volunteered. "I would like to talk to you about a job."

His con turned interesting, and I was curious to see where it would go. "I don't turn tricks for the circus either."

"That's not what I have in mind." He studied my face for a long time and then tucked my arm through his. "Come along. I'll buy you dinner and you can tell me about yourself. I think we have a lot to discuss."

He was a pushy old thing, but I was hungry. "Okay, but if you try anything, I'll hack your thing off."

Instead of being disgusted, he laughed. "I think we're going to get along famously."

That made one of us.

ONE

PRESENT DAY

*D*etroit.

    I didn't like returning. I hadn't been here in years. The return trips with Mystic Caravan Circus were few and far between, and I was fine with that.

Still, this was my home. Technically. Of course, I didn't think of it that way. The circus was my home now. Max made it my home when he saw something in me that others didn't. Then, the people I met with the circus became my family. I was comfortable traveling now. Being on the road was freeing. If I didn't like my location I only had to wait a week. Then I would be someplace new.

I'd seen most of the continental United States with the circus. I'd broadened my horizons, enhanced my knowledge and learned about being a real person. Being back where it all started, where my journey began, was unnerving.

I don't get nervous, yet I couldn't stop staring out the window. I wouldn't even recognize the faces any longer. A decade can change a person. Still, I expected to find a familiar one on the street corners as we passed. I couldn't stop searching.

My boyfriend Kade Denton was a different story. His eyes were keen, too, as he navigated the Detroit streets. He was out of his element. He wasn't used to a gritty city like this. He grew up in California, for crying out loud. Even their grittiest city couldn't compare to Detroit.

There was nothing in the world comparable to Detroit.

"You look like you're about to hop out of the window and run away," he noted as he frowned at the brake lights igniting in front of us. "What's this?"

I shifted my eyes out the front windshield and shrugged. "Probably an accident ... or maybe road construction. Michigan has the worst roads in the country. There's always road construction."

"The worst roads, huh?" He looked amused. "That's quite a claim."

"It's true. Look it up."

"I just might do that." His hand snaked over the console and rested on top of mine. "Why are you so agitated?"

I'd been expecting the question. That didn't mean I was prepared to answer it. "I'm not agitated."

"I've never seen you this jittery before. It's ... interesting."

I liked the word "jittery" even less than "agitated." My temper was raw today and I had to bite back a hot retort. "I'm not jittery either. I'm just ... taking it all in."

"You grew up here."

"I remember."

"Tell me about it."

Kade is the sensitive sort. I think it comes from being raised by a single mother. She taught him that emotions weren't to be feared. She was gone now. It was her death that spurred Kade to join the circus. At the time, he thought he was merely accepting a lucrative offer from a family friend. It turned out that "friend" was actually his father.

Max, the man who had plucked me from the street and gave me everything I never thought I would have, only recently had the chance to bond with Kade on a familial level. Their relationship was still a work in progress. It was going better than it had been, though, and I was grateful for that.

"Tell you what?" I asked, genuinely curious. "What is it that you want to hear?"

Kade arched an eyebrow. He obviously recognized the edge to my voice. "Only what you're comfortable with. Talking about it might make you feel better."

"I don't feel bad."

He heaved out a sigh. I recognized it for what it was. He was getting tired of my attitude. I didn't blame him. "Poet," he started on an exasperated note. He didn't follow it up with anything, so I merely stared at him.

"This relationship thing we both seem to enjoy so much only works when we confide in one another," he said finally, his tone even and measured. "I thought we agreed to open up to one another so there would be no secrets."

Now he was playing dirty. "I'm not keeping anything from you."

"Except the reason you're so upset."

"I'm not upset!" I practically exploded. Only the seatbelt kept me from hopping on top of the dashboard. It was at that moment that I realized he was right. I was completely out of control. Taking out my anxiety on him was not only unfair, it was ridiculous. I had to get it together. "Fine. It's just ... I keep thinking I'm going to see them."

"Who are you talking about?" He shot me a look before turning back to the road. "Your parents died when you were a kid. I didn't think you were fond of any of your foster families. Are you afraid of seeing the people who took care of you?"

"No. Although ... I really don't want to see them either." That was the truth.

"Did they hurt you?" His gaze was dark, his knuckles white as he tightened his grip on the steering wheel.

"No. I ran away before anything like that could happen," I reassured him. "I'm not keeping some deep, dark secret that would crush your soul. You don't have to worry about that."

"I can't help but worry. I love you."

Even though I was determined to remain in a foul mood, my lips curved upward, unbidden. That was a new thing. Admitting we loved each other, I mean. It was only recently, at a stop in northern Lower Michigan, that we'd professed our feelings. It still felt like a novelty, which wasn't entirely bad.

"And I love you." Just saying the words released some of the pressure building in my chest. "I don't mean to be a pill. It's just ... this place isn't exactly full of good memories."

"That's why I want you to talk about it. If you tell me, the memories won't be haunting shadows in the back of your mind any longer. You'll be able to let them go and move forward. I want that more than anything for you."

He wasn't the only one. Oh, hell, it was worth a shot. "When I ran away, I was in a home in the suburbs. We're talking about five miles north of Detroit. It wasn't like this."

Kade grimaced as he moved forward a few feet, his eyes immediately going to the abandoned building to his left. "I certainly hope not."

His distaste made me feel better for some reason. "It's not so bad when you're used to it. I mean ... the city has its struggles. I've read a few articles online. It's seeing a revitalization of sorts."

"Oh, yeah?" He didn't look convinced. "There's a prostitute over there trying to solicit the revitalized mailman."

I followed his finger and shrugged. "She has to make a living."

Realization dawned on his handsome features and a bit of color drained from his face. "Did you have to ... ?" He couldn't even finish the sentence.

I leveled a hard gaze on him. "How would that make you feel?"

It wasn't a denial, which is what he wanted. "It would make me feel really sad," he said on a breathy exhale. "It wouldn't change how I feel about you. Nothing will. It's just ... I never really thought about it. You were a minor making your way on the streets. How did you survive?"

It was a fair question. It's the first everyone asks. "I didn't engage in the life," I replied after a beat. "Not *that* life, at least. I knew a few people who had no choice. Surviving out here isn't easy. People get broken down by the system and they find themselves doing things they wouldn't normally do. For me, that came in the form of picking Max's pocket."

"You've mentioned that before." Kade's smile was charming. "But I've never heard the story in full detail."

Telling him the story of Max was better than telling him the other stuff, so I acquiesced. "It was a weird day. A guy I knew had just died and we were warned away from the alley we slept in."

He frowned. "You were sleeping in an alley?"

I was amused despite myself. "How did you imagine living on the street worked? Did you think I checked into a hotel every night? If so, then you're Hollywood-ing it up. We slept on the street ... or in parks ... or sometimes in abandoned buildings, but that brought on a different set of problems."

"What sort of problems?"

Internally, I sighed. It appeared we were going to get into this after all. "The drug dealers used the buildings for buys. The prostitutes used the buildings for tricks. The bangers used the buildings for merchandise exchanges.

"If you were lucky, you could find a building that no one wanted to do business in, but those were usually so run down that you didn't want to risk staying in them. The floors had gaping holes, rats had built nests and the druggies were likely to take them over.

"There were entire buildings in the Cass Corridor that had hundreds of druggies taking up real estate inside ... and when they overdosed and died, they were just moved to a corner and forgotten about," I continued, my mind traveling back. "The people I hung with were generally young, so it wasn't safe to stay in those buildings. If you did, you risked rape and a few other things, because people got so high they forgot who and what they were."

Kade's mouth dropped open. "And you thought it was better to stay on the street than in a foster home? Why didn't you report what you suspected and get a different placement?"

"It doesn't work that way. They need actionable information. I didn't have it. I couldn't exactly tell them I saw flashes from the guy's mind with my telepathic powers. They would've put me in a hospital ... and believe it or not, those are actually worse."

"Oh." He looked sick to his stomach. We were still stuck in traffic, so keeping up the conversation seemed the only viable option. He wouldn't simply let me drop it now anyway.

"It wasn't all bad," I reassured him. "No, really. I had a small group of friends. I was even tight with another girl. Creek. She was ... not meant for street life. She couldn't go back home because her mother's boyfriend was a rapist. Her mother chose to believe the boyfriend over her daughter, so Creek made a break for it.

"When she first showed up, she had big plans," I continued. "She thought she would be able to get a decent job at a Starbucks or something. She was convinced it wouldn't be difficult. She didn't realize that nobody wants to hire someone who doesn't have a permanent address. We all went together to get a post office box at one point, but that didn't help."

"What happened to her?"

That was a good question. "I don't know. I was looking for her the night I met Max. There was a lot going on. Noble was dead and there was a question about whether it was suicide or murder. Shadow warned me to stay away from the alley for at least that night because he was convinced the cops would consider us suspects."

"Shadow? Noble? These can't be real names."

"Most people on the street don't use their real names," I replied. "The general rule is that you pick a name that fits your personality."

"You named yourself?"

"Yes."

"What was your name?"

"Poet. No one realized it was my real name. They thought I chose it because I was always jotting down ideas and stuff in a notebook. They assumed it was poetry. In reality, it was my plan for getting out. I couldn't tell them that, because it's considered bad luck to give voice to future hopes and dreams."

"Why is that?"

I shrugged. I honestly didn't have the answer. "The street has rules. You either learn them fast or get used up. I had an advantage. I could read people's minds — even though I was still figuring out how all that worked — and it was easier for me than others.

"Anyway, Shadow hung with a biker gang," I said, returning to the story. It was best to get it over with now. "They were pretty rough guys and almost killed him at one point. We found him and nursed him back to health. I could tell he was a good guy under all that leather. Plus, well, he was really hot."

Kade's eyes turned suspicious. "You had a crush on a biker dude?"

"What can I say? The heart wants what the heart wants," I teased, poking his side. "He wasn't a bad guy. After he got better, he was always checking in on us. He would bring us food and toiletries. He didn't want the other bikers to know, because he thought it would make him look weak. We kept his secret, and he gave us a helping hand when he could."

"And Noble?"

"He was a Gulf War vet who had a few quirks. He was a drunk, which didn't help matters, but he had legitimate mental problems. Someone should've been available to help him. I realize that now. Then, he was just a funny guy we often checked on.

"He was hanging from an overpass when I last saw him," I continued. "I don't know if he did it to himself or not, but at the time I didn't think it was possible because he wasn't suicidal in the days leading up to his death. Now I realize that doesn't necessarily mean anything.

"Shadow warned us that one of the drug dealers could've taken him out. He was quiet, so he often saw things we missed. It's possible he was right. Groove was there that night, I remember. He was the gangbanger who ran that particular turf. He never gave us grief, because he liked to use us for cover.

"I remember that Creek was off with Tawny, a prostitute who was teaching her the tricks of the trade," I said, my mind working fast as I embraced the memory for the first time in a long while. "I was on my way to find her — I had Junk and Hazy with me — and I ran into Max. I picked his pocket out of habit. I had other things on my mind at the time.

"I ran things a specific way back then," I explained. "I would use my powers to make my marks believe nothing was happening. That's what I was doing with Max when he caught me. He seemed amused more than anything else. He was also intrigued. He invited me for a meal, which I quickly turned down, but he was persistent."

"Did you leave with him that night?"

"Essentially. I had dinner with him, listened to his spiel, and then said I needed time to think. I went looking for Creek but I didn't find her. I went back to the alley to take a look and found Shadow was right. The area was crawling with cops. They were questioning Groove when I made my decision, and he was pointing the finger at street kids who often stayed in the alley.

"The thing is, I didn't want to end up like Tawny and I thought that was a legitimate possibility if I didn't catch a break," I continued. "I also didn't want to end up like Noble. That was another possibility. If I wanted a chance to break from the cycle, I had to find a way out. Max was offering me a way out.

"Sure, he could've been a pervert walling off his mind so I couldn't read it, but I had a good feeling about him. The idea of joining the circus was kind of fun. I figured if it didn't work out I could always return ... or find a warmer climate to live in. That's a constant dream on the street, because the winters are brutal."

"I can't believe you lived like that," Kade noted. "That's just not how I see you."

"I'm not the same person I was. Max changed things for me. Then Luke changed them even more. And you, well, you changed them a lot, too. I wouldn't even recognize the girl I was if she was standing right in front of me."

"What about your friends? I mean ... did you say goodbye to them?"

"I said goodbye to Junk and Hazy because they were the only ones I could find. Shadow was in the biker bar and I couldn't risk it. I left a letter for Creek and Shadow with Junk, but I'm not sure they ever got it. Heck, I'm not sure if Creek ever came back to find me. She might've moved on."

"Or something might've happened to her," he surmised. "You said her life was going a certain way. It's probably best that you got out when you did."

I couldn't argue with that. "Yeah. But I can't help but wonder if they're still here. When I think about them, they're still kids and young adults. I'm not sure any of them had the wherewithal to get out."

"You did." He squeezed my hand. "That's the most important thing. You got out and you're here with me. You don't have to dwell on the past when the future looks so bright. You don't have to hide yourself away from me either. If you feel nervous and agitated, tell me. We can talk about anything."

The words warmed me all over. "Thanks. I guess I was more amped than I realized."

"Just a little."

"I'm okay now." I mostly meant it. "It's weird being back."

"I can see that."

TWO

*I*t took us a full hour longer than it should have to reach the fairgrounds. We were being lodged on the former Michigan state fairgrounds, an area in downtown Detroit that featured interesting buildings and green space plopped down in the middle of an urban jungle. The grass and foliage was something of a luxury in an industrial city that was as old as Detroit.

"This isn't so bad," Kade noted as we exited his truck. He lifted his arms over his head and stretched, his back popping a few times as he sent me a slow grin. "I was expecting a lot worse."

"That's because you believe what the media has to say about Detroit," I countered. "It's not as bad as you think. It probably couldn't be as bad as you think. There are pockets of revitalization."

"So you said. Twice now. What kind of revitalization? My understanding is that this place is practically abandoned now. I heard Max talking about it before we left Hemlock Cove yesterday."

My heart did a little somersault at the mention of Hemlock Cove. I'd been dubious when we first arrived in the small hamlet. I believed the town too small to contain the big personalities we traveled with. I'd been wrong. The town had even bigger personalities, and I'd found a sense of calm there that I hadn't known in many other places. "We'll have to go back for a visit one day. I liked it there."

"I agree." His grin was flirty. "That's the place we first said 'I love you' ... without being able to blame it on a drunken slip, that is. It definitely deserves another visit. I think we should wait until just the two of us can go. It's not that I'm not fond of our co-workers, but we sometimes need quiet time, and I think Hemlock Cove is the perfect place to be quiet."

"Good point. We'll work in a visit when we can."

"We definitely will." He slipped his arm around my shoulders and kissed my temple as he looked over the area. "So ... where should we set up?"

The Michigan state fairgrounds differed from our other locations. The property housed numerous buildings, all of which were empty. I wasn't sure positioning our trailers too close to those buildings was a good idea. "I think they sent a map with a spot circled on it," I noted, moving to search my bag, which rested on the floor of the truck. "Let's see what we've got."

While I rummaged for the map, my best friend Luke appeared at Kade's side. His gaze was dubious as he looked at the neighborhood across the road, but he made a big show of shuttering his emotions when I focused on him.

"This is nice," he enthused. "I mean ... it's really nice. I think it's going to be a great visit."

I drew my eyebrows together. "You're not just saying that because you think you'll hurt my feelings if you tell the truth?"

"Of course not."

I waited. I'd known Luke most of my adult life. I could tell when he was lying. More importantly, he knew I could tell.

"Fine," he said finally, blowing out a sigh. "It's not good. I don't like this place at all. I mean ... there's a cemetery across the road."

"There is?" Kade craned his neck to look in the direction Luke gestured. He'd obviously missed that tidbit when we first pulled in. "You're right. Eternal Sunshine Cemetery. Weird name for a cemetery, huh?"

I'd heard worse. "People try to make death cheery, so they come up with ridiculous names," I volunteered. "It doesn't make anyone feel better about losing a loved one, but it makes the developers feel as if they're doing something important. I think they should just be named things like 'Plant Your Dead Here' and be done with it."

"I can see your head is in a good place," Luke drawled, shaking his head. "Are you anxious about being here?"

"No." It was an automatic answer and I pinned Kade with a pointed look to make sure he didn't contradict me. "I'm not anxious in the least."

"She's not," Kade agreed. "She's been calm and pleasant the entire drive."

Instead of being satisfied with the answer, Luke snorted. "Oh, please. I don't know who you're trying to fool with that load of crap. Who has known Poet longer than anyone?"

"Max," I answered without hesitation.

Luke ignored my one-word answer. "That's right. Me. I'm her best friend. I can just imagine how she was during the drive. Why do you think I insisted she ride with you?"

Kade made an exaggerated face that caused me to chuckle. It felt good to laugh, which helped alleviate even more of the stress that I'd been carrying.

"You didn't insist on riding with me," Kade countered. "You tried to trick her into riding with you. It was only six hours ago. Do you think I've forgotten that fast?"

Luke's stare was withering. "You're imagining things. That's not what happened at all."

My memory coincided with Kade's, but I saw no reason to start an unnecessary fight. "It doesn't matter," I offered. "I'm fine. You don't have to worry about me. Either of you."

"Did she tell you the story of the ruffians she used to live with down here?" Luke queried. "She told me the tale not long after we met. I still have nightmares."

"She told me how she met Max," Kade volunteered. "That sounds like a mildly funny story. I bet he was surprised someone was ballsy enough to go against him in the magic department."

"I think that's probably true," Luke agreed. "When he returned to the circus grounds that night, he said he'd found a new performer and she would be joining us the next day. I didn't find out until after the fact that Poet hadn't agreed to anything of the sort ... at least not yet. She told me a few weeks later and seemed in awe that Max was powerful enough to see the future."

I was sheepish when Kade slid his eyes to me. "At that point, I had no formal training when it came to magic. It was something I'd hid for a very long time. Max told me it was nothing to be ashamed of. He helped me learn thereafter ... something I'm profoundly grateful for."

"Me, too." Kade squeezed me tight against his side. "I mean ... think about it. What are the odds that Max would be walking down the alley at the exact moment you were leaving it? What if you hadn't tried to pick his pocket? He would've just carried on without talking to you. We never would've met."

I hadn't looked about it that way before. "Life is a series of small events that lead to larger ones," I noted. "It's weird to think about, but there it is."

"It's definitely weird to think about," Kade agreed.

We lapsed into silence for a moment, the three of us content just to stand there and think about what could've been. Then our resident lamia, Raven Marko, completely ruined the moment.

"If you're done lazing about, can we figure out what's going on here?" she challenged, her long silver hair pulled back in a loose bun. She didn't look happy. I wasn't alarmed by her expression, though, because she never looked happy. "I would like to have the basic layout complete before dark. I don't think this hellhole is the sort of place you want to run around in after dark."

I scowled. "We're working on it," I snapped. "Just ... hold your horses."

"Scales," Luke corrected. "She has scales, not horses."

Raven ignored him. "Work faster," she ordered. "I don't have all day."

"Yeah, yeah, yeah."

THE FESTIVAL ORGANIZER, Larry Wilcox, arrived and directed us to the location where we were supposed to set up. It was on a corner parcel that opened us up to danger from every direction. Generally we have woods on at least one side — sometimes even three — and that makes designing protection easy.

That's not how things would be on this trip.

"Will this work for your needs?" Larry asked, his eyes bouncing around the group until they fell on Kade. He must've decided he was in charge, because he directed his full attention in Kade's direction and puffed out his chest. "I was told this would be fine by some woman I talked to on the phone."

This was hardly the first time I'd been discarded as an authority figure. It grated all the same. "I was the woman you talked to on the phone," I volunteered.

"That's lovely." Larry's smile was indulgent. "Are you his secretary?" He pointed at Kade.

"No, I'm second-in-command at Mystic Caravan," I replied, bristling. "I handle all the bookings."

"Does that put you in command?" Larry remained fixated on Kade, allowing Luke and I to make faces behind his back without risking notice.

"I'm head of security," Kade replied. "Poet is my boss."

"Really?" Larry appeared flabbergasted by the news. "That is ... interesting."

"Yes, because women in Detroit aren't allowed positions of power," Raven drawled, making a face. "This is the corner we're staying in, right?" Her eyes were on me. "If so, I suggest putting the Midway on the Woodward side and clown row along Eight Mile. I've heard enough about that street, so I think that's the best set-up for our particular needs."

I had to bite back a laugh. "This isn't the same part of Eight Mile you saw in that Eminem movie," I offered. "But I'm fine with that configuration. That will leave the entrance close to the parking lot, which is for the best."

"I agree." Raven offered Larry a snide curtsy before slipping behind me. "We need to put the dreamcatcher up as soon as night falls," she whispered so only I could hear. "This area isn't safe ... for more reasons than one."

I knew what she was talking about. She was worried about crime from our human neighbors for a change rather than paranormal interlopers. The dreamcatcher was a magical net that drew in evil paranormals and humans alike. It helped protect us. Even though I wasn't keen on her knee-jerk reaction regarding the area, I understood what she was saying. "Absolutely." I smiled at her so Larry wouldn't pick up on any strife. "Get the trailers up as soon as possible. Then we'll have dinner and go from there."

"Aye, aye, Captain." She saluted me and then cast some serious side eye in Larry's direction. "Good day, sir."

I held it together despite Raven's show, but Luke wasn't as professional. His shoulders shook with silent laughter as Kade fixed the festival manager with a tight smile.

"Is there anything else we need to know about the area?" Kade asked. "Do you have any specific requests?"

"The area is fairly safe," Larry replied, seemingly oblivious to the silent conversations sparking all around him. "Some of the local kids occasionally party in the cemetery. If you hear them in there, don't hesitate to call the police."

"Of course," Kade said congenially.

"There isn't a big transient population in the area. They seem to congregate in the Cass Corridor. If you see anyone who looks homeless you're also supposed to call the police. We're trying to keep this place clean."

I frowned. "How do you tell if someone is homeless just by looking at them?"

"Oh, you can tell." Larry's nod was knowing. "If you can't tell by sight alone, get close enough to smell them. Homeless people don't shower. It's horrible."

Sensing trouble, Kade moved his arm around my back. "We'll keep an eye out," he said, anchoring me tight to his side. "Is there anything else?"

"Just know that I don't want any carrying on," Larry replied. "I don't know if you guys do crazy rituals ... or have clowns running around willy-nilly ...

but I would prefer you not draw attention from the neighbors or police. Can you handle that?"

Kade's smile never wavered. "I believe we can manage that."

"Great. Then we won't have a problem."

I had serious doubts that was true, but I decided to keep them to myself. At least for now.

DINNER WAS A CASUAL AFFAIR. We barbecued hamburgers and hot dogs, limiting side dishes to pasta and potato salad. Raven's suggestion that we erect the dreamcatcher early had become a priority. In just a few hours, I'd noticed we were garnering unwanted attention from the people who lived in the area. That was on top of the group of men hanging at the corner across the road, resting their backs against the cemetery wall. They watched us with a mixture of fascination and enthusiasm. They didn't look like the family-friendly-fun sort.

"We need to go in small groups," I announced as we gathered around the picnic tables after dinner. The dishes had been washed and put away. All that was left was securing our borders. "I don't think anyone should be alone for this."

"Speak for yourself," Naida groused. She was our water pixie and she was clearly agitated by the lack of lakes in our immediate area. "I'm not afraid of those little punks across the road."

"Well, that's great for you," I said. "But if you go alone you'll draw attention. That's another reason for the groups. We don't want people asking what we're doing. We simply want them to think we're wandering around as couples or small groups of friends. It's the easiest way to avoid detection."

"Poet is right," Raven interjected. "We have to be careful not to draw attention. These neighborhoods are thick with dealers and druggies. I'm pretty sure those guys across the street are even worse. If they think we have something worth taking — even if it's magic — they'll come for us.

"I'm not worried about them being able to harm us," she continued. "We can easily take them. The thing is, I don't want them to even try. Right now they think we're circus freaks and they're merely curious. We need to keep it that way."

"How do you want us to break up?" Dolph, our strongman, asked. He was somber and ready for action, which I appreciated.

"You and Nixie take that way," I ordered, gesturing toward one side of the parking lot. "Nellie, you and Naida take the other side of the parking lot. Make sure the wards are tight."

Nixie and Naida are sisters, but they are complete opposites in temperament. Nixie almost looked excited for a new adventure. As for Nellie, our bearded lady was really a male dwarf from another dimension. He simply enjoyed cross-dressing. He was also good with an ax. His appearance alone would be enough to dissuade looky-loos.

"No problem." Nellie nodded his approval.

"Raven, you and Percival should take the Eight Mile corridor. Take Seth with you."

Raven made a face. "Why do I need an extra bodyguard?"

"The corridor isn't exactly safe," I replied. "An attack could come from that direction. And no offense to Percival, but he won't frighten anyone. Seth looks like a legitimate threat. You are the real threat, but I'd rather not throw out our magic if we can help it."

"Fine." Raven looked resigned. "I guess that leaves you, Kade and Luke with the cemetery side."

"Yup. Kade and Luke should dissuade those idiots hanging on the corner from doing anything stupid. We need to work fast."

WE MADE AN INTERESTING THREESOME.

Kade and Luke walked in front of me, carrying on inane conversation about Detroit sports teams and how bad they were. They acted as cover for me as I muttered curses and wards, and used my magic to draw an endless series of lines to form the dreamcatcher.

Raven and I had designed it together. Along with Naida and Nixie, we erected it at every stop. It kept us safe and allowed us to fulfill our real purpose, which happened to be eradicating dangerous monsters. Nobody outside of our tight circle knew that.

I worked fast. I was an old hand at working the magic. I could do it from memory. It seemed Naida, Nixie and Raven were doing the same, because I could see the ethereal lines of the dreamcatcher — only a paranormal being could recognize them — strengthening in record time.

By the time I'd finished, I was tired. I'd expended a lot of magic in a short amount of time. I was ready for a good night's sleep and some quiet time with Kade. When I lifted my head to tell them I was finished — opting to wait until they were done talking about the Red Wings' former greatness — I was almost jolted out of my shoes when my gaze locked with that of a woman across the road.

I wasn't sure when she had arrived. It wasn't even clear where she came from. I was, however, certain I'd met her before.

"Tawny," I muttered on an exhale, my mind briefly clouding. I couldn't believe it was her. After all these years, all the miles I'd traveled, my past really had caught up with me. I wasn't sure there ever was a true escape.

3

THREE

A blaring horn drew my attention to where the men were standing in front of the cemetery. Several of them were out in the middle of the road now, taunting cars as they passed and generally making a nuisance of themselves. When I turned back to where Tawny had stood, she was gone.

I spent a long time scanning the street to see if I could find her. It was possible she'd only changed her location. It was a fruitless endeavor. If she really had been there – and I was starting to have doubts – she was gone now.

"Is something wrong?" Kade asked, rubbing his knuckles along my spine as he stared at the spot that had caught my attention. "Did you see something?"

That was the question. "I thought I saw something," I said finally. "I think my mind was playing tricks on me. There's obviously nothing there."

He slid me a sidelong look. "Are you sure?"

I forced a smile for his benefit. "Yeah. I might be a little haunted right now. It will pass."

He slipped his arm around my waist and tugged me to him. "I guess it's good I like my women haunted."

His reaction was charming, and it allowed some of the agitation hanging over me to drop away. "I don't understand why all men don't chase after haunted women. They're much more interesting."

He smacked a loud kiss against my lips as Luke rolled his eyes. "I agree. How about I take my interesting woman over to the fire and get comfortable for a few hours? I would like to keep my eyes on things for a little bit and put off going to bed. Just to be on the safe side, I mean."

He wouldn't come right out and say it. That wasn't his way. The neighborhood made him nervous. Sadly, I had news for him. Compared to the streets of certain Detroit neighborhoods – including the Cass Corridor – this area was actually peaceful. It felt relatively safe, too. That was the last thing he would want to hear, though, because he'd already convinced himself we were in a bad area. "A fire sounds great." Briefly, my eyes flitted to Luke. He was still watching the men on the street. His expression was hard to read, but I felt waves of annoyance and suspicion washing off him. He wasn't thrilled with the locals either. "Come on, Luke." I kept my voice even as I grabbed his arm. I didn't want him deciding he needed to play with our new friends. That would just get ugly. "Let's have a fire. You can tell fun stories and eat s'mores."

His lips curved mischievously. "Who doesn't love talking about me and eating s'mores?"

No one I wanted to associate with.

IT WAS ALMOST TEN BEFORE WE decided to call it a night. Nellie and Dolph doused the fire as the members of our group dispersed to their trailers. Raven and Percival were the first to retire, but since everyone recognized they were obviously going to play weird clown-and-chaps games, no one said anything when they departed.

As for the rest of us, we would need to start early to get everything done. That meant a late night was a bad idea. No one put up a fuss, so it was obvious they agreed. Kade and I were the last standing as we double-checked to make sure the fire was out and slowly walked to our trailer.

"Are you still haunted?" he asked, his voice low.

I shrugged, unsure what answer he sought. It was entirely possible that he was trying to be romantic and wanted me to say yes so we could play our own set of games once inside our trailer. Or, he could be genuinely concerned. I was tired enough that I was having trouble deciphering his reaction.

And then it didn't matter.

A scream so bloodcurdling it caused the hair on the back of my neck to stand on end tore through the night, causing me to snap my eyes toward the cemetery.

"What was that?" Kade asked, readjusting his stance. He looked ready for action … and yet dubious all the same. "Do you think they're trying to coax us away from the safety of the dreamcatcher so they can attack us?"

He was overthinking it. I couldn't really blame him. This wasn't the sort of environment he was used to, and keeping everyone safe was his responsibility.

"I think it's someone in the cemetery." I moved closer to the property line and peered into the gloom. Unbidden, an image of Tawny floated through my mind. What if she was the one in trouble? What if she really had been there and didn't disappear of her own volition? "We need to go over there."

Kade didn't offer up a word of argument. He once told me that he trusted my instincts above all else and didn't think they would lead us astray. True, at the time he'd been trying to romance me and we were saying schmaltzy things to one another to see how much we could make the other laugh. Still, the statement felt true then ... and he was continuously ready to prove it.

"Okay. Stick close to me. I don't want us getting separated."

I couldn't agree more.

Traffic was practically nonexistent this late at night, so it wasn't difficult to jog across the road. The men who had been holding court earlier were gone, and I couldn't help but wonder if they were responsible for whatever was happening beyond Eternal Sunshine's fences.

There were five of them. I'd counted earlier. Kade and I would have no problem taking five of them. Er, well, at least if they weren't paranormal. If they had gifts, it might be more difficult. As the son of a half-mage, Kade was still growing into his powers. He wasn't comfortable using them most of the time and insisted he needed more practice. I thought the best way to practice was throwing him into the middle of a battle to see how he reacted.

He respectfully disagreed.

We were flying high on love and gooeyness these days, so we didn't push things too far.

"Which way do you think?" Kade's eyes scanned left to right once we were beyond the wall. It was dark, but the location of the cemetery – so close to busy areas – meant there was a decent amount of ambient light.

Slowly, I raised my finger and pointed to the right. "I think it's that way."

As if to prove me correct, another scream ripped the air, this one much closer.

"You stick close to me," Kade repeated, breaking into a jog. "There's something off about this situation."

He wasn't wrong. Screams in the middle of a cemetery rarely led to good news.

I sensed a presence before I saw it. When we crested a hill, we found ourselves surrounded by old mausoleums. This part of the graveyard reminded me more of a New Orleans cemetery. It was clear the graves here belonged to wealthier individuals.

"Where … ?" I didn't get a chance to finish the sentence. Another scream assailed my ears, causing me to look to the right.

A woman in a white dress – no, seriously – raced through the cemetery. She had long black hair and unnaturally pale skin. Her eyes were dark, almost onyx, and she wailed as she tried to evade the man following her.

Kade instinctively moved to help her, his features ashen, but I grabbed his arm before he could intercede. I understood what was going down … and it wasn't good. It was, however, necessary.

"Don't."

Kade widened his eyes as he looked at me. "He's going to kill her. He's carrying a freaking sword."

I hadn't missed the sword. On the contrary, it was one of the first things I'd seen. "Of course he's carrying a sword," I replied dryly. "That's one of the only ways to kill her."

"What?" Kade's eyebrows practically flew off his forehead. "You're just going to sit back and let him kill her?"

"As a matter of fact, I am."

It didn't take the man long to back the woman into a corner. His dark hair gleamed under the moonlight and his eyes – which seemed an odd purple color – were harsh and pitiless as he stared down the woman.

"You shouldn't have stayed after you killed him," the man intoned. His smirk told me he was enjoying himself, which set my teeth on edge. "You were greedy and wanted the soul. You should've run. Your kind isn't known for its intelligence, is it?"

"What does he mean?" Kade queried. "What is she?"

I opened my mouth to answer, but the man picked that moment to attack. He swiped in a broad arc the blade of the sword – which looked to be genuine silver – cutting through the woman's chest and causing her to let loose an unearthly scream. It sounded as if a coven of witches were about to be burned.

"Are you sure we shouldn't do anything?" Kade wasn't the sort to stand on the sidelines and do nothing when a woman was being slaughtered. His hands were clenched into fists at his sides as he watched the man rear back. "This is it."

I pressed my hand to his back to reassure him. "She's not human."

Despite the woman's best efforts, she couldn't hold off the flurry of sword slashes. The man overpowered her within seconds and for the coup de grace severed her head with a flourish.

"Oh, geez," Kade muttered.

Instead of her body dropping to the ground, glittering dust filled the air as the creature emitted one final anguished scream – even as her head detached – before ceasing to be.

Absolute silence filled the cemetery after that. Kade was the first to recover.

His mouth dropped open and his breathing turned into gasps. "What was that? Was that a vampire? Vampires turn into dust, right?"

It was the same series of questions he'd asked before, although I hadn't answered then. Not really. "It wasn't a vampire." I focused on the man, who didn't appear bothered in the least to catch us watching him. "Who are you?"

His grin was cheeky. "Who are you? Wait, don't tell me. Are you a stripper? You've kind of got that look about you."

Kade was recovered enough to take offense at the remark. "She is not a stripper ... and don't you look at her that way." He extended a warning finger, which the man seemed to accept with a good-natured shrug.

"It doesn't matter who I am," he replied, returning my gaze. He looked as if he wanted to ask a question, as if he had suspicions of his own, but he clearly thought better of pressing me. "I should probably be going. All that screaming is going to draw a crowd."

"You can't just leave without telling us who you are," Kade argued, planting his hands on his hips. "I want to know what that thing was."

"A banshee," I answered automatically, unfurling my magic and stretching it toward the stranger's head. It wasn't difficult to get inside. He was supernatural, but not magically powerful. His mind was open ... and apparently he thought about sex and food nonstop. "Did you really have Mexican and ice cream for dinner?" I blurted out the question before I thought better of it. "I mean ... that's a weird combination."

The man cocked an eyebrow. "How could you possibly know that?"

I didn't have an answer for him. "If you're not sharing information, we're certainly not."

"That's a shame." He looked me up and down, his grin widening. "You look interesting. You're a little dressed down for my normal taste but I'm willing to make an exception."

"She's already spoken for," Kade snapped, his arm snaking around my waist as he puffed out his chest. "Don't look at her that way."

Under different circumstances I would've laughed, but I couldn't shake the feeling that we'd just witnessed something important. I wanted to know more about it. "Do you have many banshees around here? I thought they were more of a West Coast thing."

"They've been popping up," the man replied, frowning when he looked in the direction we'd come from. "Uh-oh."

I looked over my shoulder, my heart sinking when the familiar blue and red flash of police lights brightened the night air. "They must have heard the scream."

"I'm guessing that's the case," the man agreed. "We should run. They'll never catch us."

That sounded like a horrible idea. "We're staying at the fairgrounds across the road. It won't be hard for them to catch us."

He didn't look sympathetic. "I believe that falls under 'your problem' on the list of things I don't care about."

He was a smug pain in the ass. "If you run, I'll describe you and say you were chasing a woman around the cemetery with a sword. They'll check cameras for you."

He sighed. "I can't believe you're a tattletale. You're way too hot to be a tattletale."

"Try me."

He frowned, and then crossed his arms over his chest and jutted out his lower lip. His distaste for what was happening was obvious, but he must have read the stubborn tilt of my head correctly because he wisely refrained from fleeing.

"You remind me of my sister," he said after a moment.

"She must be fantastic," I drawled.

"I guess it all depends on the direction you're coming from. What are you going to say to the cops, by the way? I need to know which lie to spin."

I shook my head. "Just shut up and let me do the talking. I've got everything under control."

"Yup. That's something my sister would say."

I kind of wanted to meet his sister.

THE COPS SEEMED confused by my explanation of what had happened.

"I'm sorry. My boyfriend and I were looking through the cemetery – the mausoleums are so pretty I couldn't resist – and I accidentally tripped and screamed. He had to catch me so I didn't bash my head in on one of the benches."

The uniformed officer closest to me blinked several times. "That's it?"

"That's it," I confirmed. "We're staying at the fairgrounds across the way. I'm Poet Parker. I'm second in command at Mystic Caravan Circus."

"Ma'am." The uniform tipped his hat and then looked to his partner.

That allowed me to focus on the stranger, who gave me a silent hand clap and a smug smile when nobody was looking in his direction. I couldn't wait to get him alone and wipe that smile off his face.

"You should be careful," the uniform said finally. "A cemetery isn't the place to play games ... even if they're romantic games." His eyes were on Kade when he said the words, causing me to bite the inside of my cheek to keep from laughing.

"You have my word," Kade reassured him. "We won't play games here again."

"That's all I ask." The officers turned to leave but pulled up short when another man joined the group. This one was dressed in jeans and a simple black shirt ... and he looked tired more than entertained.

"What's going on here?" the new man asked.

"Detective Taylor, we didn't know you were coming." The two uniformed officers exchanged looks and then gestured toward us. "They were running around and making noise. We warned them to quiet down."

I kept my expression neutral as I caught the detective's gaze. "We're very sorry."

Instead of focusing on me, he turned his attention to the black-haired stranger. "I'll take it from here, guys. Thanks for being so diligent and keeping the cemetery safe."

"No problem, sir."

The four of us remained silent as the two uniformed officers vacated the premises. Finally, the detective spoke.

"What are you doing here, Redmond? Wait ... I don't want to know." He held up his hand. "You're supposed to be home helping your sister with the baby. You're not supposed to be gallivanting about."

I was caught off guard. "Wait ... you two know each other?"

The man referred to as Redmond looked sheepish. "He's my brother-in-law."

"Griffin Taylor." The detective extended his hand. "And you are?"

I introduced myself – and Kade – and then fixed my full attention on Redmond. "No wonder you weren't worried about taking out a banshee in front of witnesses. You have a protector in the Detroit Police Department."

Redmond shrugged. "It pays to know people in high places. As for my sister, I'm heading back now. Cillian stepped in to take my shift in the baby rotation. You don't have to worry about Aisling. She's well taken care of … and that baby is already spoiled rotten."

"Don't I know it," Griffin muttered, shaking his head. "Either way, you need to be more careful next time, Redmond. Luckily it sounds as if Ms. Parker here covered for you. Yeah, I heard her story as I was coming down the hill. Next time you might not have it so easy."

Redmond brushed off the warning and winked at me. "I have to get going. I really am supposed to take care of my sister. She just had a baby and she melts down all the time. I'm a saint for helping her. Women like saints, so … I figure you're probably already halfway in love with me."

I rolled my eyes. "You think a lot of yourself, don't you?"

"If you play your cards right, you could think a lot about me, too."

"I think I'll pass."

He held my gaze for a long moment and then shrugged. "Fair enough. I should get going." He clapped Griffin on the shoulder before skirting around him. "As for you, Ms. Poet, I'm sure I'll be seeing you around."

"I wouldn't count on it."

"Oh, never say never."

4
FOUR

*G*riffin stared at us for a few moments and then shrugged. "I don't know what I'm supposed to say to you," he said finally.

"You don't have to say anything," I offered. "I get it. Your brother-in-law is a monster hunter and you cover for him."

Griffin shrugged. "Something like that. I need to head out. I'm working the late shift so I don't have to the rest of the week. If I'm too late, my wife will melt down."

"Is your wife like her brother?" Kade asked pointedly.

Griffin chuckled. "Sometimes. More often than not, she's her own brand of terror. As for what you saw, well, I'm not sure what's going on with you guys. You seem nice enough. You're not screaming about paranormal creatures and the end times. I'm guessing that means you understand what was happening, and probably better than I do."

That was only half true. "We know enough."

"That's good, because I couldn't expand your knowledge base anyway. The only reason I bothered to come out here is because I'm familiar with the cemetery and figured it was possible whoever was creating the disturbance I heard about on the radio was now a member of my family."

He didn't appear bothered by the admission, which I found interesting. "We're fine. Don't worry about us."

"That's great." He flashed a weary smile and then turned to leave. "I wouldn't hang around here at night," he called back. "Weird things tend to happen in this place after dark."

He sounded as if he was talking from experience. "We're leaving." I cast one final glance over my shoulder and then slipped my hand into Kade's for the trip across the road. "Just out of curiosity, what sorts of things happen here?"

"Things that are best not talked about in mixed company," Griffin replied. "You said you're staying across the road, the fairgrounds? Why are you staying there?" He slowed his pace.

"We're with the circus," I replied automatically. "We're setting up for the festival at the end of the week. It's supposed to be some big thing."

"Yeah. They're trying to revitalize Detroit. To do that they have to draw people to the city. Most of the locals spend their time in the suburbs because they figure it's safer and there's more to do."

"I used to live here. I know how that goes." The admission slipped out before I realized I was going to say it.

Griffin arched an eyebrow, surprised. "You lived here? In Detroit?"

"I grew up in the suburbs and then spent a bit of time in the city when I was a teenager," I said. There really was no reason to tell him the story of my teenage woes. "After that, I joined the circus and have been traveling ever since. We've stopped in the city a few times since I joined up with the troupe, but ... I haven't really been in this area for a very long time."

"What's a long time?"

"Twelve years."

"Well, then you might be in for a surprise. A good one, I mean. The city is seeing a lot of growth. Young professionals are moving into lofts in the downtown area because it's hip and trendy now. Unlike before, all the sports teams are housed in the city now."

"Where were they before?" Kade asked. He was a big sports fan, so of course this was the topic that piqued his interest.

"The Pistons were in Auburn Hills, and the Lions in Pontiac. Only the Red Wings and Tigers were always in the city. They both have bigger stadiums and arenas now. When you add in the casinos, which are a big draw, and Greektown and Mexican Town, things are starting to look up."

My mind went back to when I was younger. "They used to have this weekend market thing. It was one of those places where a lot of vendors visited."

"Eastern Market." Griffin bobbed his head. "It's bigger than ever. There are, like, forty-five thousand visitors on Saturdays if the weather is good.

They have great food and crafts. If you guys are still here then, you should check it out."

"I would like to, but we have work." I sucked in a breath when we escaped from the cemetery and landed on the sidewalk in front of the facility. "Why don't they lock this place at night? It seems like that would be the safest bet in this neighborhood."

"It usually is locked. Someone must've fallen down on the job. I'll place a call." His eyes traveled to where we'd set up our operation. "How many of you are over there?"

"Fifty or so. We're divided into performers, midway workers, manual labor peeps and clowns."

A visible shudder worked its way through Griffin's body. "Ugh. Clowns?"

"Nobody likes them," I offered. "You don't have anything to worry about."

He chuckled hollowly. "Good to know." He fell silent again, but I could tell it was fatigue weighing him down rather than worry. "Just be careful. You're a big group and you seem to understand what's happening. You should be fine."

That was an interesting way to phrase things. "Do you have reason to believe we have something to worry about?"

"Not particularly. But I've learned that nothing in life is what it seems." He checked his watch and then shook his head. "I need to get going. I have to return to the station and fill out some paperwork."

"And then home to your wife?"

A small smile played at the corners of his lips. "And daughter ... and brothers-in-law ... and father-in-law. We're essentially one big clan."

"That's good."

"In this case, it really is." He offered us a half-wave and then started moving down the street. "Like I said, be careful of the cemetery at night. You should be fine otherwise."

Kade remained silent until Griffin was out of sight. "What do you think?" he asked finally.

"I don't know." I pressed the heel of my hand to my forehead and rubbed. "Banshees aren't usually found in this part of the country. They're drawn to mist and a lack of sunshine. Redmond mentioned this one had killed someone. They must have been tracking it."

"So ... that's it?" He was new to the paranormal world, so Kade often needed things spelled out. "We just pretend that creature never existed and go on with our lives?"

"Pretty much. Can you live with that?"

"Do I have a choice?"

"Not really."

"Then I can live with that." He gave my hand a squeeze and tugged me toward the road. "Come on. It's getting late. We have a long day ahead of us. We should get some sleep."

"Sleep?" I was dubious. "I was certain when we were heading to bed earlier that you had a few other things on your mind. Sleep makes you sound old."

"Is that a fact?" His eyes lit with mirth, the previous horror seemingly forgotten. He released my hand and gave me a playful shove. "You should start running."

"Why?"

"Because it's more fun when I have to catch you."

I understood exactly what he was talking about. "Okay, but I'm going to make you work for it."

"That's what I want to hear."

KADE WAS STILL ASLEEP when I woke the next morning, his breath steady and even in my ear. We'd played well into the night, both of us slipping into dreamland after midnight.

Generally I was the one who had to be dragged out of bed kicking and screaming. I was something of a slow-starter. I was awake long before I had to be this morning, though, and there was no going back to sleep.

So as not to disturb Kade, I slid from beneath the covers and showered quietly. I checked on him long enough to make sure he was still sleeping before leaving a note on the pillow next to him and slipping outside.

I was unsettled.

There was no other way to describe it. I'd slept well for the time I was out, but my dreams were muddled messes, the past colliding with the present and creating a hodgepodge of insanity.

It was too early to start breakfast. Even the earliest risers would sleep another hour. The sun was rising, casting a warm pall in the air, and I felt safe even though I was on my own. I couldn't stop myself from staring at the cemetery. It drew my attention at every turn.

I thought about seeing Tawny there the night before. Had she been real? I'd certainly thought so at the time, but the notion was so easy to push aside when I lost sight of her that I thought there was a chance I'd imagined her. I was worried about seeing faces from my past.

Maybe it was only a woman who looked like Tawny. Heck, maybe she didn't even look like Tawny at all. Maybe it was the banshee I saw.

I knew that was wrong. Tawny had brown hair, not black. Also, the woman I snagged gazes with wasn't wearing a white dress. She was dressed in leggings and a low-cut top. It was the top, I realized, that really convinced me I was dealing with Tawny. It was so risqué that it immediately made me think of her.

I shifted from one foot to the other as I stared at the cemetery wall. It looked quiet. Most people weren't awake yet, even though the sun was bright enough to chase away the haze of night. That meant paranormals were likely not hanging out. If I wanted to visit the cemetery alone and get a feel for it, now was the time.

I wasn't doing anything wrong and yet I felt guilty, enough so that I stared at the trailer for a long time, debating whether I should wake Kade and tell him my plans. He would be crabby upon waking, but insist on going with me. He was good that way.

I didn't need him, though. I didn't sense danger from the cemetery. I simply wanted to look around.

I'm not sure when I decided to make my move. I only know I was halfway across the street before it registered that I was acting on a plan. The gate was still open from the night before – obviously no one had come to fix the problem with the lock – and I easily slipped through it.

The terrain appeared different during the daytime, but it wasn't hard to retrace my steps. Within two minutes, I'd cut through the cemetery and was back among the mausoleums. I wasn't, however, alone.

The first face I saw belonged to a handsome man with hair that brushed the top of his shoulders. If I hadn't spent several minutes talking to him the night before, I would've assumed this was Redmond wearing a wig. The new man looked just that similar ... and he boasted the same set of lavender eyes, the color remarkable in the sun.

Next to him was a woman. She boasted black hair as well, although it was streaked through with deliberate hanks of white. She shared the same lilac eyes. She stood next to Griffin, who didn't look any more rested than he had the previous evening, and was in the middle of a tirade.

"I told you to stay home and get some sleep," the woman barked. "You look like death warmed over."

"Thank you, baby," Griffin drawled. "You know exactly how to make me feel like a loved husband."

"Oh, whatever." The woman rolled her eyes until they landed on me. She didn't jump or scream when she saw me. She also didn't start babbling to cover her actions. Instead, she simply eyed me with overt curiosity. "You're the chick from last night. The one with the weird name."

"That's rich coming from you, Aisling," the other dark-haired man chuckled, shaking his head. His eyes were curious when they met mine. "You are exactly as Redmond described you."

"She is not." Aisling made a face. "He said she was panting after him and wanted him bad. This woman clearly doesn't need to lower herself to that. Redmond is full of crap."

I couldn't stop myself from smiling. "You must be the sister he mentioned last night," I said finally. "He said he was due home to help you with a baby."

"Yes, my daughter." Aisling folded her arms across her chest and regarded me with an unreadable expression. "I'm Aisling Grimlock-Taylor. I'm still getting used to the Taylor part. I think it makes me sound like a banker."

That was a bit of an overshare but amusing all the same. "I figured. I've heard your name twice now. I'm Poet Parker."

Aisling stilled. "Wait … your name is really Poet? I thought for sure Redmond was making that up. He said your words were poetry to his ears."

I'd heard variations on that from horny men for the better part of my life. "Your brother is … interesting."

Aisling snorted and handed a baggie to her husband. I couldn't make out what it contained, but it looked like dust. Very interesting.

"My brother is full of himself," Aisling corrected. "He must have seen you as a challenge. That would appeal to him."

"Especially because she was with her boyfriend," Griffin added, displeasure written all over his face when he held my gaze. "I thought I told you to stay out of the cemetery."

"No, you told me to stay out of the cemetery at night," I corrected. "You didn't say anything about during the day."

"I guess that's fair." He placed the baggie in his pocket when he realized I was trying to get a better look at the contents. "Is there a reason you came back? Do you have unfinished business?"

"Was the banshee a friend of yours?" Aisling added.

"The banshee definitely wasn't a friend of mine," I replied, shaking my head. "We only ran over here because we heard the screams. We wanted to make sure an innocent wasn't in danger."

"So … you're brave. Did you hear that, Cillian? They ran over to save someone. She didn't run over because she was hot to trot for Redmond's body, which is what he told us."

My mouth dropped open. "You can't be serious. He really said that?"

"He's a complete and total putz," Aisling volunteered. "He feels the need to act out because he's the only one in the family who's still single. He says it doesn't bother him, but he's full of crap. As the oldest, he fears life is passing him by while the rest of us move on to greener pastures."

Cillian – the name fit him because he had an oddly sexy and smart allure – pinched his sister's flank. "Where did you learn that nonsense?" he complained. "You sound like a television psychologist. Like Dr. Phil, or one of those Kardashians pretending to be smarter than they really are."

Aisling's gaze turned dark. "Don't ever compare me to a Kardashian. I'll beat the crap out of you if you do."

As entertaining as I found the sarcastic woman, I had other things on my mind. "You warned me not to come into this cemetery at night," I reminded Griffin again. "I want to know why. Is something bad here? Are you hunting for something specific? Is that why you hid evidence in your pocket when you thought nobody was looking?"

I had to give him credit; Griffin's expression never changed. Even though I'd purposely baited him he was calm in the face of my pointed questions.

"We're here to make sure that Redmond didn't leave any evidence behind last night," Griffin replied without missing a beat. "It wouldn't go over well for anyone if somehow things get tracked back to Redmond."

I could see that, but I sensed more was going on. Because I felt that she was the most likely to run her mouth, I focused on Aisling. "Would you hang around this cemetery at night?"

She shrugged, blasé. "I've been in this cemetery so many times after dark that I've lost count."

"And nothing bad ever happened?"

"Oh, I wouldn't say that. There have been fires … and sword fights … and a zombie infestation that only I understood and everyone else doubted."

"Way to bring that up again, Ais," Cillian muttered.

"Yes, we don't hear about how you were right and we were wrong nearly enough," Griffin added.

Their interaction made me like them. Aisling's relationship with Cillian reminded me of the one I shared with Luke. And Griffin, well, he was apparently unflappable. They looked good together.

They were still lying. I could feel it in my very marrow. There was no way to force them to tell the truth without revealing my magic. And, while I got a basic reading on Redmond the night before, I knew it was entirely possible that his sister was more powerful. In fact, the more she talked, the more I started drifting toward that likelihood. If I revealed myself, I would make myself vulnerable to them.

I wasn't ready to do that.

"Well, okay." I cleared my throat and forced a smile. "I don't want to take up much of your time. I just stopped by because I wanted to take a look around in the daylight. I'll leave you to your activities."

"I think that's for the best." Griffin lobbed a smile at me, but it didn't make it all the way to his eyes. The three of them were desperate for me to leave. "Be careful crossing the street ... and have a nice day."

"Don't worry; I've been crossing streets for as long as I can remember. I'll be perfectly fine."

And with that, I was dismissed ... and I had even more questions than when I'd started.

5

FIVE

$\mathcal{K}$ ade was up when I returned to the fairgrounds. I told him about my adventure. He wasn't happy to hear I took off on my own given what went down the previous evening, but he didn't appear angry.

"So, what do you think their deal is?" he asked as he watched me pull out a variety of breakfast foods and prepare to start cooking. "Do you think they're monsters?"

The question seemed ludicrous on its face, but I'd seen my fair share of monsters hide behind snark and sarcasm. Most weren't quite as adept as the Grimlocks. "I don't know," I replied finally, handing him a loaf of bread. "They don't feel evil. In fact, they sound like a normal family. They tease one another, make jokes at each other's expense. There's talk of a baby at home."

"For all you know it could be the kid from *Rosemary's Baby*."

I had to laugh. "This is true. But that doesn't feel right. Griffin looks tired, has circles under his eyes. He mentioned he had to work a night shift, which is probably difficult for a new father. Aisling talked smack about her brother, but I'm betting she would race to his rescue in a heartbeat. They seem like a normal family."

"Except they're hanging around a cemetery and collecting evidence they're trying to keep on the down low."

There was that. "I don't know." I made up my mind on the spot. "It doesn't really matter. We probably won't see them again. They might've been there to make sure there was no evidence to track back to Redmond. That's smart in this particular situation, especially because those uniformed officers showed up."

"I guess." Kade rubbed his chin, his eyes thoughtful as they scanned my features. "How did you sleep?"

The swift topic shift threw me. "Fine. I slept fine. Why do you ask?"

"You were up with the sun. You usually like to hide from it until I yank the comforter off the bed and you mainline coffee for an hour before facing the world. You were up early today. I figured that was because you couldn't sleep."

He knew me too well. "I didn't sleep great," I admitted. Even white lies were frowned upon in our relationship, so I opted for the truth. "Actually, I slept okay. I fell out quickly. I had weird dreams, though. They woke me and I knew there was no drifting under again, so I headed out for a bit.

"You don't have to worry about me," I added with a laugh. "I'm more than capable of taking care of myself. Besides, things turned out fine. If danger was lurking in that cemetery, I'm sure I would've sensed it."

"I would like to believe that. Still, I can't help but worry. You seem on edge. I think most of that has to do with returning to your old stomping grounds. What happened last night didn't help."

"I'm fine." I meant it. "I don't want you sitting around worrying about me. I'm not going to fly off the handle and do something stupid. That's not who I am."

"I know." He reached over and grabbed my hand, his fingers warm as they wrapped around mine. "It's just that … well … I love you."

I smirked. "I love you, too, but I thought we were done with that competition. Luke swears he'll rip out our tongues if we keep saying 'I love you' ten times a day."

"You let me worry about Luke." He leaned over and gave me a soft kiss. "I thought we could spend the morning working around here and then head out for lunch before picking up groceries. How does that sound?"

"Sounds like a plan."

CIRCUS WORK IS LABOR-INTENSIVE and physically draining. Four hours spent arranging tents, cleaning interior and exterior bleachers and checking on the big top to make sure it was being erected properly was tiresome. By the time noon rolled around, I was ready to make my escape.

"Ready?" I asked Kade when I found him securing the animal tent. Mystic Caravan didn't really work with animals. We had shifters in disguise. That saved us in some ways … and put us in danger in others. We had to pretend we were taking care of animals even if they were out of the public eye, so we were always careful when positioning the tent. We didn't need trouble catching an outsider should one attempt to sneak in.

"I'm ready." Kade leaned over and gave me a kiss as he watched Seth and Luke argue about where to place the pegs used to tie off the flaps. They were shifters, both alpha in their own right, and they got off on torturing each other. It was a dance of sorts. "You don't think they're going to get into it, do you?"

He looked genuinely concerned, so I decided to squelch this spat before it could get away from them. "Hey!" I stomped my foot to get their attention. "Stop acting like imbeciles," I ordered. "It doesn't matter where you tie off the flaps. One of you pick the location. Then, at our next stop – which is in Ohio, so you'll both be bored out of your minds – the other one can pick the anchor locations. It's fairly simple."

Luke made an exaggerated face. "Oh, thank you, wise one. I don't know what we would do without you."

"Probably rip each other's eyes out." I turned back to Kade. "Ready?"

"Yup. I need a break from the fighting." He slid his arm around my shoulders as we ambled through the circus grounds. "Things are coming together quickly. We should have plenty of time to make sure everything is ready."

"That's good. I ... ." The sound of feet pounding against the ground caught my attention. I wasn't surprised when I swiveled and found Luke giving chase. "Uh-oh."

Kade followed my gaze and scowled. "He's going to invite himself along, isn't he?"

If I was a betting person, I would put big money on that. "It will be fine," I reassured him. "Luke will be on his best behavior."

"I didn't agree to that," Luke groused as he fell into step with us. "We're getting lunch, right?"

"We are," Kade confirmed.

"Great. What sort of restaurants do they have around here?"

I smiled at the seemingly innocuous question. "I think you're going to be pleasantly surprised."

MARVIN'S CONEY ISLAND WAS CLEAN, brightly lit and smelled like my childhood. I almost started drooling the second my memory and olfactory senses collided with the rich scent of chili and onions.

"Oh, geez. Do you smell that?"

Luke wrinkled his nose. "Grease?"

I elbowed his stomach. "No, smart guy. I'm talking about the coneys. I used to love coneys because all the restaurants – and there are at least fifteen different chains in this area – would run ninety-nine-cent sales one day a week. We could eat like kings a few times a week for only a few bucks. It was awesome."

Kade looked pained when he met my gaze. "I would rather not hear stories about you being hungry."

"Me either," Luke agreed, wrinkling his nose. "That's a bummer of a tale."

I sighed and shook my head. "That wasn't meant to be a bummer story. Those days we got to eat coneys were the best. Especially when it was cold outside. We could come inside, clean up in the bathrooms and spend a bunch of time in front of those hand dryers because they could warm us all over."

"Oh, geez." Kade's hand automatically moved to my back. "You're going to make me cry if you keep it up."

"And nobody wants to see that," Luke intoned, lifting his chin to scan the diner. "There's a booth over there."

Luke took the lead, Kade following, and I brought up the rear. I was feeling nostalgic, the delightful scent of grill grease clubbing me over the head with memories that didn't seem so bad when looking back. Slowly, I let my gaze drift over the faces in the booths and I only grinned wider. It was the same sort of clientele. Apparently some things really never change.

And then I practically tripped over a face that seemed familiar. It was so jarring I came to a complete halt. I was so close to Kade that I slammed into his back. His eyes were full of concern when he stabilized me, but I was too busy staring at the woman and child in the booth to my left.

"Creek?" Her name came out a strangled gasp.

Her eyes, always so bright when we were younger, were dull and lifeless when she lifted them. Her hair, which had always been glossy even though she couldn't wash it regularly, was dull and drab. "Do I know you?"

I didn't know if she was pretending not to recognize me or if she'd simply forgotten me. I could walk away and put the past where it belonged or I could be brave and talk to her. I was no coward.

"Poet."

Slowly, her eyes cleared of the haze they'd been hiding behind. "No way."

"Yeah. Um ... yeah." I shifted from one foot to the other, uncomfortable. "How are you?"

"Oh, you know, living the dream." Her snort was derisive and then she inclined her head toward the little girl sitting in a booster seat next to her.

The child's clothes were worn and frayed at the edges, but her hair was clean and neatly pulled into pigtails. She had the glow of youth and seemed happy enough. The smile she sent me was infectious.

"Hi." I waved at her, suddenly awed that the same girl I lived with on the streets was now a mother. I couldn't imagine that. "Is this your daughter?"

"Hannah." Creek smiled fondly at the child and then handed her a crayon before looking me up and down. "You look the same."

That was ridiculous. Twelve years had passed. Nobody looked the same after twelve years. "I think you're exaggerating."

"Not really. I mean … you look a little older. You mostly look the same."

I wished I could say the same about her. The years had not been kind. The young, spirited woman I'd met had been ground into nothing. I felt inexplicably sad for her. Kade picked that moment to clear his throat and bring me back to reality.

"Oh, right." I gestured toward him and Luke in turn. "This is Kade Denton and Luke Bishop. We all work in the circus together."

"Right." She bobbed her head. "I heard you joined the circus. That was the rumor anyway. I wasn't sure if it was true or if something happened to you."

I frowned. "I left you a letter."

"You did?" She furrowed her brow. "I don't think I got it."

"I left it with Hazy and Junk."

"Oh, well, if you left it with those guys … ." She finished on a hollow laugh. "What are you doing back in Detroit? I would've thought this is the last place you would ever want to visit. I mean … you got out. Nobody ever gets out. Why would you come back?"

She sounded bitter. I could see why. Obviously the girl who had big dreams of escaping and becoming famous, of making something of herself, had died a tragic death. The person left behind was … well … . Something like that would be impossible to overcome for a woman like Creek.

"We're here for a week to put on a show," I replied, choosing my words carefully. "We're at the old fairgrounds."

"Yeah? I hear they've been working on the neighborhoods over there, cleaning them and stuff. You want to be careful if you're actually spending the night out there."

My interest was officially piqued.

"The cops are in and out of there three times a night. They'll drag you in for possession, even though it's a stupid charge that barely gets them any money. They're serious about cleaning that area up."

It shouldn't have come as a surprise that she was talking about a subject I couldn't relate to. The second I'd left Detroit, our lives diverged. Obviously, things got better for me. She wasn't so lucky.

I cleared my throat to push away the melancholy. "How about you? Are you married?"

She shook her head. "I never saw the need. Are you?" Her gaze shifted to Kade and Luke. "Or are you guys a threesome or something?"

Kade made a face and I could tell a biting retort was on the tip of his tongue, but I slowly shook my head in warning. He carefully snapped his mouth shut and then gestured toward the booth. "Luke and I are going to sit down. When you're done, you know where to find us," he said.

"I'll be over in a few minutes," I promised. I was sad to see him go because his mere presence was enough to ground me, but he and Luke were obviously making Creek nervous. I didn't want her to feel out of place. The conversation was awkward enough.

"What about the others?" I asked. "Do you ever see them?"

"What others?" The question obviously annoyed her. "There've been a lot of 'others' in my life over the years. You'll have to be more specific."

"Hazy. Junk. Shadow."

"We only saw Shadow once after you left. He stopped in to see us at Hart Plaza. When we told him you'd disappeared, he was mad and yelled at us. He never came around after."

I felt bad for not saying goodbye to him. "I left him a letter, too."

"Well, I don't think he got it. Hazy and Junk went their own way after. They were running with the crew that hung in the Cobo parking deck. They wanted to be with their own kind. They didn't have room for me."

"I'm sorry." I meant it. "I couldn't find you that day. I didn't have much time."

"I don't blame you. You got out. You should be thankful."

"Yeah, but … ."

"I survived," she added. "I had to do things I never thought I would have to do, but I made it. I even have a house now. I'm not on the street."

"Good for you. That's great."

"Yeah." She didn't look as if she appreciated my empty words. "It wasn't easy. I spent two weeks trying to find you because I was certain the druggie duo couldn't be right about the message they said you gave them. I mean … the circus. How could you join the circus?"

"It's a good job," I offered hurriedly. "I get to travel. I have good friends."

"That's great." Her face was blank. "I bet you make sure to say goodbye to them when you leave."

"I tried to find you."

"It doesn't matter." She waved off my lame attempt at an apology. "Like I said, it was two weeks. After that I gave up. I went to Beacon for help because I didn't know what to do. He got me into a job-training program, and I managed to survive."

"What do you do?"

"I work." Creek took a napkin and dipped it in her glass of water before wiping the corners of Hannah's mouth. "It was great seeing you, but I really have to go. We only stopped by for a quick lunch."

"Yeah, I … ." I wasn't even sure what I was going to say. There was nothing really to say. Our lives had diverged and I wasn't sure we'd ever had anything in common. Not really.

I stood rooted to my spot and watched her leave the diner, and then slowly I tracked my gaze to Luke and Kade. They were watching me with a mixture of concern and curiosity. "It's fine," I said hurriedly, sliding in next to Kade and taking the menu he handed me. "It was weird to see her, but it's fine."

"Okay." Kade moved his hand to my neck and started massaging at the stress there. "Are you sure you're okay?"

"I'm … fine." I directed my attention to the menu even though I'd lost my appetite. Luke broke the silence.

"She said the name Beacon," he started. "I've never heard you mention that name before. Who is it that helped her?"

"He was a local guy who worked at one of the shelters," I replied, searching my memory. "I never liked him, but he was friendly enough. Sometimes we would try to stay at the shelter when it was really cold. There was a lottery, and not everybody could get in. If you were lucky enough to get picked, the others wouldn't hold it against you. Beacon ran the lottery. She says he helped her get a job. I guess I should be happy about that."

"The little girl is cute," Kade offered lamely. "At least she's a mother."

I wanted to explode. "Let's focus on lunch," I demanded. "I don't want to talk about this. We have a bunch of shopping to do this afternoon. Let's make a list."

Let's not talk about this, I added again silently. Anything but this. If we talk about this for another second the guilt will probably consume me. I can't look back. It's too hard. I don't know why I even tried.

SIX

*L*uke was familiar with coney dogs. Kade had only heard about them. He was dubious when I ordered, although he followed suit. The look on his face when his plate was delivered was priceless. It did a lot to loosen the invisible fist gripping my heart.

"Don't they smell amazing?" I briefly shut my eyes and inhaled. "Umm. I used to dream about that smell right after I left. It was a long time until I forgot about it."

Kade's eyes were hard to read when I opened mine.

"What?" I asked finally, self-conscious. "Did I drool or something?"

That was enough to garner a laugh. "No. I just ... it's hard for me," he said finally. "I don't like to think of you suffering."

"I didn't suffer."

"You were on the street. You had a friend learning how to turn tricks. From the looks of her, I think she was forced down that road. Friends died ... and disappeared ... and you couldn't go into certain buildings for fear of being hurt by other people. If that's not suffering, I don't know what is."

I'd never really thought about it that way before. "It wasn't as bad as you make it sound. There were good times, too."

"Oh, yeah? You haven't told me one good story from back then."

"I told you about ninety-nine-cent coney day" I protested.

"That is not a good story."

"Hey." Luke, who usually loved when we fought, reached across the table.

It wasn't me he was trying to comfort. "You're going to drive yourself crazy if you keep going down this road," he advised Kade. "I've been where you are. Picturing it is worse. You've got to put it out of your head. She came out the other side and survived."

They were being ridiculous. "You guys keep seeing the ugly in it, and I don't like that. There was good stuff, too."

"Enlighten us," Kade shot back.

"Fine. In the summer we would head out to Belle Isle for the beaches ... and the aquarium. The people who worked there took pity on us and gave us free passes to look around whenever we wanted. They weren't suspicious or anything."

Kade stilled. "That's it? You got to visit an aquarium for free? How awesome."

My temper started to build. "There was a fire escape on the side of the Detroit Opera House. We could climb all the way to the top and sit and listen to great music while looking at the stars. We knew the good places to eat ... and visit ... and we never went hungry for more than a few days. We survived and, yes, there were times we had fun doing it."

Kade's expression was impossible to read. He almost looked as if he was being strangled as he searched for whatever words he thought would make the situation better. "Poet, I'm not looking down on you."

"I didn't say you were."

"That's how you're acting." He was unbelievably calm. "I love you."

"Oh, don't start this again," Luke whined.

Kade ignored him, keeping his gaze focused on me. "I love you and I don't like thinking about you living on the street. I'm glad you have good memories of it. I think that if you didn't the bad ones would swallow you whole. That's a defense mechanism."

"Since when are you a professional psychologist?" I shot back, my fury building. "I think I know if I was happy or not. There were parts of living out there that weren't so bad. We were together, a unit."

"And you just saw one of your friends from back then." Kade refused to back down. "You said on the drive that she was a dreamer, that she had big plans to get out. You made it sound as if she was a ray of shining light. Look at her now. I don't think things worked out for her."

He was right, of course. Things clearly hadn't worked out for Creek. I couldn't help feeling guilty about that. Perhaps I shouldn't have left.

As if reading my mind, Kade slowly shook his head. "What would've happened if you stayed?" he asked gently. "You would be right there with her.

We'd have never met. You never would've found your niche in the circus. That's where you belong. You did the right thing."

I rubbed my forehead and focused on my plate. This conversation was sucking the spirit out of me. "She was angry. I guess I can't blame her."

"I noticed the anger." Kade unwrapped his flatware and stared dubiously at his plate. "It looks like somebody already ate this."

"Dig in and shut up," Luke instructed, reaching for a napkin. He'd already plowed through one coney and was tackling his chili fries. "It's fine." He focused on me. "Even if you had stayed, I know we would've found each other. Some things are meant to be, like you and me."

He made me laugh. He always did. "I do think we would've found each other," I admitted, my eyes traveling back to the table where Creek had been sitting. "She said she didn't get the letter."

"I heard." Kade moved his hand to my back and rubbed. He still hadn't touched his food. "I'm sorry if that upsets you."

"She also had a big scar on her arm," Luke pointed out. "I mean ... huge. It looked like it never healed correctly because she never got treatment."

I'd noticed the scar. I wasn't good at judging things like that, but I had to estimate it was at least five or six years old. "She still looked like Creek," I hedged, my eyes falling on a newspaper that the people in the next booth had left behind. On a whim, I reached over and grabbed it, something on the front page catching my eye. "She just looked beaten down. She says she owns a house."

"And I'll just bet it's picturesque," Luke muttered.

I glared at him. "There's nothing wrong with not having a million-dollar house. Shame on you."

He balked. "I didn't mean it that way. I just meant she probably doesn't clean it. Oh, don't look at me that way. I can't gracefully escape from this conversation, so I'm going to eat my lunch and pretend I didn't say anything stupid."

"That would probably be best," I agreed, as I scanned the front of the newspaper.

"What's that?" Kade asked, peering over my shoulder.

"It's an article about missing girls in the Corridor," I replied, my stomach doing a terrifying flip as I read through it. "At least four have gone missing, maybe more, and the cops are suggesting that females in the area buddy up so they're never alone."

Kade tilted his head to the side, considering. "Maybe that's what Griffin was really collecting evidence for," he said. "Maybe the girls aren't missing. Maybe they're banshees."

Two months ago he would've jumped to a "normal" conclusion. Now he went straight for the paranormal. That was interesting. "Maybe." I'd considered that myself, although the article was woefully short on details. "I don't know. There's not enough information here."

"Maybe the girls aren't missing," Luke suggested. He'd plowed through the better part of his food. Kade still hadn't touched his. "Maybe, like you, they left. They're calling them 'street girls' in the headline. That could refer to homeless teenagers or prostitutes."

His tone grated. "Not all street kids turn tricks. I never did."

"I know." Luke's eyebrows hopped. "I was just saying ... the cops might not really be looking for them. They're throwaways. One of the journalists clearly stumbled over the story and gave it some good play. How long will that last? If you don't have tearful parents standing in front of news crews pleading for the return of innocent children, the news cycle will chew you up and spit you out. That's what's going to happen here."

He had a point. Still ... . "Eat your lunch," I instructed Kade, cutting into my first coney with determination. "If you don't like it, order something else. Just know that I'll lose all respect for you if you don't like it."

He glared. "This looks as if it's already been eaten."

"You'll live."

"ABSOLUTELY NOT."

I instructed Kade and Luke to drop me downtown and carry on grocery shopping without me. The story about the missing girls bothered me, and I wanted to drop by my old stomping grounds for a visit. I wanted to make the trip on my own.

Kade, however, was dead set against it.

"I'll be fine," I reassured him, refusing to back down. "Nothing can touch me there now." I wiggled my fingers. "I'm powerful."

"I know," Kade shot back. "But it's still not a safe area."

"Poet, I don't want to agree with him — you know that gives me scurvy — but I think he has a point," Luke said. "You really shouldn't go down there alone."

"It will be fine. I know the area."

"Just ... let me go with you," Kade pleaded. "I'll feel better if you're not alone."

I understood what he was saying. He would worry about me the entire time I was gone. He wouldn't be able to help himself. But I couldn't bring him with me. The street kids would scatter if someone like him showed his face. He gave off a militaristic air.

"The kids won't talk to you," I said. "You look like a cop."

"What about me?" Luke challenged.

"Yeah, what about Luke?" Kade brightened at the suggestion. "He's better than nothing."

"Oh, I think I'm going to get a T-shirt made up with that saying," Luke sneered.

I ignored their squabble. "Luke would fit in better, but he tends to make things about himself," I replied. "I need to talk to these kids, see if I can get a handle on what's happening. They'll only talk to me because I used to be one of them. I know what I'm doing. You don't have to worry."

"Fat chance," Luke grumbled.

Kade almost looked bitter. "Poet, please don't do this."

I was resolved. "I have to at least try. I won't be gone long. I'm sorry for leaving you guys to do the shopping, but you have the list. I'll probably be back at the fairgrounds before you return."

Kade glanced around the area. He didn't look happy. "Honey ... ," he trailed off. He realized there was nothing more to say.

"I'll be fine," I insisted. "I'll text regularly to let you know I'm okay. That's the best I can do. You can't change my mind, so we're just wasting time here."

He nodded and pressed his hand to his forehead. "Text every few minutes or I'll have an aneurysm or something. I mean it."

"It will be fine." I was sure of that, and I put as much of my belief as possible into the kiss I graced him with before hopping out of the truck. "I'll catch an Uber back to the fairgrounds. This is my turf. Don't worry."

"There's no stopping us from doing that," Luke lamented. "Just ... watch your back. I'm sure things aren't exactly like you remember."

"The street never changes."

IT TOOK ANOTHER FIVE minutes of cajoling to get Kade and Luke to leave. I wasn't sure they would, but once I was alone I was all business.

I remembered the neighborhood. Some of the buildings had undergone a facelift, but I remembered everything.

I remembered the shortcut through the tiny abandoned lot, which was still there and piled high with garbage. I remembered the alley behind the pizza place. The name of the business was different, but the smell was the same.

I remembered the park off the Corridor. The playground equipment had been switched out, the old, rusted stuff that was there a decade before replaced with sleek plastic playsets. There were no kids playing on it, though. Instead, dealers, pimps and bangers took up various positions around the park to show off their superiority.

That was the same, too.

I paid them little heed as I strolled through the open expanse. I'd dressed in simple capris and a T-shirt this morning, grabbing a hoodie before heading out. I didn't look wealthy or as if I was trolling for a hit. That didn't stop people from calling out to me.

"Hey, honey," a man in red pants and a black leather coat barked. "If you're looking for a job, I think I can put you to work right away."

I slowed my pace and glared at him over my shoulder. "I don't think you're man enough to handle me," I called back.

One of the druggies from across the way hooted at my response as he slapped his knee and then broke into a terrifying coughing fit. I was so focused on him I didn't notice the big man standing in my path until I almost ran into him. I knew better than to show surprise on the street, so I retained my position and slowly tracked my eyes to him.

"Groove," I muttered, looking away from him.

The big man looked the same. He was more than six feet of muscle and attitude. He seemed surprised to see me.

"Whatchoo doin' round here, girl?" he challenged. "You don't live here no more."

I folded my arms across my chest and narrowed my eyes. "I'm back for a visit. I thought it might be fun to look around all the old places." And ask a few questions, I added silently. "In fact, I was having breakfast this morning and happened to read a news article about girls going missing in the Corridor. You don't happen to know anything about that, do you?"

Groove looked legitimately puzzled as he scratched the side of his head and sneered. In the years since I'd last seen him, he'd had his teeth replaced with what looked like a gold grill. It was disturbing on a variety of different levels. "I have to wonder why you care," he said, still not making eye contact. "You left this place without saying goodbye to your friends. That other girl, the one that looked like a shiny toy, she looked for you for days."

Creek. I felt sick to my stomach. I didn't want to hear that. "I've already seen her," I shot back. "I left her a letter back then, but she apparently never got it."

"Ain't that sweet?" Groove spat. "You left her a letter. You always were an uppity thing. You thought you were better than us, didn't you?"

"Than you? Yes. Than the others? No. You were special," I said. He didn't scare me. I knew he had a gun in his waistband, but he would never get the chance to use it. He had a weak mind and I could easily overpower him if it came to it. "I just want to know about the missing girls," I pressed. "What are you hearing?"

"Why you care?" he challenged. There was something in his eyes I couldn't immediately identify. It almost seemed to be hope.

"Because I remember what it was like to be out here when a predator was on the loose," I answered. "I remember the fear ... and the way we all had to sleep in groups ... and I want to help."

He tapped his chin and remained silent for what felt like forever. Then he asked me an odd question. "Did you really see your old buddy?"

"Yes. I didn't seek her out. I wouldn't have known how to find her even if I tried. She just happened to be in the same restaurant."

"Uh-huh. What about you? You really join the circus?"

His curiosity had me reconsidering my earlier opinion on him. It was possible he was simply putting on a show to make sure nobody jumped him. That was a standard way to keep potential rivals off your back in the dealing world. Groove had managed to survive this long. He had some tricks.

"I did," I confirmed.

"You hang out with clowns and stuff?"

"Nobody likes the clowns."

He cracked a legitimate smile for the first time since I'd arrived and shook his head. "I don't know that I have anything to tell you. The girls are here one second, gone the next. There's no rhyme or reason. People are on the lookout for whoever is doing this, but we don't have no ideas."

I was afraid he was going to say something like that. "That sucks."

"Yup." He nodded, his eyebrows drawing together as something over my shoulder drew his attention. "Well, will you look at that?" he drawled. "Looks like everybody coming home this week."

I slowly turned and found myself staring at another face from my past. This one I was certain I would never have the fortune of seeing again. Apparently I was wrong.

"Shadow," I said on an exhale, my heart skipping a beat at the sight of him. "What are you doing here?"

"I was just about to ask you the same thing," he snarled, extreme displeasure sparking in his eyes. "Why did you come back here? You can't stay. Get out."

"That's quite the welcome."

He held up his hands. "I don't want to hurt your feelings or anything, but ... get out. You don't belong here. You never did. You need to get out right now."

SEVEN

*H*e looked pretty much the same. Twelve years had been good to him. Of course, he'd been young back then. If he topped twenty-five, I would've been surprised. Still, his reaction to seeing me was a jolt.

"And a happy hello to you," I drawled.

His lips quirked, as if he was holding back a smile. "You shouldn't be here." He was firm. "Why are you back?"

"She be asking the same questions as you, pig boy," Groove offered. "She wants to know about the missing girls."

"Why?" The question was directed at me, not Groove.

"I'm curious," I replied on a shrug. "I didn't realize that was against the law."

Groove narrowed his eyes at me. "You know."

"Know what?"

"That he's a cop. How could you know that? The truth didn't come out 'til he took down the Vipers. That was at least a year after you left."

The news didn't surprise me. I could read minds, after all. I saw a hint of it in his head back in the day. Not all of it, of course. I wasn't trained back then. I didn't know how to peel back the layers like I do now. The visions I saw then made sense with additional information, and the truth made me smile.

"I always had a feeling," I said. "I knew that he was more than he pretended to be."

"I think that could be said for all of us." Shadow held up a finger. "You wait right there. I want to talk to you. I have some business to discuss with Groove first."

I smirked. "I have no intention of running. I'm an adult now, and I'm not afraid of the police."

"As long as you don't do anything illegal, there's nothing to fear."

"That ain't true," Groove protested. "I'm a fine, upstanding citizen and this mook is down here giving me a hard time at least twice a week. Do you want to know why? It's because I'm a black man. The cops is always trying to keep the black man down."

I shot Groove a derisive look. "Yeah. You're pure as the driven snow."

"I am." He adopted an innocent expression. "I can't believe you'd doubt me, girl. I took care of you back then. I'm the only reason you weren't taken and forced to be someone's plaything. Rodney wanted you something fierce back then."

A chill went down my spine. I'd forgotten about Rodney, he of the leather jacket and ugly scar on his face, until Groove mentioned him. I'd probably pushed him out of my mind on purpose.

"You didn't save her from Rodney," Shadow countered. "That was me. He had a hard-on for her and Creek. I warned him something bad would happen if he went after either of them."

"He was afraid of you?" Groove arched a dubious eyebrow. "Word on the street is the girls saved your life and you was a weakling who hung around with bikers because you wanted to look tough."

"Do you want me to tell you the word on the street about you?" Shadow shot back.

I sensed the conversation getting out of control and, while it was none of my business, I wasn't in the mood to watch them urinate verbally over one another for dominance. "Didn't you say you had something to talk to him about?" I reminded Shadow. "You should probably get to it so he can return to his business."

"Yeah, well ... ." Shadow didn't look happy about being reminded he had a task. "I want to know what you know about the missing girls, Groove."

"Aw, man." Groove shook his head and looked up the street. "I told you before I don't know nothing about that. You've asked me twice. If I knew something, I'd handle it."

"There have to be whispers," I pressed, ignoring the dark look Shadow sent in my direction. "The street is always thick with gossip. You must have heard something."

"What would you know 'bout the street?" Groove snapped. "You haven't been on the street in years. You look all soft now. If it wasn't for those blue eyes and that hair, I wouldn't even have recognized you. You don't fit in here."

I was thankful for that in some ways. An odd shiver of guilt rolled through me, though, because so many others hadn't been as lucky. "You'd be surprised where I can fit in," I replied. "I've been all over the country. I fit in wherever I go."

Groove snorted, the sound full of phlegm. "Please. You didn't fit in here and I doubt you fit in there. You a nothing, and you always will be."

Once, long ago, that statement would've upset me. Now it didn't bother me in the slightest. I'd come across men like Groove numerous times. No matter their race, creed or nationality, there was only one way to deal with the type.

"Do you need me to get a ruler so you can make sure yours is bigger than his?" I inclined my head toward Shadow. "This show you're putting on is for his benefit. He's not impressed."

"I'm not," Shadow agreed. "But I'm used to it. This is a serious situation, Groove. It affects you as much as anybody. If these girls keep going missing it's going to be bad for business because we're going to have to station cops down here twenty-four hours a day. They'll have nothing better to do but hassle you. Is that what you want?"

Groove's gaze only darkened. "Why you gotta be that way? Are you showing off for her?" He jerked his thumb at me. "I always had a feeling you were hot for her. She's a big girl now. Maybe you want to see if there's something there after all. At the very least, you want a peek under those ugly pants."

Shadow's eyes filled with fury and I was legitimately worried he would attack Groove. It was completely unnecessary.

"Don't let him get to you." I raised a hand and pinned Groove with a pointed look. "You've already got your ear to the ground on this."

"You don't know nothing about me."

"Don't be so sure ... Edwin." I dropped his real name with a smirk. I was stronger than I used to be and had easily picked it out of his head.

"How ... you ... ?" He was flabbergasted.

"Does your mom still call you Eddie Spaghetti?"

"You shut your mouth!" The finger he pointed at me promised mayhem. "You don't know the trouble you're messing with."

I moved until I was standing directly in front of him, chest to chest, and held his gaze. There was no fear in me. I wasn't the same child he remembered. I let him see that. "You don't want to mess with me," I countered, my voice low. "You've been looking into this. There's no shame in it. I'm sure it's because you want to protect your business, but you have been looking."

I dug deeper in his head and found a whole lot of conflicting information. "Some people think it's a trafficking ring," I offered. "There's a story going around about men in black sedans picking up girls, tossing them in trunks and then driving them over the bridge into Canada. From there, supposedly they're sold to men in different countries."

Shadow's expression was incredulous. "How can you possibly know that?"

"I'm with the circus," I replied simply. "It's part of my job."

"Aren't you an acrobat or something?"

The question caused me to choke on a chuckle. "I tell fortunes."

"I see." His tone told me he didn't, but he allowed me to continue messing with Groove.

"Other people are whispering that you have a community cleaner on the loose and he's looking for girls who embrace the trade," I said. "You don't believe that because you knew some of the girls. Not all of them were turning tricks."

"Get out of my head, girl," Groove growled.

"There's not much here, so I'm almost done." I offered him a serene smile. "You're legitimately confused about what's going on because there's no pattern. The girls were alone when they disappeared, but they weren't far from groups. If they'd called out, someone would've heard them. That means whoever is doing this is stealthy ... and can move around the area unnoticed."

I took a step back as I considered the new information. Groove was the pragmatic sort. He didn't believe in the paranormal. That meant it didn't occur to him that they could have a different sort of predator in the mix.

It occurred to me, though, and I didn't like it.

"You done?" Shadow asked.

I nodded. "Yeah. There's nothing else in there."

"You're telling me." His smile was tight before shifting his eyes to Groove. "Keep your ear to the ground. I'll be back." He motioned for me to follow him, waiting until we were on the other side of the park to speak. "That was impressive. Did you really see that in his head?"

It was an interesting question. "Yes." I saw no reason to lie. I was billed as "the greatest fortune teller the circus had ever seen." If he didn't believe me, there was no harm in it. If he did, I might be able to help him.

"Well ... that's more than I knew a few minutes ago, so I guess I'll take it." He looked me up and down. "I never knew your real name."

"Poet Parker."

"Poet's your real name? I think you missed the whole reason people make up street names. It's a survival thing."

"I survived. And because people thought that was my street name, they never questioned me. It all worked out."

"You did survive. I'm glad for that, but I was worried when you first disappeared. I looked for you. I was afraid ... ."

He left it hanging. "You were afraid something happened to me," I finished. "I don't blame you. If it's any consolation, I left letters for you and Creek with Junk and Hazy. I guess they didn't deliver them."

He chuckled. "They weren't exactly the reliable sort. You should've realized they would forget."

That was true. "I didn't have much time. The circus was pulling out, and if I wanted to go with it, I had to do it then. I was torn, but ... I sensed it was the only legitimate chance I would probably ever get. I wanted to take it."

"I'm glad you did. Although ... the circus?" His lips curved. "Really?"

"It's a good life. I have friends who are really my family. I fit in there. I can be who I was always meant to be."

"That's good, because you certainly didn't belong out here. You were always the one I worried about most."

"Yeah, well ... you didn't need to. I'm stronger than I look."

"I knew that about you. Still ... I thought about you over the years. I wanted you to be safe and happy. Disappearing the way you did left me with a few dark thoughts. I also had happy thoughts, because they allowed me to imagine you on grand adventures."

I thought of the monsters we'd taken out, the people we'd met and places we'd visited. "I've definitely been on grand adventures."

"I bet. Well ... come on. I'll give you a ride back to wherever you're staying. You really shouldn't be out here, even though I enjoyed the way you made Groove whine like a big baby."

"Sure. I'm over at the old state fairgrounds."

"That's close."

"Just one thing," I called out, stilling him. "What's your real name? It feels weird to call you 'Shadow' given the fact you're a police officer."

"Can't you pick it out of my head like you did with Groove?"

"I could, but it's invasive. It's also easier if you just tell me."

"Logan Stone. I'm an FBI agent, not a police officer, although I was with the Detroit Police Department back then. I've been promoted fairly regularly since the Vipers were removed from power."

I was impressed. "Awesome. Logan fits you. Although ... I thought Shadow fit you, too."

"Come on. Let's get you out of here. I want to see this circus."

"Okay, but if you think the street is weird, the circus is going to rock your world."

"Now I'm definitely looking forward to it."

THE FAIRGROUNDS WERE BUZZING WITH activity when we parked. I didn't miss the look of appreciation on Logan's face when we coasted to a stop in the lot and he could see the hustle and bustle for himself.

"Wow! When did you guys arrive?"

"Yesterday."

"And you did all this in less than twenty-four hours?"

I shrugged as I got out of the Ford Escape. "We're a well-oiled machine. Totally professional and on top of our game."

The moment the words left my mouth, Nellie appeared. He was dressed in a flowery spring dress that put his hairy legs and armpits on full display. "Where have you been?" he snapped, ignoring Logan. "And where is the food? I'm hungry. You know I need my afternoon snack or I get cranky."

Logan arched an eyebrow as I rolled my eyes.

"Luke and Kade are getting the groceries today," I replied. "They shouldn't be too far behind me. I had them leave me downtown because I had an errand to run."

"An errand?" Nellie shifted his suspicious eyes to Logan. "Looks like a Fed to me. Have you traded in your security stud for him?"

I scowled. "I knew him a long time ago. He gave me a ride and wanted to see how we operate."

"That's right. I forgot that you used to live here." Nellie's gaze turned thoughtful. "I never imagined you hanging around with a Fed."

"It's a complicated story," Logan offered.

"One that's none of your business, Nellie," I added. "You don't have to worry about him. He's not here to give you grief."

"I don't know," Logan hedged. "He looks the sort that might need some grief."

"Oh, better men have tried," Nellie sneered. "If you don't have food for me, you're useless. You'd better hope that your boyfriend and sidekick show up soon. I'll eat them if they're not careful."

"I'm sure they're on it."

Logan chuckled as he watched Nellie go. "He's ... interesting."

"He's a good guy with a big mouth. He's harmless – mostly." Except for the ax he carried around at night so he could behead monsters, I silently added. Of course, Logan didn't need to know about that.

"This is amazing," Logan said, leaning against the front of his vehicle and tucking his hands in the hip pockets of his pants. "And you guys travel around together from one end of the country to the other. Does that mean you don't have a home base?"

"We have a home base in Florida, but we're only there for two months in the winter. It's the closest thing we have to an anchor."

"Do you wish you had a home?"

"I have a home. These people are my home. It's because of them that I didn't end up dead or ... something worse. I saw Creek today, by the way."

"I haven't seen her in years. She was searching for you right along with me for a few weeks, but she distanced herself from me fairly quickly. She had hope at first. You could see in her face when it faded. I'm pretty sure she thought you were dead. It was easier than believing you would take off the way you did."

Guilt, hard and fast, barreled into my chest. "I didn't have a choice."

"I'm not blaming you. I didn't really live on the street. It only felt like it because I was undercover for so long. For her, it was different. I think there was some jealousy involved. Groove was telling people that some rich pervert took you off the streets and married you. The rumor went around that you were living in the lap of luxury ... but selling yourself to do it."

"Not quite."

"The circus rumor went around. That came from Hazy, so most people didn't believe it."

I could see that. "Well, I really did join the circus. As for the man who found me, he's still here. His name is Max, and he's not a pervert. He's a good guy who is pretty much like a father to me, although that's weird because I'm dating his son."

Logan barked out a laugh. "Sounds complicated."

"Maybe on paper, but it's not really. We're a tight-knit unit. Well, we're a segregated but tight-knit unit. Nobody likes the clowns and we try to keep away from the midway workers as much as possible because they're crazy."

"Crazier than the little guy wearing a dress?"

"He's our bearded lady."

"Ah. I guess that makes sense?"

"Yeah." I was amused by his expression. "Do you want to look around? It really is a different world."

"Why not? At least now I won't have to imagine how you live."

"There's that."

"I also want to talk to you about the missing girls."

"There's that, too. I want to help if I can."

"I'm not sure how you can, but I'm willing to give it a shot. I don't like what's happening out here."

I didn't blame him. "I'll do what I can. I think there's more to the story. Groove has been looking, but he hasn't found acceptable answers."

"Then we need to tap resources he hasn't."

EIGHT

*L*ogan took a tour, met several people — including Nixie and Naida, who were enamored with him — and then sat with me at a picnic table so we could talk about the missing girls.

"They're all from bad homes," he explained. "They're on the street for a reason. You can always tell when a kid has a bad home life." His gaze was pointed. "You never mentioned what you were doing on the street. I assume you're not visiting anyone else while you're here."

He'd never really asked about my history, but that made sense. He was undercover and there was so little he could do for us without blowing his fake persona that it was probably easier not to know the specifics.

"It was different for me," I replied. "I had good parents. They died when I was a teenager. I bounced around between families after that. Some were really good, but the placements were only temporary. Not many people want to take on a bitter kid who is almost an adult."

"You didn't run from a good placement."

"No." That was definitely true. "I ran from one that had the potential to go bad."

He furrowed his brow at the way I phrased things. "Did you do that mind-reading trick of yours to figure that out?"

"Basically."

"And you thought the streets were better than reporting him to the foster care system?"

"Back then, I didn't believe they cared enough to do anything. I'm an adult now, so I see things differently. They were overwhelmed, not negligent. Still, I'm not sorry about how things turned out. I ended up here."

"Yes, in your own kingdom of ridiculousness."

"It's not so bad."

"I can see that." His eyes traveled to trailer row, to where Percival — our clown with the fake British accent — was trying out a new routine in full makeup for his girlfriend's benefit. Raven didn't look impressed. I often wondered how their relationship survived, because he seemed the exact opposite the sort of man she would seek out. Of course, as a lamia, she'd been alive for centuries. Perhaps she was simply looking for something different.

"Percival notwithstanding." I snickered as he shot water out of a flower and it hit her in the face. The look she shot him promised death ... or some very kinky sex games that she would dominate. "You can't choose your family. We're a family. Sure, it's a different kind of family, but it's still a family."

"I'm glad you have them. In fact ... ." He trailed off, his eyes going to a spot over my shoulder.

When I turned, I found Luke and Kade heading in our direction, their arms laden with groceries. "Hey, guys. I told you I would be fine. You had nothing to worry about."

Kade didn't look happy. "Is your phone broken?"

I cringed when I realized I'd forgotten to text him. It had slipped my mind. "Oh, um ... ." I dug in my pocket and found my phone. I'd muted it before heading into the park and it looked as if I'd missed twenty-five messages ... all of them from Kade and Luke. "I'm sorry." I felt real contrition. "I got distracted."

"Blame me," Logan interjected quickly. "We got to talking, sharing information, and time got away from us."

Kade's eyes were dark when they landed on the FBI agent. "And who are you?"

"Logan Stone." He extended his hand. "I knew Poet a lifetime ago. I ran into her in the park."

"You were friends with a Fed?" Luke made a face as he looked Logan up and down. "That doesn't sound like you, Poet."

Now it was Logan's turn to frown. "How do you know that? Are you guys sharing information or am I wearing an invisible sign that reads 'FBI agent'?"

I chuckled at his discomfort. "In this line of work you learn to recognize law enforcement pretty fast."

"Who else identified him?" Luke asked.

"Nellie."

"Of course." Luke's expression was hard to read, but he couldn't drag his eyes from Logan. "I'm Poet's best friend. Luke Bishop." He extended his hand. "If you like her, you have to like me. Those are the rules."

Instead of being put off, Logan laughed. "Well, I can tell already that I'm going to like you." His eyes were clouded with doubt when he turned to Kade. "And you?"

"Kade Denton." My boyfriend was more reticent when it came to shaking hands. It was expected, so he did it, but I could feel his annoyance.

"Another best friend?" Logan teased.

"Boyfriend," Kade quickly corrected, and then darted a look in my direction. He was obviously worried I would think he was unnecessarily marking his territory. I wasn't in the mood to argue, so I let it go.

"They live together," Luke volunteered helpfully. "I live next door."

He was acting weird, even for him, and I was suspicious of his motivations until I realized what he was doing thanks to a few stray surface thoughts. "He's not gay," I offered, causing Luke to frown.

"That's not what I was thinking," Luke protested. When I didn't immediately respond, he pointed a finger. "You stay out of my head. You're supposed to mind your own business where I'm concerned."

"Then don't think so loudly."

"I'm going to get the rest of the groceries," Luke supplied after a moment's contemplation. "I'll leave you guys to ... whatever it is you're doing."

"We're talking about the missing girls." I patted the open spot next to me so Kade would sit rather than stand and glower. "There's not much information about them, even from a law enforcement perspective."

Kade's nose might've been out of joint a bit, but he was nothing if not a consummate professional. "Did you find out anything while you were down there?"

"There are a lot of rumors, but few facts to back up any of the rumors. One second the girls are there and the next they're gone. It's ... distressing."

"That's putting it mildly," Logan said. "We're forming a task force among local departments. Four missing girls is a big deal, and if we have a serial predator on our hands we need to stop it before it gets out of control."

"Yeah." I rolled my neck. "Are you going to be hanging around the old haunts?"

"Until it's solved," he confirmed.

"How did you two meet?" Kade asked.

"He was undercover with a biker club back then," I replied. "I knew he was different from the rest, but I hadn't pegged him as a cop. It made sense when I heard the news today. He looked out for us, brought us food sometimes. He always checked to make sure nothing bad was going down."

Something occurred to me. "That last day, you warned me to get out of the park because the police were coming," I noted. "Is that because you called them?"

He nodded. "I was undercover, but I couldn't ignore something like what happened that day. I couldn't just pretend I didn't see Noble's body."

"Yeah." I rubbed my forehead, suddenly weary. "I'll keep my ear to the ground. What about the girls? Do they have anything in common?"

"They're all brunette — brown or black hair — and their eye color varies. They're between the ages of sixteen and twenty. They're all thin and none look ... used up by the street."

Kade knit his eyebrows. "What is that supposed to mean?"

"I understand what it means," I volunteered. "After a certain amount of time, you start looking different when you live on the street. It's something you can't really shake. I'm sure you saw it today with Creek."

"She looked as if life had beaten her down and she forgot to get back up," Kade said.

"That's the look."

"You're lucky you got out before you got the look," Logan said, getting to his feet. "I'll be in touch if I can. I'm not sure what my schedule will be like. If I can't stop by, don't take it personally. I'm glad to know you found your people and I can put the sad stories to rest."

"I'm glad to know that you took down the Vipers. They were jerks."

He smiled. "Thank you. Stay safe if you go wandering around. Groove isn't the only old friend who might recognize you. Some of the others are still around."

"I'll be careful. I know how to take care of myself."

"And she has me," Kade added.

"And I have him." I smiled as Logan shook his head. "We really are fine. There's very little this city can throw at us that we can't take. Trust me when I say we can handle ourselves."

"I don't doubt it. Still, watch the shadows. Whoever this is somehow gets in and out without being noticed. I want to make sure that doesn't happen to anyone from your group."

That made two of us.

. . .

KADE'S MIND WAS FULL OF questions for the rest of the afternoon, but I refrained from calling him on it. I was curious about how long it would take him to break and ask, but to my surprise, it wasn't until we were getting dinner ready. And then, when he finally did ask, I was stunned by what he wanted to know.

"Do you think what's happening to these girls could be paranormal in origin?" he asked as he helped me shuck corn. "I mean ... you didn't come right out and say it, but you had that look you get when you're not showing all your cards."

He was observant ... and determined not to come across as jealous. I had to give him credit.

"Seeing the banshee last night was jarring," I admitted. "She was young. I wish I had taken a better look at her so I could compare her face to those of the missing girls. I'm not sure I would recognize her ... and I'm not sure all the disappearances have been reported."

"That's not really an answer," he pointed out.

He was right. "I think there's more going on here than meets the eye." I chose my words carefully. "I poked around in Groove's head. If he knew something, he wouldn't have been able to hide it from me. He's an open book ... and he samples a bit too much of his own product from time to time. He doesn't know, and he's been searching for answers."

"What does that tell you?" Max asked, appearing from behind and giving me a small jolt.

"I didn't know you were here." I smiled at him. He rarely joined us for dinner, although he'd been making exceptions more often so he could spend time with Kade. "Are you eating with us?"

"Unless it's an imposition." He sat at the picnic table and nodded in thanks as Nixie handed him a glass of iced tea. "What does that tell you?" he repeated.

"On the street, it's really hard to keep a crime secret," I answered. "Not from the cops, but from other people. There's an inherent need to blab for some reason. If someone knew what was happening out there, word would've spread and someone like Groove would be the first to know. The fact that the news hasn't spread makes me think that something else is going on."

"Can a person turn into a banshee?" Kade asked. "I mean ... you said you didn't get a good look at the banshee's face. Does that mean you think it could be one of the missing girls?"

"That's what I'm starting to wonder," I admitted. "Banshees are rare in this part of the world. There has to be a reason one turned up now."

"Banshees spring from great loss," Max volunteered. "At least that's how it started. During wars especially, women would band together when their men were overseas, and when one of those men fell in battle the women would join together and keen. This was mostly something that happened in Europe, mind you."

Confused, Kade drew his eyes together. "Keening?"

"That's what we heard last night," I explained. "She wasn't screaming. She was keening."

"How can you tell the difference?"

"Practice. I've come across my fair share of banshees. Most on the West Coast. There was a nest of them in New Orleans that one year, and we took them out. I've never heard of them in Michigan before, though."

"Why would that be?"

"I don't know. Max is right. They started as mourning women. They've grown a bit over the years, expanded their reach. Not all banshees are born of loss. Human suffering can breed them."

"Isn't human suffering and loss the same thing?"

I exchanged a weighted look with Max. It was difficult to explain.

"Not exactly," Max replied finally. "The thing is, the early banshees were created when the women lost something ... or rather someone. And, before you ask, banshees are always women. If there's a male counterpart, I've never heard of it.

"Not all women widowed during war became banshees," he continued. "It was only those hit particularly hard. I once heard it explained that when someone loves someone with their entire heart and then they lose that person, there's a rending of the soul. When a heart breaks to this degree, a banshee is born."

"You said not all banshees were born out of loss," Kade pressed. "How else are they born?"

"It was first noticed during the Holocaust," Max replied. "Or that's when it was reported. It started as whispers."

"Wait ... were you there?" Kade was confused. "Are you older than you look?"

He chuckled. "No. I was not there. Others were, including Raven."

Kade's mouth dropped open. "Raven was in a concentration camp?"

"Raven ran an underground railroad out of Germany to save people," I corrected. "She put her life on the line and was a hero. Of course, she also killed a bunch of Germans and didn't pay attention to whether they were guilty or not, so her actions really kind of evened each other out. That's a story for another time."

"I see. What happened?"

"Many of the individuals who lost loved ones were ripped asunder by what was happening," Max replied. "Of course, not all of them turned into banshees. Apparently some of the women, however, held up as long as they could ... and then they could do so no longer. They became a different sort of banshee."

"See, it seems like you guys are talking around each other," Kade noted. "I don't understand."

"It's not a simple issue," I volunteered. "Banshees can't be saved. At least ... I've never heard of one being saved. Once you're turned, that's it. Your soul has to be fractured for it to happen.

"It used to be that grieving wives turned into banshees and people in the small villages knew what to look for and headed off any issues," I continued. "In the cities, it wasn't as easy, but banshees don't hide, so they were easy enough to track down. The banshees that grew out of the second World War, however, were vastly different."

"How so?"

"They were smarter, more agile," Max replied. "They kept more of their wits about them and didn't become thoughtless monsters. The suffering from which they were born was the sort that nobody should ever have to face."

"Like torture?"

"Yes ... and the loss of multiple children ... and the torture of children ... and gas chambers ... and you can imagine the terrible things that were being done. Some of the deaths were quick and merciful. Others were drawn out for weeks, months and years. It was those who endured the torments of the damned for an extended period who were more susceptible to becoming the new breed of banshee."

Kade nodded, the information slowly sinking in. "So ... is that what you think we're dealing with here?"

"We don't even know what's truly happening," I countered. "I need to take another look around that cemetery after dark."

"Griffin warned you against that," Kade reminded me.

"Yeah, but ... that's not really going to stop me. I need to take a look around when I can investigate freely."

Max's eyes twinkled. "I think that can be arranged. Kade and I are having one of his magic lessons this evening. I thought maybe you would like to watch and see his progress."

"Absolutely." I wanted Kade to get a handle on his magic more than anything. He was a powerful ally, but he was often timid and afraid he wouldn't be able to control what was happening. That made him indecisive. We needed to break him of that habit. "I would absolutely love to see the lesson."

"I'm thinking the cemetery is the perfect place for it," Max noted. "You can investigate while I teach him a few new tricks. Nobody will be alone, and if another banshee shows up, we'll deal with it our way."

"Do I even want to know what that means?" Kade asked.

"Probably not," I replied. "Just leave it to us." I grinned as he went back to shucking corn. "I still can't believe you didn't jump all over me because you had questions about Logan. That's what I was expecting."

"I'm saving those questions until we're alone and you can pacify my ego with a massage."

My smile slipped. "You just had that one sitting around in your back pocket, huh?"

"Hey, whatever works."

NINE

*M*ax was in a jovial mood as we crossed the street. He seemed to be happy, lighter than I'd ever seen him, and I knew it was because he was bonding with Kade.

As for Kade, he was obviously still grappling with the fact that his mother had lied to him his entire life about the identity of his father. He was angry that Max had never told him the truth and he was struggling with learning that he was a magical being when he'd lived his entire life believing paranormal powers were nothing more than fairy tales.

Now, not only was he sharing a roof with a magical being, he was manifesting magic himself. It was a big step.

I thought he was handling it with aplomb.

"Your friend seemed nice," Max noted as we crossed toward the opening to the cemetery. "Did you know he was a police officer when you were younger?"

I lifted an eyebrow, surprised. "You didn't meet him when he was around."

"I didn't, but I met him twelve years ago."

I was taken aback and slowed my pace. "What?"

Max chuckled at my expression. "Don't act so surprised. I knew there was a magical being in that park before I entered. I was looking for you ... though I had no idea who you were at the time. Didn't you ever wonder why I was in that particular location?"

I'd never considered it. Now that he brought it up, I was intrigued. "You were looking for me?"

"I was looking for a magical girl who could make people do things against their will. I'd heard whispers about you. While I was out looking, I ran across Officer Stone. He was leaving the police precinct. I went there to try to find a location for you. I actually used my magic to get them to open their files.

"I found you pretty quickly, if you must know," he continued. "There were numerous notations about you in the system. There were a few conspiracy theories — that you were really undercover with some elite police group and no one had mentioned it to anyone else — but they all agreed on one thing."

"Oh, yeah? What?"

"You didn't belong on the street," Max replied without hesitation. "I knew that the minute I saw you. I watched you a bit in park. I followed Officer Stone, because his name was in several reports and I knew he would know how to find you. He seemed worried, but his hands were tied. He did his best for you guys, but lived in constant fear. He was the one who propelled me to take you with me right away. I knew you were in a bad situation and I could change your life if I removed you from the situation."

"You did change my life." I was surprised when I realized my throat felt thick and my eyes pricked. "I would probably be dead if it weren't for you."

"Don't say that," Kade chided, sliding his arm around my neck. "I don't like hearing you say things like that."

"Yeah, well, the truth is the truth. Returning to that place today was ... surreal."

"It's wonderful that you want to discover what is happening to those girls," Max offered. "I'll help. As for the banshees, I'm still at a loss. I know a few people in the area, though — scholars and such — and I have every intention of tapping those resources tomorrow."

"It couldn't hurt," I agreed, sliding my hand into Kade's as we slipped through the gate and into the cemetery. "All we can do now is keep our eyes and ears open."

"Then that's what we'll do."

I LET KADE AND MAX PICK the location where they wanted to practice. I wasn't surprised when they traveled deep into the cemetery and chose a spot hidden between mausoleums.

Max was taking it slow with Kade, which was wise. Three times a week they worked on a particular skill, keeping to the same skill for the entire week. Max wanted to ingrain the lessons into Kade's head so they would essentially become second nature, but it was an ongoing process.

"I can't do this," Kade complained when he fumbled a simple defensive shield, rubbing his arm ruefully as he checked the tender spot where Max sent a bolt of magic to singe him. "I'm bad at it. I don't think I'm geared for this."

"Nonsense," Max countered. "You've got a military mind. You know how to protect yourself and others. Your block is coming from the fact that your magic isn't something you draw on automatically." He slid his eyes to me. "Ideas?"

I had only one, and I didn't think it was something Kade would like. "Actually, I do. I think it's going to cause an argument, though."

"Then I'm all for it." Max was matter-of-fact. "What's the idea?"

"I don't think you should attack Kade," I replied. "He doesn't think of himself before others when it comes to protection. Besides, he knows you won't really hurt him. I think you should attack me."

Kade's mouth dropped open and he immediately started shaking his head. "Absolutely not," he hissed. "I won't allow you to be hurt so that I'll learn faster."

Amusement at his reaction slid through me. "See, this is why I think it'll work. You want to protect me, so you'll be more engaged in the process of learning."

"Absolutely not." Kade was adamant. "I won't stand by and allow you to be hurt."

"Of course you won't," I agreed. "You'll protect me." I nodded in Max's direction. "Do it."

"Wait. No!" Kade held out his hand to stop his father, but it was already too late.

Max knew what he was doing. He whipped a magical cage in my direction, essentially trapping me. I didn't fight the cage. There was really no point. If Max wanted to hurt me, he could've done it a long time ago. He was the most powerful being I'd ever encountered. The key to this endeavor was to motivate Kade ... and it seemed to be working.

"What is that?" he whined as I made a big show of cringing inside the cage. I didn't say anything. Somehow it added to the mystique. In truth, I wasn't in pain. Max had a soft hand. At most, I itched a little. Kade didn't need to know that, though.

"I can't tell you what that is," Max replied. "You need to figure it out and repel it to save Poet. Just ... reach out with your magic. Instinctively, you should know how to remove it."

"I don't like this." Kade moved closer to me. "She's in pain."

"She's fine," Max shot back. He knew I was putting on a show. "Just focus on getting her out."

Kade whimpered, but met my gaze, sucking in a breath as he focused on what he was doing. He clenched and unclenched his fists at his sides, inhaled and exhaled at regular intervals, and focused on me.

The first hint I got that something was happening was a tickle across my cheek. When I turned, there was nothing there, and yet I was certain I'd felt something. Then it happened again, and this time I was positive I caught a glimpse of a wispy tendril.

I flicked my gaze to Max and found he was watching the same show. He seemed intrigued. Kade continued to pressure the magical tendril, and before I even realized what had happened it doubled in size. Then it doubled again ... and again ... and again. Within seconds it was huge ... and it was barreling right for me.

"What's that?" Max was in awe.

I didn't get a chance to answer because the magic was already overtaking me. It didn't stop when it reached the barrier Max's magic had put in place. Instead, it ran roughshod over that magic and engulfed me.

Instantly, the itchy feeling I'd been laboring under before was replaced with a warm, comforting sensation. It was almost as if I was being hugged. I smirked as Kade's magic burst into millions of small particles of dust that rained down around my head. I was a bit charmed when the dust started falling like romantic (and dry) rain around me.

"What was that?" I was almost breathless.

Kade didn't take a moment to enjoy his victory. Instead he strode directly to me. "Are you okay?"

He looked so serious I had to take pity on him. "I'm fine." I patted his hand. "Max would never hurt me. That spell made me a little itchy, nothing more."

"But ... ." Kade made a series of protesting sounds with his mouth. "You acted as if you were being hurt." His tone was accusatory.

"No, I acted as if I was uncomfortable. I was. That thing you did, though, it was amazing."

"It certainly was," Max agreed, moving closer to study the fine particles that were still falling. "I've never seen an approach quite like that. What did you do?"

Kade appeared caught off guard by the question. "I ... um ... I'm not entirely sure."

"Just walk me through it," Max insisted.

Kade was huffy, but did as asked, causing me to smile as I took a step away from them and studied the ornate window in the nearest mausoleum. Whoever did the craftsmanship was a master. I flipped my eyes to the name over the door and read it out loud: "Grimlock."

I remembered the woman I'd met earlier in the day. She'd introduced herself as Aisling Grimlock.

"Did you say something?" Max called.

"No. I was just reading the name." I moved a bit to study the dedication plaque on the front bench. While the rest of the mausoleum looked old, the bench looked relatively new. "You taught us faith, love and loyalty. We live in your honor," I read out loud. "Redmond, Cillian, Braden, Aidan and Aisling." For some reason the names clogged in my throat.

"What are you looking at?" Kade asked, suddenly focused on me. It was as if he could read the change in my mood.

"Lily Grimlock," I replied. "That guy we met last night ... and the guy and girl I met today ... it's their mother."

"That's sad," Max noted as he moved closer to me. "She was young when she died."

"Yeah." My mind was busy with possibilities. "I wonder if her being here is a coincidence."

Max was puzzled. "How do you mean?"

"Her children were here yesterday and today. They killed a banshee. It wasn't far from this area. It just seems weird to me."

"Perhaps it was a coincidence."

"I'm not sure I believe in coincidences," I said as I turned my eyes back to the window. There, in the reflection, I caught a hint of movement that didn't belong. I swiveled quickly, my eyes immediately moving to a small grove of trees standing between the Grimlock mausoleum and another one that boasted the name Olivet.

"What's wrong?" Kade was instantly alert as he turned. "Do you see something?" He raised his hands, as if he was going to get into a fistfight, which I found absurdly amusing.

"I don't ... ." Something clicked in my brain and I turned away from the mausoleum and headed toward the trees. Something — or someone, rather — was there. I could feel it in my very bones.

A danger alarm went off in my brain at the very last second and I immediately stepped to my left as a figure jumped out from behind the tree. The light was limited so I couldn't immediately see a face, but I recognized the voice as a sword shot in my direction.

"I've got you now!"

I was beyond annoyed as I magically slapped the sword away, causing it to fly five feet before it fell harmlessly to the ground. "Knock that off," I ordered Redmond Grimlock, shaking my head as I met his gaze. "What do you think you're doing?"

Redmond took a moment to stare at me and then straightened his shoulders, smoothing the front of his T-shirt as he lobbed an imperious look in my direction. "May I ask what you're doing here?"

His reaction was funny enough that I had to bite back a laugh. He clearly hadn't been expecting me. That meant he'd set a trap for something else. "I believe that's supposed to be my question," I shot back.

"Hey, Redmond, did you catch her?" Another man, this one boasting the same black hair and purple eyes, rushed out from the shadows and pulled up short when he saw me. "Hello. It's a wonderful evening for a walk in the cemetery, isn't it?"

I had no doubt this was another Grimlock. I'd met three of them so far, and apparently their genes were so strong they could be mistaken for twins. "You must be Braden or Aidan." I involuntarily chuckled. "Hey, that rhymed."

The man didn't immediately answer, instead pinning me with a suspicious look. "And who are you?"

"She's the circus chick," Redmond volunteered, dusting off his shirt. "You remember, I told you about her."

"The one you said was ridiculously hot and warm for your form," the man surmised. "This is her? You're right about her being hot. She doesn't look like she's hot for you, though."

"I'm most definitely not," I agreed.

"Definitely," Kade echoed, moving in behind me.

For the first time, Redmond's eyes moved from me to my partners in crime. "She doesn't go anywhere without you? That's a bummer."

"Not for me," Kade shot back.

"Leave it to you, Redmond, to fall for a chick who already has a guy ... and one that could clearly beat the snot out of you." The second man looked more amused than annoyed. "That's so ... you."

"Shut up, Braden," Redmond snapped.

Well, that answered that question. There was only one Grimlock sibling I'd yet to meet. "What are you guys doing out here?" I challenged.

"We were about to ask you the same thing," Braden replied smoothly. "You know this cemetery is off limits after dark, right?"

He acted as if that was the most normal thing in the world to say despite his location. "And yet you're here," I pointed out.

"We got turned around while taking a walk."

As far as lies go, it was a weak one. He delivered it without a hint of hesitation, though, so I had to give him props for that.

"I thought maybe you were visiting your mother." I pointed to the mausoleum I'd just been standing in front of. "I read the dedication plaque. It's sweet."

For an instant, a dark look swept across Braden's features. He looked genuinely evil. "You didn't touch my mother's grave, did you?"

I was taken aback. "Of course not. I ... why would you think that?"

Braden didn't immediately answer. In his stead, Redmond offered up a hollow chuckle and moved to his brother's side, lightly resting a hand on his shoulder.

"You'll have to forgive Braden," Redmond offered. "Our mother's death isn't exactly something we enjoy talking about. We're sensitive."

"I didn't mean to upset you." That was the truth. "I was merely curious when I saw the name."

Braden found his voice. "Which doesn't explain what you were doing over here. I thought you were warned to stay out of the cemetery."

"I'm kind of curious why that rule is supposed to apply to me but not you," I shot back "I want to know why you guys were setting a trap — with swords, mind you — in the same cemetery where I saw you banishing a banshee last evening. Are you hunting another one?"

Redmond didn't miss a beat. "What's a banshee?"

I narrowed my eyes. If he thought he was being cute — and the way his lips curved told me he did — he'd severely missed the mark. "You're not fooling anyone," I pressed. "You guys are up to something. We're not idiots."

"That's good," Redmond supplied. "I would hate to think people hanging around a cemetery in the middle of the night and throwing magic at one another were idiots. What was that, by the way? We assumed the red spark meant you were evil. But I'm always keen to be corrected. If you have a whip, you can teach me a lesson." His smile was devilish.

Kade growled as he moved closer to me. This clearly wasn't his day ... although that defensive spell he'd whipped up was something special, so I was hopeful it balanced out everything else.

"We have no idea what you're talking about," Max replied smoothly. "We didn't see any bright lights. We were just taking a walk, enjoying the fine night air."

Braden made a hilarious face. "In a cemetery?"

"You seem to be enjoying the same night air in the same cemetery," I reminded him.

"We're local," Braden argued. "We know how fine the air is in this cemetery. You're new. You couldn't have figured that out yet."

Redmond snorted. "Smooth, dude. Truly masterful."

I didn't want to encourage Redmond, so I kept my expression neutral. His reaction made me want to laugh. "What are you doing here?"

"Leaving," Redmond replied after a beat, keeping a firm hold on the back of his brother's shirt and tugging him in the opposite direction. "We're leaving ... and you should do the same. Cemeteries aren't safe to hang around after dark, especially in this neighborhood."

"You should perhaps heed your own advice," Max noted.

"Perhaps." Redmond winked at me and kept pulling at his brother. "Have a lovely evening."

I watched as they turned and walked toward the front of the cemetery. They continued talking as if we couldn't hear the conversation.

"I told you she was hot," Redmond said.

"She's also running around with her father and boyfriend. I don't think you have a shot," Braden argued.

"I always have a shot. Can't you tell how badly she wants me?"

"No."

"Then you're blind. Have you considered having your eyes checked?"

"I'm done talking to you for tonight," Braden complained on a sigh. "You make me tired. I should be home with Izzy and in bed. Instead I'm here with you. I hate it."

"That's because you've gone soft. We need to fix that."

"Yeah, yeah, yeah."

TEN

The next morning, I was still bothered by our meeting with the Grimlocks. Once separated from the encounter — and with a full night's sleep under his belt — Kade was feeling pretty good about himself. If it were someone else, the show of ego might've bothered me. He'd been so unsure about his burgeoning magic, though, that I was more amused than annoyed.

He puffed out his chest and reenacted the event for anyone who wanted to listen, and given who we were, he had an engaged and captive audience.

"That sounds rather intriguing, mate," Percival enthused, his fake accent on full display. He'd been discovered as a fraud — just on the accent; he really was a clown — yet he insisted on throwing out the British accent whenever possible. "I would think that marks tremendous growth."

Luke rolled his eyes. "Mate?"

Raven pinned him with a dark look, practically daring him to say something. Most days Luke would've taken that challenge. This morning, however, he was in a pouty mood and wisely opted to refrain from poking the beast.

"I'm just upset that I wasn't invited along on this late-night excursion," he complained, fixing his eyes on me. "I mean ... what were you thinking, Poet? You might've needed me for backup."

Nellie let loose a derisive snort. "Max was with her, *mate*." He smirked when Luke glowered at him. "She didn't need you when she had the big dog."

"I didn't technically need anyone," I reminded them. "It was supposed to be an easy outing, a way for Kade to practice without prying eyes."

"It doesn't sound like it went that way," Raven pointed out, using a spot of magic to keep her spoon continuously circulating in her mug of coffee. "It sounds like outsiders saw what he could do. Should we be worried?"

It was a fair question. "I sincerely doubt it. They were there for a specific reason."

"And you think they were hunting banshees?" Naida asked, sliding a platter of bacon on the table and making a face when all the men eagerly reached for it. "What a bunch of gluttons," she groused. "We made enough for everybody. It's not as if you're going to go hungry."

Luke, five slices in his hand, merely smiled. "We can't help it. It's a man thing. The smell of bacon turns us into wild animals."

Naida looked to me for confirmation. "Is that true?"

"That they're wild animals? Yes. I don't think it's the bacon, though. They simply have poor manners."

"Ah. That I already knew." Her gaze was dour as it landed on each man in turn. Only Dolph, our strong man, had the grace to look abashed.

"We're growing boys," Nellie explained. "We can't help ourselves."

"Some of us are growing more than others," Luke noted. "That pink dress of yours is looking a little tight, by the way. You might want to lay off the bacon ... and leave it for me." He reached for more but Nellie gripped his fork in such a manner that it looked as if he was about to use it as a weapon and Luke backed off at the last second. "Of course, I've always thought that a few extra pounds is something to exalt."

"You'd better think that," Nellie growled.

I ignored the raw showing of testosterone and returned to the matter at hand. "As for the Grimlocks, I think they're paranormal ... although I'm not sure what they are. Never in my life have I seen such strong genes. The four I've seen look exactly alike, even the girl. It's ... eerie."

"You said you liked the woman," Kade pointed out, forgetting about his magical triumph long enough to focus on security issues. "I have to believe you'd recognize if they were evil."

He had a point. "I didn't sense anything evil about them. I mean ... they're snarky, don't get me wrong."

"Who isn't?" Luke challenged.

"The best people in life are snarky," Nellie agreed. "That's not a reason to behead them. But I'm not ruling out beheading them if it becomes necessary."

I wanted to freeze that compulsion quickly. "That's a terrible idea," I countered. "We don't know that they're evil. In fact, from where we're sitting, they could be allies. They did take out the banshee, after all. They could be just like us."

"It seems to me that you should've been able to pin down a species after three run-ins," Raven argued. "Maybe you're off your game."

"Or maybe they're something we've never encountered," Nixie shot back. She was loyal to a fault. She rarely argued with anyone, but if she was going to throw down, more often than not it was Raven on the receiving end of her ire.

Raven was philosophical. "I guess that's possible. Unlikely, but not impossible."

"I don't know what they are. They obviously know about the paranormal world. They're not going to talk to anyone but each other about what they saw. We're fine."

"Okay then." Raven held up her hands. "What do you want us to do about the missing girls? It's become apparent that you plan to track down the culprit before we leave. It'll be easier if we all work together."

She wasn't wrong. "I don't know where to look yet," I admitted. "It's ... frustrating because I can't even be sure we're dealing with a paranormal monster. For all I know, it's a monster of the human variety."

"We take those monsters out, too," Raven said. "I have no problem ending an evil human. With that in mind, I plan to head down to the area in question and see if I can poke around some heads. Maybe I'll get somewhere."

The territorial part of me wanted to fight her on that, but I knew it was a ridiculous reaction. "Just be careful. Don't wear any jewelry or you'll look like a mark."

"I've survived a very long time," she reminded me. "I know what I'm doing."

"What are you going to do?" Kade demanded. "I can see your mind is already working."

It was, and he wasn't going to be happy with my answer. "There's a shelter about three blocks from here. Er, well, there used to be. I'm hoping it's still there. The guy who used to run it kept his ear to the street."

"What are the odds he's still there?" Luke asked. "I mean ... a lot changes in twelve years."

"It does, but he struck me as a lifer."

"I'm assuming you want to make this trip on your own," Kade noted. He didn't sound bitter as much as resigned.

"I think it would be for the best, at least for now," I replied. "These kids don't trust easily. We're going to be outsiders venturing on their turf. At least I used to be like them. I should be able to blend in better. If the kids are taking refuge at the shelter even though the weather is good, some of them probably have a reason."

"Like they heard stories about bad things happening on the street," Kade surmised. "That's smart. I still wish you would let me go with you."

"It's better this way. I don't know how to explain it. This entire thing is throwing me for a loop. I need to talk to Beacon alone if he's there. It's been a long time. He'll be more likely to open up to me if I'm alone."

"Did you know him well?" Naida asked. "Were you close?"

I turned grim. "I wouldn't say that."

BEACON HILL SHELTER WAS IN the same building, though it had grown since my last visit. Unlike some of the others I ran with back then, I was never keen to stay in the facility. It was usually my last resort.

At the time, I told myself it was because they locked down the facility at night. Once you entered for the evening, you were stuck there. I hated feeling penned in. It was more than that, though. The place always made me uneasy.

Beacon was on the front sidewalk talking to two street kids when I rounded the corner. I slowed my pace so I could watch the interaction without him registering my presence. An intense conversation seemed to be taking place, and none of the participants were happy.

"I don't know what you want me to say," one of the girls offered, her blond hair dirty. She looked like she'd showered — even recently — but a layer of grime that could never be laundered away coated her clothing. She'd been on her own a long time. "I didn't do what you're saying."

"Come on, Cotton," Beacon chided. "We both know that's a load of crap. You were caught offering blow jobs for meth. Two of the workers overheard you. I'm not here to judge your lifestyle. I know it's hard out there. But you can't bring that in here. That's one of the rules."

Cotton — and I couldn't help but wonder how she chose that name — worked her jaw. "You can't send me away." She almost sounded pitiful. "It's not safe right now. I ... won't do it again."

"You've said that before."

"Yeah, but ... I promise this time."

Beacon looked caught. I remembered that expression from when I knew him before. His job wasn't easy. He wanted to help everyone, but there were some kids who couldn't be helped. He set rules for a reason, and there was a zero-tolerance policy in place for breaking the rules. It had to be that way or everybody who tried to stay would run rampant and create an unsafe environment.

"I need to think about this for a bit," he said finally. "I know it's not safe out there, but it has to be safe in here. That's non-negotiable. Come back after dinner and I'll tell you what's up. Until then ... stay safe."

"Fine." Cotton jerked her head so the other girl would follow, and when they swiveled they walked in my direction. Cotton immediately started complaining under her breath. By the time they reached me her expression had changed, and her eyes shined with keen interest as she looked me up and down.

Like the previous day, I opted for simple capris and a T-shirt. They were casual clothes and I didn't stand out in them. Still, I was out of place in this neighborhood now. I no longer fit in. I figured that out the day before, but the notion being reinforced still stung.

"You lost, lady?" Cotton asked. "I'll point you in the right direction for five bucks."

She was a hustler, understood that she had to keep moving or the world would swallow her whole. The demons chasing her were essentially sharks and she would sink and serve as dinner if she didn't keep moving.

"I'll give you twenty bucks if you do me a favor," I countered, fixing her with a pointed look. I didn't want her to think I was a mark, but I couldn't ignore her plight.

"I don't roll with chicks," Cotton shot back. "Although ... you look kind of clean. Double it and I'll consider it."

"That's not what I'm talking about."

Cotton, world-weary and jaded, looked intrigued despite herself. "Oh, yeah? What do you want?"

"If you guys are up for some day jobs — we're talking manual labor, cleaning and whatnot — head over to the fairgrounds and go to where the circus has been set up. Ask for a guy named Kade. Tell him I sent you and that I said I would pay twenty if you do some work."

"Kade?" Cotton made a face. "What kind of name is that?"

"What kind of name is Cotton?"

"Fair point." A shrewd negotiator, Cotton wasn't ready to agree until she'd thought out all the angles. "That's twenty bucks each, right?"

I nodded. "I'll also allow you to sleep in the main tent, although there aren't really any beds. You'll be safe in there and not on the street. Just in case you can't come back here, I mean."

She appeared intrigued. "Seriously?"

I nodded. "There are a lot of us. I promise you'll be safe."

"Well ... we'll think about it."

I knew they would be at the circus before I was finished talking to Beacon. "Just ask for Kade. He'll take care of you."

"No problem." Cotton added some swagger to her step as she strolled down the street. "Oh, hey, wait." She slowed. "What's your name? You said to tell Kade that you sent us, but I don't know your name."

I opened my mouth to answer but someone else responded before I could.

"Poet," Beacon volunteered, causing me to jerk my head in his direction. "Her name is Poet ... and she used to run these streets much like you about twelve years ago."

Cotton didn't appear impressed by the news. "Okay, well ... you don't look like much of a street kid now."

"I got out," I replied. "We'll talk about that when I get back in a little bit. For now, you guys head that way. I need to talk to Beacon."

"Sure." Cotton flashed a peace sign before taking off. This time when she started whispering to her friend she sounded excited.

Beacon waited until he was sure they were out of earshot to speak again. "Been a long time."

"It has," I agreed. "Rick Baxter, right? That's your real name."

"It is, although I think of myself as Beacon now. The name just sort of ... fits." He folded his arms across his chest and regarded me with an unreadable look. "You're one face I never expected to see around here again. I always knew you would get out."

"I've heard that a lot the last few days."

"Most people thought you were dead," Beacon offered. "I knew better. I figured you were too smart to stay on the streets for long. I didn't foresee you joining the circus, but stranger things, right?"

If he only knew the truth. "I'm only here for a few days. I've heard some of the street kids talking. There's a predator on the loose. Some of the girls have gone missing."

"Why do you think I was considering taking Cotton in again tonight despite her breaking the rules? She's vulnerable."

"That's why I offered to help."

"She's also an opportunist," he added. "She'll steal if she can, try to sell sex to your workers for drugs. That's who she is. She can't help herself."

"My workers won't engage in that and I'll keep an eye on her." His tone rankled. "I remember how the street works."

"Do you? You've been gone a long time. Even when you were here, you were never really 'street.'"

"I survived. If I can, I'll help them survive."

"You can't save them all."

"Are you afraid I have a martyr complex? I'm well aware I can't save them all. I can try to stop a predator, though. That's why I'm really here. You must know what the kids are whispering about. If I had a lead ... .'" What? I couldn't exactly tell him what I planned to do if I caught this guy ... or monster.

"You always were the type who thought with your heart instead of your head." Beacon made a clucking noise with his tongue. "I guess it's not my place to tell you what to do."

"It's not," I agreed. "I want to see if I can help. I don't have much time. I figured you'd be a good place to start for information."

"I'd agree, except I don't have information to share." Beacon let loose a heavy breath as he leaned against the building and rubbed his forehead. "It's been going on for weeks now. When the first girl disappeared, everyone thought it was a fluke. Kids go missing out here. A lot of the time it's of their own volition. I mean ... you woke up one day and just walked out without a backward glance. Sometimes others do the same thing."

"Not without a backward glance," I countered. "I looked back. I simply opted to keep going forward. I saw it as my only shot."

"And it was. I'm glad you got out. Coming back now seems a strange choice. It has me questioning what I always believed about you."

"I'm back for work. We were hired to run a festival at the fairgrounds. I heard about the missing girls after we arrived. There's no reason I can't do two things at once."

"Fair enough. I don't have any information to offer. There are a lot of rumors and no facts. I've heard twenty different stories — including aliens and evil witches."

The second part of that statement caught my attention. "Evil witches?"

He chuckled and nodded, obviously mistaking my interest for amusement. "Yeah. Some of the kids are saying that witches, the sort that scream constantly and try to rip out people's throats with their teeth, are behind the disappearances. I like the alien stories better."

"So ... you don't put any stock in their stories?"

"I've been here a really long time. I've heard every story imaginable. There's a monster out there — I'm sure of that — but it's not a witch. I hope they find him soon."

He wasn't the only one. "Well, thanks for your time." I started to leave and then something occurred to me. "You're not familiar with the Grimlock family, are you? They're not on the street or anything but I've seen several members of the family around. I would like to track them down."

Beacon looked puzzled. "Redmond Grimlock?"

Bingo. "Yes. He was one of them I met."

"He lives in Grosse Pointe with his father, Cormack. The old man is a big philanthropist. They've given to my shelter multiple times."

"Great. Thanks." It was a place to start. "Wait ... he lives with his father?" The dude had to be pushing thirty, if not sliding over the line. "How does that work?"

"They're a tight family."

ELEVEN

*I*t wasn't hard to track an address when I got back to the circus. I booted my computer, connected to the wi-fi hotspot and had a location in less than five minutes. Now I knew where to find them, which meant I needed a ride to one of Detroit's ritzier surrounding areas.

"I put your new friends to work," Kade announced as he entered the trailer. "They seem gung-ho about earning their twenty bucks and didn't complain a lick when I told them to wipe down all the bleachers in the big top. They're in there doing it right now."

"Thanks for that." I meant it. "I plan to let them sleep there if it becomes necessary. It's not safe for them on the street."

"Just for the record, the one named Cotton offered me a blow job for meth."

I cringed. "Yeah, well ... ."

He chuckled at my expression. "You'll be happy to know I turned her down. The other one is shy."

"I never did get her name."

"Michelob."

"Ah." All I could do was shake my head. "I'm sorry. I couldn't just leave them to fend for themselves."

"I'm not upset. I warned the others what to expect, and put Nellie and Luke in charge of them. I figured they were the ones most likely to be able to handle whatever weird stuff Cotton throws at them."

"That's a good idea." I programmed the address into my GPS and then turned a hopeful look to Kade. "Are you busy?"

"That depends. What do you have in mind?" He wiggled his eyebrows in the direction of the bedroom.

"On any other day, I would take you up on that. I tracked down the Grimlocks, and I want to talk to them."

He sobered. "I see. I'm allowed to go on this mission with you?"

I bit back a sigh. "I'm not trying to cut you out. You have to believe that. It's just ... this is hard for me. I can't help remembering what I was like back then and I don't want to take up too much of your time chasing this if it turns into nothing. I feel off my game."

He stepped in front of me and ran his hand down my hair, a soothing gesture that caused me to turn my cheek into his palm as he pressed a kiss to the top of my head.

"I love you, Poet," he whispered. "Time spent with you is never a waste. I feel off my game, too. I don't want to push you, because this is clearly affecting you. I don't know what to do to make this okay."

"We can't make it okay. But we can catch a monster. Beacon didn't have any information. He said he's heard a hundred stories, including ones about evil witches. We need someone who understands about the paranormal world and isn't afraid to tell us the truth. That means the Grimlocks."

"And you want to invade their turf?" He didn't look thrilled at the prospect. "What if they attack?"

"They won't."

"You can't be sure of that."

"I have a really good feeling." That was true. "I need to talk to them. You don't have to come if you don't want to. I can go alone."

"Oh, that's fighting dirty." He poked my side and smiled. "I'm going. You don't even have to ask. It's you and me to the end, right?"

"That's the plan."

"Then let's visit the Grimlocks."

I hopped to my feet, excited. "They live in Grosse Pointe. That's a ritzy area. You'll be much more comfortable there."

"You say that now, but if I have to kill them it's not exactly going to be a comfortable experience."

"Good point."

I EXPECTED A BIG HOUSE. What I got was a castle.

"No way!" I was flabbergasted when I climbed out of the truck and fixed my eyes on the behemoth of a house.

"I guess now we know why he's still living with his father," Kade said. "This house is big enough for everyone to pick a wing and then never see each other again."

Even though I'd spent only a bit of time with the Grimlocks, I seriously doubted that's how they operated. "Let's get this over with."

It was the middle of the day, something I didn't think about until I was knocking on the door. There was every chance the Grimlocks were at work ... or sleeping because they spent their nights hunting monsters. I wasn't surprised when a man in a dapper suit opened the door. I was, however, surprised when he gave me a churlish look.

"Deliveries are made in the rear." He moved to shut the door.

Kade reacted faster than me and held out a hand to stop him. "We're not here to make a delivery," he said quickly. "We're here to ... ."

"See Aisling," I finished. Of all the Grimlocks, she would probably be happiest to see me. "We're here to see Aisling."

The butler — we learned later that's what he was — narrowed his eyes. "You know Miss Aisling?"

"We do."

"Do you wish to do her bodily harm?"

That wasn't the question I was expecting. "No. Why? Do people who want to do her harm stop by often?"

"You would be surprised." He held open the door. "Please come in. You'll have to wait in the foyer until I ask Miss Aisling if she's available to guests. If you have weapons, I expect you to leave them on the front table."

"Okay, well ... we're unarmed."

The foyer was as impressive as the outside of the house. The floors were marble and the statues stationed at either side of the room looked to be carved from the same. They were huge lions, sitting resplendent as they stared at each other across the room. They were creepy, but I was hardly an interior decorator.

"Oh, it's you." Redmond appeared in the doorway the butler had disappeared through. He was smiling when he poked his head through the door. The smile evaporated quickly. "I thought maybe someone from Aisling's past showed up and wanted to pull her hair."

"Does that happen often?" I asked.

"You would be surprised."

That was the second time someone had uttered that phrase. I was starting to regret my decision to track down the Grimlocks. "We need to talk," I started. I'd come this far, so there was no sense turning back. "I think you know something about the disappearances on the street and I'm here to find out what that is."

In his home environment, Redmond was even cockier than normal. He crossed his arms over his chest and leaned against the door jamb. "You came here to demand answers from me?"

"Actually, I was hoping to see your sister. She seems the most capable of your group."

He snorted. "That just shows you haven't spent enough time with her. She's dealing with a tiny monster right now, so she can't visit with you. Maybe you should stop by tomorrow or something."

He was trying to put me off. That wasn't going to work. "Is there someone else here I can talk to? Cillian or Braden, perhaps? They seemed more open to conversation ... and less likely to grunt their way through it."

"Oh, big talk." Instead of being offended, Redmond looked amused. "We're not used to inviting strange people with magical powers into our house. How do I know you're not here to kill us?"

"Why would we knock if we were here to kill you?" Kade questioned.

"That's happened a few times, too." Redmond's gaze was thoughtful as he watched me for a long moment. "Okay. I'm going to let you in, but if you move on the baby we'll cut your heads off without thinking twice about it."

"Fair enough."

He led us through the house, which somehow seemed bigger on the inside, and didn't stop until we reached a large office at the end of an ornate hallway. There, sitting behind a huge mahogany desk, was the source of the Grimlock children's looks.

"This is my father," Redmond began as he led us through the door. "He thinks we should've killed you at the cemetery last night, but I stood up for you – mostly because you're hot. He's agreed to hold off on the murder for now. No worries."

I focused on the patriarch. His hair was black, although there was a bit of gray at the temples, and his eyes were violet and full of suspicion. "Hello, sir." I extended my hand. "My name is Poet Parker."

He stared at my hand for a moment and then took it. "Cormack Grimlock."

"She's with the circus," Redmond volunteered.

"So you've said." Cormack gestured toward two open seats in front of his desk. "I understand you're here to talk."

"Is the house bugged or something?" I sat in one of the chairs, Kade taking the other, and tried to get comfortable.

"Not last time I checked," Cormack replied, his gaze on Kade. "And you are?"

Kade introduced himself. It was clear he felt out of his element, but he was determined to stand with me. He was loyal and trustworthy, and even though we were outnumbered he wanted the Grimlocks to know he wasn't afraid. I was fairly certain they were all talk, so I wasn't particularly worried.

"We want to know about the missing women," I started, frowning when I heard an infant start wailing in another part of the house. "Are you babysitting?"

Cormack sighed and rubbed his forehead. "Not exactly."

"Then ... ?"

"Just wait for it," Redmond instructed, his eyes on the door we'd just passed through. Sure enough, moments later, Aisling strode through it with a baby perched on her hip. She looked as if she had enough – of whatever it was.

"Take her," Aisling ordered, shoving the baby at her father. She pulled up short when she saw me. "Hey. What are you doing here?"

"Actually, I came to see you," I replied, smirking when Cormack obediently took the baby. He put a burp cloth over his shoulder and immediately shifted the infant so he could softly pat her back. "I was hoping to get some information about the girls who are going missing downtown."

"And you thought we would know about that?" Aisling arched an eyebrow. "That's kind of weird. How did you even find us?"

"It wasn't that hard. I knew most of your names — first and last — and I asked the guy who runs the shelter around the corner from the cemetery. He not only knew you, but said you were philanthropists. Once I had a city, it was a simple matter of Googling an address."

"Well, look at little Miss Nancy Drew," Redmond teased.

Aisling had the honor of cuffing him. "Shut up. Trixie Belden is way better than Nancy Drew. If she's anyone, she's Trixie Belden."

Redmond screwed up his face as he rubbed the back of his head. "You've turned vicious since becoming a mother."

"She's just tired," Cormack countered. "The baby had us up all night."

"Not that you helped," Aisling said pointedly.

"I was on an assignment with Braden," Redmond said. "Some of us have to work late shifts more than we used to because you're not available to go out unless you feel like it."

"Leave your sister alone," Cormack ordered as he patted the baby's back. "Lily is a handful. Your sister is still getting used to things."

I focused on the baby, taking a moment to do a brief mind probe. Lily was indeed a handful. She was only a few months old but had already figured out how to manipulate all the people in her life ... which meant constantly crying because she liked the attention. She was probably going to grow up to be her own breed of monster. That was really none of my business, though.

I cleared my throat to get everybody's attention. "I really don't want to invade your personal space. I get that you don't want to tell me what you are. It's smart to protect your identities. But I want to figure out what's going on, and I think you guys know."

"I think you're giving us too much credit," Aisling countered, throwing herself on the small settee on the other side of the room and planting her feet on the stool as she regarded me. "May I ask why you care about this so much? You're not local. None of the girls who were taken are related to you, right? It seems like a weird thing for you to be obsessed about."

"I'm not local," I confirmed. "I was at one time. I lived here until I was eighteen."

"Whereabouts?" Cormack asked.

"I was in the suburbs until my parents died. Then I was moved to various foster homes. After that ... I took off on my own. I was a street kid until I managed to get out thanks to a friend. This very well could've happened to me if it occurred back then."

Realization dawned on Aisling's face. "Oh. You're trying to keep the kids safe because nobody ever kept you safe."

That was a simplistic answer. "Not quite. I'm not convinced what's happening isn't paranormal in origin. I mean ... I did watch Redmond take out a banshee with a sword the other night. I don't really believe in coincidences — and banshees don't normally spawn around here — so I'm wondering if the two are connected."

Cormack and Redmond exchanged a weighted look before the elder Grimlock shifted the baby against his chest. She'd fallen asleep and seemed perfectly content in her grandfather's arms.

"We've been wondering that, too," Cormack admitted, choosing his words carefully. "Here's the thing: We don't know you. My instincts say to trust you, but I'm a father first and I put my children's safety before my own. I just don't know how we can help you."

Aisling's gaze never moved from my face, and when she spoke, it appeared to be off the cuff. "We're reapers," she announced. "What are you?"

"Reapers?" I'd heard the term, but I wasn't familiar with the actual beings. "Like ... grim reapers?"

"Yup."

"Aisling, you have a huge mouth," Cormack complained. "I can't believe you just did that."

"It's fine." Aisling seemed sure of herself. "She's not our enemy. If she was, she would've already attacked ... that first night, or the next morning, or again last night. You heard Braden and Redmond. They're magical, which means they're probably more powerful than us."

Cormack heaved a sigh. "You are an incorrigible child," he muttered.

"I'm right." She smiled at me. "We absorb souls after the dead depart and then act as ferrymen of sorts. We transfer the souls to the regional gate, and then they're transferred to another place."

Kade stirred. "Where?"

"Onward."

That wasn't really an answer. Of course, she might not have an answer. Either way, it wasn't important to our reason for being here. "I'm psychic," I explained. "There is no real name for what I am because I seem to be a hodge-podge of things. I can read minds, direct energy and control others if need be."

"You can read minds?" Redmond was suddenly intrigued. "How does that work? Wait ... you don't need to explain. Just tell me what I'm thinking right now."

It didn't take a mind reader to recognize the smug smile on his face. "That you want my boyfriend to beat you up," I automatically answered.

Kade looked intrigued at the prospect while Aisling dissolved into gales of laughter.

"You really are a pervert, Redmond," she said when she recovered. "As for the missing girls, we're not sure what's happening. All we know is that some of our souls have gone missing, too. We managed to track one of them the other night. That's how Redmond found the banshee."

I was confused. "So ... you literally absorb souls?"

Aisling bobbed her head. "We have scepters."

"But ... I've never seen a reaper before," I admitted. "At least not that I'm aware of. Wouldn't I have seen a reaper before?"

"Are you often around death?" Cormack asked.

"Actually, yes. We're more than a circus. We're monster hunters. We have a variety of paranormals in our service."

"Told you." Aisling looked triumphant. "I knew I was right about you." She leaned forward, eager. "What kind of monsters do you hunt?"

"Any that we can find." That was the truth. "Right now I want to know who is taking young girls from the streets and what's happening to them."

"We would like to know that, too," Cormack said, the baby sleeping sweetly in his arms. She didn't look like much of a monster when she was passed out cold. "We're simply unsure. Redmond was on the hunt for his soul — sometimes they run, but this one was taken — when he crossed paths with the banshee."

"She ran, so I chased her," Redmond said, taking over the story. "She headed straight for the cemetery. I had every intention of following her to find her lair, but she started screaming when she realized she was being followed and I knew I had to dispatch her before someone heard. Unfortunately, it was already too late for that."

"And that's all you know?" I couldn't help being disappointed.

"So far," Cormack conceded. "We're not giving up. We want to help those girls. The odds of them still being alive are slim ... but we're digging as hard and fast as we can."

I fought the dejection threatening to overwhelm me. "Well, great. That's not really what I wanted to hear."

"It's all we have."

I rubbed my forehead and then realized Aisling was staring at me. "What?"

Her grin was wide. "What other kinds of paranormals do you have in your group? Do you have a vampire? I've always wanted to meet a vampire."

"We have a lamia who sleeps with a clown who wears leather chaps."

Aisling flashed an enthusiastic thumbs-up. "That's even better. Tell me about them."

I needed time to absorb and think, so I acquiesced to her demand. What? The butt-less chaps story is always a crowd pleaser.

TWELVE

*T*he Grimlock house was utter chaos.

At first, I thought it was because we'd invaded their space and they weren't used to other paranormals under their roof. I was quickly disabused of that opinion. This was simply how they lived.

Braden and Cillian arrived in short order, mentioning the fifth brother was detained over planning a wedding with his fiancé, a man named Jerry who they told a series of raucous jokes about. Cillian was the easiest to identify because of his longer hair. Braden and Redmond looked so much alike I often had to look closely to be sure which was speaking. Of course, they had very different energies.

Redmond was all boastful jests and inflated ego. Braden had an ego, too, but he seemed to be distracted with something else and was constantly on his phone. The vibes I got from him told me it was a woman ... and he was altogether smitten.

"What are you smiling at?" Kade whispered, leaning close. He was much more relaxed now than when we'd first arrived. Apparently seeing the way the Grimlocks interacted with one another was enough to ease any suspicion he might've had. It wasn't as easy for me.

Aisling must've judged that, because at one point she motioned for me to follow her out of the office and into the main house. She gestured toward the stairs and I followed, leaving Kade to entertain himself with the testosterone trio and their long-suffering father.

"It must have been cool to grow up here," I offered halfway up. I didn't know what else to say to her.

"It was," Aisling confirmed, turning down a hallway. "We got in a lot of trouble, but we were always entertained. Even on snow days."

"I can see that."

"We created games and tortured one another. My father ultimately had to separate us into different wings of the house as we got older because we fought so much."

"You seem to get along okay now."

"Oh, we still fight." Her smile was mischievous as she turned into a bedroom. "We just don't hold grudges like we used to."

The bedroom was enough to take my breath away. There was a huge sleigh bed in the middle of the room — I always dreamed of having one when I was a kid — and stuffed toy sharks littered the floor, which I found odd.

"Oh, sorry." Aisling scooped up the sharks and tossed them toward the bed. "Things got out of hand last night."

I was confused. "With sharks?"

"It's a game I play with my brothers ... and husband. He's really gotten into the spirit of it since the first time he played and thought we were nuts."

I took a moment to study the room in greater detail. Everything was a hodgepodge. There didn't seem to be a unifying decorating scheme. In fact, if I had to guess, the room had been decorated when Aisling was a child and only mildly updated as she aged.

"Huh." I was thoughtful as I glanced around. "I'm confused," I admitted after a beat. "Where is all your baby stuff?"

"Lily has her own room down the hallway."

"Oh. Of course." No, it was still weird. "Doesn't it bother you to still live with your father?" It was a blunt question, but I was curious. "I mean ... don't you ever want to venture out on your own?"

Instead of being offended, she was amused. "Oh, I don't live here. I mean ... you wouldn't know that from how often I spend the night these days. Griffin and I have our own place. It's right next door to the townhouse my brother and his fiancé share."

That was a relief. She wasn't nearly as weird as I originally thought. "That's good. Do you like your brother's fiancé?"

"Yes. Jerry was my best friend first and then he and Aidan fell in love. My nose was out of joint for a bit because I thought Aidan was stealing my best friend — we're twins so we've always been competitive — but I'm happy now.

They're even on a list to adopt a baby. I've offered to give them mine, but they don't seem interested."

I knew she was kidding. Even as she mentioned her daughter, a wave of love rushed through her ... and then weariness. I think I finally understood.

"You're just staying here because your father and brothers help with the baby," I surmised. "You're a little frightened you're going to screw up, and they're your safety net."

Aisling looked impressed. "So ... you really are psychic. That was pretty impressive."

"I wouldn't need to be psychic to see that. It's all over your face. You love your daughter, but you're used to being the center of attention around here. Having to be the provider for a helpless infant has you terrified ... and you want your daddy."

Aisling snorted. "Wow. I'm glad I'm so easy to read."

"It's not a bad thing," I offered hurriedly. "I would assume that everyone who could take advantage of a situation like this would."

"I'm lucky." Aisling sounded intensely grateful. "My father and brothers have stepped up. My brothers pretend they want to be Lily's favorite — and I'm sure that's true on some level — but they're really trying to help me. I haven't gone back to work full time yet. I offered to go back full time, but my father thought it was better to ease me in. I tend to find trouble when I'm reaping."

"How does it work?" I was genuinely curious.

She shrugged. "It's not a big deal. We get a list from the home office and it tells us where to go. Sometimes we can get in and out without a problem. Sometimes we have to wear rings that make us invisible. Sometimes there are wraiths at the sites looking to steal the souls. Other times it's quick and easy. I tend to be a talker, so my jobs are never quick and easy."

I tried to picture what she described and found it difficult. "Being invisible must be cool," I said finally.

"You would think. But it loses its luster after a bit."

"Yeah, well ... what do you think is going on with the missing girls?" I wanted her opinion even more than the others. She was more intuitive, though I wasn't sure she realized it.

"I don't know. I think it's bad." Aisling was thoughtful as she turned to me. "Do you think it's possible to create a banshee for a specific purpose?"

Her take interested me. I'd been wondering that. "I don't know. I know a little about them. One type springs from grieving. The other type, the more dangerous type, happens when the sum of human suffering for one individual becomes too much. Is that what you think is happening here?"

"It's possible. No bodies have been found. That's the part that bothers me the most. Most people here dump bodies in the Detroit River because of current that allows them to disappear. We were curious and sent people from the home office out searching, but they couldn't find anything."

"You have people who search the river for bodies?" I wrinkled my nose. "What a fun job."

"Gargoyles," she corrected. "They can fly over the area and smell death. We have several who work for us. They came up empty."

My mouth dropped open. "You have gargoyles working for you?"

She seemed amused by my reaction. "Doesn't everybody?"

"Um, no."

"Well, they're useful ... at least when they're not trying to kill you."

"How often do they try to kill you?"

"Not much lately. That's a bonus. For now, I don't know that we have enough information to form a solid opinion. We need to keep digging. It could take days ... or weeks."

That's what I feared. "I don't have weeks. We'll be out of here on Monday."

"It's not your responsibility," she pointed out. "This doesn't fall on you."

"No, but I feel I should help. This used to be my turf. I want to save them if I can. If they're out there and need help ... I want to find them."

"So do we. The thing is ... when you deal in death, you come to expect it. I think the odds of finding these girls alive are slim."

I thought about the banshee Redmond had dispatched. "I wish I would've gotten a better look at that banshee. We could've sketched her face and showed it around to the street kids. At least that would be something."

"We can't go back and make that happen. We can only move forward. For now, that means holding the course. There's nothing more we can do."

I hated that she was right.

WE LEFT OUR CONTACT INFORMATION with the Grimlocks and returned to the circus. Kade seemed reluctant. He was having a good time. But I was adamant. We couldn't shirk our duties to hunt for a monster — man or beast — when we didn't know what we were seeking. We were rudderless, so we had to focus on our regular work and leave the hunting for later.

Larry was at the fairgrounds, wearing khaki pants and a white shirt with a weird badge affixed to the pocket. As we drew closer, I realized the badge declared him the "official festival organizer." It was laminated, and I couldn't help wondering if he'd made it himself.

"Is something wrong?" Kade asked, instantly alert.

"I'm here to check on the progress of things," Larry replied, his tone crisp and official. "So ... what is the status of things?"

I was confused by the question. "Good?"

He flashed a smile that I understood was supposed to feign patience, but there was an undercurrent of annoyance about him that wasn't easy to ignore. "Are things on time?"

"Yes. Why wouldn't they be?"

"Well, I heard you hired extra help and I figured that was because you were behind."

So that's what he was worried about. He'd heard two street kids were working with us and wanted to know if we were up to something nefarious.

"If you're talking about Cotton and Michelob, they're just earning a few extra dollars by cleaning bleachers. I ran into them this morning when I was visiting the shelter around the corner and offered them money for a few chores. Do you have a problem with that?"

Larry's insincere smile never faltered. "Do I have a problem with you bringing drug abusers onto the property and allowing them to run wild for what's supposed to be a family-friendly event? Um ... just a little."

His tone rankled. "How do you know they're drug abusers?"

"Are you saying they're not?"

I recognized the slippery slope. I couldn't deny it. Frankly, it was none of his business. "I'm saying that the girls are working for me and we'll take care of them. Do you have specific knowledge of them somehow ruining the festival? I'm guessing not since it hasn't even started."

"Young lady, this festival is a big deal," Larry shot back, imperious. "Do you understand that we're trying to revive a family tradition here? For years, the state fair was the premier event in the entire state. Now, we're not bringing the state fair back to this location, but we are bringing family activities back. We want this festival to be synonymous with clean and wholesome fun. We don't want it mentioned in the same breath with dirty fun. Frankly, I don't want my name associated with dirty fun, and there's no one on the steering committee who wants that either."

His unintended double entendre had me struggling to keep a smile from my face. Thankfully, Kade picked that moment to swoop in and play security chief extraordinaire.

"I don't think you ever have to worry about anyone thinking you offer dirty fun," he said with a straight face, which only made it harder for me to hold it together.

"I don't think so either." Larry obviously missed the sarcasm flying fast and furious between us. "Now, I would like to talk to you about the entertainment lineup for the festival. Is now a good time?"

I wanted the guy out of here as soon as possible. He gave me acid indigestion. He was technically in charge, so there was nothing I could do about it ... which was beyond frustrating.

"What lineup are you talking about?" I asked.

"Well, for starters, I know you have a trapeze crew," he started. "I want to make sure the costumes aren't too skimpy. I was thinking a nice sparkle bodysuit that completely covers the bosoms would be appropriate." He moved his hands over his chest for emphasis.

"You don't want boobs hanging out," I noted. "That's what you're saying? Well, you don't have to worry about that. Our costumes are chaste and cover everything."

"That's good." He beamed happily. "I would also like to talk about your fortune teller."

Instantly my antenna went up. "Excuse me?"

"I understand you're the one who reads fortunes, correct?"

"Yes."

Clearly sensing trouble, Kade moved closer to me. He looked as if he was ready to jump between Larry and me should I decide it was time to kill him.

"Well, we've been discussing that in the committee meetings, and we think it would be best if you only delivered happy fortunes."

"Do you?" My temper was bubbling hot and threatened to grab me by the throat.

"We thought about canceling the fortunes altogether because we don't believe in promoting hocus pocus, but, surprisingly, many of the committee members were against that. They said the fortunes were a popular draw. Of course, they were all women, so that explains that."

"Oh, so women believe in hocus pocus and men are rational and only believe in the real?" I challenged.

"Yes." He didn't seem bothered by the change in my tone or the aggressive stance I'd adopted. Clearly, he wasn't afraid of me. That probably had something to do with the fact that I was a woman.

"Now you listen here ... ."

Kade extended a hand and pressed it to my chest to keep me from throwing myself on Larry and expressing my out-of-control rage. "Mr.

Wilcox, the thing is, Poet is truly gifted. She doesn't decide between what's happy and sad. She volunteers the readings she gets in a truthful manner. You're not saying you want her to lie, are you?"

Larry's face was blank. "I don't believe in psychic powers."

I was so furious I considered putting on a display to silence him, but even through the haze of red I saw that was a bad idea. I was never going to bring Larry around to my way of thinking. He was a narrow-minded individual and that would never change. I should simply agree and send him on his way. Besides, I had other things to worry about.

I couldn't quite make myself do it.

"I'll do my absolute best to make sure my customers are satisfied," I gritted out. "That's the promise I make at every venue."

"And she's good," Kade interjected quickly. I could tell he was worried, but he really needn't be. I was already over Larry and his ridiculous attitude. I wanted to move on ... and get him away from us. "She's always our biggest draw."

"I would've assumed the games were the biggest draw," Larry argued. "I mean ... isn't that where you make most of your money?"

"I meant outside of the games," Kade said quickly, cringing when I murdered him with the darkest look in my repertoire. "Personally, I think Poet's show is the best thing we have to offer, far and away better than the games."

"Yes, well, people like all different types of things," Larry drawled. "I happen to be a game person."

"I'm sure you are." I managed to rein in my temper, but just barely. "Is there anything else you would like to discuss?"

"That's it for now. Just make sure you don't allow those ... urchins ... out in public. We don't want homeless people on the fairgrounds during the festival. That means you have to get them out before we open. We've spent a great deal of time and money cleaning them out of here already."

To him it was a simple statement. To me, it was something more. "What is that supposed to mean?"

"Just that. We hired security to keep the homeless from squatting on this property. They're unsightly. Normal people don't like seeing them because it creates an atmosphere of discomfort."

I would show him an atmosphere of discomfort when I shoved my foot up his ... .

"We've got it," Kade snapped. His good nature had been completely eradicated. "You don't have to worry about your precious festival. We'll make sure the girls are taken care of. If that's all, you really should go. We have things to do."

"That's all." Larry graced Kade and me with his smarmiest smile. "This was a productive meeting. I'll be back tomorrow with further tweaks. Keep up the good work."

With those words, he was gone, happily waving and calling out to people as he exited the grounds.

"Get Nellie," I hissed. "Tell him to bring his ax."

"You know we can't do that." Kade sounded practical, which only served to tick me off more. "You just have to ignore him. He's hardly the first jerk we've met in recent months. Don't give him the satisfaction of riling you."

He was right, and I hated it. "I have work." I disengaged from Kade. Wisely, he made no move to follow me. "I'm going to set up my tent and prepare myself for happy fortunes. It would probably be best if you didn't follow me for a bit. I'm ... upset."

"I gathered that." His lips curved up. "I'll check on the girls. You know where to find me if you need to talk ... or have someone talk you down from a ledge."

The only thing I needed right now was to vent ... and I knew exactly where to go to do it.

THIRTEEN

I checked on Cotton and Michelob and found them diligently working. I took a moment to observe them when they weren't looking and found their conversation interesting ... mostly because Michelob seemed soft-spoken, as if she couldn't speak above a whisper. Her voice was ragged. She was slow and deliberate in choosing her words.

"Hey." I pushed back from the wall to approach them. It was rude to eavesdrop, after all, and I wanted the girls to trust me. "How are things going?"

"We're making our way through all the benches like good little girls," Cotton offered with a sassy salute. "We're holding up our end of the bargain."

"I never had a doubt." I moved to Michelob and sat on the bleacher bench next to the one she was cleaning. She was an enigma, and I felt sorry for her. "How are you doing?"

The girl's eyes widened. She was clearly surprised to be addressed. I had a feeling that Cotton served as their official spokeswoman.

"She's fine," Cotton replied. "She's working hard."

"That's not what I asked." I pinned a pointed gaze on Cotton, one that warned I meant business. "I was talking to Michelob."

I didn't want to make the quiet girl nervous, but I was curious about her voice. "Do you mind?" I tentatively stretched my fingers toward her throat. "I just want to see what's going on in there."

"Are you suddenly a doctor or something?" Cotton snapped. "If you're not, we don't want you doing no witch doctor magic on her."

"Quiet," I ordered, mustering a small smile for Michelob's benefit. "It's okay. I just want to see."

Michelob appeared uncertain, but she hesitantly nodded.

I was gentle when I touched her throat, frowning when my fingers brushed against a set of the most inflamed tonsils I'd ever felt. "How long have they been like this?" I asked.

"It's just a cold," Cotton interjected. "She'll be fine."

I ignored her. "It's okay. You can tell me." I nodded to prod Michelob. "I want to help."

"Mostly since I was a kid," Michelob finally rasped. "A doctor said they needed to come out, but my mother didn't have the money. It's okay. I'm kind of used to it now."

I caught a fleeting glimpse from inside her head of what her mother needed the money for. It looked to be crack. I was momentarily overtaken by a wild impulse to track down the woman and give her a piece of my mind. That wouldn't help Michelob. It would only make me feel better.

"I think we can help you," I offered. "Do you trust me to try?"

Michelob looked to Cotton for confirmation. The chattier girl was mired in suspicion.

"Is this where our payment comes in?" she asked darkly.

"No. This is where I try to help. I used to be just like you. I understand about struggle. I think we can fix this."

Michelob immediately started shaking her head. "I don't want to go to the hospital."

"You don't have to. We have an alternative medicine practitioner here."

Cotton snorted. "See. I told you they're witch doctors."

I fought the urge to strangle her. The kid had a mouth ... which probably had kept her alive to this point. "She's not a witch doctor. She's really good. She's fixed me numerous times. I think she can fix this ... and for good. You won't need surgery and this problem won't pop up again."

Michelob's eyes went wide. "For real?"

"Yeah."

"What do I have to do?"

"Just trust me and her. Can you do that?"

"I'll try."

"That's good enough for me."

NIXIE'S HAIR WAS LONGER AND orange today. She changed the way it looked often — sometimes daily — and I had to admit the cut she'd picked was flattering to her sculpted face.

"Hi." Nixie was the chirpy sort. The pixie was more than a century old and yet was blessed with eternal enthusiasm. When I called her on my cell phone she was happy to drop what she was doing to help. She was a giver, and I was almost certain she would be able to help Michelob.

Michelob moved closer to Cotton, obviously afraid.

"It's okay," I reassured her, internally cursing myself for not warning Nixie to come in with a more muted personality. Bright and shiny people were always something to worry about on the street because woe was the currency they traded in there and happiness was a limited commodity. "She's good at what she does. I promise you that."

Nixie isn't often effective when it comes to reading a room. She sees what she wants to see. Today, though, she picked up on the fear coursing through the girl and allowed her smile to fade. "I am good," she agreed. "I just need to see. Can I see?"

Michelob, still mistrustful, finally nodded and opened her mouth at Nixie's prodding. The pixie used a small flashlight to stare at the back of her throat and then shook her head.

"Good grief. How can you even swallow?" Nixie was horrified. "I guess that's why you're so thin. You can't eat more than soup."

"That leaves more bread for me," Cotton said jovially.

"Not for long." Nixie opened her bag. It looked like a standard doctor's bag, but it was filled with powder packets and potion vials. When she finished rummaging around, she tugged out a bottle of green liquid and handed it to Michelob. "Drink this. In about eight hours, you should be all better."

Michelob only stared at the green liquid.

"That looks like poison," Cotton announced. "She ain't drinking no poison."

I wanted to shake Cotton until sense started filling her head. In truth, I didn't blame her. I remembered what it was like to be suspicious of everybody. It was a necessity on the street, because if you trusted the wrong person, you could literally die. Cotton was just being pragmatic.

"It's not poison." I took the vial from Nixie and opened it, downing a sip. "See. I'm fine."

Cotton narrowed her eyes. "And you just expect us to believe that this is going to fix her? If that potion is real, why didn't the doctors offer it when she was a kid?"

"Because it's not from this world," Nixie replied without thinking through her words. "It's from another world."

Cotton rolled her eyes. "See. They're witch doctors."

"Stop saying that." I extended a warning finger. "I swear we're not trying to hurt you. We want to help. This can help, Michelob. You'll feel like a different person tomorrow morning. We're here to help. I know you don't believe me, but it's true."

Michelob looked caught. She was clearly in a lot of pain. Still, she trusted Cotton with her life. If the girl continued to fight the effort, Michelob wouldn't drink the tonic. I had to entice Cotton to believe if I wanted to gain traction with Michelob.

"Do you want your friend to be in constant pain?" I challenged Cotton. "Winter will be here in a few months. With tonsils like that, she could get sick enough to die. We can fix it and then she can start eating more and get hardier. This will be good for her on every level. That means it's good for you, too."

Cotton pursed her lips. "I ... ."

"It's worth a shot," I supplied before she could come up with an excuse. "You have nothing to lose."

She let out a resigned sigh. "Fine." She nodded at Michelob, who almost looked eager when she stepped forward to accept the vial. "If she dies, I'll murder you in your sleep."

It was clear she meant it.

Michelob made a face as she downed the potion. When she finished, she looked to Nixie expectantly.

"Eight hours," Nixie instructed. "You need a good night's sleep. When you wake up, you'll feel like an entirely different person."

"Do you think you could make her a celebrity so we can live in a mansion?" Cotton asked.

"Not with this potion." Nixie winked at her before reclaiming the vial. "I'll check on you in the morning. You're sleeping in here, right?"

"They are," I confirmed. "They'll be joining us for dinner."

Surprised, Cotton cast me a sidelong look. "You don't have to feed us."

"We'll have plenty of food. It's part of the service."

"Well, if you insist." Cotton's grin was impish. "I'm starting to think you're a fairy godmother instead of a witch. I think it was lucky we ran into you ... but I'll change my opinion if my friend dies in the next ten minutes."

I chuckled. "You'll both be fine. I'll make sure of it." It was a promise I couldn't make and yet now that I'd uttered the words, I wanted nothing more than for them to be truthful. Once we left the area, though, it was out of my hands. I had no idea how I could fix this for them, but I was determined to find a way.

DINNER WAS A FESTIVE AFFAIR. Cotton had managed to charm much of the staff. Dolph doted on the two girls as if he was their long-lost father and Nellie gave them fashion tips while whispering and gossiping about everyone at the table. Luke kept flirting with them — in a completely sexless way, of course — and it was obvious they found him entertaining. It was Kade who Michelob kept sliding her eyes to, and I was certain she'd developed a crush on him. I found it cute.

"How are you feeling?" Raven asked as she took the seat next to Michelob. Obviously word had gotten around about her ailment.

Michelob didn't immediately answer, so Raven put her hands to the girl's throat without asking. I opened my mouth to admonish her, but Michelob seemed so in awe of the silver-haired lamia that she didn't put up a struggle.

"They'll be better by morning," Raven announced, her eyes hard to read. "After you guys finish in the big top tomorrow, you should come to the House of Mirrors. I have some work for you there."

Raven wasn't known for being giving of spirit. Out of nowhere, though, she was offering help to two girls she'd never met. I couldn't fathom her motivation.

"Sure." Cotton nodded enthusiastically. "I went to a House of Mirrors once when I was a kid. It was cool."

"I'll pay you. And I also have some clothes that have basically moved with me for years now. They're nothing fancy, but you're welcome to anything you want."

"It's like a circus miracle," Luke whispered, leaning closer to me.

Even though Raven was across the table from us, it was obvious she picked up on his remark. She shot him a dark look that promised retribution later. I had no idea what had gotten into her, but I was thrilled with the way the girls seemed to be warming to her. They clearly sensed she was a straight-shooter — which was true — and were eager to work with her.

"That sounds like a great idea," Kade enthused. "I'll make sure you guys get blankets and pillows."

"I've got some bedrolls tucked away," Dolph offered. "We'll make sure you're comfortable."

Pride — and something else I couldn't quite identify — washed through me. These people were my family, and yet I'd never been this proud to claim them. They'd fought monsters and saved countless people. The way they insisted on adopting two street kids caused me to choke up. I focused on my plate so nobody would notice.

Kade, obviously sensing the change in my mood, moved his hand to my back and lightly rubbed his fingers over my spine. His smile was small but heartfelt. He understood what I was feeling.

I wanted to say something, find the right words to thank everybody. But for once, I was speechless. I had no idea what to say. Even as I opened my mouth to blurt something out, the intention died on my lips when the dream-catcher alerted.

Everyone hopped to their feet and started scanning the perimeter for an enemy. Only Cotton and Michelob remained seated ... and stunned.

"What's wrong?" Cotton asked. She'd gathered her plate close because she didn't want to lose it if something bad was about to happen.

"It's the security system," I replied without thinking.

"What security system?" Cotton looked bewildered as she glanced around. "I don't hear anything."

"It's something only we can hear." There was no way I could explain the dreamcatcher in any detail that she could accept. "You guys need to go inside right now."

Cotton looked as if she was ready to bolt, plate or not, but Kade was calm as he helped Michelob gather her food and inclined his head toward the trailer we shared.

"Come on guys," he prodded. "I'll put you in the trailer and you can eat in there. You'll be perfectly safe."

Cotton didn't look convinced. "Maybe we should run."

"No." I immediately started shaking my head. "You guys need to stay inside. Nothing will get near you. I promise."

Kade directed the girls away from our group. I remained silent until I was sure they were out of earshot. "We need to split up," I ordered. "Something is out there ... and we need to figure out what it is. Nobody is to go out alone."

"We've got it," Nellie said. He'd already retrieved his ax, gripping it in anticipation. "We know what we're doing."

"Try to capture it first," I insisted. "Whatever it is, it might have answers to what's happening on the street."

"No promises." The delightful glint of mayhem in Nellie's eyes told me he was already on the hunt. "Let's move. Our turf is being invaded. Let's show this crazy SOB exactly what happens when the circus comes to town."

Luke made a face. "That was totally over the top."

"That's how I roll."

KADE CAUGHT UP WITH LUKE and me as we strode toward the sidewalk across from the cemetery. For some reason, that's where my instincts told me to go, and I wasn't disappointed. We were barely past the trailers when I saw movement.

"What is that?" Kade asked, confused.

It was hard to make out in the limited light — the clouds had gathered thick and fierce, threatening a storm — and it took me a moment to realize what I was seeing. "Oh, my ... !"

"There are four of them," Luke said, awestruck. "They're all wearing white dresses. I ... don't understand."

That made two of us. The creatures straddling the line of the dream-catcher — they'd obviously identified it as something to be wary of — were all dressed alike. They had dark hair, long and hanging past their shoulders, and their filmy white dresses lent an ethereal flair to their presence. They looked like stereotypical ghosts, but they were obviously much, much more.

"Banshees," I muttered, reaching out with my mind. "All four of them. They're banshees."

As if to prove my point, the women lifted their heads in unison — as if they were all thinking with the same brain — and screeched.

"Well, that won't draw any attention," Kade complained, his gaze immediately going to the corner where the local toughs often congregated. It was deserted, a small blessing.

"We have to capture them ... or kill them," I muttered. "We should at least try to get one of them for a reading or something."

"That's easier said than done," Luke countered. "They're working together. It's almost as if they're operating from a hive mind, like the Borg."

The look I shot him was withering. "You watch too much television."

"You obviously know what I'm talking about, so maybe you watch too much television."

"Yeah, yeah, yeah." I focused on the nearest girl. There was something familiar about her features. I was almost certain she was one of the missing girls whose photo I saw in the newspaper. She looked different, more gaunt, but I was positive it was her. "I don't think our theory that someone is creating banshees is all that far off."

"Yeah. I think you were spot-on there," Kade agreed. "That doesn't change the fact that we need to get rid of them. All this screaming will draw atten-tion. The last thing we want is the cops showing up to ask questions."

He wasn't wrong. "We have to silence them. Maybe ... ." I didn't get a chance to finish my sentence because a shadow — this one boasting long hair and a sword — detached from the nearby fence line. I hadn't even noticed him until he was practically on top of us.

"Cillian?" My confusion turned to horror a split-second before I realized what he was going to do. "Wait!" I took a determined step forward to stop him, but was too late. He arced out the sword, attacked the banshee closest to him, and caused her to scream as the blade cut through her ... and rendered her to dust.

Shocked terror coated the faces of the other three banshees when they registered one of their own had fallen. As if in slow motion, they all turned on Cillian and started shrieking. That's when utter chaos descended.

FOURTEEN

The remaining banshees formed a half-circle around Cillian, who had their full attention. They were advancing on him with a clear purpose ... and that purpose was death. One of their own had been destroyed. They wanted to repay the favor.

"Get out of the way," I ordered, vaulting past the dreamcatcher line and extending my hands. I meant to slam a debilitating spell into the heads of the banshees. I had no idea if it would hurt them, but it would at least delay the telepathy they were displaying. I didn't get a chance, though, because a burst of magic blew from behind me and smacked into the nearest banshee, igniting her dress.

The banshee screamed in distress, her comrades turning to her rather than continuing their pursuit of Cillian. They flapped their hands around the dress to extinguish the flames, which they managed to do ... but not without considerable effort. When they lifted their heads again, they looked between Cillian and Kade, who was standing behind me. They looked right through me and focused on the two individuals who had hurt them. Instinctively I recognized that they were marking them.

Slowly, they began to slink away. The banshee in the scorched dress walked with something of a limp, but she made good time as she hit the road. I wasn't surprised when they headed toward the cemetery. They were always drawn there for some reason. They probably had a nest in one of the mausoleums ... but now was not the time to search for it.

Cillian looked as if he was going to give chase, but I offered him a firm headshake. "Don't."

"They dangerous," he persisted."

"They are, but there's something else going on here. This isn't normal behavior."

"What was your first clue?" he asked dryly.

"And you were my favorite until the unnecessary sarcasm," I muttered under my breath.

"Don't lie. My sister is your favorite."

He wasn't wrong.

Cillian exhaled on an exaggerated sigh. "Well, that was exciting, huh?"

I could think of a few other words to describe it. "Not so much," I countered. "What are you doing here?"

"Hunting," he replied simply. "I lost another soul tonight. The banshees took it, absorbed it into what looked to be a pendant of some sort. It was amber in color. They were fast ... and apparently hungry. It was over before I even realized what was happening. I followed them here. They looked to be heading toward the cemetery, but then changed direction and started going for you."

Not so strange. The dreamcatcher called to them ... or it should've called to them. That's what it was designed for. It was practically impossible for the banshees to ignore it. "We can talk about that later," I supplied. "We need to talk about a few other things right now."

"Like the fact that your boyfriend can shoot fireballs out of his hands?"

"Actually, that wasn't on my list." I cast Kade a small smile. "That was nice. Good job."

Kade was sheepish. "I didn't really plan it. It just sort of happened. I saw you were going to land in the middle of them and ... well ... ." He didn't finish. He didn't have to.

"You raced to my rescue." I was amused more than anything. "Max was right. You respond better when someone else is in danger. We need to work on that."

"Sure. Later."

I turned back to Cillian. "Those aren't normal banshees."

He didn't react to the statement with anything other than curiosity. "How do you know that?"

"Because I've faced off with banshees so many times I've lost count. They're prevalent on the West Coast."

"But not here in Michigan?"

"No. These are the only banshees I've ever seen in Michigan. It's weird."

"Life is weird."

"This is *really* weird." I was adamant. "Banshees don't usually hunt in groups. They're solitary creatures. That's the basic structure of their creation. They're born out of mourning and human suffering. That almost always means they're alone. If they had a proper support system they never would've turned in the first place."

"Fair enough. Can you explain why these banshees are acting the way they are?"

"I can posit ideas all day, but I need more information. The one closest to me, the one Kade set on fire, I'm almost positive she's one of the missing girls. She looks like one of the photos from the newspaper. The banshee was thinner, but I'm ninety percent sure it was the same girl."

"Thinner doesn't necessarily mean anything," Kade noted. "She was a street kid. That photo was probably taken before she ended up on the street. She would've lost weight because she had less access to food."

I glanced over my shoulder at the sound of voices and footsteps. The rest of my crew were descending, and they were obviously curious as they glanced around. "You missed the show," I called out, relating the tale in a succinct manner. They could ask further questions later. This was enough for now.

"Should we go to the cemetery?" Nellie asked. "We might be able to catch them."

I hesitated before answering. "I'm not sure."

Raven's eyes were shrewd when they locked with mine. "You're not thinking you can save them, are you?"

The question irked. "Of course not." I averted my eyes and turned back to Cillian. "You should probably go home. We'll handle it from here."

"No offense, but I can't really do that," Cillian argued. "I have a job that's separate from what you guys are trying to do. I'm part of this."

"I get that, but ... there's nothing else to do right now. We need more information."

"Because the banshees aren't normal?" he asked.

"Pretty much."

Raven made an exasperated sound. "Oh, geez. You do believe you can save them. What are you thinking?"

I didn't want to answer the question, but she'd called me out in front of an audience. "I'm thinking that they showed cognitive thinking," I replied.

"They also showed hive activity," Luke reminded me. "That means someone else was controlling them. That cognitive thinking that you think you saw could be a byproduct of whoever possessed them."

Even though I was annoyed that he didn't take my side — we always sided with each other on issues like this — part of what he said struck me as particularly interesting. "You think they were possessed?"

He appeared surprised by the question. "I think they clearly weren't in control of what they were doing. They attacked as a unit, Poet. That means someone else was controlling them. They were returning to the cemetery for a reason ... because that's what they're programmed to do. They were waylaid by the dreamcatcher because the lure of it was more powerful than their programming."

"What's the dreamcatcher?" Cillian asked. He had a logical mind and he was obviously curious.

"Later," I muttered, never moving my eyes from Luke's face. "If they're programmed, we can deprogram them."

"And what if there's nothing left when you strip away the programming?" Raven challenged. "I didn't see these things in action — although I wish I had — but I would bet that they're essentially carved-out vessels that someone is using to enact some plan."

"What plan?" My temper came out to play. "What could you possibly use banshees to do that would benefit anyone?"

"You already have the answer," Cillian interjected. "It's the souls. They're stealing souls from us, absorbing them somehow. Maybe they're collecting them for someone else to absorb."

"What can you do with a soul?" Kade asked. "I don't mean to sound daft, but I don't understand all of this yet."

"Souls are coveted," Cillian explained, his smile kind. "They can fuel people to live for extended periods of time, but the souls and the individual ingesting them are essentially destroyed in the process."

"What eats souls?"

"Wraiths for starters."

"Wraiths?"

I furrowed my brow, my interest officially piqued. "They're former humans who try to unnaturally extend their lives. To do it, they essentially have to fracture their souls by ingesting the souls of others. They live off the energy of the souls, but it's not a full life. It's a depressing half-life."

Cillian looked impressed. "You've done your homework."

"We've crossed paths with wraiths before," Raven volunteered. "They're easy takedowns and walk right over the dreamcatcher like babies coming for candy. They're never a threat."

"They're a threat for reapers," Cillian countered. "We've had a real problem with them here in recent years. They hid in a lot of the abandoned buildings, created an army of sorts. They were organized by a charismatic leader who set them against us because she was trying to extend her life."

That sounded like a lead. "Who is their leader? Maybe we should go after her."

His expression turned sad. "That's not possible. She's dead."

"How can you be sure?"

"Because she was my mother, and Aisling killed her."

I was flabbergasted at his matter-of-fact reaction. "W-what?"

Weary, Cillian let loose a long sigh and dragged a hand through his hair. "It's a long story and I don't really want to go into the specifics. Suffice to say, we thought our mother died when we were teenagers. In a fire while she was collecting a soul. It turned out she survived, but the people who took her kept her alive at a cost."

"They turned her into a partial-wraith," Raven mused. "I've heard of that. It's been centuries, though."

Cillian arched an eyebrow. "Centuries? Are you telling me you've been alive for centuries?"

Raven smirked. "I've been around the block a few times. I'm familiar with the process you're talking about. Are you sure your mother died? If not, using banshees would be a unique way to collect souls."

"I'm sure she's dead. We all saw it." Cillian took on a far-off expression and then purposely blanked his face until it went neutral. "The thing that came back wasn't my mother. We got to see her before the end, but the creature was definitely dead. We made sure of that ... and then buried the body in our family mausoleum."

I thought of the inscription I'd read. "I'm sorry about your mother."

"I am, too. But she's not responsible for this. That doesn't mean one of the factions left behind when her regime fell isn't. We need to ask around."

"Do you have any ideas on that front?"

"A few. I ... ." He trailed off, his eyes darting to the left at the scuff of feet.

I expected to see one or more of the street toughs returning. They'd conveniently gone missing for the attack, which I filed away to think about later. Instead, it was Logan who appeared out of the darkness. His eyes were keen as they scanned the crowd, not stopping until they landed on me.

"Do you want to tell me what's going on here?" he asked gravely.

That was a loaded question. "Oh, well ... ."

"What are you doing lurking around here at night?" Kade asked, taking control of the conversation. He pinned Logan with a suspicious look. "Have you been watching us?"

"Would it be a problem if I was watching you?" Logan asked. "You shouldn't care if you're not doing anything illegal."

Realization dawned on Cillian's face. "Ugh. Who invited the Fed?"

Logan's expression twisted. "Seriously, how do you people keep figuring out I'm a federal agent?"

"It's the suit," Raven and I answered in unison.

Even though he was obviously here for a serious reason, Logan's lips curved. "I guess I'll have to buy more suits."

"That's probably a smart idea," Raven agreed. "As for what we're doing, there's really not much to say. We were merely giving my new boyfriend a tour."

"New boyfriend?" Kade slid his eyes toward the other members of our group who had assembled at the back of the crowd. Percival wasn't amongst them, which was probably a good thing.

"Yes, my new boyfriend." Raven's glare was pointed as she sidled over to Cillian and linked her arm through his. "It's a fresh love, but an intense one."

I had to swallow my laughter at the expression on Cillian's handsome face. He looked to be the shy sort — at least more reticent than the other members of his family — and the mortification rolling off him was profound.

"So ... that's who you are?" Logan pinned Cillian with a dark stare. "You're dating a circus woman who is here for a few only days? Does that mean you're local? I'm pretty sure you weren't here when I visited yesterday."

"He's local," Raven answered for him. "We just met yesterday. It was love at first sight ... although we've been corresponding over the internet."

"You just said you met yesterday for the first time," Logan pressed. "How have you been corresponding over the internet if you just met?"

"We just met in person for the first time yesterday," Raven clarified. She was masterful under pressure and didn't as much as shiver when Logan cast doubt in her direction. "We've been corresponding blindly over the internet for a very long time."

"So ... you guys hadn't even seen each other until yesterday?" Logan clearly didn't believe them. I couldn't blame him. It was a ridiculous story. "I guess it's lucky that you're both pretty, huh?"

Raven fluttered her eyelashes. "Oh, agent, you do go on. I'm a loyal woman. You can't tear me away from my boo."

Luke made a choking sound behind me as Cillian blinked several times in rapid succession. This situation was quickly spiraling out of control and there was little I could do about it.

"Oh, don't be silly," Raven said, her voice high and girlish. "We sent each other naked photos before meeting. How else would we know that we were destined to be?"

Logan worked his jaw. I could practically see his mind working. If Raven's intention was to confound him until he forgot he was here looking for specific information she'd done a wonderful job. Still, Logan was determined. He wouldn't allow her to completely derail him.

"I'm here because the neighbors across the way reported screams," he started, his eyes moving back to me. "Did you hear anything?"

"Maybe a little," I admitted, ignoring the glare Raven lobbed in my direction. "They weren't scary screams. They were romantic." I jerked my thumb at Raven and Cillian, who looked as if he wanted to find the nearest hole to hide in, and offered a shrug. "They were playing games. I'm sorry if it got too loud. We didn't really think about it because they were having so much fun."

"We won't allow it to happen again," Nellie volunteered. He leaned on his ax as if it was a walking stick, which made me want to throttle him for drawing attention. "We're very sorry that Raven is such a slut."

Anticipating her move, I slid in front of Raven so the magically-packed smack she planned to land on the back of Nellie's head smacked into my back. I managed to keep my expression neutral despite the pain.

"We really weren't doing anything, Logan," I lied. "We were just screwing around and forgot about the neighbors. We're usually in more remote areas. We forget ourselves when we're surrounded by suburban life."

"Basically she's saying we're heathens," Nellie added.

Logan glanced between faces a moment and then shook his head. "Well, who am I to be the thief of fun?"

"I bet more than one person has asked that question of you," Raven shot back.

He burned her with a dark look and then turned back to me. "I was in the area because I wanted to make you aware that I've been put in charge of the missing girls' investigation. The case has been taken away from the Detroit Police Department and given to me. It was official about an hour ago. That means we'll be able to share information if it becomes available."

Uh-oh. I sensed trouble.

"You took it from the Detroit Police Department?" Cillian asked, his eyes going dark. "Why would you do that? They were working diligently on that case."

Curiosity etched its way across Logan's face as he regarded the reaper. "Are you familiar with the case?"

"Don't be stupid," Raven interjected. "He heard Poet talking about it earlier. That's it."

"Yeah, well ... ." Logan shook his head and then took a step away from us. "I should probably be going. I don't want to interrupt whatever shenanigans you guys are up to. Poet, I'll be in touch tomorrow so we can share information. Will you be around?"

I felt Kade bristling next to me. There wasn't much I could do about it. "Absolutely." I nodded. "I can't wait to hear what you've learned."

FIFTEEN

$\mathcal{C}$otton and Michelob seemed more excited than upset about what had transpired outside. Of course, they'd only seen limited snatches of action. The banshee — and Cillian taking her down — was well out of their line of sight. That was for the best.

We escorted them to the big top, situated them on the floor in the corner — Dolph came through with the bedrolls — and then plied them with snacks to make sure they were comfortable.

"You know where the bathrooms are?" I thought of the nearby building. The path to and from it was dark. "Here." I handed Cotton a heavy-duty flashlight. "These grounds are safe. Still, if you have to go to the restroom, go together."

Michelob solemnly nodded. Cotton, of course, was mouthier.

"What if we aren't the types who like going to the bathroom together?" she challenged. "Should we just go right in here?"

I shot her a quelling look. "I'm sure you'll be fine. Go to sleep. We have more chores for you tomorrow."

"And eggs, hash browns, toast, sausage and bacon for breakfast," Kade added with a wink, as Michelob's cheeks flushed pink. Her crush on him was adorable.

"Yes. There will be a big breakfast. We'll talk then."

"No problem." Cotton's salute was sassy. "We're looking forward to breakfast. All the candy you've given us should tide us over until then."

"We aim to please."

Kade was silent as we left the tent. I wasn't surprised to find Raven, Nixie and Naida strengthening the wards around the perimeter. They understood the real worry here. If the missing girls were being turned into banshees, we had to keep Michelob and Cotton from that fate ... by any means necessary. That included magic, which we were trying to hide from the girls.

"They should be snug in there," Raven announced when she finished and joined us. "If they leave, I'll know." She was so matter-of-fact I had no doubt she was telling the truth.

"If they leave, they're probably only going to the bathroom," I supplied. "They know how well they've got it here. Their next step will be to see how far they can push things."

"Is that what you would've done in their place?" Kade asked.

"Most definitely. Cotton is smart. Tomorrow, they'll wake up and realize Michelob is better. They're not users in the sense that they want to hurt us, but they're not used to having anything, so they will try to press their advantage."

"So what?" Raven countered. "If they're in need, we can provide."

There were times Raven came off as a bitter woman with no soul. She was practical to the point of being blunt, disinterested in most people she met, and only vaguely aware of the human condition as a whole. There were other times — like now — when she was absolutely fabulous and giving of spirit.

"We'll take care of them," I agreed. "You can keep them busy in the House of Mirrors tomorrow. That's good, because I have a feeling I will be out of the mix for part of the day."

Kade stirred. "And where are you going? Please don't tell me you're having lunch with your second boyfriend."

There was an edge to his voice that I recognized. Even worse, Raven recognized it. She lifted an eyebrow, chuckled, and then waved as she started to break away from us. "I think I'll leave you two to your domestic squabble. I need some sleep. I'll be up early to make sure the girls are okay. If they do any wandering tonight, I'll handle it."

"Thank you." I waited until I was certain she was gone to speak again. "As for you ... ." I slid Kade a look and sighed when I saw there was more lurking in his eyes than belligerence. "You know you have no reason to be jealous, right?"

"I didn't say I was jealous." Kade was calm, but that edge remained in his tone. "Why would you assume I was jealous?"

"Just a hunch."

"Well ... I'm not jealous." He was firm and held it together until we were inside our trailer. Then he kicked off his shoes and sank onto the couch, his expression dark. "Fine. I might be a little jealous," he conceded. "But I think I should get a pass, because I'm almost never jealous."

He was unbelievably cute. Still, I didn't want to encourage this behavior. Of course, Logan was at the center of a unique situation.

"I think it would be best if I explained things," I offered, sliding onto the couch next to him and plopping my feet in his lap as I got comfortable against the armrest.

"I take it you want a foot massage while you're explaining things," he muttered. It sounded like a complaint, but he didn't look all that unhappy to have something to do with his hands while we talked. "Am I going to like this conversation?"

"I don't know." That was the truth. "The thing is ... I didn't exactly peg Logan for a cop back then. I knew there was something slightly off about him. I saw things in his head — he has something of a hero complex like someone else I know — but I didn't realize what I was seeing at the time. I was too new at what I was doing to realize exactly what he was."

"I don't have a hero complex."

I ignored his statement. "All we knew about him back then was that he showed up one day, said his name was Shadow, and started hanging around the bikers. They were volatile enough that we knew to keep away from them. Shadow was different. He never yelled or threatened us. He didn't pay much attention to us, but he wasn't overly aggressive.

"At some point he made the hierarchy suspicious and earned a severe beating," I continued. "We found him in an alley. He was close to death. We offered to drag him out in the open and call an ambulance, but he kept saying 'no hospital.' Now I would know better than allowing him to call the shots, but back then we were young and dumb.

"We sat with him, took care of him the best we could, and somehow he didn't die. I still don't know how he survived. It was a full week of taking care of him twenty-four hours a day before he was truly out of the woods. After that, once he was well enough to start getting around again, he always visited us.

"He brought food ...and medicine ... new clothes and even makeup and other stuff." I smiled at the memory. "He was a good guy. More than that, he listened to us. He warned us if there was going to be trouble. He made sure we were out of the line of fire when bad things were about to go down."

"He protected you," Kade confirmed. "Is that when you developed your crush on him?"

If he thought the question would embarrass me, he was wrong. "Yeah. He brought chocolate sometimes. He said the candy was bad, would rot our teeth, but he made sure we had fresh toothbrushes and paste all the time. I couldn't help myself. To me, he was a hero."

"Of course he was. He didn't take advantage of that crush, did he?"

I was amused despite myself. "No. He was a rule follower. In fact, he reminds me a lot of you. You would've done the same thing for us. You're doing the same thing for Cotton and Michelob."

"You took them in first."

"And yet you've sort of taken over to make sure they're okay," I supplied. "You have no intention of taking advantage of their crushes, do you?"

He screwed up his face. "I would never."

"See. You're just like him. He would never either."

"Yeah, but ... you're an adult now," he pointed out. "It wouldn't really be a crush any longer."

"Wouldn't it?" I wasn't so sure of that. "He's always going to be the guy who helped keep me alive when I was a kid. One of the first things he said to me when he saw me in the park was that he always imagined me ending up in a good place. But occasionally a weak thought would creep in and he'd succumb to the worst. He was glad he'd run into me so he could push the bad thoughts from his head."

"That doesn't mean he's not as fond of you as you are of him."

"It's not the same." I caught his gaze, held it. "We met and fell in love as equals. Shadow was an authority figure who loomed large and brief in my life. He saved us as often as he could and we reciprocated. It's not the same kind of attraction."

"No?" Kade's smile was rueful. "I guess I'm glad to hear that."

"You don't have to be jealous."

"I know. I also know that you don't want to be with anyone but me and I should suck it up. Still ... *still* ... there's always a twinge when another man looks at you the same way I do. I can't help myself."

"He was not looking at me the same way you do. Trust me."

"It felt similar."

"Tonight he was looking at me as a suspect because he could tell we were hiding something. We weren't very stealthy."

"Do you think he'll return tomorrow?"

"Yup. He knows we're trying to find answers on the girls. He might think we're the type to take matters into our own hands if we catch the individual responsible. He doesn't understand about banshees ... or the paranormal ... or the fact that we have an ax-happy dwarf in our midst. He only sees us acting squirrely."

"How are you going to counter that?"

"I have no idea." I leaned forward and rested my forehead against his cheek. "I don't really want to think about it right now. I was hoping you could distract me with something else for a bit."

His lips curved. "What did you have in mind?"

"How about I show you in the other room?"

"Now you're talking."

I HAD AN IDEA THE NEXT morning. Tawny. She came to me in a dream. I'd almost forgotten I was positive I saw her the night of the first banshee appearance. I wanted to track her down now. Unfortunately, I had no idea where to start looking for her.

I left Kade and Raven to handle Cotton and Michelob. Kade wanted to go with me ... until I explained where I was going. He immediately stepped back when he realized this was a task I needed to complete on my own.

It wasn't hard to track Creek. She was still going by that name. Whether it was her legal name, I couldn't say. I sincerely doubted it. Still, when I Googled Creek Castle — she chose the last name she adopted because she always wanted to live in a castle — I found numerous mentions – all of them linked to strip clubs at which she'd performed. The current establishment she worked at was Stockings & Stilettos on Woodward. It was early, but the website boasted about being open twenty-four hours a day, seven days a week, fifty-two weeks a year. They didn't even close for Christmas, which I figured had to be the mark of a fine establishment.

The bouncer gave me serious side-eye as I strolled toward the door. I tried to look as if I belonged there, but it was a tough sell.

"Hello. I ... um ... is there a cover charge?" I felt out of my element.

"I've got this," a voice volunteered from behind me and I stiffened when I felt a familiar presence at my back. *Luke.* Where had he come from? I hadn't seen him at all before I left this morning, which was most unusual. "I've got enough for both of us. We like to do this as a couple."

I kept my smile in place, but just barely.

The bouncer accepted the money from Luke, pressed ink stamps to the backs of our hands, and motioned us inside. He didn't ask a single question about why I would be present at a strip club. I was mildly disappointed.

"How does he know I'm not some sort of weird pervert?" I complained as I stepped over the threshold.

"Strip clubs wouldn't exist if it weren't for weird perverts," Luke replied, pressing his hand to the small of my back. "Now, come on. Let's try to find your friend ... although something tells me she won't be happy to see us."

I slowed my pace and pinned him with a serious look. "I'm not trying to embarrass her or anything. It's just ... I saw something the first night. I almost forgot about it. It was a woman we both knew back in the day ... and I'm almost positive it was her. Not long after the whole initial banshee thing happened. That can't be a coincidence, right?"

Luke shrugged as he frowned and looked over the bar. Garish strobe lights fractured the room filled with small pits at even intervals across the space, and naked women dancing on tables as men sat in the chairs beneath them and watched. The entire set-up was depressing.

"I can't believe this." The words were out of my mouth before I thought better of them. I quickly caught myself ... or as quickly as possible. "I mean ... we should get a drink so we don't look so out of place."

Instead of readily agreeing — Luke was always up for some day drinking — he moved his hand to my shoulder to still me. "You wouldn't have ended up here."

I was dumbfounded. "How did you know what I was thinking?"

He shrugged, his grin impish. "Who knows you best?" He tweaked the end of my nose, which would've irritated me under different circumstances but, surprisingly, made me feel better today. "You didn't escape the same fate as Creek. You were never meant for this.

"And, before you start wondering if you could've saved her from this life, you're not omnipotent," he continued. "You did the best you could for her when you were together. You can't fix everything. You can't take the weight of the world on your shoulders. You're strong, but you'd buckle under that weight. Anyone would."

Tears pricked at the back of my eyes. "I just can't believe she ended up here. I thought she would do more."

"Did you?" Luke's eyes were clear as they held mine. "Did you really think that she was going to be a movie star ... or model ... or happy housewife? When you really look back at how things were going at that time, what do you see? I'll bet it was the beginning of a road that was always going to end here."

I hated that he was right. "I don't want to think about that." I was emphatic as I shook my head. "I just want to find Creek, ask her about Tawny, and then get out of here. I very much doubt she'll be happy to see us either."

"Oh, I can guarantee that." Luke was dour as he inclined his head to his right.

My heart sank as I turned in that direction, a sick feeling bubbling up when I saw Creek standing on a table, no one around her, glaring at me. "Nope. She's definitely not going to be happy."

"That doesn't change the fact that we have questions for her," Luke pointed out. "I also want to give her a tip to keep sweaty glitter from clumping ... because it's obvious no one has shared that little tidbit with her over the years and she desperately needs the help."

"Don't talk to her about sweaty glitter," I snapped. Out of the blue, something occurred to me. "How did you know where I was?"

"What do you mean? I followed you."

He was a terrible liar. "No. Kade sent you." I went back over the conversation we'd had this morning. I thought it was too easy when he readily agreed to allow me to visit a strip club in a rough part of town without batting an eyelash. "He wanted you to protect me."

"Not protect you," Luke countered. "He didn't want you to be alone for this. He understood how difficult it was going to be for you. For some reason, he thought a strip club was the perfect environment for my special breed of charm. That's a direct quote, by the way."

I didn't want to laugh, but I couldn't help myself. "You really are the best friend I've ever had."

"I am," he agreed without hesitation. "She was a good friend at one time, too. Don't forget that, no matter how surly she's about to be. It's unfortunate, but ... it is what it is. We can't change her past or future. We can only share information, and that's what we're here to do. Remind yourself of that as often as necessary."

"Since when did you turn into the practical one?"

"We each play to our strengths. Now, come on. The longer we stand here looking like idiots, the angrier she's going to get."

I didn't think that was possible, but we had no choice. It was time.

SIXTEEN

reek definitely wasn't happy to see us. The anger on her face was enough to cause an avalanche of shivers to race down my spine. Never the shy sort, I hung behind Luke as we approached her station because I didn't know what else to do. I felt smaller than I had in my entire life ... and it wasn't a good feeling.

"Hey." Luke never let anything get him down and Creek's overt disdain wasn't any different. "We're here for the show." To my utter surprise, he pulled a crisp hundred-dollar bill from his wallet and put it on the table.

Creek's eyes lit with interest when she saw the money. I never would've thought of going that route, but Luke was clearly ahead of me on this one. I was grateful.

"What do you want?" she asked finally, suspicion lacing her words. She wanted the money desperately. I could see thoughts of what she might be able to do with it floating through her mind ... and all of them revolved around her daughter, who apparently needed new shoes. She wasn't the sort to acquiesce without knowing what she was agreeing to, though.

I found my voice. "Information."

"You want information from me?" She was incredulous. "What could I possibly tell you?"

"We're looking for information on the missing girls." I stalled, unsure how much I should tell her. Mentioning the paranormal stuff was clearly off the table. Explaining our interest was a thorny concept. "Logan Stone approached me on the street the other day when I was hanging around our old stomping grounds. He mentioned what was happening. We'd like to help if we can."

Bafflement etched across a face that looked ten years older than it should. "Who is Logan Stone?"

"Shadow."

"The cop?" She made a face. "I can't believe you found him right away. Oh, wait ... yes I can. He was the one you cared about most." Bitterness, hot and dark, flowed freely from her.

"It was a fluke," I countered. "I was actually talking to Groove when he approached. I would've much preferred Hazy or Junk. They would've at least been good for a laugh, but Groove is what I got."

"Junk is dead." Creek delivered the news with blasé detachment. "He died about eighteen months after you left."

The news hit harder than it probably should have. "He overdosed?"

She shrugged. "They found him in one of the abandoned buildings with a needle in his arm."

I wasn't surprised. Junk was the sort who was destined to die in the throes of addiction. "I'm sorry to hear that." I meant it. "I guess, in the back of my head, I kept hoping he would find a way out."

"He did find a way out. It just wasn't as fancy as the way you found." Creek glanced over her shoulder and met the gaze of the man behind the bar. She was grim as she climbed on top of the table. "He has to think I'm working," she supplied as she started moving. "I'll answer your questions if I can ... but I ain't no snitch."

"I don't want you to snitch on anyone. I'm looking for Tawny."

Creek's eyebrows, which were patchy and bare in spots, migrated north. "Tawny? Why would you possibly be looking for her?"

"I think I saw her the other night. It was close to where a witness thought she might've seen one of the missing girls. I don't think she did anything," I added hurriedly. "She might've seen something. We need information, and she's a potential witness."

"You're talking Tawny the ho, right?"

I hated that word. I always had, even when it was being tossed around like popcorn at a scary movie. "I only knew one Tawny when I was here. You were with her the night I went looking for you. Before I left. I couldn't find you guys."

"Are you blaming it on her?"

"I'm not blaming anything on her."

"Oh, so you're blaming it on me. That's why you didn't say goodbye."

I figured this would come up. "I tried. I looked everywhere. You were nowhere to be found."

"I was working." She let loose a sneer that turned my stomach. "I was just supposed to be watching, but she found two good guys that night and they had cash. It didn't go exactly how I thought it would. I assumed it would be easier. That was my introduction into a new life."

I felt sick in my heart for her. "I'm sorry. I ... don't know what to say." I held my hands up, helplessness washing over me. "I didn't want any of this to happen to you. I really did think you would get out." It was a lie. I wanted it to happen for her, but I always knew the street would chew her up. I couldn't have admitted it back then, but clarity comes with age.

"You're sorry?" she seethed. "You're sorry? That's just ... so stupid." She shook her hips and turned her back to us so we couldn't see her face. I had a feeling it was because she needed to collect herself and didn't want us to see her crack.

"I am sorry," I promised. "You have no idea how sorry I am. I didn't want to leave, but ... I had to. It was the best shot I was ever going to get. I really did want to find you and say goodbye. I looked hard."

She turned back to us, a mask of indifference in place. "I suppose it never occurred to you to ask them to wait, to take me with them?"

Honestly, that had occurred to me. "I was afraid they would think I was more trouble than I was worth if I rocked the boat. I believed they would leave me behind." Now I knew Max would've waited. Even if he had to send the others on without him, he would've waited. I didn't know that then. "I don't know how else to apologize. I feel horrible."

"You feel horrible." She jiggled her breasts at Luke, who was much more interested in the glitter situation than the cleavage she offered. "Well ... as long as you feel horrible." She shook her head and sighed. "I can't help you with Tawny. I don't think you saw her. She's been gone for years. She didn't last more than two years after you left. Maybe a little more than that. The timeline is a little hazy. She got a ride west with someone. She was desperate to get to where the weather was better. And she heard some story about a woman who was working the streets and got discovered by an agent and turned into a big movie star."

"I believe that's the movie *Pretty Woman*, although she just got the rich guy, not an Oscar," Luke offered helpfully.

Creek glared at him. "I'm familiar with *Pretty Woman*. I didn't say I believed the story. I said she did. I haven't seen her since. I don't think she's here."

Crap. That wasn't what I wanted to hear. "What about the missing girls? Have you heard anything about them?"

"I don't live on the street anymore. I haven't in years. My house may not be great, but it's still a house. I don't hear anything ... mostly because I don't care to listen. It's too hard."

I wasn't sure I believed her. Ultimately, it didn't matter. She wasn't going to talk to us. "Well, thanks for your time." I moved to stand. I was ready to put as much distance between the club and me as possible. "I really am sorry about what happened back then. I tried to find you."

"Yeah."

Luke put his hand to my back in a show of solidarity and then cast his eyes to Creek. "Hairspray," he offered.

Creek was already stuffing the money he'd left in her bra. Her forehead wrinkled. "What?"

"Hairspray," he repeated. "If you spray it on your body and then put the glitter on and let it dry before you start dancing it won't clump. Make sure it's the hair spray that's geared for humidity."

She worked her jaw. "You know a lot about glitter," she said finally.

He smirked. "I'm a man of many talents."

"Yeah, well ... ." She looked pained as she focused on me. "There is one person I can point you to for your questions. She's ... a weird chick. I mean *really* weird. She knows what's happening on the streets, though, and she's always gathering and giving information."

My interest was officially piqued.

"Madame Maxine," Creek volunteered. "She reads fortunes down the road."

"Around here?" I couldn't picture a place like that in this neighborhood. "How has she not been rolled?"

"Not here. Six miles down the road, in Royal Oak."

Oh, that made more sense. "And her place is right on Woodward?"

"Yeah. Tea & Tarot or something like that. She might be able to help."

It was the grandest gesture she had to offer. "Thank you." I meant it to the depths of my soul. "I know I can't make up for what happened, but I wish you the very best. If you ever need anything ... ." On a whim, I dug in my pocket until I came back with a business card. "We're always traveling. We never stay in one place very long. I'll do what I can if you ever call, though. I promise."

Creek's expression was thoughtful as she stared at the card. I thought she might rip it up and throw it in my face, but she tucked it in her bra. "Thanks.

You should get out of here. You're going to make my boss suspicious if you're not careful."

TEA & TAROT WAS EXACTLY what I expected. Royal Oak was vastly different from Detroit. It had an artsy vibe, with studios, ritzy shopping, fancy restaurants and deluxe coffee shops on every corner. It was the sort of town Luke thrived in. Even I had to admit it looked pretty great as we met in the parking lot.

"Now this isn't so bad." Luke's smile was wide. "This place looks cool."

Of course he would think that. "This woman might be a quack," I reminded him.

"Maybe. I still think it's cool."

I couldn't admit it out loud because I was still recovering from our meeting with Creek, but I wholeheartedly agreed.

The wind chimes near the door emitted a whimsical sound as we entered the store. The first scent that assailed my nose was the muskiness of cloves. The second was anise.

"It smells awesome in here," Luke enthused. "I don't ever want to leave."

I couldn't blame him. I was a fan of the scent, too. "It's nice," I agreed.

"Nice? It's orgasmic."

"It's *really* nice," I conceded. "I ... ." My internal radar pinged and I swung my head to the left, frowning when I caught sight of Redmond leaning against the counter. A woman with pretty gray hair stood with him, an ankle-length skirt in wild colors setting off the rich olive tones of her skin. They looked amused as they watched us.

"Were you just talking about me?" Redmond teased.

His joviality annoyed me. "Why would you possibly think that?"

"I'm pretty sure I heard the word 'orgasmic.' When you look it up in the dictionary, my face is right there. No joke."

Luke snorted. "This guy." He didn't seem bothered by the appearance of a Grimlock. Instead, he strode in Redmond's direction and extended his hand. "You must be Madame Maxine." We'd looked her up online before leaving the strip club parking lot. "I'm Luke Bishop and this is my life mate Poet Parker. We're not romantically involved, but we're soul mates all the same."

Madame Maxine's eyes sparkled. "I bet you are. I know another set of platonic soul mates just like you."

Redmond snorted, but I didn't get the joke. "We're here for some information," I started, frowning at Redmond. "I'm assuming he already asked the same questions we're trying to get answered."

"That would be my guess," Madame Maxine agreed. "You're asking about banshees?"

I glanced around the store to make sure nobody was listening. "Oh, well ... ." The store was empty other than the four of us.

"It's okay," Redmond reassured me. "Madame Maxine knows her stuff. She's a regular resource for us, which is why I tapped her this time. We're still searching for information, just like you."

"I assume your brother told you what happened last night."

"He did." Redmond's smile slipped. "He's still traumatized because the hot silver-haired chick made jokes about him being her love muffin. He lives with his girlfriend and he's worried that can somehow be construed as cheating."

"He didn't do anything to worry about."

"Yes, but he's something of a whiner. Everyone in my family is that way. I'm the only one who that unfortunate family trait skipped. I've been whine-free since I was in diapers."

He was so full of himself. He was also charming. It was an annoying combination. "How great for you," I drawled. "Your brother is fine. Guilt-free. Where is he?"

"He's at the reaper library digging into research. He's bothered that you think the missing girls are being turned into banshees. He feels guilty about killing one of them."

"You can't cure a banshee," I pointed out.

"No, you can't," Madame Maxine agreed. "But I'm not sure we're dealing with banshees."

I moved closer to the woman, intrigued by the surge of power I felt emanating from her. I wasn't sure what she was, but she was more than some meek store owner who only had information to offer. She could hold her own in a battle. She was ... interesting.

"What do you think they are?" Luke asked.

"That, I don't know," she answered. "I'm going to dig into some research, too."

"I've seen two of them now," I reported. "If they weren't banshees, then someone is doing a wonderful job of faking it. I mean ... they had all the hallmarks of banshees."

"Have you seen many banshees?"

"Yes."

"Can you define 'many'?" she pressed.

"I'd estimate more than fifty."

For the first time since we'd entered the store, Madame Maxine straightened. The look she gave me was full of respect. "Really. What are you?"

"A hodgepodge. I don't think there is any real definition for what I am. I lean more toward mind magic."

"She can make people do things," Luke offered. "That's how she got me to eat avocado toast even though it looked like someone had thrown it up."

Madame Maxine's lips quirked. "I see."

"What are you?" I asked.

"I'm psychic. Brujas run in our family. I sense you might have a bit of bruja in you. You're definitely powerful."

"Like Izzy?" Redmond asked.

"Who is Izzy?" I asked. "Is that another sister I've yet to meet?"

Redmond chuckled. "Thankfully I have only one sister. You've met her."

"Yes, Sassy Sourpuss," Madame Maxine intoned. "I haven't seen her since before she gave birth, by the way. I think you should send her my way so I can read that baby."

Redmond snorted. "Yeah. She'll jump all over that. You know how she loves it when you climb inside her head."

"She needs to get over that."

"Aisling doesn't get over anything she doesn't want to get over," he argued. "As for Izzy, she's kind of a new member of our clan. She runs the gate on Belle Isle."

Luke was enthralled. "What gate are you talking about?"

I was curious about that, too.

"The gate between planes," Redmond replied. "When we collect souls, we transport them to her and she sees they pass over. She's powerful in her own right. She's Maxine's niece and Braden's girlfriend."

"She's a good girl," Madame Maxine confirmed. "She might be able to help us on this."

"I still don't know what this is," I reminded her. "I'm pretty sure we're dealing with banshees. They're not that difficult to identify."

"Unless they're not really banshees," she argued. "It's possible that someone created something new. It would hardly be the first time. That's how half the creatures in the paranormal world came into being, after all."

She had a point. "What do you think we're dealing with?"

"I don't know yet. You can bet I'll be delving into the research. Before you get ahead of yourself — and I only say this because I can feel the compassion wafting off you — I very much doubt these women can be saved.

"You're positive we're dealing with banshees, and I think it's something close but not exact," she continued. "You would recognize the void of a soul. The two creatures you've seen have been soulless?"

Reluctantly, I nodded. "Yes." In my head I knew that saving the women was probably out of my wheelhouse. However, my heart wanted a loophole.

"The odds of wedging a soul back in a body are slim. I don't know that it's possible, especially in this case. We'll check every avenue."

"With that in mind, I think you should come to dinner at my father's house tonight," Redmond interjected. "He was going to invite you himself, but I just saved him a trip. I think we should compare notes again. We should have more information tonight."

"I'll be bringing a few friends," I warned.

"Your boyfriend and platonic soul mate?" he teased.

"Maybe a few others."

"The more the merrier. Seriously, dinners at our house are a big event. You could bring an army and my father would still have enough food. It will be fine."

I found myself nodding before I even thought about what I was agreeing to. "That will work."

"Great." His charming smile was back. "I look forward to spending quality time with you again this evening."

"You're looking forward to annoying Kade," I corrected. "You take perverse pleasure in it."

He didn't as much as blink. "That, too. But don't sell yourself short. I find you adorable."

I rolled my eyes. "Has that line ever worked on anyone?"

"You'd be surprised."

SEVENTEEN

Once back at the circus grounds, I filled Kade in on the new plan. He was a go-with-the-flow guy, so he readily agreed.

"That was easy," I noted.

"I bet they have good grub."

I could picture that, too. "I'm heading over to the cemetery for a bit. I want to do some thinking, clear my head ... and maybe see if I can figure out where the banshees are holing up."

He was instantly alert. "I'll go with you."

"That's not necessary. Besides, you have things to do here ... including making sure our new refugees are taken care of. I'll be fine. Banshees don't attack during the day."

"Luke says they're not regular banshees."

I frowned. "When did you talk to Luke?" And why did he always have to open his big mouth before I was ready to deal with things on my own timetable?

"I saw him when he got back. That's how I knew you were on your way."

Yeah, speaking of that ... . "You sent him after me, didn't you?"

Kade was unruffled. "Sent him? I don't know that I would use those exact words. I mentioned that you were about to embark on a difficult task and suggested that, as your best friend, he might be helpful. He did the rest himself."

I was surrounded these days. "I was angry when I first realized he was there," I admitted. "But he was a big help."

"He didn't give me much of an update on that," Kade admitted. "I thought maybe you would tonight, when we have some down time."

"There's not much to say. She's been holding a grudge about the way I disappeared for a long time. I can't really blame her. If our positions were reversed, I wouldn't be a happy camper. I feel guilty even though I know I didn't have much of a choice at the time and I would do the same thing again. It is what it is."

His eyebrows rose speculatively. "Wow. That was a lot to take in over one morning."

"We were at a strip club to boot."

"Yeah. I saw the search on your computer. Looked like a picturesque place."

"That's the real reason you sent Luke."

"I didn't want you to be alone, and I thought that was a weird outing for us to participate in as a couple. I didn't want to be a distraction. I figured Luke would have a lot to offer when it came to strip club trivia."

"He has seen *Striptease* about a hundred times."

"There you go."

"And *Showgirls* about a hundred and fifty."

"That's mildly disturbing."

On a whim, I reached over and offered him a heartfelt hug. "I thought you were being a busybody, but I needed him so ... thank you."

He returned the embrace, resting his cheek against my forehead. "I love you. I want to do whatever I can to make things easier for you."

"I love you, too."

"I said it first, so I get the credit."

"We're not playing that game any longer ... and I get double the credit because I whispered it to you before you woke up this morning."

"I whispered it to you after you fell asleep last night."

"This is getting sick."

"Yeah." He briefly tightened his arms around me and then planted a soft kiss on my lips. "I want to do what I can to help you here, but I'm trying really hard not to step on your toes. It's a balancing act, and if I overstep my boundaries, I'm sorry. It comes from a place of love."

I knew that before he said it. "Thanks."

"You're welcome."

"I'm still going to the cemetery alone. I'll be perfectly fine. They won't move during the day."

"I'm going to trust your judgment on that. But if I see anything hinky, I'll be there like a shot."

"Fair enough."

THE CEMETERY WAS QUIET AS I strolled the well-worn paths. I took a circuitous route this time, because I was looking for a hidey-hole. It made sense that wherever the banshees were located was in the part of the cemetery where the first creature was killed. She was fleeing, hoping to hide. She might not have wanted to lead Redmond to her sisters, and that was the thought that fueled me as I walked the cemetery.

Was Madame Maxine right? Had someone created an entirely new breed of creature? I didn't want to believe it, but the banshees didn't act as they normally would. There was no doubt about that. Banshees were solitary creatures. They didn't live in hives ... or think as one. That meant something else was clearly going on.

But what?

"This doesn't look like a good place for a walk," a voice called out.

I swiveled quickly, frowning when I saw Logan leaning against a mausoleum, his arms folded across his chest. He looked amused ... and curious. He'd also managed to sneak up on me, something that bothered me on a different level. I was supposed to be aware of my surroundings. Obviously I was off my game.

"What are you doing here?" I slowed my pace and regarded him with curiosity. "Do you have this place staked out or something?"

"Do you think I should?"

Definitely not. That would ruin any late-night excursions we were forced to make. "I don't see why."

"Neither do I. I'm actually here looking for you. Your boyfriend said you were here. He didn't look happy to see me, by the way, but he didn't give me any guff. I'm kind of glad about that. I'm trained, but so is he."

That was a deliberate slip. He wanted me to know he'd researched the people I was closest to. The question was: Why? "He's former military."

"I know. He has an impressive record. I'm good, but I think there's a legitimate chance he could take me."

With the magic to call on, Kade could crush Logan. "He's a good man. You don't have to spend all your time crawling through his records. He's not dangerous."

"I wasn't crawling through his records. I was simply ... making sure he was worthy of you. What? Don't look at me that way. To me, you'll always be the teenager who risked your life to take care of me. You sat vigil beside me for days, going without food yourself, and I appreciate what you did. That could've ended badly for you."

"I never want anyone to die if I can help it. You were no different."

"Probably not, but you could've called for an ambulance and wiped your hands of me with a clear conscience. You didn't. You did what I asked — saved my undercover assignment in the process, although you didn't know that's what you were doing — and took care of me. I know that Creek wouldn't have done the same if you weren't calling the shots."

"I don't know if that's true. Back then she was ... softer."

"That's a fair assessment," he conceded, pushing away from the mausoleum and closing the distance between us. "I've seen her over the years. Her path was much harder than yours. She was never going to get out."

He was right and yet frustration bubbled up all the same. "What makes her different from me? Why did I get a shot and not her?" I already knew the answer. It was the magic. Without it, Max would've passed by and never stopped. The magic called to him and united us. It still united us in a singular goal.

"You can't think of it that way," Logan chided, shaking his head. "You didn't make it because she didn't. You made it because you were always meant to make it. You're a survivor."

"So ... what? Are you saying Creek was a throwaway from the start?"

"I would never say that." He was adamant. "The thing is, you had everything working for you. She had nothing. Sometimes that's the way things align and there's absolutely nothing you can do about it. I'm sorry about if that upsets you, but it's the truth. You weren't ever supposed to be out here."

That might've been true. I wouldn't trade my time on the streets for anything, though. It helped mold me into the woman I am today, and I'm fairly proud of her ... at least most of the time. "I know what you're saying makes sense. It still bothers me."

"Why?"

"Because ... because we all should've had a chance to get out," I replied finally. "I saw Creek today. I visited her at work. I wanted to ask her some questions about the missing girls. I thought she might still keep her ear to the ground. She kind of unloaded on me a little bit."

"She blames you for her misery, huh?"

"How did you know that?"

"Because Creek was a bubbly kid who lost a little bit of hope every single day she was out there," he replied without hesitation. "She had big dreams. The street didn't beat those dreams out of her in a single day. It took years, and it was a thorough job.

"There's probably a fixed point in Creek's mind where she knows she crossed a line," he continued. "My guess is it coincides with your escape. She's linked the two things in her memory even though they're not on the same level."

"You're pretty insightful for a former biker."

He chuckled. "I minored in psychology and still take classes whenever I can with the Bureau. That's another reason I was constantly checking on you after the fact. I could see what you were, that you would get out, and I wanted to make sure you actually made it happen.

"There was relief the day I showed up and heard you'd left," he continued. "There was sadness, too. I knew I was going to miss your face and the way you used to pretend you were reading people's minds for money."

I kept my face neutral. "I still read people's minds for money."

"You've turned it into a lucrative shtick. I'm glad for you."

He didn't understand. He couldn't. "I feel out of place here," I admitted, circling the small clearing. "This was my home at one time, but it doesn't feel like this was ever my life. Not really. I don't know how to explain it."

"Part of you originated here. Your roots, so to speak. You spread your wings and flew away. You made a new home with the circus, which I never would've believed was a viable option for anybody until I saw you with your friends. You've created a new life.

"I once heard someone say — and I can't remember where I heard it, but I was impressed at the time — that to thrive, you need both roots and wings. When you were here, you didn't have wings. With them, your new friends, you have both. You've done well."

"I felt that way until I saw Creek."

"You can't take responsibility for her life. It's not fair to either of you."

"I know. It's just ... I wonder what would've happened if I'd asked Max to bring her along. I was scared at the time, thought he would rescind the offer. I know now that he wouldn't have done that."

"And what would Creek have done with your circus?"

"I don't know. She could've worked the midway or something."

"While you were a headliner? That doesn't sound like an arrangement she would've been happy with. Jealousy was always going to consume her where you're concerned. You can't see it because you're too close. The seeds for her bitter discontent were already taking root even back then."

I sighed. He had a point. "Yeah, well ... I still feel guilty."

"You need to get over it. You're living your best life. There's no sense feeling guilty about that. It's not necessary or right."

"I guess." I rubbed my forehead and sighed. "Were you looking for me for a specific reason?"

"Actually, yeah. I wanted you to know that we're taking a contingent of agents into the shelter this afternoon. You can't come, before you ask. There's no way I can get clearance for that. I just wanted you to know that I would share information should I get it."

"Why are you raiding the shelter?"

"Not raiding," he corrected. "Beacon invited us in. The kids are terrified and he wants to put them at ease."

That made sense ... in a way. "Won't the kids balk at the Feds being on the premises? Won't they run?"

"He searches them for drugs before they come in. He doesn't let them turn tricks. The kids lucky enough to stay there are pretty clean. I don't think they'll run. If a few do, well, we'll deal with it then."

I hated to admit it — mostly because it seemed like an invasion of privacy for the kids — but it was a good idea. "Well, I wish you luck."

"Where will you be if I learn anything?"

"At the fairgrounds. I still haven't put my tent together – even though I've made the attempt about three times now. I need to hit that. We open tomorrow. I've been distracted. Usually I'm set the second day after arrival."

"I think it's okay to let momentary distraction seep in."

"Yeah." I rolled my neck "You can find me over there when you need me."

"Okay. Good to know. We'll be going in about an hour from now. I'll keep you informed."

"Thanks."

I REMAINED SITTING ON ONE OF the ornamental benches after he left. I wasn't done searching the cemetery, but I didn't want him to know what I was really doing. I trusted him implicitly, but he was still a federal agent. He wouldn't understand what we were doing and I didn't want to be the one to shatter any illusions he had about the world he lived in.

"Hey."

I sensed Melissa a few seconds before she spoke. My protégé had her own magic and was learning the ropes of the circus. She'd been quiet of late thanks to a scary event on the West Coast. She'd grown in leaps and bounds since then, though, and was finally starting to settle.

"Hey." I cast her a sidelong look. "Are you watching me for Kade?"

She laughed at the notion. "Not exactly. He did send me over here to warn you that the Fed was coming. He didn't want you to be caught unaware. Unfortunately for me, he was already with you by the time I found you. I couldn't do anything but hide and wait."

"And listen," I surmised, smirking. "Did you hear anything of interest?"

"I would like to help with the research on the banshees."

"Sure. Anything else?"

"Just one thing." She looked hesitant as she licked her lips and shifted from one foot to the other. "The thing is, I don't like that you feel guilty because you couldn't save this Creek person. The Fed is right. It's not fair to you."

"I don't think anything in this world has ever been fair to Creek."

"Maybe, but have you ever considered that if you'd stayed behind because of her you never would've met Luke ... or Kade ... or me. Sure, Max would've been fine. Eventually Kade would've even joined him. Kade wouldn't have stayed without you, though. You were his anchor.

"What about Luke? You're the only reason he doesn't float away some-times because of his big head. You can't tell me that he would've been the same person without you. What about me? You plucked me out of a festival in the middle of nowhere and gave me a new life. I would probably be dead by now if it weren't for you."

I didn't believe that and yet I understood what she was saying. "Life isn't one thing," I mused. "Life is a series of actions."

"Your choice to join the circus changed multiple lives, and all for the better."

"Raven might not agree with that."

"She would agree. You two drive each other nuts, but you're both better for knowing each other. The thing is, I can see your mind working even now. You want to find a way to fix Creek's life. Not everything is fixable. Not everyone can be helped."

"I still have to try."

She exhaled heavily. "Of course you do. That's who you are. You can't let your self-worth hinge on whether you make it happen, though. She's not your responsibility."

"I can't just forget about her. Not a second time. There has to be something I can do for her."

"And what if she doesn't want help?"

"I ... ." I wasn't sure how to answer.

"You can't force her to live the life you want for her. You need to prepare yourself for disappointment, because she's not capable of being the person you need her to be. If you have one shortcoming, it's that. You sometimes expect the impossible."

"And you think this is one of those times?"

She was emphatic. "Yes."

"Well, I'll give it some thought. Until then, I need to search the cemetery and then get back to the fairgrounds. I still have to put the tent together."

"I've already done that. You can stay here as long as you want."

"Really?" I was impressed. "Thanks for that."

"You saved me," she repeated. "I wanted help, so I was willing to meet you halfway. If Creek won't meet you halfway, you can't do everything for her. It's just not possible."

With those words, she turned on her heel and left me alone with my thoughts. I had a lot of them.

EIGHTEEN

My conversation with Melissa left me with a lot to think about. She wasn't always demonstrative, choosing to be stoic. If she felt the need to come out of her shell like she had, I realized I must be emitting a certain vibe ... and it wasn't one that I was especially proud of.

I needed to think more about that if I wanted to fix it, but I didn't have much time because everybody was bopping around and getting cleaned up for dinner at the Grimlock house when I returned. There was no way I could take all of them ... which meant making cuts.

"No way." I was firm as I shook my head in Nellie's direction. "I'm not taking you there."

"That's discrimination." Nellie was hissy ... and I didn't necessarily blame him. "Just because I wear a dress doesn't mean I'm not a person."

I shot him a withering look. "That's not going to work on me. I think you're a fabulous person wearing a fabulous dress. That doesn't mean everybody can go. We have to limit the number of invitations extended."

Nellie shrewdly narrowed his eyes. "Did they give you a limit?"

He was trying to trip me up. "They told me to use my best judgment."

"So ... ."

I firmly shook my head to cut him off. "So I'm using my best judgment. You're not a good match for an already combustible situation. Only a few of us are going."

"And who is that?"

I'd been expecting the question, and for once, I had an answer. "Me, Kade, Luke ... ."

"Of course the three musketeers are going," Raven groused.

"Max," I added pointedly.

"Me?" Max looked up from the table where he'd been drinking coffee and enjoying the show. "Why do you want me to go? I'm fine staying here and keeping an eye on the others until you return and regale us with stories."

Nellie's hand shot in the air. "I claim his place."

"You're not going," I repeated, glaring. "As for you, Max, you are going. You're the patriarch of our family. Cormack will respond better to someone trying to keep his children safe. We're not really your children but ... ."

"You're all my children," Max countered. "You've been my child since you tried to pick my pocket on the street several miles from here. I haven't forgotten that day, or where it happened. I'm fine going to dinner."

I exhaled in relief. I wasn't certain he would agree.

"Is that everyone?" he asked.

"No, we need one more," I replied, my eyes slowly drifting over the crowd until they landed on Raven. "We need someone who understands the history of banshees because she was there. There's a lot of talk about these creatures being different. I need someone who can debate that fact."

"You want me to go?" Pleasure tinged Raven's cheeks, but she quickly shuttered and turned neutral. "If you get to take your boyfriend, I get to take mine."

I should've seen that coming. "Fine." It wasn't worth quibbling over. "That's the extent of the group. I want everyone else to stay here and watch the perimeter. If the banshees come back while we're gone ... ." I purposely left it hanging.

"I'll cut their heads off," Nellie replied without hesitation. "Hey, don't look at me that way. If you're going to keep me from an excellent dinner, I'm going to kill whatever I want."

I could do nothing but roll my eyes. "Knock yourself out. Keep an eye on Cotton and Michelob. I don't want them wandering into trouble."

"We'll keep them safe," Dolph promised. "You can trust us."

I had no doubt about that. Every person I was leaving behind — well, except for the clowns and midway workers — would sacrifice their lives to keep those girls safe. We were strong and united for a reason. That wouldn't change because there was strife about dinner.

"We won't be late," I promised. "We're going to share information and that's it."

"Have fun." Dolph offered a wave as Nellie continued to glower. "Everything will be absolutely fine here. You have nothing to worry about."

KADE AND I HAD ALREADY SEEN the house, so we didn't stare as long as the others when we pulled into the driveway. Max was too cool to stare (although I didn't miss the way his eyes appreciatively roamed the turrets at the top of the house), but Luke, Raven and Percival's eyes were busy.

"Does Dracula live here?" Luke asked finally. "This looks like the sort of place a deadly vampire would live while seducing women and wearing a velvet cape."

I slid him a sidelong look. "That's a very detailed fantasy," I pointed out after a few seconds, causing him to chuckle. "No, seriously."

"It is a detailed fantasy," he agreed. "This place, though, ... I can't wait to see inside."

"The inside is even more impressive," Kade reassured.

The same stuffy butler from our previous visit opened the door to us. He looked resigned rather than excited when he gestured for us to enter. "This way."

"Cool." Luke beamed as he strode past the man. "Thanks for the warm welcome, Jeeves."

Even though I found the butler stiff and annoying, I felt the need to apologize to him. He was only doing his job, after all. "Sorry. Everyone is just excited to be here."

He slowly tracked his eyes to mine. "You needn't apologize. There's nothing your group can throw at me that the Grimlock children haven't already lobbed ... and with slingshots."

Oddly enough, I felt that was true. "Well ... ."

"You're expected in the parlor. The family is already gathered there."

That sounded ominous. I followed the trail of voices through the house, assuming someone was leading Raven and Percival, who were at the front of our group. Sure enough, we halted in one of the most ornate rooms I'd ever visited ... and it was filled with Grimlocks.

"Ah, you're here." Cormack was on his feet and already zeroing in on Max. He introduced himself, nodded with polite interest as Max did the same, and then the men settled in chairs at the front of the room to talk.

That left the rest of the room for the kids to play ... and I wasn't sure it was going to be a comfortable meeting of the minds.

"You have a baby here," Raven announced, her eyes landing on the infant

Griffin held against his shoulder. He was patting her back, giving me the impression that baby Lily was feeling unsettled.

"We do," Cormack confirmed. "That's my granddaughter." His eyes lit with joy and, for a moment I felt a warm flash of love emanate from him. He loved his family more than anything, was proud of them. His granddaughter was a particular marvel to him, though. "Lily."

"That's a beautiful name." Max beamed at the baby. "She's a beautiful girl."

"She is," Cormack agreed. "She looks like her mother."

"I'm sure that was inevitable given the genetic freak show you've got going on here," Luke offered. "I mean ... why do your kids all look exactly the same?" He looked from face to face. "Were you and their mother brother and sister?"

Cormack scowled. "Excuse me?"

"Ignore him," Max interjected smoothly. "He's addicted to attention. It doesn't matter if it's positive or negative. He'll take anything he can get."

"That sounds like someone else I know," Cormack said dryly, his eyes landing on Aisling.

"I'm sitting here being good," she protested.

She'd been quiet since we entered, contemplative. Her gaze followed Raven. I wanted to question her, but wasn't keen on the idea of doing it in front of an audience. "So, what did you guys find out today?" I asked, launching to the heart of the matter.

"Really, Poet, we can have a little small talk before we get to that," Max said, catching me by surprise. "Sit down and have a drink. You don't always have to be so vigilant."

I thought about arguing, but the look Kade shot me told me he thought that was a bad idea. With nothing better to do, I settled on one of the ornate settees — Luke and Kade taking up positions on either side — and watched with fascination as Raven circled the baby.

"What are you doing?" Griffin asked finally, protectively sheltering his daughter. "She's not on the menu if you're looking to eat her."

Raven snorted. "Please. I haven't done that in centuries."

Griffin's mouth dropped open. "What?"

Max chuckled nervously. "You'll have to excuse Raven. Her manners aren't the best. She's drawn to the baby. She can't help herself. There's something different about the child ... I'm not sure what it is."

I'd also sensed something interesting about the baby. "She's got a bit of magic," I offered, causing numerous eyes to snap in my direction.

"Magic?" Redmond leaned forward in his seat. "What do you mean by that?"

I shrugged, unsure how to explain. "She's too young to really get a read on her. I would guess whatever it is starts manifesting when she's a little older — probably five or seven — and then you guys will be able to make better preparations for when she acts out."

"You're not the first person who has suggested that Lily is special," Cormack noted, his eyes traveling to the door as Braden strolled through it. He had a striking woman with him, long black hair and cheekbones so sharp they could cut salami. She seemed bubbly as she held Braden's hand, relating an amusing anecdote to him. "And there's the other person now."

Braden and the woman pulled up short, glancing around.

"You guys could at least applaud if you're going to stare like that," Braden announced, earning a snort from Aisling.

"What's going on?" the woman asked a bit nervously, slowly tracking her eyes around the room. They lingered on Max, Kade and Raven before finally settling on me. "Who are you people?"

"That's not a very polite greeting, Izzy," Cormack chided, although he looked more amused than upset. "These are our new friends from the circus." He introduced us in turn — although he had to gather names to complete the task because he hadn't yet met everybody — and when he was finished Izzy turned her full attention to me. "Is there something wrong, my dear?" He looked concerned as he studied the striking woman.

Her coloring was similar enough that people might assume she was part of the family from a distance. Her eyes were different, though, and she practically bubbled over with magic. She wasn't the strongest being I'd ever come in contact with, but she was up there.

"You're a bruja," Raven announced before I could decide how I was going to address the woman.

Izzy didn't seem bothered by the assertion. "I am, but what are you? I keep seeing a snake in my head."

Luke snorted. "You're not far off."

Raven ignored him. "Lamia."

"Really?" Izzy brightened considerably. "I was under the impression that most of your kind were extinct."

"There are very few left."

"Well, then I'm really glad to meet you." Izzy's thoughtful gaze turned to Max. "You're a mage."

"I am." Max wasn't ashamed to admit it. "Half mage, to be exact."

"And he's quarter-mage." Izzy jerked her thumb at Kade.

"If you don't mind my asking, how did you know that?" Max queried. He looked genuinely curious.

"I spent most of my childhood in New Orleans," Izzy volunteered. "There's a decent amount of mages trying to hide among the bruja down there."

"Fascinating." Max smiled. "I didn't realize that. We visit New Orleans every year. In fact, we're due to visit in a few weeks. I will have to research that tidbit."

"They shouldn't be hard to find," Izzy offered. "They stick to the French Quarter because it's easier to blend in with the voodoo folk."

"That's good to know. Thank you."

That left me, and when Izzy finally focused on my face she looked more puzzled than anything else. "What are you?"

It wasn't until she asked the same question I'd uttered a thousand times that I realized how rude it sounded. "I seem to be a potpourri of things."

"I'll say." Izzy released Braden's hand and walked closer. "May I?" She didn't wait for an answer, instead resting her hand on top of my head. "Fascinating."

"Izzy, you're being weird," Braden complained, dragging her away from me before I had a chance to grow too uncomfortable. "You can't pet her like that."

"I'm not petting her. I'm just ... you're not one thing." Izzy, frankly, looked amazed. "You're kind of a mixture. You must've had a lot of magic folk in your lineage because you're utterly fascinating."

She'd used that word twice now. I wasn't comfortable with it. "I don't really know," I admitted. "My parents died when I was a teenager. Before then, they wanted me to hide what I could do. They were insistent that I be quiet about it. Once they were gone, there was no one to ask."

"I'm sorry." Izzy was sincere. "I lost my parents when I was little. Luckily I had my grandfather to raise me in New Orleans."

"We met your aunt," I pointed out. "We were in her store today."

"Aunt Max. She's great."

"She's convinced that we're dealing with mutant banshees," I noted, taking the conversation full circle to the serious topic. I didn't care if Max thought it was rude. I wanted to get to the heart of matters. "She thinks they're different. What do you think?"

"I've yet to see one of them," Izzy admitted, rueful. "My home base is Belle Isle. I have a new employee who is set to come in any day now and I'm down one worker. I've been stuck on the island for the past two weeks."

"Which is stupid," Braden muttered as he shook his head. "I haven't had an omelet bar all week."

I was confused. "What's an omelet bar?"

No one answered. The Grimlocks were avidly watching Braden and Izzy instead.

"You didn't have to sleep on the island," Izzy pointed out primly. "You could've slept here — with your brother and father — and left me to my work plight alone."

Braden made a face. "Oh, don't be like that. I wasn't blaming you. I was just saying that I happen to love a good omelet bar."

"Who doesn't?" Aisling enthused, climbing to her feet to join Griffin in the corner as he settled the baby. Lily wasn't making much noise, but it was obvious the baby didn't want to relax. I had a feeling I knew why.

"You know the baby is aware that she's the center of all your worlds, right?" I finally announced.

Griffin lifted his chin, surprised. "You read Lily's mind?"

"I tried, but there's not much I can see," Izzy admitted. "You must have stronger mind magic."

"Maybe," I hedged.

"No, you definitely excel with the mind magic," Max agreed. "That was the first thing I noticed when we met. You were trying to push me into believing it was a beautiful evening and at the same time trying to make sure I didn't realize my wallet was being lifted. As a mage, you shouldn't have been able to budge me. You gave me a little shove, though, and that's how I knew you were special."

My cheeks flushed as Kade grinned and rested his hand on my knee. "There's definitely a lot of magic in this room."

"There is," Max agreed. "Given that magic, we should be able to work together and figure out what's happening. We need to come up with a plan."

"Izzy needs to see one of them first," Braden countered, his hands continually roaming his girlfriend's slim back. He seemed to constantly need to touch her, which had me guessing that they were a relatively new couple. They were clearly into one another, but they hadn't yet walked through fire to save each other.

That was still to come ... and it would be interesting.

"I spent the afternoon searching the cemetery," I said. "I think they have a home base there, but I'm not familiar enough with the grounds to know if there's a place they could be hiding ... other than the obvious, I mean. I don't want to invade any of the mausoleums, but I think that might have to be our next step."

"We invade mausoleums there all the time," Aisling offered, waving her hand before taking the baby from Griffin. Lily immediately seemed to settle a bit when her mother started swaying back and forth — especially when Griffin moved to the other side, so his chest was against Lily's back and he was facing his wife — the new parents essentially wrapping her in a cocoon. "We can do it again if we have to."

They were forming a human swaddling machine to make the baby comfortable. I wondered if they realized it or instinct caused them to protect her this way. They were good parents without even realizing it.

They also were going to have their hands full for a very long time.

"We can take a trip to the cemetery after dinner," I suggested. "Maybe if we're all there as a group we'll be able to figure things out. It can't hurt."

"It can if the cops come back," Cillian challenged. The woman sitting next to him on the settee — she'd been introduced as Maya and had Griffin's coloring – smiled serenely at his discomfort. She was Griffin's sister, if I remembered the family connections correctly. It seemed there were a lot of intricate ties in the Grimlock world. It was very much like our world ... except most of the people in our world didn't look exactly alike.

"We'll post lookouts outside the cemetery to make sure that nobody can sneak up on us," Max insisted. "I think a cemetery search will be good. If we can find these banshees sooner rather than later it will benefit us all."

"Then we're agreed to go on a banshee search after dinner," Cormack announced. "We have prime rib and a potato bar for dinner, so everyone should eat up before we head out."

"Prime rib?" Luke was tickled. "Do you guys eat like that all the time?"

"When you have as many children as I do you learn to bribe them with food at an early age."

"There's even an ice cream bar for dessert," Aisling added, grinning as she pulled away from Griffin. The baby was finally asleep. "Gummy sharks and everything."

Cormack's smile was indulgent when aimed at his only daughter. "I got you gummy owls, too, because you said you wanted them."

"Score!"

I couldn't swallow my laughter. It was like being in a surreal new world set inside an urban castle in which a doting father spoils the crap out of his children and sees nothing weird about it. It was unrealistic ... and yet I kind of liked it. I had no idea why.

"Dinner first," Cormack insisted. "Then we'll come up with a plan."

"Definitely dinner," Braden enthused. "What did you get me for the ice cream bar?"

"Coconut-covered sprinkles. They're multiple colors."

Braden nodded. "Good choice."

NINETEEN

*T*he group heading back to the cemetery was massive.

Maya volunteered to stay behind with Lily. Apparently she wasn't keen to go on an adventure, but she offered to patch up anybody who was hurt after the fact. I thought that was weird until I was informed she was a nurse. Aisling demanded to be included, so Griffin insisted he had to be part of the team, and by the time we were finished we had a six-vehicle caravan traveling to the cemetery.

We parked at the fairgrounds to exchange information with our people. Now that the action had shifted, there was no keeping Nellie out of the fray. He scampered off to get his ax before I could inform him that we wanted to keep the hunting party manageable. It was too late. Apparently everybody was going.

If Cormack was bothered by the army we'd brought with us from across the road when we met at the cemetery gate he didn't show it. He apparently had a the-more-the-merrier mentality, which explained why he had so many kids.

"Seth, I want you and Dolph to take up position on either side of the cemetery," I instructed as I tied my hair back in a bun. "Keep on the lookout for Agent Stone particularly. It wouldn't surprise me at all if he's hanging around ... and if he sees all of us heading into the cemetery he'll be curious. Text me so we can at least pretend we're doing something normal."

Aisling slid me a sidelong look. "What normal thing could we possibly be doing in a cemetery after dark?"

"Having a séance," I answered without hesitation. "Perhaps your father, being a rich man, decided he wanted me to contact the spirit of his dead wife and jumped at the chance to hire us."

"Wait ... can you really conduct séances?" Braden looked intrigued.

"Yes, but they're not like those you've seen in television and movies. Why?"

Izzy put her hand on Braden's shoulder and leaned in to whisper to him. Some of the tension left his body, which I took as a good sign.

"We'll talk about a séance later," Cormack instructed. "For now, we need to get moving. I think we should break into teams."

That made the most sense, except for one thing. "Do you really want to trust some of your kids — like Redmond — to run around with someone like Nellie?" I gestured toward my cross-dressing friend. His eyes were lit with excitement because he hadn't beheaded anything in days. He became almost manic when he had to go without action.

Cormack heaved out a sigh. "Good point. I guess we're going as a group."

"It will be easier to explain if we get caught by Logan," I offered. "Then we can use the séance excuse."

"Fair enough." Cormack put his hand to Aisling's back and prodded her in front of him. It was a protective move, one designed to make sure that his lone female child wouldn't fall by the wayside and into trouble. I had no idea if that was normal behavior for him — if he favored her over his brothers or simply watched her more closely because she was a new mother — but I found it interesting.

As for Aisling's brothers and Izzy, they seemed thrilled to meet new people and didn't find Nellie's ax off-putting in the least.

"That's a nice one," Redmond commented as he matched paces with our bearded lady. "How many notches do you have on it?"

"If you can count your kills, you're doing it wrong."

"Does that mean a lot or only a few? I'm not sure if you're trying to be smug or psychological."

"I have more kills than you have years behind you."

"How old do you think I am?"

"Don't make me behead you," Nellie shot back.

Kade and I fell into step behind Aisling, Griffin and Cormack. They took the lead because they seemed to know the cemetery well.

"I take it you guys are here often," I said to their backs. It seemed silly not to talk. "Do you collect souls here?"

"Souls should be collected as close to the time of passing as possible," Cormack countered. "It's not always feasible, but we do our best. You shouldn't have to absorb a soul at the cemetery. It should be done long before then."

"And you absorb every soul?" I was naturally curious. "If that's true, how do you explain ghosts?"

"We *try* to absorb every soul," he explained. "Despite our best efforts, I would say that at least five percent of them are either missed or flee."

"That's not a terrible percentage," Kade pointed out. "Most people would kill for a ninety-five-percent success rate."

"Yes, but the five percent of souls left behind usually fall victim to a horrible existence."

"Ghosts," I surmised.

Cormack nodded once. "In some instances. Most souls become manic or crazed when left without a body for too long. They draw attention to themselves, which allows us to track them after the fact. Very few are quiet ... and they're the ones to be more concerned about. That usually means they're more aware of their surroundings and can turn vicious."

I'd never really given it that much thought. "You said that only some of them become ghosts. What about the others?"

"They are absorbed by wraiths." Cormack's voice went grim. "When that happens, the soul is lost forever. It's destroyed to fuel the wraith ... although wraiths only live a half-life, so the souls aren't even put to good use. It's sad, really."

It sounded sad. "What about the souls that you've lost recently?" I was curious about the process and decided to take the opportunity to ask the question that had been plaguing me since things started going sideways. "I mean ... you guys have said the banshees are stealing your souls. What do you think they're doing with them?"

"I don't know." Cormack's gaze was grave when he stopped and turned to me. "My guess would be ingesting them. I can't think of another purpose. I'm not all that familiar with banshees. They're soulless beings, correct?"

He seemed to be asking for a history lesson, so I decided to give it to him. "Banshees were created in times of great mourning. They're Irish in origin."

"Hey, so are we," Redmond chirped from behind me.

"The keening is their main identifier. It stems from Scottish and Irish traditions." I explained. "Those who mourned hardest and couldn't get over their grief turned into banshees."

"And they're always women?" Griffin asked.

"Yes, but I don't have an explanation for that. I would think there had to be cases of men mourning hard enough for lost loves or children that they would turn. But the phenomenon seems to happen only to women."

Aisling glanced at her father. "Yeah. I've known people who grieved hard and never had that happen. So, it's a woman thing. That doesn't explain what's happening on the streets right now."

"It definitely doesn't," I agreed. Cormack was leading us to the old section of the cemetery, to the place where the mausoleums and tombs were built. I wasn't surprised. I figured that's where the banshees had to be hiding. "There's another type of banshee, though."

I explained to them about human suffering and the phenomenon that occurred during World War II. When I was finished, Aisling looked disgusted and Cormack was intrigued.

"Ugh. Weren't those poor people put through enough?" Aisling complained, annoyance obvious. "I mean ... really."

It was a valid question. Cormack had another one.

"Do you think that's what's happening here?"

I expected him to ask. That didn't mean I was sure how to answer. "I don't know," I said finally, organizing my thoughts. "The thing is, the girls have been missing for only a few weeks. Human suffering of this magnitude usually takes longer than that. We're talking about a soul-cracking force. That takes a lot of effort. It doesn't simply happen willy-nilly."

"We know a little something about soul fractures," Cormack started, clearly choosing his words carefully. He risked a glance at Aisling and immediately slipped his arm around her shoulders when he saw the way she was looking at him. Her expression was not exactly accusatory. It wasn't loving either.

"I would agree that fracturing a soul, breaking bits off, takes longer than a few weeks," he continued. "I don't have an exact timetable — nobody does, because suffering doesn't follow guidelines — but I get what you're saying.

"If these girls have been transformed into banshees — whether the traditional sort or something new — then something truly terrible had to happen to them," he continued. "The thing is, even when a soul has been fractured, goodness remains. Sometimes it remains in only one half of the soul. That doesn't mean that all is lost."

He was speaking from a place of specific knowledge.

"You're talking about your wife."

Cormack jerked his eyes to Aisling, perhaps sensing she was the one to tell me. "I ... you know about that?"

"A little. Not much. I know the basics, and that's okay. The thing is, I've seen two of these banshees die so far. There were no souls hanging around that I saw."

"She's right," Redmond interjected as he hurried to catch up with his father and sister. "The one I killed ... there was no soul left behind. Not only that, when I killed it, there was only dust left. That usually indicates the absence of a soul."

He said it in such a matter-of-fact manner I had to take a moment to consider it. Once I thought about it, I decided he was right. Soulless beings often faded to dust when killed. That was beyond interesting ... and something to think about down the road.

"You want to know if we can save them, don't you?" I asked Cormack pointedly. He didn't respond, just held my gaze. "I don't know if we can. My gut says no. The two we've seen go down were easily defeated and gone within seconds. Nothing remained behind to save."

"They're thinking as a unit," Kade pointed out. He kept my hand firmly in his as we closed in on the part of the cemetery we were headed for. "They reminded me of the human dolls we faced out on the West Coast."

I tilted my head, considering.

"Human dolls?" Aisling looked horrified at the thought. "Is that a real thing?"

Kade launched into the tale of the crazy witch who subverted human girls so she could feed off them, giving me time to decide if I thought it was an avenue worth pursuing. When he was finished, Aisling was even more screechy than usual.

"Ugh. I hate dolls," she complained. "I don't know how you managed to deal with that. I mean ... gross."

"They were still humans underneath," I murmured, rubbing my chin. "They still had souls."

"What are you thinking?" Cormack asked. "I can practically hear the gears working."

"Maybe they're rusty," Redmond suggested, earning a firm cuff from his father.

"There are spells to track souls," I said. "They're mentioned in books, but I've never used them. I have used a modified version of the spell to track other forms of monsters. We might be able to try to find the souls ... although that might be a wasted effort. I need to give it some thought."

"It's not a wasted effort if we can help the souls move on," Aisling persisted. "It's not the outcome we wanted — which is to save these girls — but it's better than nothing."

"I need to conduct some research," I said. "I have some books to check. I'll do it first thing tomorrow morning."

"Good. I ... ." Whatever Cormack was going to say died on his lips as a peculiar scratching reverberated through the area. It sounded like a brick wall was moving, perhaps opening, and it put us all on alert. "Spread out," he hissed. "Find the source of that noise."

No one needed to be told twice. We were two separate groups who hadn't worked together before, yet we moved as a seamless unit. Everyone knew what they were doing. Even Nellie was quiet as he hunted with his ax.

"Which direction?" Kade whispered, his hand in front of me as if he was trying to keep me from running headlong into danger. "Which way should we go?"

I didn't have an answer. "I ... ." The hair on the back of my neck suddenly stood on end and I swiveled quickly. It was an odd time of day. It wasn't quite dark and yet the sun was offering no illumination. I had to squint to make out anything thanks to the growing haze, and it took me almost a full ten seconds to find the source of the feeling.

The girl had dark hair. I couldn't determine her age, but she was so small I figured she couldn't be older than sixteen. Her eyes looked sunken and there was no glow to her skin. She was a pallid creature, but she was alive. Her head moved, her eyes bounced from face to face, and her hands were extended and ready for battle.

"Where did she come from?" Redmond asked, moving to my side as he prepared to take her down.

"I'm not sure," Kade replied. "She just appeared."

"It can't be far. We should kill her and go looking for the others." He made a move to do just that, but I shot out my hand and grabbed his arm.

"Not yet," I hissed.

His eyes widened. "Why not? I thought we agreed we couldn't help them. They're soulless."

I mostly believed that, but a niggling doubt remained. "Just let me try to talk to her," I insisted.

He was incredulous, but took a step back. "Fine. Talk to the banshee. See where that gets you."

His tone grated, but I ignored him and focused on the girl. "Hello." I held my hands out to my sides in a peaceable manner so she wouldn't fear me. "Can you hear me?"

The girl blinked several times rapidly and glanced between faces. Finally, after what felt like a really long time, she focused on me.

"You can hear me?" I forced a smile that probably came across as creepy rather than soothing. But she was a monster. Perhaps creepy was comforting ... although I sincerely doubted it. "I would like to help you," I offered. "I know you don't trust me and you're probably confused, but I would definitely like to help you."

The girl cocked her head to the side, reminding me of a dog I once saw. The vacant expression in her eyes told me the dog had understood more than this girl.

"Do you understand me?" I pressed. "Can you communicate with me?"

The girl hissed but didn't speak. Of course, I didn't really expect her to.

"Listen, we want to help." Tentatively I took a step in her direction. She shrank back, but I was determined to get close enough to touch her. If I could make that happen, I was certain I would be able to see whatever was happening inside her mind. If it was nothing, so be it. If it was something, I might be able to find a way to help her.

"I only want to touch you," I reassured, adopting the calmest voice I could muster. "I won't hurt you. I have no intention of hurting you. I just want to ... ." My fingers lightly brushed against her hair and a lightning-quick flash filled with screaming and brick walls filled my head. "Oh, geez!"

I slowed my pace, which was a mistake. The banshee decided at that moment that I was a threat and she needed to take me out. She extended her fingernails into brutal claws and moved to leap on me. I was just deciding how to react — with deadly force or something softer — when Nellie appeared behind the woman.

I knew what he was going to do. I'd spent enough time with him to see exactly how this was going to end. I opened my mouth to scream at him to stop, but it was already too late.

He brought the ax down on the back of the girl's neck with an exuberant precision that took my breath away. The girl froze for a split second, her eyes filling with something I couldn't quite identify, and then dissolved into dust and poofed out of existence.

The hand I was reaching for crumbled to nothing, and I was left standing alone next to the mausoleum. What had once been a young girl I was certain had hopes and dreams, was no more.

"Are you okay?" Kade rushed to my side.

I was too angry to answer. Thankfully I didn't have to because that's when a shadow I hadn't noticed before started moving. This one was lower, set close to the ground, and it appeared to belong to an animal.

We weren't out of this yet.

"There!" I extended a warning finger and everyone turned in anticipation. I held my breath as the beast padded forward.

When the creature stepped forward enough for me to make out its features, I was horrified. It looked like some sort of mutant dog ... or as if it was the outcome of what would happen if a dog and owl mated.

"Holy ... !"

Kade shoved me behind him and took the position closest to the creature. "I don't know what you are, but if you touch her I'll kill you."

Instead of bearing teeth or growling, the animal started laughing ... like a human.

"Oh, I love it when you people say stuff like that," he chuckled. "I mean ... it's so funny. Aren't death threats funny? I love them." His expression shifted quickly. "Oh, wait, I don't. You're all douches and I don't want to know any of you. Are you happy? I mean ... geez. What is wrong with you people?"

I was starting to wonder that myself.

2 0

TWENTY

"*What* the hell is that?"

Luke practically jumped into my arms he was so eager to get away from the creature. For a guy who could shift into a killer wolf, he had a lot in common with Shaggy from *Scooby-Doo*.

"I don't know, but I want to mount that head on my trailer wall," Nellie announced, gripping his ax tighter. "Come here little ... owl-dog thing." He looked uncertain as he eyed the creature. "Hey, is that your tail or ... nope." He averted his eyes quickly. "Wow. I think we know why there aren't many of these things in existence. They'll kill anything they try to procreate with."

Aisling made a sound that was halfway between a snort and a chuckle, and bent at the waist. I couldn't tell if she was getting sick or laughing.

"He's a gargoyle," Cormack announced, shaking his head as he moved to the front of our group. "What are you doing here, Bub?"

Bub? That thing had a name. Still ... I'd always wanted to see a gargoyle. I couldn't stop myself from leaning to the right so I could peer around Cormack and study the creature. I knew better than to look at its tail — or whatever it was — but I couldn't stop myself. An involuntary cringe fluttered through me when I saw the appendage jutting out. "Oh, holy ... !"

"Yeah, it's better if you don't look at it," Aisling announced, raising her head and moving to her father's side, amused tears glistening in her eyes. "By the way, I told you he looked like an owl-dog. I'm not the only one to notice."

"An owl-dog isn't a thing," Bub shot back, his eyes narrowing as he looked Aisling up and down. "Hello, littlest Grimlock. I haven't seen you in weeks. I was starting to think the worst."

Aisling snorted. "Oh, you were not. You were probably throwing a party."

"Believe it or not, you're the fun one in your family," Bub countered. "I keep running into that long-haired brother of yours in the library, but it's not the same."

"I'll try to stop by for a visit when I can. I have a baby now."

"I heard." Bub lifted his chin. "Where is it? I want to see it."

"He probably wants to eat it," Luke whispered much louder than he probably intended.

"Totally." Nellie bobbed his head. "That definitely looks like a creature that eats babies. That's why I want his head for my wall."

"You're not beheading him," Cormack barked. "He works for the reaper council."

"Besides, we kind of owe him," Aisling added. "He's helped us a few times when we really needed it. He's, like, ... well, not family. He's like the neighbor's dog you're loyal to because he keeps robbers away."

"Thank you so much for that." Bub's sneer was withering. "I'm actually here for a reason. Believe it or not, I don't enjoy spending my time skulking around cemeteries and talking to the likes of you."

"You silver-tongued devil," Nellie intoned.

Bub ignored him, although he regularly checked to make sure the ax wasn't flying in his direction. "I'm here to warn you about an infestation of banshees," he announced.

Redmond pursed his lips and gestured toward the glittering dust that was still settling. "We're aware of the banshees."

"So I see. I just heard about them tonight. I don't hang with the old crew as much as I used to. They were whispering hard this evening, and I couldn't ignore them."

"What are they saying?" Cormack, all business, asked. "Do they know why the banshees are acting the way they are?"

"They're being controlled."

I decided to insert myself into the conversation, even if it seemed rude. "How? I've never heard of banshees being controlled."

Bub slowly turned his eyes to me and made an odd hiss as his expression went dark. "Romani."

I frowned. "Excuse me?"

"You're Romani?"

"What's Romani?" Redmond asked, bewildered.

"Romani are called gypsies or Roma," Cillian volunteered, his eyes unreadable as they found me in the crowd. "They're an Indo-Aryan ethnic group who are usually itinerant. They originated in Indonesia more than a thousand years ago."

"Is that why you're magical?" Redmond asked.

"She's magical because she's descended from, like, eighty different things and they joined together in a hodgepodge," Izzy answered, pushing forward until she stood directly in front of Bub. "Romani hate is not pretty. You should let it go. There's no need to be prejudiced."

Bub scowled. "I don't need you to tell me what to do, *bruja*."

"Apparently you do." She wagged a finger. "Tell us about the banshees. I didn't get to see this one that closely. It appeared to be listening to Poet, but I don't think it understood her ... and it didn't try to communicate."

"Banshees can't communicate," Bub pointed out. "They're soulless eating machines ... kind of like the Grimlock boys."

Redmond threw something I couldn't make out at the gargoyle. "You're a delight. We need to know what's going on with the banshees. I mean ... how did you even know to warn us?"

"That's a good question," Cormack interjected. "How did you know we were here?"

"I wasn't really looking for you as much as the banshees. I thought I could confirm their existence and then sell you the information. I had a plan ... which you people shot all to hell."

"You were going to sell us information?" Aisling folded her arms over her chest. "Why? You used to like dropping in and giving us information for free."

"That's when I had someone else funding my needs," Bub shot back pointedly, causing Aisling to shake her head. "Your mother was evil, but she bought good eats."

Cormack furrowed his brow. "Are you saying you need money?"

"That's exactly what I'm saying. None of the rogue reapers will hire me because they say I turned on them. I'm in a bind."

"What about the reaper council?" Aisling challenged. "Doesn't it pay you for working in the library?"

"Not until I pay off my medical bills. Apparently they didn't save my life after that last battle for free."

Aisling looked disgusted. "Don't worry about it. I'll talk to them and fix it."

Cormack rolled his eyes. "You're not going to fix it. You're going to whine to me until I fix it."

"It's the same thing."

Cormack let loose a world-weary sigh and dug in his pocket to retrieve his wallet. He came back with a stack of bills and handed them to Bub, who greedily grabbed them without uttering a word of protest. "That should tide you over. I'll talk to the council about your pay. Is there anything else?"

"Just that there's talk about a bigger magical force creating the banshees. Warlock, maybe demon. I can't be sure. What's happening isn't a natural occurrence."

"We figured that out ourselves," Aisling replied.

"That's all I have for now. I can do more digging. Now that I'm not going to starve, I mean."

"See what you can find out," Cormack instructed. "We'll do the same. Three of these creatures have been taken out. I want to know how many remain."

"And where they're coming from," I added. "Obviously that banshee was sent out to either distract us or kill us. My guess is the former because she was woefully outnumbered. They're being housed nearby."

"We'll search a bit longer, but we can't stay too long. That Fed who is sniffing around is bound to show up eventually. I would rather not explain our presence."

That made two of us.

I SLEPT HARD. THE SEARCH WAS fruitless and once Seth texted that Logan was on the move we slipped out through the cemetery's back gate and went our separate ways with promises to keep in touch.

My dreams were ragged, a potpourri of the present and past overlapping. I was on the hunt in the dreams, and I kept circling to people I knew. Some of them, like Creek, Logan and Beacon, were still around. Others, like Noble and Junk, were long gone. I asked them questions, pestered them for answers, and yet they offered me nothing.

Kade was already awake when I opened my eyes the next morning, his fingers gentle as they brushed my hair away from my face. He seemed lost in thought.

"Did I wake you?" he asked when he realized my eyes were open.

I shook my head. "Just time to get up."

"We open today."

"Not until noon."

"I guess that means you have plans before then," he noted. "And here I hoped we could spend half the day in bed and do nothing but worship each other."

It was a nice thought, but we didn't have time for it. "I need to speak to Beacon again. I have more information, and I think he might be able to help me."

"And you don't want me going."

"I want you to stay here and make sure everything is ready for our grand opening."

He nodded.

"It's not that I don't want you with me," I added. "You know that's not it. Beacon has always been difficult. I just want to ensure my best shot of getting information out of him."

Kade rubbed his thumb over my cheek as I rested my head on his chest. "I don't want to demand you take me."

"That's good, because that would cause a fight."

He chuckled. "I don't like the idea of you running around by yourself. This thing feels ... convoluted. I think we're missing a layer, maybe more."

"Oh, we're definitely missing layers." I was certain of that. "I'll be fine going to the shelter. It's right around the corner. Besides, I think the gargoyle only comes out at night, and he's the only thing I'm currently afraid of."

"You mean the dog-owl?"

I laughed, as he'd probably intended. "That wasn't his tail."

"I noticed." He leaned forward and pressed his lips to my forehead. "I won't lie; I'll be happy when we're out of here. It feels as if you're being stretched in multiple directions."

The admission surprised me. "Like ... away from you?"

"No. Not exactly."

"Nothing could stretch me so far I'll slip away from you," I reassured him.

"I might have said that wrong. I don't think I'm losing you. Don't worry about that. It's just ... people are pulling at you. Luke and I are always pulling at you, so you're used to that. Now you have Cotton and Michelob to worry about, too. Then there's Creek, and I don't care what you say, you're still worried about her. Then there are the Grimlocks, and they form their own army. It's a lot."

He wasn't wrong. "You still take precedence."

"That's sweet but unnecessary. I don't expect to be the most important thing in your life every second of every day going forward."

"That's good because I think Luke would pitch a fit if you demanded that."

He chuckled and tightened his arms around my back. "This place holds a lot of memories for you. You feel guilty for getting out when others didn't. You look at Creek and wonder what you should've done to save her. The thing is, I don't believe there's anything you could've done. You can't take the weight of the world onto your shoulders."

He made sense, and yet I was still troubled. "I can't focus on Creek right now. If I can think of a way to help before we leave, I will. These missing girls are my biggest priority. We might not be able to save the ones already taken, but we can save the ones still out there. I'm determined to try."

"I know." He pressed a series of kisses to my cheek. "You're nothing if not diligent."

"Do you want me to show you how diligent I really am?"

Interest sparked in his eyes. "Yes, please, Ms. Parker. Show me your diligence."

I had plenty of time for that. Life had to go on, right? I could look forward while still straddling the line to my past, and that's exactly what I planned to do.

BEACON WAS IN THE LOBBY when I let myself into the shelter. I was familiar with the set-up. They locked the doors at night. No one in or out. That was for safety purposes, and I understood it. During the day, though, the doors were open so kids could come and go. They had to pass certain checks at the front desk to be allowed in the back, but I wasn't really here for lunch and lodging.

"Poet." Beacon didn't look happy to see me when he slid into the lobby. "I thought perhaps you'd left by now."

"We're here through Sunday. We'll be out of here on Monday."

"Good to know." He dragged a hand through his sandy blond hair. He looked frustrated, a little weary and rundown. The breadth of what was happening on the street was weighing on him. "How are the girls you took in? Are you taking them with you when you leave?"

"We can't take them." Even if I wanted to take the girls, it wasn't possible. We were monster hunters, after all. We couldn't protect them forever. Eventually they would figure out we were lying to them ... or worse. "I wish we could, but they're underage, and that's against the law."

"I never realized you were such a stickler for the law."

"I'm responsible for the people I work with. I'm second in command. I fill out all the paperwork and handle payroll. People would lose their jobs if we just up and left the state with two kids."

"So ... you decided to wine and dine them, and then dump them?" Beacon challenged. There was an edge to his tone. "That sounds fair."

I knew better than to argue with him, but I couldn't stop myself. "We're not wining and dining them. We're feeding them and keeping them safe at night. We tackled Michelob's tonsils. By the way, she's speaking normally now. She's still quiet compared to Cotton, but it's not because she's in constant pain."

Anger sparked in the depths of Beacon's eyes. "Are you blaming me for that girl's condition? I tried to get her to go to a hospital for months. She refused. I can't make her go."

"I'm not blaming you."

"It sure sounds like you are."

"Then maybe you need to clean out your ears."

We stood glaring at each other for a long moment, anger building to a crescendo that caused the air to feel thick and hot, and then we stepped away from each other at the same time.

"I'm sorry," Beacon said finally, shaking his head. "I don't know why I reacted that way. I should be happy you helped Michelob. The girl has been struggling for as long as I've known her. There were months in the winter she was so sick I feared she would never return."

"It shouldn't be a problem now," I reassured him. "We took care of it. As for wining and dining them, it's not like I'm going to make them scrounge for food while they're helping us. They're not getting lobster and steak either. We cook burgers and hot dogs ... homemade pasta salad and other fixings."

He held up his hand. "I shouldn't have attacked you. It's just ... it's weird seeing you back. I convinced myself you were nothing but a dream. I know that sounds weird, but these kids held you up as some sort of beacon, a symbol of hope.

"In the weeks after you left, Creek was complete and total trouble," he continued. "She would tell the other kids these ridiculous stories about how you joined the circus and were just waiting for your moment to return and pluck her up, too. You just had to make sure they trusted you before you added her into the mix. That's what she said, anyway."

My heart plummeted. "She thought I was coming back?"

"Yes."

I hated the feelings of guilt coursing through me. I did nothing wrong. Deep down, I knew that. The guilt was still overpowering. "I did what I had to do," I said. "I had exactly one shot to get out. I couldn't find her. She was off with Tawny." I rubbed my forehead. "You probably don't even know who that is."

"I remember Tawny." Beacon sighed as he slid into one of the chairs at the edge of the room. "She was a working girl who tried to recruit you and Creek to her team. She failed with you and was victorious with Creek."

I made a derisive sound in the back of my throat. "She didn't try to recruit me."

"No?" Beacon arched a challenging eyebrow. "Why do you think she spent so much time with you? It wasn't because she enjoyed your company. It was because her pimp ordered her to be on the lookout for fresh meat. You and Creek fit the bill."

"But ... no." I was good at reading people. I always had been. If Tawny had ulterior motives, I would've picked it up from her head. I mean ... I would have, right? I wasn't so certain.

"I can't believe you're just now realizing this," Beacon supplied. "It was obvious to everyone in the know. Why do you think the biker who turned out to be a cop was watching you so closely? He warned Tawny what would happen if she touched you."

That was news to me. "Well ... great. I didn't know that."

I regrouped. "I just want to make sure that you let in every girl who needs shelter the next few nights. I know you have a budget and rules, but I can help. Just tell me how much money you need and I'll find a way to get it to you. I need to keep these kids safe and we don't have room at the circus." We also didn't have walls to keep out the monsters, but I left that part out.

"To what end? They'll still be in danger when you leave."

Not if I could help it. "We're working on that. We're going to find who's doing this."

"How do you plan to do that?"

"I'm not sure yet, but I'm determined to see it happen."

"You always were determined above all else." He shook his head. "I'll do what I can," he said finally. "I can't make any promises."

"That's all I ask." I started for the door, but stilled when he called my name.

"That family you built back then wasn't real," Beacon offered. "It was an illusion. There was never a future for the group of you together. You have to realize that."

I swallowed hard. "Why are you telling me this?"

"Because I think you need to hear it. You're trying to make up for some perceived slight that you believe you made years ago. You don't have anything to apologize for. You survived. You made it out. It is what it is."

"I'm still going to save these kids." I was firm on that. "I need your help to do it. Don't turn them away."

"I won't."

"Good. I'll figure out the rest."

TWENTY-ONE

The circus bustled with activity when I returned. I disappeared to my trailer without greeting anyone so I could take a few moments to decompress. That turned into an hour, and by the time I exited I was dressed to impress in one of my favorite ankle-length skirts. I'd pulled my hair back in a turban and wore an over-sized peasant blouse to sell the rest of the ensemble.

Kade glanced up from the picnic table, where he sat reading a newspaper, and let loose a low wolf whistle when he saw me. He was the only one around.

"Where is everybody else?" I asked, glancing around to make sure we weren't about to be descended on by circus locusts.

He smiled. "They're off doing their thing. You don't have anything to worry about. We're a well-oiled machine."

Uh-huh. That didn't sound like our group at all. "Where are they really?"

"I asked them to give you some time," he replied, sheepishly patting the bench next to him. "I saw you when you came back. You looked a little shell-shocked."

"And you didn't kick in the trailer door to get to me?"

"You didn't look like you wanted company."

I searched his face for hints that he was upset about that and then, finding nothing, sighed. "It's harder to be here than I thought it would be."

"See, I think it's exactly as hard as you thought it was going to be. You put on a good show for the rest of us, but I should've caught on sooner that you were keyed up for this visit. I can't help feeling a little guilty."

That was ridiculous. He had nothing to feel guilty about. "Don't feel guilty. You've gone above and beyond the last few days. I know you've had to stuff your feelings down deep a few times, and I'm sorry about that. You're the best man I know. If you feel guilty, I'm going to be angry."

"That's kind of how I feel about you. Not that you're the best man I know, but you are the best woman. I don't like you feeling guilty. If I can't feel guilty, neither can you."

Yup. I'd walked right into that trap. "I'm doing my best to get over the guilt." That was mostly true. There were times I found myself mired in it no matter how hard I tried. "It's harder than I thought. When we're on the road it's easy not to think about it. I'm happy. I have you ... and Luke ... and even Raven. I love my life."

"Coming back reminds you of how things could've been," he surmised. "One missed turn, one errant step, and you think you wouldn't have made it here."

"That's the truth."

"See, I don't believe that. I think you were always meant to end up here."

"Destiny?"

"You don't believe in destiny? Come on, after all you've seen, how could you believe in anything else?"

It was a good question. "I don't know. I just don't see how I would've found you if it weren't for Max helping me instead of ignoring me that day."

He lowered his forehead to mine. "I would've found you. There's no way I could live my life without you. This was always meant to happen."

I wrapped my arms around his neck for a moment, fought back tears, and collected myself. When I pulled back, there was a genuine smile on my face. "I love you."

"I love you."

"I'm still ahead on saying it."

He pressed a solid kiss against my mouth. "In your dreams."

THE CIRCUS OPENED AT NOON and people began lining up outside my tent shortly after. Oddly enough, I found I was happy to return to my normal routine, if only for a few hours. It helped clear my head.

Unfortunately, not all the visitors to my tent were of the relaxing variety.

"I want to know if my husband is cheating on me," Cathy Hogan announced. She was a pleasant-looking woman in her forties, cute freckles sprinkled across the bridge of her nose, but the anger in her eyes was enough to have me checking any jokes I might feel like unleashing.

"Okay. May I ask why you think your husband is cheating?"

"Aren't you psychic? You should already know the answer to that." Her tone was frigid. That led me to believe something had happened recently to make her suspicious.

"Fine." I shuffled the tarot cards and held them out to her. "Cut."

She did as instructed and watched as I doled out the cards. "Thinks he can lie to me about why he needs two phones," she muttered under her breath.

I studied the cards for a few minutes, debating how I wanted to handle the woman. Larry had been insistent when he said only happy fortunes would do. That wasn't reality, though. If I lied to this woman and delivered a happy fortune, it could do real harm.

"He's cheating," I announced with little preamble.

"I knew it," she hissed. "I just knew it."

I had to bite the inside of my cheek to keep from laughing. It wasn't a funny situation, but she was so animated she was like a cartoon character.

"What's her name?"

Should I answer? It was easy enough to snatch the name from the ether. It might not be a good idea, though. Oh, well, I was mildly curious about what would happen. "Desiree."

"Desiree?" Cathy's eyebrows flew up her forehead. "How can you possibly know that?"

I merely tapped the side of my head as a response.

"But ... Desiree ... it can't be her. That's ... I mean ... no way. That's gross."

"I take it you know her." I pressed my fingertips over the Tower card and frowned. The card was often misread, but there was every chance it really could point to catastrophe in this particular lineup.

"Of course I know her. She's my mother."

Oh, well, I hadn't seen that part. My mouth dropped open. "Are you kidding me?"

"No. Are you kidding me?"

"Unfortunately not." I licked my lips. "Why would your mother steal your husband?" It seemed the obvious question, so I asked it.

"Because he was her husband first. Dang it!" Cathy slapped her hand on the table. "I can't believe she did this to me."

I was still behind. "I'm sorry, wouldn't her husband have been your father?" I was on the verge of freaking out.

"No. My father was her first husband. Jack was her third husband. They were married just two months because Jack and I fell in love. It wasn't our fault. We're soul mates."

"So ... Jack divorced your mother and married you?"

"Yes." She bobbed her head as if it was the most normal story in the world.

"Do you have children?"

"Two."

"And how did your mother feel about all of this?"

"She was fine with it. I mean ... well ... she was angry at first. She didn't talk to me for a full year. Then she got over herself and we were fine again. She was even starting to date someone and thought it would be fun if we went on double dates. Things were getting back to normal."

Something niggled in the back of my brain. "I see. Did it ever occur to you that your mother didn't forgive you, and instead only pretended to make up so she could steal back her husband?"

Cathy turned huffy. "Um, no. He's my husband."

"He was her husband first."

"Then he became my husband. Possession is nine-tenths of the law."

She had me there. "Yes, but ... now that the roles are reversed, can you ever see yourself forgiving your mother for sleeping with your husband?"

"Of course not. She's a dirty skank."

"What were you when you slept with her husband?"

"Overwhelmed by love. Those are two entirely different things."

Of course she would think that. "Well, I guess you've got a busy night in front of you." I pressed my hands to the table and stood. "You should probably think long and hard about what you're going to do."

"Oh, I know exactly what I'm going to do."

I figured. "A gun is a terrible idea," I offered.

She narrowed her eyes to slits. "I didn't say anything about a gun."

"No, but ... just stay away from the gun idea." Her head was so full of twisted ideas I couldn't separate them. "In fact, I think you would be much better off if you forgot all about this and kicked your husband out. You can do better."

"I'm not kicking him out." Cathy was aghast at the suggestion. "I'm kicking my mother out."

"Wait a second." I reached out and snagged her arm before she could escape. "Your mother lives with you?"

"Yes. She lost her house and needed a place to stay. I think that's why she finally forgave me."

Oh, I had news for Cathy. Her mother didn't lose her home. She sold it ... and cleared out everything Cathy's father left in trust for his daughter after the mother's passing. She'd moved all the money to a hidden bank account, and she and Jack were planning to clean out Cathy's bank account as an added bonus before fleeing in a few days.

But I couldn't tell her that. She would melt down and one of those horrible possibilities I saw in her head would turn into reality.

"I think you should check into a hotel and take a twenty-four-hour mental health break," I suggested. "Decompression is a good thing when you've been handed a life blow such as this."

"I'm not staying in a hotel."

"It doesn't have to be an expensive hotel. Just something with a spa so you can sweat out your aggressions."

"Oh, stuff it." She jerked away from me. "I know exactly what I'm going to do. I have everything under control. She is not going to get away with this."

Cathy was out of the tent before I could stop her. Thankfully, Kade poked his head inside to check on me in the wake of her fit.

"Everything okay?" he asked with a grin. "That didn't look like a happy fortune."

"Definitely not," I agreed, hurrying through the opening and pulling him with me. "I need you to follow that woman. Make sure you don't lose her, and call the police. She's going to murder her mother and husband."

"Why?"

"Because they're sleeping together."

His eyebrows migrated north. "Seriously? That's kind of gross."

"There's even more to the story, but I don't have time to tell you. Make sure she doesn't get away. I don't know how you're going to pull it off, but ... ."

"Don't worry." He squeezed my wrist and grinned. "I have an idea. I'll take care of it."

I hoped that was true. Otherwise, I would have two murders on my conscience. Sure, they were horrible people, but the kids had done nothing to deserve being orphans, and that's exactly what they would become if their mother pulled the trigger.

TWO HOURS LATER, I DECIDED to take a break. I'd kept to Larry's "happy fortune" edict for the rest of the afternoon, and I wasn't sorry. I was, however, a little bored.

I decided to grab a snack and check on the girls. They'd been excited when they heard they would be allowed to work throughout the weekend. I refused to hide them away as Larry suggested. Instead, Raven dolled them up in bright costumes and allowed them to help her at the Hall of Mirrors. That's where I headed now.

"Looking for someone specific?" Raven asked after creeping up on me in the mirror house foyer. I had an elephant ear and was happily munching while looking for the girls. "If so, I have Kade tied up in my back office and I've been doing naughty things to him."

I slid her a sidelong look and frowned. "You're not funny."

"I think I'm hilarious."

"And I think you need to look that word up in the dictionary." I did a double take at her outfit. She'd gone all out and dressed in an ornate black dress. "Why are you so gussied up?"

She shrugged and slid onto a nearby bench. "Do you want the truth?"

"No, I want you to lie to me."

"Okay. I wore this dress because it belonged to my grandmother and she would've wanted me to wear it. I believe in honoring my elders."

"You're centuries old. Your grandmother, if she's even still alive, would be centuries older than that. There's no way that dress is five-hundred years old."

Raven smirked. "You said you wanted me to lie to you."

I continued eating and stared at her.

"Fine." She blew out a sigh. "When Cotton and Michelob were looking through the clothes they found this dress. I haven't worn it in a long time. They wanted to see me in it."

My lips curved, unbidden. "So, basically you're saying those two girls have turned you into a big softie."

"Watch it." She extended a warning finger. "I might be soft for them, but I'll still beat the stuffing out of you."

I knew she was strong enough to give it a good try, so I decided to let it pass. "I think it's nice you've been spending so much time with them. I hoped I would be able to give them more time, but ... it just hasn't turned out that way."

"You've got your hands full with the ghosts of your past. It's okay. No one begrudges you the time you're spending working on this. Besides, the girls have charmed almost everyone. Even Mark likes them."

Mark Lane, the slimy midway chief, was pretty much my least favorite person working for Mystic Caravan. I'd brought up my distaste for his attitude numerous times to Max, who had the final say on all hiring decisions. Unfortunately for me, Max refused to fire Mark because the man made too much money. He may have been a horrible individual, but he was a smart horrible individual, and Max liked that.

"He hasn't been hitting on those girls, has he?" The idea made me sick to my stomach. "I'll tie his you-know-what into a knot if he tries."

Raven shook her head. "I already warned him what would happen if I even caught a whiff of impropriety. He knows I'm not kidding. I'll do worse than tie knots. The problem is, Cotton continuously falls back to her go-to move to make money, which is offering people blow jobs."

My stomach gave an uneasy heave. "I told her not to do that."

"She can't help herself. Yelling at her won't fix it. She's a product of her environment. The only way she can really be fixed is to get her off the streets."

I sensed where this conversation was going. "We can't take them."

"Why not?" Raven's silver eyes flashed with annoyance. "We took that little urchin you found in Nebraska and brought her with us."

"Melissa was an adult," I reminded her. "She wasn't a runaway. We weren't breaking federal laws by transporting a child over state lines. Cotton and Michelob are underage."

"They won't be forever. We only have to hide them for a little while."

I'd never seen this side of Raven before. I didn't want to discourage her, but I couldn't give her hope. "We can't take them. We can, however, call the state to see if we can get them taken into custody."

Raven immediately started shaking her head. "There's a reason you fled custody when you were a child."

"There is," I agreed. "I saw what would happen if I didn't. Not all homes are like that. The bulk of the people who volunteer to take at-risk children like this are wonderful individuals. Besides, we now have a weapon at our disposal that we didn't have then."

"And what's that?"

I tapped the side of my head. "We can read these people's minds. Even if we have to fly back to double-check placement, we can manage it. We'll make sure they end up in a good place."

As if on cue, Michelob and Cotton strolled into the room, laughing and having a good time. They looked healthier than they had days before, had a bit of glow to their skin. Michelob's voice was no longer raspy and she wasn't in constant pain. There was happiness in their eyes, and I remembered that same feeling from way back, when I thought I'd struck it rich on the street a few times.

They would be crushed when we left, but we weren't the right fit for them … at least not right now. That didn't mean we couldn't find someone to fit.

Raven lowered her voice as the two started cavorting in front of the mirrors. They were having a good time seeing their reflections distorted and barely paid any attention to us. "I know what you're saying is true. It's just ... they're vulnerable. I don't like sending them into the system when they're so vulnerable."

"It's only until they're adults. That might not be all that far into the future. We can talk to them, explain things. Once they're legal, then we can make arrangements for them to join us. They'll be your responsibility when that happens."

Her eyes went wide. "Mine? Why?"

"Because you're Mommy Raven as far as they're concerned. They've bonded with you most. That means you'll be the one looking out for them. That's the only way this will work."

She looked pained. "You know exactly how to annoy me."

That was true. "Are you willing to give it a shot?"

She chewed her lip, uncertain. Finally, she nodded. "I want to make sure we find them a good home. Together. They can't be separated."

I agreed wholeheartedly. "I'll put Logan on it this afternoon."

"What makes you think he'll help?"

"He doesn't want to see them suffer." I was certain of that. "They'll be okay." I turned to stare at the girls, amused at their antics.

While laughing with Raven, something odd caught my attention. The reflection in Michelob's mirror changed, and the image staring back wasn't the happy girl in front of me. Instead, it was a pale girl, with sunken eyes, wearing a long white dress ... and she was screaming.

I looked over my shoulder to make sure someone hadn't snuck behind me to plant a fake image in my head, but no one was there. When I turned back to the mirror, the reflection remained. I glanced at Raven, but she obviously didn't see it. That meant only I could.

It wasn't really there. It was a prophetic vision. It wasn't happening now, but it would someday.

Michelob was marked to become a banshee ... and there was no way I would allow that to happen. I had to stop it.

But how?

TWENTY-TWO

I didn't know what to do.

I stood frozen in my spot so long that Raven noticed I was no longer speaking — she's often self-absorbed, so it took a while — and fixed me with a considering look.

"What is it?" Her voice came out a hiss. "You sense something."

That was true, but it was something I couldn't share in front of the girls.

I managed to keep my smile in place as I watched the girls cavort. They really were having a good time and I didn't want to ruin it. Even more, I didn't want to terrify them. If they knew what I was worried about, Cotton's inclination would be to run. That would probably be their undoing.

"What did you see?" Raven demanded once we were in front of the House of Mirrors. She paid little heed to the guests filing into the building.

"Not here," I muttered, dragging her away from the stream of traffic and glancing around to make sure nobody was trying to eavesdrop. Once it was just the two of us, I realized I had to be very careful when it came to unveiling what I saw. Raven was the type to anger quickly and start smiting every potential enemy she could find.

"What did you see?" Raven's fingers dug into my wrist.

"I saw Michelob," I replied, my voice raspy. "It was her reflection ... except it wasn't. It was a harbinger."

Raven frowned. "You're saying you saw a psychic flash in her reflection. You know what's going to happen to her in the future."

"I saw a possibility," I corrected. "It's something I won't let happen."

"Was it one of the foster homes we were talking about? I'm not kidding. I'm willing to kidnap her to keep her from that situation."

I had no doubt that was true. "It's not the foster homes."

"Then what did you see?" She drew her eyebrows together as she worked to puzzle it out. Then, realization dawned and her eyes turned so dark I thought a storm might break out. Naida could control the weather, but Raven looked as if she was willing to give it a shot. "She becomes a banshee, doesn't she?"

I swallowed hard and nodded.

"I won't let that happen to her." Raven was adamant. "I don't care what you say. I'll take them before I let that happen."

"So will I," I snapped, my temper coming out to play. "Do you really think I'd just sit around and let them be hurt that way? Really?"

Raven had the grace to be ashamed. "No. You'll fight for them. It's just ... they should be untouchable on this property. They should be safe. What kind of moron would cross the dreamcatcher to get to them?"

That was a very good question, and one I hadn't considered. "I don't know. The dreamcatcher hasn't alerted since the other night, when the banshees were testing it."

Raven's gaze was sharp when it landed on me. "You think they were testing it?"

"They didn't cross the line. They alerted, but never stepped over. That either took unbelievable willpower — which I don't believe they possess — or someone was controlling them and recognized the dreamcatcher for what it was."

Raven worked her jaw, thoughtful. "You think they're completely empty vessels? Like the human dolls."

I was coming to a different conclusion. "No. I think they're worse than the dolls. I think their souls are already gone. They can't be saved, and I'm guessing their souls were swallowed during the course of their transformations. With the human dolls, their souls were still there. They were simply suppressed and slowly being eaten away. I think by the time these girls are transformed into banshees their souls have already escaped."

"You mean you think they're dead."

Arguing about death semantics didn't seem wise, but we obviously both needed the clarification. "I think these girls are being taken to a place so low and foul they wish they were dead," I said, choosing my words carefully. "I think that's what needs to happen to create the banshees. In the past, it was the tortured soul that created the banshee, so the creatures were fueled by despair.

"By getting the girls to the point where death would be better than whatever they're going through the person in charge creates a void in them," I continued. "They embrace death, but somehow their souls escape. That leaves empty shells behind for this creature — and we're obviously dealing with another paranormal — to use the banshees however he or she wishes."

Raven tapped her bottom lip, considering. "That makes sense," she said. "I didn't really think about it from that angle, but it makes sense. No souls are being released when we take out the banshees. That means they were already released."

"And not collected by the Grimlocks," I added. "They haven't found any of the girls. I asked at dinner the other night because I was curious whether it was possible to discover souls that weren't on their lists."

"Yeah, I've been trying to picture what they do, and it's not easy," Raven admitted. "Still, they obviously serve a purpose."

"So do we. Our purpose is to keep those girls safe. That means they can't be alone from here on out."

"That's easier said than done," Raven argued. "They're used to sleeping in the big top by themselves. If someone tries to go in there to sleep with them, even if we try to play it off as a game, they'll figure out something is wrong. They're just now getting comfortable with us, and I still see Cotton's mind going a mile a minute occasionally, like she's trying to figure out our angle because she doesn't believe we could really want to give them something for nothing."

I'd seen the same doubt reflected from Cotton on more than one occasion. "Then we'll have to enchant the tent tonight after everyone is gone. We'll make sure they're safe inside and no one can get in. Then we'll post guards around the fairgrounds to be certain."

Raven didn't immediately say anything, instead holding my gaze for an extended beat. Ultimately, she nodded. "I don't see that we have much choice. If we try to close ranks, they'll be frightened and run. What you saw will happen to them. If we don't do anything, we'll obviously miss something. You were shown that vision for a reason. We're meant to save them."

She sounded sure of herself. Oddly enough, it made me feel better. "We still need to keep an eye on them this afternoon. They're having a great time, but they could wander off if we're not careful. I don't want to tell them what's happening because ... well ... I don't think they'll believe us."

"They'll think we're nuts," Raven agreed. "They don't believe in the paranormal. Why would they? There are enough monsters on the street without adding fantastical new ones."

She understood. That made things easier. "I was paranormal myself and I had trouble believing back when I was one of them," I admitted. "Meeting Max felt kismet. I believed in magic that day. That's what helped me get out."

"You were always going to get out," Raven countered dismissively. "You were too big for this life."

"I believed that about a lot of people."

"Did you really?" Raven's question wasn't mean as much as probing. "I heard about the girl you ran with. Luke described her, said she was a stripper now. I heard him talking to Kade. Before you get worked up, they thought they were alone. I just happen to enjoy eavesdropping."

I gave her a dirty look. "You should try to break yourself of that habit."

"I'll give it serious thought," she said dryly. "Your boyfriend and that whiner you call a best friend are worried about you. They think you feel guilty about leaving this cesspool. They're not sure how to approach you, and don't want to make things worse. I don't have that problem."

Raven's expression was stern as she held my gaze. "You were never truly one of those kids. You realize that, don't you?"

"I was one of them," I shot back. "I slept on the streets with them. I ran from the cops with them. Heck, I feared for my life with them. I most definitely was one of them."

"No, you weren't." Raven's tone was measured more than argumentative. That was rare for her. That didn't mean I wasn't agitated by her words. "You were in an untenable situation and you didn't have many choices. You didn't realize that you could take out your foster father with a simple thought, because that's not who you are. I would've jumped to that conclusion right away. Not you, though.

"You were always a good girl who thought about others before yourself," she continued. "You ran because you wanted to keep yourself safe, but you also ran because you sensed you had the power to hurt others and you didn't want to embrace that. Why do you think you only went so far as to pick pockets when you could've forced people to give you their homes?"

I was flabbergasted. "I would never force someone to give me a home."

"Of course not. You're a saint. Anyone else in your position would have, though. You were cold, hungry and constantly frightened. You were also powerful. You were never destined for the street. Those other kids didn't have a choice. You did."

"I don't feel comfortable talking about this," I offered, taking a step back.

"We have other things to worry about. I am not the center of everyone's world. We need to concentrate on the missing girls."

Raven let loose a petulant sigh. "You are ... unbelievable." She shook her head and planted her hands on her hips. "You just don't want to see what's right in front of you. I don't get it."

"You never will. Those people were my first family."

"No. They were people you survived with. Your first family was your parents. You lost them, and you rarely talk about them. Your second family was Max and Luke. You bonded with them from the start.

"Slowly, you expanded that family," she continued. "Nixie, Naida, Nellie, Dolph, Seth ... and right down the line. You've added Kade and Melissa, as well. They're your family. Those kids you knew back then were simply people you were forced to hang with because you were afraid to be alone. There's a difference."

I didn't want to hear it. "We need to focus on Cotton and Michelob. Can you watch them all afternoon?"

Raven threw up her hands. "Yeah. I'll watch them. If there's something I need to do, I'll put Nixie and Naida on the case. I very much doubt a banshee will be wandering around the fairgrounds in the middle of the day."

"I doubt it, too, but what about the person controlling the banshees? There's nothing stopping that individual from wandering around and taking new victims to up their banshee army."

Raven's lips curved down. "I didn't think about that. You have a good point. I'll be diligent."

I knew she would be. "We'll figure out protection charms for the tent tonight. For now, we just need to keep an eye on them so they don't wander away."

I WAS ON MY WAY BACK TO MY tent to give readings when I caught sight of a familiar face. Logan, a soda in hand, reclined on a bench and watched the activity. His eyes were busy as they bounced from person to person. He appeared more contemplative than anything else.

Out of the corner of my eye I saw a hint of movement. When I turned, I found Kade watching Logan from behind Naida's tent. He didn't look nearly as conflicted as I felt and immediately set off in Logan's direction.

I sensed trouble and gave chase.

"Hello, Mr. Denton," Logan drawled as Kade closed the distance. Apparently he wasn't as unaware of Kade's presence as I'd assumed.

"Agent Stone," Kade said. "I didn't realize you were visiting today. Is there something specific you want to see?"

Logan's voice remained friendly. "I want to see everything. I'm a big fan of the circus."

"I think you're a big fan of Poet," Kade shot back. "She's the one you're looking for, isn't she?"

"She's the one I've found," Logan countered, inclining his chin in my direction.

Kade's expression didn't reflect happiness as he slowly turned and met my gaze. "I didn't realize you were standing there. I ... ." He didn't finish what he was going to say. It was obvious why.

"Were you about to duel for my honor?" I asked, only half serious.

"I was going to ... figure out what he's doing here."

"That's interesting. I was about to do the same." I moved closer, cast him a warning look while resting my hand on his arm, and then focused on Logan. "This seems a weird place for you to be hanging out given the fact that you've got a killer on the loose."

Instead of immediately answering, Logan narrowed his eyes. "I thought we had a kidnapper," he countered. "We haven't found any bodies. Do you know something I don't?"

Well ... crud on a cracker. I walked right into that one. I didn't think before I spoke and now I was in trouble. Of course, Logan was already suspicious. He didn't think we were killers, but he was convinced we were odd and potentially dangerous to killers. He'd gotten it in his head we were vigilantes. I saw the notion there a few times the past few days. It wasn't going away.

"No. I just find it difficult to believe these girls are being taken and warehoused somewhere. I'm probably being pessimistic — most of my co-workers think I'm sour on life — but I can't help but assume these girls are dead."

Kade slid me a sidelong look. He was reacting to the "sour on life" comment. He'd told me more than once that he thought I was upbeat and earnest. I found that funny given the life I'd lived. But this was not the time for another argument.

"I guess I'm not as pessimistic as you," Logan said. "I have hope we'll find them. Human trafficking is real. It was a real thing back when you were on the streets — and I was genuinely worried for you and Creek — but it's worse now. I think someone might've taken these girls and sold them."

Of course he did. He was thinking as a human. He didn't know the missing girls were turning up as banshees and stealing souls. How could he? Every banshee we dispatched turned into dust. There was no body to dispose of.

"I hope you're right. I really do. I just don't see things going that way."

"So, in your head, they're already dead?"

"Yes."

"I see." Logan stroked his chin and shifted his eyes between Kade and me. "You guys seem tight," he said. "You're always searching for one another in a crowd ... that is if you're not already on top of each other. I'm glad you found happiness."

"You don't seem glad," Kade argued before I could find the correct words to address the topic. "You seem more wistful than happy when you see her. I think you had feelings for her twelve years ago and perhaps you still do today."

Leave it to Kade to charge in first without thinking about what he was saying. That was so ... him.

"I did have feelings for her," Logan agreed, causing my heart to skip as stunned disbelief washed over me. "She kept me alive. I knew she didn't belong on the street. I was terrified something bad was going to happen to her.

"I was a young cop back then," he continued. "Idealistic. I thought taking the gang down from the inside was going to do some good. Now, I guess I'm more jaded. I know that when you take out evil, new evil simply moves in and takes its place.

"As for Poet, I was genuinely fond of her. She saved my life, as I said. It was her more than the others. They were frightened and wanted to leave me. She was determined ... and she's the reason I'm alive. That doesn't mean I have romantic feelings for her. You don't have to worry about that."

"I'm not worried," Kade replied. "We love each other. I'm not living in fear of you or anyone else. She had a crush on you back then. She feels guilty for not saying goodbye before she left ... to you and to Creek. You're manipulating that to your advantage."

Logan balked. "How do you figure that?"

"You think she has answers on the missing girls that she's not sharing. That's why you keep showing up. That's why you have people watching the fairgrounds. Don't bother denying it. I can recognize an unmarked federal car from a mile away. I was with the military and did a stint with intelligence. You can't hide the truth from me."

I expected Logan to argue, deny the charge. Instead, he merely shrugged. "Fine. I'm watching you. I can't help myself. You're in the middle of the hot zone and there's a lot of activity in this place after dark. I think you're searching for whoever is doing this. I also think you plan to do something horrible with this person when you find him."

Kade wasn't expecting that answer. "What?"

"He thinks we're vigilantes," I interjected. "He assumes we plan to find this person and kill him or her and then dispose of the body."

"You've got to be kidding." Some of the tension left Kade's body, replaced with amusement. "That's just so ... ridiculous."

Was it? Technically that's what we planned to do. We simply weren't the sort of vigilantes Logan envisioned. We were something more.

"How do you know what I think?" Logan challenged. "I didn't mention you guys to anyone."

I got a quick flash of him sitting in his car and watching the hoopla with the Grimlocks as we gathered to enter the cemetery the night before. Apparently he'd arrived before our sentries alerted to his presence. He was good at being stealthy, which sucked for us. "Let's just call it a hunch," I replied. "And, if you're worried about what you saw last night, you don't have to be. We were conducting a séance to contact their mother. The Grimlocks, I mean. They wanted to talk to her."

Logan worked his jaw, clearly annoyed by the fact that I'd read him so easily. "You really can read minds, can't you?" he asked finally.

"I can."

"What am I thinking now?"

"That you don't trust me like you used to." The realization hurt a little. "You think we're odd and you don't trust any of us."

"I trust you," he shot back. "I wouldn't be here if I didn't trust you. I do think you guys are weird, though. I won't lie about that."

"Yeah, well ... we are weird." I opted for the truth. "But we're not what you think we are. We're not trying to find this individual just so we can kill him or her and rid the streets of a predator. We are trying to keep the girls safe. That's pretty much the only thing I can guarantee."

"Then I guess we're at a standstill."

As much as I didn't want to, I had to agree. "I guess we are."

TWENTY-THREE

*L*ogan didn't leave. We talked to him a bit longer, but it was obvious he had no intention of going anywhere. The realization threw me ... and opened a crack in my foundation that allowed a bit of sadness to creep in. He'd said he trusted me, but that obviously wasn't true. He was suspicious. The bond we'd built twelve years earlier couldn't survive time and missing girls.

In truth, I didn't blame him for hanging around. He thought we could lead him to answers. It was gratifying that he didn't believe we were responsible for causing this mess — the disappearances started happening long before we arrived — but he recognized we were up to something. He was always good at reading people, which is probably why he advanced through the ranks so quickly.

I kept it together for the rest of the afternoon, closed my operation in time to watch the big show in the main tent, and joined Raven so she wasn't alone in keeping an eye on Cotton and Michelob. They'd taken seats at the front of the action and couldn't stop laughing at Luke's hijinks on the trapeze. They were completely enamored ... and unaware that we were watching their every move.

"Nixie, you need to watch them as we clear the fairgrounds," I instructed when she joined us a few minutes later.

"No problem. They won't get past me."

"Don't tie them up or anything," Raven ordered. "They'll think we're weird and run."

"You are weird," Nixie reminded her. "But I'll watch them. I heard what you saw in the mirror, Poet. I'll make sure they're safe."

I pinned Raven with a hard look. I hadn't shared my vision with anyone other than her. I was waiting until after dark to spread the news. "You have a big mouth."

She shrugged. "I do," she agreed. "I figured the more people in on the secret, the better in case something happens to me."

She had a point. "Fine. Just hold it together for a bit longer and then we can start herding these people out. It will be easier to watch them once the grounds are cleared."

Nixie bobbed her head in agreement. "What are we going to do after that? We need to figure out a way to draw in whoever is doing this."

I'd come to the same conclusion. "Yeah. I know. I haven't a clue how to do it. We'll figure it out."

WHEN THE PERFORMANCE ENDED, our people sprang into action. We were masters at directing traffic.

Dolph took the lead, calling everyone toward the big top opening, and then leading them directly toward the parking lot. Seth, who had been in his tiger form in the tent, was back in human form minutes later and helped Dolph draw people toward their vehicles.

The second the tent was empty, I started barking orders. "I want the entire place cleaned out as soon as possible." I focused my attention on Michelob and Cotton, who were boasting smiles so wide they almost swallowed their entire faces. "Girls, I want you to straighten up and sweep the floors. By the time you're finished, it will be dinner time. Nixie will supervise."

Cotton made a face. "Yo, you're acting like you don't trust us. We've been here for days."

"I'm not acting like I don't trust you," I countered. "I'm acting like we have certain things we need to cross off our list to make sure there aren't any insurance claims." She would understand about not wanting to pay extra money, so that's the story I went with. "If our premiums go up, we can't pay you two."

She made a face. "You just don't want to clean the tent yourself."

"There is that," I agreed, grinning. "It won't take long, and then it will be time for dinner. This is part of the job you take on when you're with the circus."

"We're just freelancers," Michelob pointed out. It was the first time I'd heard her speak with any conviction. It was obvious she was no longer in pain and was feeling bolder, both of which I wanted to see. "If we were full-timers, we might be propelled to work even faster."

I understood what she was getting at. They wanted to stay. They were going to start feeling us out. It wasn't possible, but I didn't want to crush their spirits with that brutal news and cause them to run away when we were in the thick of things. "We'll talk about that later."

I didn't miss the excited look the girls shared.

"For now, we all have jobs to do and I expect everybody to do them."

EVERY WORKER AT MYSTIC CARAVAN KNEW what was expected of them. Even Michelob and Cotton, who were temporary and new, understood what needed to be done. Because of that, it took only twenty minutes to clear the grounds.

Kade, Nellie and Luke immediately went through again to make sure there were no laggards, as Dolph and Seth directed traffic. In less than thirty minutes it was as if nobody had ever been on the grounds.

"You guys are good," Cotton announced, grinning as she moved toward the picnic table. Raven and I had already begun food preparations.

"We are good," I agreed, inclining my head toward the table. "You two should sit."

Cotton, always the suspicious sort, narrowed her eyes. "Are you about to drop bad news on us?"

"What makes you say that?"

"Because you have the look my mother used to get when she was about to tell me she had another new boyfriend and he was going to move in. Usually she added a 'You don't need to live here if you're going to complain about it' yell to everything when it was happening."

My heart gave a little lurch. "I don't have a boyfriend who wants to dislodge you."

"But you're with Kade?" Michelob asked, smiling happily when Naida delivered a soda to her. "Thank you."

Naida smiled and ruffled the girl's hair before joining us in preparing the food.

That's when it truly hit me; everyone here was fond of them. It wasn't so much the girls' personalities. Those were works in progress. It was the fact that we all recognized we could've probably been these girls at some point in our lives. Even Raven, who had been around for centuries, knew what it meant to suffer. No one wanted the girls to suffer.

"Kade and I are together," I confirmed. "Don't worry. I'm not giving you grief for having a crush on him."

Michelob's cheeks flooded with color and she stared at her Coke. "I don't have a crush on him. Why would you say that?"

Raven snorted. "Yeah, right. Don't worry about it, Michelob. He's hot. I had a crush on him when he first arrived."

"You did?" Suspicion flitted through her eyes. "He didn't want to be with you?"

"Actually, right from the start, he only had eyes for Poet," Raven volunteered, taking me by surprise with her fortitude. She usually enjoyed messing with me rather than bolstering my ego. "It was very annoying. It took me a bit to realize that he only liked boring women, but once I did, I figured out they belonged together."

Ah, there it was. I knew she couldn't get through it without taking a jab at me.

"It's true," I said solemnly when Cotton and Michelob focused on me. "Kade only likes boring women. That's why we're perfect for each other."

Cotton chuckled and shook her head. "You guys are funny."

"We're a laugh riot," I agreed, my eyes tracking to the parking lot as Seth and Dolph gave it a final sweep.

"We're funny, too," Michelob offered, her transition anything but subtle. "We would fit in well with you guys."

I met Raven's gaze for a beat and bit my lower lip before responding. "How old are you two?" I asked finally.

"Eighteen," Cotton replied perfunctorily.

I pinned her with a dubious look. "How old really?"

"We're eighteen." Cotton didn't as much as blink. She was good. Unfortunately, I had a talent she couldn't have foreseen, and I simply slipped inside her head to take a look around.

"You're sixteen," I replied finally. "You turn seventeen in two months."

Cotton's eyes went wide. "How can you possibly know that?"

"I'm a mind reader," I reminded her, turning to Michelob. "You're seventeen, but there are several problems with your file. You've fled custody four times when social workers tried to medically intervene over your tonsils. You're not going to be allowed to leave until you're eighteen no matter what."

"That's not true." Michelob immediately started shaking her head. "We can leave whenever. In fact, we're ready to go right now. There's nothing keeping us here."

"The law is keeping you here."

"But ... we don't care about the law." Michelob's voice cracked, causing a lump to form in my throat. "You just don't want to take us with you."

"That's not true," Raven countered, swooping in as I struggled to get my emotions under control. "We think you're a good fit, but you can't join us until you're adults."

"Who will even know?" Cotton protested. "It's not as if people will ask for our IDs. We'll be with you guys."

"Actually, that's not true," I offered, drawing their eyes to me. "There are certain municipalities where we have to provide work permits for everybody. It's standard procedure, and we have to follow the letter of the law. We can't lie."

"Why not?" Michelob sounded pitiful. "Why can't you lie? It's only for a little over a year."

"If we get caught, we'll lose our license and there won't be a circus." I opted for honesty. That was the biggest reason. Sure, there was that pesky business about hunting monsters, but that could wait for another time "You don't want that to happen any more than we do."

"No, but ... ."

I held up my hand. There was no reason to let this conversation completely unravel. "We've already talked about this and come up with a plan."

"You have?" Cotton darted her eyes between Raven and me. "You two came up with a plan? I didn't think you liked one another."

"We like each other fine," Raven countered. "We also like to mess with each other. That's what friends do. We've discussed things and we're willing to compromise with you."

Cotton folded her arms over her chest, disdain evident. She was a businesswoman, and was doubtful. "How?"

"You're going to have to go into the system for a year and a half," I answered, bracing myself for an onslaught of complaints. They came like clockwork.

"That's never going to happen," Cotton argued.

"They lock you in cages and don't feed you in the system," Michelob whined.

"They don't lock you in cages," I countered. "There are bad foster families out there. I'm not going to lie. We'll find you good ones."

"How can you guarantee that?" Cotton shot back. "You're not God."

"No, but I can read minds." I tapped my head again. "This is the best way, guys. We're going to find a home to get you in together, check in with you regularly, and then bring you to us when you turn eighteen."

"But ... that's not what we want," Cotton protested

"You can't always get what you want," Raven reminded her. "You two know that better than most. We can provide you with a real shot. We just can't do it now. You'll have to hold up your end of the bargain for a year and a half to make this happen for all of us.

"Then, when it's time, I'll pick you up myself," she reassured them. "You'll come back with me, to wherever we are at the time, and then I'll be your boss."

Michelob knit her eyebrows. "I thought she was the boss." She pointed at me. "That's what everybody says."

"I'm Raven's boss," I volunteered. "That won't change. I'll still be her boss. She'll also be your boss. You're going to have a lot of bosses."

"Let's not push the boss thing," Raven complained. "We both know I do what I want."

I ignored her "We want to help, but we cannot take you until you're adults. We don't make the rules, but we do have to abide by them."

The girls stared at each other, misery etched across their features.

"A year and a half isn't forever," I pointed out. "Look at all you've survived. Look at the years stretched ahead of you. It can be a good life. You're just going to have to wait for a time."

"Fine." Cotton, dejected, huffed out a sigh. "I still think you're being ridiculous. The cops will never find us with you."

"You'd be surprised how often we have to deal with the cops," Raven said. "You'll have to get used to that, too. If we don't follow the rules, we can't stay in specific towns. If we can't stay in those towns, we lose money. This is a business."

"Yeah, yeah, yeah." Cotton rubbed her forehead. "This blows."

"It does," I agreed. "We'll check on you regularly. We'll call you, do video chats and visit when we can."

"We get a Christmas break," Raven volunteered. "I'll come up here to visit you guys then."

"You could just take us with you then," Michelob suggested. "You don't like following the rules, so you could break them."

"Not this time." Raven was calm, and I was grateful she didn't give them false hope. I didn't want to be the mean ogre who sent them back. "We have to follow the rules to make sure everything works out the way we want it to. I'm sorry, but ... that's all there is to it."

"Fine." Cotton shook her head. "This really sucks."

I agreed. It totally sucked.

THE GIRLS WERE STILL MOROSE after dinner. Kade and Luke offered to walk them back to the tent to perk them up. It worked, but only marginally.

Raven, Naida, Nixie and I followed, listening to the girls complain to the men — who they were trying to manipulate — as we talked in low voices about the charm we were going to cast on the tent to keep them inside ... and others out. We were going with something simple but powerful. Their safety was our primary concern.

I watched Kade slide his arms round Michelob's shoulders to console her. He was whispering something that only she could hear and I knew he was trying to make her feel better. Remorse fueled me, but my hands were tied. We could not take them with us now without risking everything we'd built.

I let out a sigh, earning an eye roll from Raven, and then let my eyes drift to the left. The circus grounds should've been empty except for us. That's why the streak of white racing down the next aisle caught my attention.

I reacted out of instinct. "Banshee," I yelled, breaking into a run to intercept her.

I had a brief moment to see Kade and Luke collapse on the girls in a protective ring.

The banshee realized I was coming, but didn't try to run. Instead, she lowered her head and increased her pace. She would attempt to push through me, run over me, instead of going around me. She couldn't deviate from whatever orders were given. That meant she had to get through me, and probably a few others, so she could grab the girls. That was her end goal. The brief vision of Michelob had shown me that.

I had no intention of letting it happen. "No." I threw up a magic wall, forming it in a split-second, and then sent it careening in the banshee's direction.

The girl let loose an unearthly scream as it slammed into her, the solid wall turning to a web and pinning her to the ground as she struggled and choked against her restraints. I was feeling pretty good about myself thanks to the fast takedown when another figure appeared at my left.

I barely had time to register what was happening before the second banshee was on me. She landed with enough force that I tilted to the side ... and screamed as she raked her fingernails over my arm. Blood gushed hot and heavy as the creature dug in. She had no intention of letting go.

Vaguely, as I tried to decide what to do, I heard Cotton and Michelob screaming and sobbing in the background. Kade barked out orders and Luke snapped back. Nixie screamed that they were under attack from another banshee, and Naida reacted by throwing her hands in the air and causing lightning to spark.

Even as I registered all that, I couldn't separate myself from the pain rushing through me. Something very bad was happening, and it was happening fast. My mind was getting muddled, the pain was spreading from my arm to the rest of my body faster than should've been possible, and someone else was screaming.

That, I realized, was happening in my mind. I was the one screaming ... and fading fast.

24

TWENTY-FOUR

*E*ven as I felt darkness closing in, I recognized that I would die if I didn't find a way to save myself. The others apparently had their hands full, which meant I had to do something ... or lose everything I'd worked so hard to build.

I had one chance, so I pooled the magic I could muster – which wasn't much, mind you – and channeled it outward. A blaze of purple fire erupted from my fingertips and barreled into the banshee, causing her to rear back. The magic made quick work of her, as she burst into flames ... and then dust. I could barely hold my head up, but I managed to give a small salute to Raven, the only one I could manage to make eye contact with before falling back a second time.

This time, as the darkness claimed me, I couldn't help but wonder if I would ever crawl out of it again.

THE SUN WAS SHINING THROUGH THE trailer window when I opened my eyes. It took a moment for me to register where I was and remember what had happened, but when I did I bolted to a sitting position ... and immediately regretted it.

"Oh, geez." I slapped my hand to my forehead and fell back against the pillow.

"That's what you get for acting like an idiot," Raven chastised, causing me to peek through my fingers until I found her sitting in a chair next to my bed. "I can see you, so pretending you can't see me seems silly."

I groaned as I shifted. "I wasn't pretending I couldn't see you. I was simply wondering if I'd died and ended up in Hell."

She chuckled. "Not quite. You're very much alive."

She sounded sure of herself, but I wasn't easily persuaded. "It felt like I was dying. It was fast. Whatever it was ... it was fast."

"It was venom from the banshee's talons. At least that's what we think. The one we captured had the same venom coating her nails. It's not naturally occurring, which means someone dosed her."

"Was anyone else infected?"

"Just you. We dispatched the others fairly quickly."

I had trouble searching through the dim memories. "How many others?"

"We took out five in total. Kade took out one on his own. The one that you captured was too dangerous to let live — she kept lashing out and trying to infect people — so she's gone."

Five banshees. Five young women plucked from the streets and killed. That was more than the four reported missing. When you added the two already dead, we were talking seven people ... and I had a feeling there were more waiting in the wings.

"We've done the math," Raven offered. "We figure there could be anywhere from five to ten more of them out there. Whoever is doing this really did build an army."

I felt sick to my stomach and rolled to my feet, gasping on a sob as I hurried to the bathroom. I tried to shut the door so I could be sick in private, but Raven was having none of it. She knelt behind me and pressed her hand to the back of my neck, making a tsking sound as she shook her head.

"I don't think this is the poison affecting you," she said.

A wretched sob escaped my throat. "No, not poison. At least ... not that type."

Raven's expression was hard to read. When she finally spoke again, it was with authority. "Get up."

My eyebrows hopped. "Excuse me?"

"I told you to get up." She didn't back down, instead standing so she towered above me and crossing her arms across her chest. "You need to get up right now. We have work to do, and you sitting here feeling sorry for yourself won't help get it done."

I wanted to strangle her. "Where's Kade?"

She didn't look surprised by the abrupt shift in topics. "Kade is outside checking on the perimeter. The dreamcatcher failed last night. We need to figure out why. Nixie and Naida are with him, working on the problem."

That didn't sound right. I knew Kade. He wouldn't have left my side. "You made him leave."

"I did." Raven nodded. "He was being ridiculous, crying like a big baby, and getting absolutely nothing done. I knew that he would coddle you when you woke, and we don't have time for that. There's a lot going on, and you can't be out of commission for it."

I wiped my hands under my eyes, annoyance and bitterness tinging the tears. "What's going on? I thought you handled the banshees."

"We did. The dreamcatcher still failed. Cotton and Michelob still saw that we have magic ... and they're asking questions. I put Nellie in charge of answering them. I thought he would be a unique fit." She looked so proud of herself I almost wanted to laugh. Almost.

"Where's Luke?"

"He also would've coddled you," Raven replied. "He pitched an even bigger fit than Kade, but that's because Kade's smarter. He's been trying to figure out a way to lure me out all morning so he can lock the two of you inside and shut out the world. He slept next to you for a few hours, but when he woke I sent him out. I didn't figure it was good for him to sit here and fret for an additional six hours."

"What time is?"

"It's not even eight. You were out about ten hours total."

I glanced down at my arm. It was covered with white gauze, and it was sore. "Can I look at it?"

"I don't see why not."

To buy myself time I removed the gauze and bandage and stared hard at the ugly mark. Only one of the cuts was deep, the other two already fading, but there was something familiar about the wounds. "Will it heal completely?"

"Yes, with time and pixie magic. The poison on the banshee fingernails was not naturally occurring. Someone concocted it."

That was interesting. "A witch?"

"I think that's a term that gets thrown around a little too often," she replied. "I don't think we're dealing with a straight-up witch or bruja either. By the way, Aisling and Izzy stopped by. They heard what happened and wanted to see you. I said they would have to wait."

"How did they hear?"

"Two of the Grimlock brothers — the mouthy one and the one dating the bruja — showed up at the tail end. They helped with the clean-up and managed to calm the girls. They were hysterical, convinced you were going to die, and wanted to know about the magic you put on display. I'm not sure that was your smartest move."

"I didn't know what else to do." That was the truth. "I didn't think I would survive if I did nothing."

"Probably not. It doesn't matter now. The truth is out. If your Fed friend was watching us closely enough last night, he saw the magic. It is what it is."

That hadn't even occurred to me. "What are we going to do now?"

Raven looked amused at the question. "Aren't you second in command? Shouldn't you already know the answer to that?"

Her superior attitude grated. "Where's Max?"

"With Cormack Grimlock. They're at the reaper library conducting research. He was very upset when he got to you last night. He worked with Nixie to heal you. Things were touch-and-go for a bit. The poison gets a foothold fast, and it took a lot of effort to combat it. We have an antidote now. They won't get past us again with that little trick."

That was good news. At least ... I hoped it was. "And the dreamcatcher? Do we have any idea about why it failed?"

"None. But we'll figure it out before nightfall, I promise you that. It won't be easy with the circus opening in four hours, but we've dealt with worse. I can guarantee the banshees will be back again tonight."

"As long as whoever is doing this sends soldiers to fight us we'll never get anywhere in finding our culprit. We need to figure out a way to track one of the banshees to her master. There has to be a magical way to do it."

Raven broke out in a genuine smile. "Now you're talking. That's a fabulous idea. You can work on that while we're trying to figure out what happened to the dreamcatcher."

"Okay." I dragged a hand through my hair. "I need to shower and see Kade first. He's probably melting down."

"In a way," Raven agreed. "He was furious when I kicked him out. He realized we were dealing with something new, though, and didn't attempt to fight me to the death. We've never had an issue like this before. The dreamcatcher has never completely failed. It makes me realize we've become complacent because we rely on it too much."

I couldn't disagree with her assessment. "Well, we need to get it up and running for tonight. We can talk about our reliance on it after we leave this place. For now, we need to find the master. That's the only way we can end this."

"Then that's what we'll do." Raven smiled as she helped me to my feet. "If I were you, I would take a long shower and brush your teeth. The security stud will be all over you, and nobody wants to kiss someone who has been puking."

I narrowed my eyes. "You're loving this, aren't you?"

"Not particularly. You almost died. It was enough to shake everybody. Kade, Luke and Max were the worst. I don't particularly like you, so I was fine."

I couldn't stop myself from laughing, although the sound was weak. "Thanks for taking care of me."

"I don't see where I had a choice. I need you to help me fix the dream-catcher."

"So ... you would've let me die if you didn't need me?"

"Oh, without a doubt."

Somehow I didn't believe her.

I FELT LIKE A NEW WOMAN AFTER showering and changing. I was in the middle of trying to bandage my arm again — explaining the injury to guests was unnecessary — when Kade flew through the door of the trailer.

"Good morning," I offered, managing a wan smile for his benefit.

"I saw Raven leave." He dragged me in for a tight hug. "Are you okay?"

"I'm fine." I awkwardly patted his back. "I'm sorry I frightened you."

"You promised you weren't going to do that again."

I didn't remember making any such promise. "I said I would do my best. It's not as if I realized they had poisoned talons. I mean ... that's never happened."

"Still." He wrapped his arms around my back and held me tight. "You have no idea how frightened I was. You were out of it and wouldn't wake up ... and then Raven kicked me out of my own bedroom."

He sounded more upset about that than my near death. "I'm sorry she was mean to you." I stroked his back. "I'm also sorry I didn't realize what was happening. It was already too late when things came into focus."

"I don't care about that." He smoothed my damp hair and kissed my cheek. "I love you. You scared the crap out of me."

"I love you."

We were silent for a beat, just holding on, and then he decided to lighten the mood. "I said 'I love you' fifty-eight times while you were unconscious last night. I'm definitely ahead."

I was delighted with the absurd statement. "I thought we weren't keeping score. Didn't we agree that was unhealthy?"

"Yeah, but I like winning ... and I'm beating the pants off you right now."

"As long as you keep it in perspective."

I let him hold me for another five minutes, and then pulled away. I was starting to feel better, stronger, and Raven was right about there being a mountain of items to tackle before guests started arriving. "Have you seen Cotton and Michelob this morning?"

"I have. They're with Nellie."

"I'm not sure that's a good pairing. They're bound to have questions about what went down, and I'm guessing you guys weren't forthcoming with answers because you were too busy taking care of me."

"That's pretty much the gist of it," he conceded, sheepish. "I might have snapped at them once or twice because they wouldn't stop going on and on about the lady vampires. That's what they called them. Lady vampires. We had to explain they weren't vampires. Er, well, Luke had to explain that. I thought maybe they were vampires and you guys somehow got confused."

I was amused despite myself. "You didn't think we could recognize the difference between vampires and banshees?"

He shrugged. "I was a little unhinged."

"So I heard." I brushed my fingertips against his cheek "I hate to say it — mostly because I was annoyed to find Raven playing nursemaid this morning when all I wanted was you — but she probably did us a favor. If she'd allowed you to stay, you would've doted all morning and we wouldn't have accomplished a single thing."

"I'm still mad."

"Okay."

"Like ... really mad."

"I understand."

"I might beat up her boyfriend as payback because I'm so mad."

I laughed. "Or you could just let it go. I'm fine. You're fine. The girls are fine ... although ... do you think we'll have to modify their memories? I didn't ask Raven about the possibility because I didn't think of it, but it's probably something we should consider."

"You're the one who has to do that, right?"

I nodded. "I'm the one."

"Do you want to do that?"

"No. I hate doing it. It's a form of raping their minds. But if they're going to expose us ... ." I left it hanging. The sick feeling was back in my stomach and I didn't want to finish.

"I don't think that's going to be necessary. Raven has talked to them. Nixie has, too. Nellie is filling their heads with horrific stories. Now they better understand why you can't risk bringing them with us until they're adults. It's a brave new world for them and they have a lot to consider."

"That's great." I meant it. "It still doesn't cover our collective behinds. They could talk. They might not want to talk, but they could get high and spill the beans at some point. Cotton does meth. So does Michelob. Although I think Michelob was doing it for pain management. They could easily blab without realizing they're doing it."

"If you were in their position, would you blab?"

"I ... no." I understood where he was going with the question. "I wouldn't blab in their position. I would recognize that we're their only chance out and suck it up for a year and a half. But they aren't me."

"They're certainly not, but I think they understand. They'll be okay. I feel it here." He took my hand and pressed it to his heart in a ridiculously romantic gesture. "I don't want you worrying about this. I'll talk to them. We'll come to an understanding. You don't have to modify their memories. I know you hate that."

I certainly did. "Thanks." I leaned forward and pressed my forehead to his and then was reminded of my arm when he accidentally jostled it. "Hey, can you put a bandage on this so I don't have to answer a bunch of questions?"

"Absolutely." He flashed a smile and reached for a bandage. "Did you apply the ointment Nixie left for you? She says it should heal eventually, but it might take longer than normal because the toxin was magical in origin."

"Raven ran me through that, and I did use the ointment."

"Good girl." He kissed the tip of my nose, causing me to smile. "Let's get you fixed up." He extended my arm and prepared to place the bandage, frowning and shifting his head to look from another angle. "Huh."

That wasn't what I wanted to hear. "What's wrong?"

"Nothing. It's just ... does this remind you of something?"

It was odd that he brought that up. "I was just thinking that before you came in. It definitely jarred me, and I figured there was a reason, but I couldn't remember what."

"That's because you're too close to it and you had a rough night."

"Does that mean you know who it should remind me of?"

"Yeah. Creek."

That's when things started crashing together in my head. Creek. He was right. "She had that scar on her arm."

"It looked almost exactly like this wound," Kade confirmed. "I mean ... if not exact, they're ridiculously similar."

I didn't know what to say. "Do you think she was attacked by a banshee?"

"I don't know."

"How did she survive without magic ointment?"

"I don't know. Maybe the talons weren't poisoned for her. She's just a normal girl, right?"

As far as I knew, that was true. "Yeah. Um ... I need to find her. I have to ask."

He sighed. "I'm guessing you want to go alone."

"Yeah. I need you to bandage me up first, though."

"Fine, but I want my complaint lodged on the record for this one. I don't think you should be running around by yourself in your condition."

"It's fine. I really think this is a conversation Creek and I should have on our own. She'll be unlikely to talk in front of you."

"Which is the only reason I'm agreeing." He perched the bandage on my arm and grabbed the roll of gauze. "You're going to owe me big time when you're feeling better. We're talking an hour-long massage here."

"I'm sure I can make that happen."

"And I want you to wear one of those coconut bras while you're doing it."

I arched an eyebrow. "Why?"

"Because I had a dream when I was a teenager and I expect you to make it come true."

I wasn't in a position to argue. "Fine. Do you want me to rub coconut oil all over you, too?"

"What do you think?"

I think it sounded like an entertaining evening. We had to get through the rest of this first. Coconut bras would have to wait.

"Once we're out of here, you can have as many massages as you want. I just want to get through this ... and save whatever girls we can."

He gripped my hand and gave it a squeeze. "We will. I promise you that we won't leave until we end this."

2 5

TWENTY-FIVE

$\mathcal{I}$t was easier to find an address for Creek than I thought. Logan had uniformed officers posted around the perimeter, including an individual one block over who had a great view of the fairgrounds. It was easy to sneak up behind him, take over his mind, and then ask him to run a simple search for me.

The man almost seemed happy as he typed in the name. "Creek Carpenter, real name Christy, lives on Alfred Street." He rattled off an address that I plugged into my phone. "Do you want her record?" he asked dully.

"Um ... sure."

"She's been arrested seven times."

I swallowed hard. Seven seemed a lot. "List the charges."

"Panhandling. Solicitation. Making up a false story about an attack. Solicitation. Burglary. Resisting arrest, though that was dismissed. Solicitation again."

My mind was busy. "Tell me about the false story."

"Um ... hmm. It says here she was discovered in an alley, disheveled and clearly high, with blood on her arm. She claimed she'd been attacked by a woman with claws for fingernails and red-rimmed eyes. She was confused, but refused medical attention. She grew increasingly worse until she fled during questioning."

That was beyond interesting. I glanced at the bandage on my arm. "Did she say what sort of creature attacked her?"

"She said it was a vampire, ma'am." The officer sounded a little dazed. I had to release the magical hold I had on him; otherwise he would start acting drunk.

"I'm assuming that's why no one believed her."

"Vampires aren't real, ma'am."

"You'd be surprised," I muttered, shaking my head. "What happened to her after she disappeared?"

"Unknown, ma'am."

"Didn't anyone follow up, make sure she got home safely?"

"Doubtful, ma'am. She was just a psych case waiting to happen. It was assumed she would show up eventually, either dead or in a straitjacket."

"That's a lovely thought." Because I could, I flicked his ear.

"Do you need anything else, ma'am?" The officer seemed eager to get away from me.

"Actually, I do. You're surveilling us under orders from the FBI."

"Agent Stone, ma'am, that is correct."

"Do you happen to know what he's looking for?"

"Missing girls. He thinks they're holed up in this area."

"Is he suspicious of the circus?"

"I don't know, ma'am." The officer's face was blank. "He didn't give us that information."

In other words, my droid could not compute. "Okay, what did he say when he positioned you here? He must've given you instructions for watching the circus performers."

"Not really. He said we were to watch the cemetery ... and keep you safe. That was his biggest concern. He said he'd be damned if he'd allow you to come back and screw up your life after you managed to get away. I don't know what that means, but he seemed adamant. We're supposed to protect you."

I was shocked. "He has you watching me specifically?"

"Keep Poet safe," he offered in a miraculous approximation of Logan's voice. "She got away. She needs to do it again."

In an odd way, I was touched that he cared enough to send a protector. That was nice. A little weird, but nice. I was also agitated. "He should've had you guys down in the Corridor watching the girls who are being targeted. I'm not important. I can take care of myself."

"You're important to him. He said you saved him and he owed you a favor."

"Any favor has long since been repaid."

"He doesn't seem to feel that way, ma'am." The officer was starting to look desperate to escape the mental hold I had on him. I couldn't blame him.

"It's okay," I soothed, sending a warming comfort to blanket his mind. "You're going to be fine in a few minutes. I have to be going. I have errands to run."

"Errands."

"Are you supposed to follow me if I leave?"

"Yes, ma'am. Your safety is my number one priority."

That was messed up given what was happening. "Well, you're relieved of duty for the day. You need to sit here and pretend you're watching me. As far as you're concerned, I never left the fairgrounds. You're going to see me with Kade ... and Luke ... and Nellie. It's going to be a quiet day. And when you report back, you're going to tell Logan I was a good girl and minded my own business."

"Yes, ma'am."

"Good." I took a step back. "You're going to stay like this for another two minutes. When you see me leaving in a vehicle, you're not going to remember that. You'll believe I'm someone else."

"It never happened," he intoned.

"Great. I think we're going to get along famously."

"Yes, ma'am."

I sighed. It wasn't nearly as much fun dealing with a robot as you might think. "One more thing." I poked my head inside the car. "No matter what happens, it's important Agent Stone doesn't blame himself. I'm in control of my own destiny. He could never change that. I'm not his responsibility."

"But ... you are. You saved him. He needs to save you."

That was such a man way of thinking I had to roll my eyes. "I can save myself."

"It's better if he saves you."

I couldn't hold back my sigh. "Yes, well, I guess we'll have to agree to disagree on that."

"Agree to disagree," he echoed.

"Just remember, I never left the circus."

"Nope. You've been here all morning running around with the little dude in the dress. Got it."

I smirked "You've got it exactly. Good job."

CREEK'S HOUSE WAS WHAT I expected. That's not to say it was horrible —

especially given the fact that she'd never managed to eke out even one break her entire life — but it needed a bit of work. Okay, more than a bit.

A blue tarp covered the roof near the garage, probably because a new roof was out of her financial reach. The front porch sagged. The brick facade was chipped and falling away in some places, and the yard was overgrown with weeds and empty beer cans.

Creek's eyes went wide when she opened the door. Her first instinct was to slam the door in my face and hide. But she held it together. I had to give her credit for that.

"I wasn't expecting you." She glanced over her shoulder, as if nervous, and then shook her head. "You shouldn't be here."

"We need to talk." I couldn't tiptoe around her feelings. I was on a timetable. "I need to ask you questions about the scar on your arm."

"My arm ... ." Creek's forehead wrinkled as she glanced at the faded marks. "I don't understand."

I held up my arm for emphasis. "The same thing happened to me last night."

"But ... how do you know it was the same thing?"

"Call it a hunch." I inclined my chin toward the living room. "We really shouldn't have this conversation on your front porch. The neighbors will think we're nutty."

"They already hate me."

"This could propel them to a new level of hate."

She sighed. "The house is kind of a mess."

"I don't care about that." I really didn't. It was obvious Creek cared. "If you think I'm judging you and comparing lives, I'm not. I've had a few stressful moments since I arrived because I assumed you were judging me for leaving. I get it. We were kids, and it was a long time ago."

She rubbed the spot between her eyebrows, something she used to do when she was stressed, and took a step back, pulling the door open so I could slide inside. Once over the threshold, I was surprised. The house was warm and even appealing. Sure, there were a lot of toys spread across the living room floor, but the house wasn't filthy.

"Where is your daughter?" I asked as I stepped around a well-loved doll.

"She's reading in her nook."

She has a nook? That was the question on the tip of my tongue before I managed to swallow it. When I looked to the left, I found the little girl sitting on a beanbag in a small alcove off the corner. She was indeed reading a book, one I didn't recognize. It was a picture book – I could see the illustrations from across the room – but she seemed to be struggling as she attempted to read the words.

"She's very smart," Creek offered quickly. "The people at the center think it's amazing that she's picking up on reading this early. I've been trying to work with her."

I was officially impressed, in more ways than one. "What center?"

"Oh, it's the Summerset Center over in Eastpointe," she replied. "Thanks to my low income, they help me with childcare. I can drop Hannah off for four hours a day, three days a week, and then I don't have to worry about paying for a babysitter. It's only twelve hours a week, but it really helps."

"Yeah." I was floored. Creek had managed to slap together some semblance of a life. Somehow, against all the odds, she was making it work. Life would always be a struggle for her. I had a few ideas on that, though. "You mentioned Beacon got you into a job-training program."

"And you're wondering why I'm stripping if I have another job. Well, right now I'm only working twelve hours a week as a paralegal as I build up experience. I have a degree and everything thanks to a program Beacon helped me enroll in. But it's a slow process. I make a couple hundred dollars a day stripping. I'm putting all that money away for Hannah's college, so she can get out of here. She doesn't need to know where it came from."

I was profoundly touched by Creek's effort. "How long will you keep it up?"

"Not much longer. She's very observant. She'll be able to figure out what I do relatively quickly if I don't keep her from it. There're only so many times I can hide pasties between the couch cushions so she doesn't ask questions. I want to sock away as much as I can before then."

"I don't blame you." I stared at the little girl before turning my full attention to Creek. "I need to know what happened when you were attacked. There's not much information. When did it happen?"

"It was before Hannah. Like, … three years. I guess that would roughly make it eight years or so ago. I … wait. How do you even know about it?"

That was a fair question. "You should probably sit down," I said. "There're a few things I need to tell you."

"Do I even want to hear it?"

"Probably not, but it might explain a bit about what happened the day I left."

"You don't owe me an explanation about that. I don't blame you for leaving. I would've jumped at the chance, too. It sucks being the one left behind, but it obviously worked out well for you."

"It has. You still deserve an explanation."

I told her everything. Well, within reason. I didn't delve into the monsters we killed in great detail. She didn't need to know, and it would only confuse her more. I did tell her about my psychic abilities ... and how I met Max. I explained about being able to be open about my talents in the circus and how that was a relief. When I finished, she didn't seem all that surprised.

"I always knew you could do things," she admitted. "I mean ... I didn't know what you could do. I could see you concentrating sometimes. You also had a way of making people do what you want, like that time it was so cold we were shivering and you convinced the guy in that office building to let us sleep in the lobby, even though he thought we were thieves. He actually said that and still let us stay."

"To be fair, I didn't realize what I was doing back then. I knew I could push people. I didn't know how far I could take it."

"How far can you take it?"

"Pretty far. That's how I found your address."

She lightly traced her finger over the scars on her arms. "And you think whatever attacked me back then is the same thing that attacked you last night?"

"I don't know. The thing is, you told the cops that the creature that attacked you had red eyes. The creature that attacked me didn't have red eyes. How sure are you about your description?"

"Damn sure!" Creek's eyes seemed to look back in time. "I'll never forget that moment as long as I live. I mean ... I couldn't believe Tawny turned on me the way she did. I thought she was just in a bad mood, but her fingers actually turned into claws — the type lions have — and I thought she might rip my throat out. I protected myself out of instinct and that's the only reason I'm alive."

I jerked my eyes to her, dumbfounded. "Tawny? What are you talking about?"

Confusion washed over Creek's features. "It was Tawny. I thought that's why you were really here, because you were asking about her before. I told the police it was her. Didn't it say that in the report?"

"No. There wasn't even a description of the suspect. They thought you were off your rocker because you mentioned red eyes."

"I was out of it. I have no idea why I got so confused."

"You were poisoned," I replied without hesitation. "The same thing happened to me. I couldn't control my environment either. The thing is, you stayed awake long enough to relate your story to the police. You must have realized they didn't believe you, because you disappeared not long after. Where did you go?"

"I wandered. I don't even know how long. Then ... I decided to lie down. I was near a restaurant. There was a dumpster that seemed safe enough. Someone found me, a man I think, and he carried me away.

"I remember thinking that he was a paramedic or something, that he thought I was dead, but I wasn't quite dead," she continued. "I figured my time was up and I would go to sleep and never wake up. I'd been thinking about that more and more during those days, was prepared for it. I thought it might be a blessing."

I swallowed the lump forming in my throat. "I'm so sorry."

"Don't be." She waved off the apology. "When I woke up, I was in Royal Oak. A woman was taking care of me. I'd never met her before, but she saved me anyway."

Something clicked into place. "Madame Maxine saved you."

Creek nodded. "Yeah. That's why I sent you to her. I thought maybe she could help you. I don't visit her as often as I should, but I still stop in to see her from time to time. She's a good woman, and Hannah loves her."

"She is." I had no doubt about that. "Tell me about Tawny. When did you realize something was off with her?"

"I don't know for certain. Some of the timeline from back then melds together. The days became a blur of trying to survive."

"Just tell me the basics as you remember them."

"I started running with a group of girls staying at Hart Plaza," she volunteered. "After Noble was murdered, everyone was afraid to go back to the alley."

I was taken aback. "Noble was murdered?"

"Yeah." She looked thoughtful. "I forgot. Word on that came down after you left. He was strung up and thrown over the side of the bridge while he was still alive. It happened to two more guys in that area before everyone scattered for a bit."

I felt sick to my stomach. "Do you know what happened to his body? I mean ... was he put to rest with a military funeral?"

Creek held out her hands, helpless. "I don't know. I'm sorry."

"It's not your fault." I meant it. Life had screwed Noble. I could hardly go back in time and make things right. "What about Tawny? You were hanging with a new crowd. Does that mean you never saw her?"

"I hadn't seen Tawny for at least six months. She disappeared like you. Well, maybe not exactly like you. She was always talking about going west. I assumed she finally went through with it ... until I saw her that night months later – actually, it could've been closer to a year that she was gone – and she attacked me. All I was doing was asking where she'd been. She wasn't even the same person. She looked normal until she grabbed my arm, and then her eyes flashed red. I swear I'm not making it up."

"I believe you." I tapped my chin as I considered the new information. "When I talked to you the other day in the club, you said Tawny went west. You never mentioned her coming back."

"Yeah, well, I didn't want to tell you about the red eyes because I assumed you would think I was crazy. I knew better than telling anyone that story because the first time I tried to get people to believe me they thought I was crazy. I have a daughter now. They'll take her away if they think I'm unfit. I buried it deep."

"Have you seen Tawny since?"

"No, and I'm grateful. I don't know what I would do if I saw her again. I think she's dead or she really did leave this time."

"No." I thought to the day we arrived at the fairgrounds. "I've seen her. I thought I was imagining it, but I've seen her."

"Did she attack you?"

I shook my head. "No. Something else attacked me. I think she created something else."

Creek looked legitimately baffled. "I don't understand what that means."

"I'm not sure I do either. I need to visit your buddy Madame Maxine again. And then I need to try to track down Tawny. I think I have an idea what might be going on here."

"Do you think you can save the girls if you find Tawny?"

That was a thorny question. "Probably not," I replied after a long moment. False hope was worse than no hope. "But at least I'll be able to save other girls from falling victim to her."

"That's better than everyone else is doing," Creek agreed. "Do you want me to go with you to visit Maxine? I can try to find a babysitter if you think it's necessary."

I looked to where Hannah sat mouthing words to herself as she smiled and flipped pages in the book. "No. You belong here." I rubbed Creek's arm and smiled. "I'm glad you found your place."

"I'm glad you found yours."

"I still wish you would've gotten the letter I sent. I kind of want to kill Hazy."

"He's still around. Owns a garage not far from the fairgrounds. He's done okay for himself. I doubt he kept the letters. He probably lost those five minutes after you gave them to him."

"Wait ... Hazy owns a garage?"

"He fixes cars." Creek beamed. "He's fixed my car for cheap a few times. He never gives me any grief about it either."

"I guess that's more important than a letter."

"I still would've liked the letter."

"Yeah." I hugged her. "I'm glad you're okay."

She awkwardly patted my back.

"I'm going to find the person doing this. I'm going to find Tawny."

"And then what?"

"Then I end it."

She pulled back and stared into my eyes. "You're going to kill her?"

"I'm going to make the streets a little safer," I corrected. "It's all I can do."

"Then you best get to it."

26

TWENTY-SIX

*M*adame Maxine was helping a customer when I entered her shop. I took advantage of the opportunity to scan the goods on display, selected a pretty dreamcatcher to replace the one by my bedroom window that was starting to show signs of wear and tear, and made my way to the counter.

When the customer left, Madame Maxine fixed her full attention on me. Her expression was hard to read, but she didn't look unhappy with my presence.

"I figured you'd be back." She motioned toward the table at the side of the shop. "Some tea?"

"Sure." I glanced at the clock on the wall. It was only two hours until the circus opened. Putting on an impatience display wouldn't get me anywhere.

Madame Maxine poured the tea and then sat back in her chair and waited. Apparently the floor was open for discussion.

"Several years ago you helped a friend of mine," I started. "Creek."

She furrowed her brow. "I remember her. She was a sad girl, seemed to have lost her spirit. She was gravely injured."

"Yeah." I removed the bandage from my arm and showed her the wound. "Does this look familiar?"

Intrigue lit her features. "You were attacked by the same creature."

"I was attacked by one of the banshees," I corrected. "Creek claims when she was attacked it was by a woman we knew. Tawny. She was a prostitute

209

who disappeared for months. When she turned back up, she attacked Creek ... and almost killed her."

"Hmm." Madame Maxine rubbed her stomach as she stared at the wounds. "Were you poisoned as well?"

"Yes. My people cured me. But I want to know what sort of poison was used on Creek ... and how this poison ties in with banshees."

"I don't know. Her story was confusing. She was brought here by a warlock who discovered her behind a dumpster in the Corridor. Apparently she crawled in there to die We managed to save her."

"How?"

"I threw every remedy I had at her. I'm not even sure if it was one that did the job or if it was all of them together. When I questioned her after, she kept talking about a demon with red eyes, or maybe even a vampire ... but I knew that was nonsense. I assumed she was mistaken or the poison had caused her to hallucinate."

I hadn't even considered that. "Have you ever heard of a banshee with red eyes?"

"No, but I haven't had much experience with banshees. They're rare here."

I pursed my lips. "I was familiar with Tawny. The thing is, the first night I arrived, I thought I saw her near the cemetery. I haven't seen her since, but I convinced myself I imagined her, that it was most likely someone who looked like Tawny. Now I'm starting to doubt that assumption."

"I should say so. Still, banshees don't survive long. They draw attention to themselves. How could this woman have survived as a banshee for that long?"

"I was hoping you would know the answer to that question."

"I don't. I'm sorry. I've been digging deep with the research — I know Izzy, Cormack and Cillian have, too — but we haven't come up with anything that explains what's going on here. No matter the outcome, I don't think we're dealing with normal banshees. This is something else."

"We're running out of time. We have to find answers ... and soon. The girls on the street are at risk." I thought of Michelob. "I can't leave without putting this to bed."

"Then we have to find answers. It feels as if we're missing a big piece of the puzzle."

Unfortunately, it felt that way to me, too.

WHEN I RETURNED TO THE circus, I didn't have time for small talk. I changed into a work outfit, put a scarf over my hair, and ventured out in time to see the front gates opening and the fairgrounds filling with people.

It was time to work ... even though my mind was elsewhere. Ah, well, it was hardly the first time I'd had to read fortunes while worrying about a paranormal monster. I would have to multi-task.

I was halfway to my tent when I caught a glimpse of movement near the opening. When I turned, the face I found watching me was one that I didn't expect.

"Groove?" I was beyond surprised, and glanced around to make sure none of his gang members were with him. "What are you doing here?"

"Looking for you." He was grim. "Is there a place we can talk?"

"Now really isn't the best time. I have to work."

"That's your work outfit?" He looked tickled. "That's just ... awesome."

I rolled my eyes. Insults from him weren't enough to derail me. They simply rolled off my back. "Can you come back later? After dark, perhaps?"

"What? You don't want me ruining your festival, huh?"

"I'm not worried about you ruining the festival, but I have to focus on paying customers."

"Yeah? I guess you don't want to hear about the girl that went missing last night then, huh? My bad." He turned to leave, but I grabbed his arm before he could take more than two steps.

"What girl?"

"I can't talk out in the open." His expression was unreadable, but sadness tinged his eyes. "You said you wanted to help."

I had indeed said that. "Fine. Come on." I dragged him toward my tent. "We'll talk over here."

His eyes traveled to the sign declaring me the best psychic in the world and he barked out a laugh. "This is so ... nuts."

From his perspective, it probably looked that way. "Just ... come on."

I settled him in a chair at my table, opened the rope so it would look like I was simply working with my first customer of the day, and then slid in across from him. "Tell me about the missing girl."

"Valentine. She's been a regular in my area for about a year. She's been gone two days."

I frowned. "Why didn't you mention this before?"

"I couldn't be sure. You know how the street is. I thought maybe she just wasn't bedding down with the others that first night. I questioned them the next day, and she hasn't come back."

"When was the last time anyone saw her?"

He hesitated.

"Groove, you've got to give me everything you have on this." I was firm. "She hasn't been missing for more than forty-eight hours. There's still a chance we can find her."

He narrowed his eyes. "Do you know what's going on here?"

"I have a few ideas."

"Tell me."

"I don't have anything worth sharing."

His temper sparked hot and fast, and he reached across the table and grabbed my arm, digging his fingernails in as he held my gaze. "Tell me," he growled, menace on full display.

"You want to take your hands off me." My voice was icy, to better face off with his fire.

"Are you going to make me?"

"Would you like me to?"

He seemed amused by the question. "I'll take whatever you can throw at me, girl. You always thought you were better than the rest of them. I saw it in your eyes. You always knew you'd get out."

"I *hoped* I would get out," I corrected. "There's a difference. I didn't know anything back then."

"You sure didn't."

I shifted my eyes back to his hand "You're going to want to take that hand off me or I'm going to break it."

"You think you can take me?" His laughter was coarse and he gripped tighter. "Tell me what you know. Tell me or I'll ... ."

"You'll what?" I was just as furious. "There's nothing you can do to me. I'm not the same girl you knew twelve years ago. It would be a mistake to assume that."

"I've learned a few tricks, too. You can't survive on the street without them. If you want to dance, we'll dance." He reached for me with his free hand, but I was expecting the move.

I slid my hand out from under his, grimacing when his jagged fingernails dragged along the wound on my arm. He couldn't see my full reaction, or the vulnerable spot on my arm. I'd covered the bandage with a long-sleeved blouse, but there was triumph in his eyes when he realized I was in pain.

It didn't last long.

I flipped my hands around and grabbed the top of his wrists, lashing out with a burst of magic that rendered him frozen. "Sit," I ordered, my voice deadly. "You sit right there."

I heard footsteps at the tent opening. I expected Kade, or maybe even Luke, to rush in. They would've heard that Groove waylaid me before I reached my tent. Gossip spreads fast in our group. It wasn't either of them. It was Redmond, and he looked ready for action.

"Did he do anything to you?" Redmond rushed to my side and then pulled up short when he realized Groove was frozen in place. "What did you do to him?"

"Nothing. Yet."

Groove could move only his eyes, and I saw fear reflected there. He made a sound deep in his throat, but he couldn't open his mouth, so no words escaped.

"You terrorized us when we were kids," I told him. It was hardly news, but he managed a smug glint in his eye. "You were desperate to make a name for yourself. You liked us because it made you look tough to have someone to kick around.

"You thought we were naive enough to believe you cared about us, or at least wanted to keep us safe," I continued. "We weren't stupid. You kept us as cover. We were your sacrificial lambs should the cops come around ... or you had a message to send to a rival gang. We were handy bodies you could drop."

Kade hurried through the tent opening but didn't interrupt. His eyes went wide as he glanced around, his gaze finally falling on Redmond. "What's happening?"

"I think your girlfriend is sending a message she's wanted to send for a long time," Redmond replied. "It's fairly fascinating. I think this guy is frozen." As if to prove it to himself, he waved a hand in front of Groove's face. "Yeah, he's frozen. He's kind of like a pose-able doll. Do you know what we should do?"

"We're not doing that," I shot back.

"How do you even know what I was going to say?"

"Your mind is an open book."

"Oh, yeah? What am I thinking right now?"

"That you're afraid I'll kill him even though he might have answers to our problem," I replied without hesitation. "That you're kind of hungry and want an elephant ear. You're also sad you didn't think ahead to bring Lily because women love a baby and if you were carrying your niece around you would attract a nonstop train of women and you could have your pick. Oh, and you're wondering how serious Kade and I really are because you're considering making a move. I wouldn't do that if I were you."

Kade pinned him with a serious glare. "I definitely wouldn't do that," he intoned.

"It was just a thought." Redmond looked sheepish. "She's hot ... and tough. I'm just sad you found her first."

Kade nodded in agreement. "I don't blame you. I'll hurt you if you move on her, though. That's after she hurts you herself. Just ... find another girl."

"Push him toward Naida," I suggested. "She's always looking for a good fling."

"Is she tough like you?"

I tilted my head, considering. "She can whip up a literal tornado in the bedroom."

"Sold." Redmond beamed and then moved so he was standing directly behind me and could stare into Groove's eyes. "What do you know about the missing girls?"

Groove didn't answer. Correction, he couldn't answer. "Asking him questions won't do anyone any good," I replied.

"We need answers."

"There are other ways to get them."

"Oh? How?"

Kade smirked as he moved toward the tent flap to keep watch. "Prepare to be amazed."

INSERTING MYSELF INTO GROOVE'S MIND was as simple as cutting through peanut butter with a dull knife. He had no mental barriers to speak of. That wasn't uncommon in humans. They simply didn't know there was another level of consciousness that could be so easily accessed.

Groove's eyes went so wide when he realized what I was doing that I thought they might bug out of his head. It was too late, though, and I entered the mind jail taking up residence in the heart of his brain with minimal effort, immediately sitting in a chair in the middle of the cell, watching him as he cowered in a corner.

"What is this?" He was dumbfounded.

"It's your brain." I glanced around, taking in the collection of items I could make out on the other side of the bars. "There's not much in here."

"Is that supposed to make me cry?" Even though he was afraid, he had no intention of backing down. He had street cred for a reason. He would die on his feet if it came to it. "I'm not afraid of you."

"You should be." I was matter-of-fact. "You should've been afraid of me back then, too. I think part of you was. That's the reason you never went after our group. You would never admit it out loud back then, to me or anyone else. Don't worry, I don't expect you to admit it now. I see more than I used to, and the memories are coming into focus."

"Oh, geez." He rolled his eyes. "You think a lot of yourself, don't you?"

"This isn't about me. It's about you."

"Ain't nothing here that's about me. I was trying to share information with you because I thought you might be able to help. I was wrong. You can't even help yourself. All you can do is ... mind tricks." He wiggled his fingers and gestured toward the walls of the cell. "I don't know how you're doing this, but I know it's not real."

"On the contrary. It is real ... and I'm not doing this. I didn't create this cell. You did."

"Bullshit."

"It's true. I don't need a cell to contain you. You're trapped in here as long as I want you to be trapped. The cell was already here. I think you created it a long time ago. I'm guessing it's because you feel trapped and there's nothing worse than feeling like you're in a cage. To you, jail would be the ultimate punishment. You might not be happy on the outside, but at least you're free."

"I'm not talking to you." He folded his arms over his chest. "Let me out of here."

"Sure." Slowly I got to my feet and walked to the cell door. I was playing a hunch, but it turned out to be true. I wasn't surprised when it swung open and allowed me to escape. I left the door ajar behind me and moved to the nearest shelf. There, amidst a collection of photographs and memories from his childhood, sat a framed photograph. It looked relatively new, and the girl in it was young and fresh-faced ... and there was a heart in the corner of the photo.

"Valentine?" I asked, gesturing toward the girl. "She looks a little young for you."

"Don't be gross!" he snapped, following me out of the cell. "It's not like that."

Something about his reaction made me think he was telling the truth. "It's not?" I pursed my lips and studied the girl's face. After a moment, I figured it out. "She's your sister ... or at least a family member. You have the same eyes."

"How do you know that?" His tone was accusatory. "How can you possibly know that? Are you a witch now?"

"I'm what I always was. I didn't know it back then. That's probably for the best, because I wasn't smart enough not to abuse my gift. I'm not a witch."

"Then what are you?"

"Something else." I ran my fingers over the photograph and watched him cringe as a series of flashes echoed around us. They were memories, and I understood better than he could've ever guessed exactly what was going on. "She's your sister. You're much older, so I'm guessing you don't share the same father."

"What do you know?"

"I know that you were trying to keep her safe. I know that you knew the street wasn't for her and were trying to find a place for her at Beacon Hill. I know you were dealing with the big man himself, but he wanted something from you in return." I frowned as I sorted through the memory. "He wanted you to do him a favor, kill a rival gang leader because he was threatening the kids at the shelter. That's ... interesting."

"What's so interesting about it?" Groove challenged. "The man is trying to keep the kids safe. He's helped some get jobs. That's what I wanted him to do for Valentine."

"But he's willing to murder in the process of getting what he wants. I just ... that doesn't seem very altruistic, does it?"

"I have no idea what that means."

"Giving. Charitable."

"I was lying. I know what it means. I don't really care what he is as long as he gets Valentine out. We was working on a deal when little girl went missing. I came to you because you're the only one I know who will be willing to help."

"Then you should've just asked for help," I challenged. "These threats you toss around, this attitude you hoard like gold, that's not how you get me to help you."

"Oh, yeah? How do I get you to help?"

"You ask."

"Just as simple as that?"

"Yup." I turned to move toward the door. "I'll do my best to find your sister. I'm not doing it for you, though. I'm doing it for her ... and the others. This needs to be shut down fast. I expect you to stay out of the way. You'll foul things up if you're not careful."

"I can't do nothing. She's all I got. My mother shouldn't have had no more kids, but someone has to take care of Valentine. She's better than me."

I had no doubt about that. "I can't promise we'll save her. I will do my very best."

"I have to do my best, too. I can't stop now."

"Then we're at an impasse. Just know, Groove, if you get in my way, I'll roll right over you. I won't have a choice."

"Just find her. Save her." His eyes were full of pleading. He wasn't the type to beg, but he was begging now. "Please. I'll do anything."

"I don't need payment. I just need information. We're missing something."

And nothing bothered me more than an incomplete puzzle.

27

TWENTY-SEVEN

*K*ade and Redmond watched me for signs of movement when I exited Groove's mind jail and rejoined the world of the conscious.

"He's not involved," I offered, getting to my feet. "He doesn't know anything."

"Then why was he attacking you?" Kade was gentle when he lifted my arm and glared at the mangled bandage. "Are you in pain?"

"I'm fine." I brushed off his concern. "He's looking for his sister. She went missing on the street two days ago."

"That's not long," Redmond noted. "She could still be out there."

"She could," I agreed as Groove took a shaky breath and began to stir. I watched him for signs of violence as he regained his senses, but the look he shot me was full of marvel rather than mayhem. "You're fine," I told him. "You can go."

"Did that just really happen?" he asked, breathless.

"Yes."

"I've never seen anything like that."

"You probably won't again. Just because I didn't trap you there this time doesn't mean I won't do it in the future. Remember that."

"I just ... that was sick." He stood on shaky legs. "That was really sick. I can't believe you would do that to me."

"I didn't do that to you," I reminded him. "You created that cell. A psychologist could have a field day with what's going on in your mind. Thankfully for you, I'm not a psychologist."

"What are you?"

"Many different things." I pointed toward the tent opening. "You need to get out of here. I don't want you getting in the way, Groove. I meant what I said to you in there. I will do my very best to find Valentine. I can't guarantee that I'll be able to save her. I just don't know enough to make a promise like that."

"Then I gotta do what I gotta do. I won't leave no stone unturned until I find her."

"You'll regret it if you do that." I'd seen a glimpse of his future while I was in his head. It wasn't pretty ... and there was no Valentine in sight, so I had no idea if we would manage to save her. "Just stay out of it. That's your best bet."

"I can't."

And, because I understood what he was saying, I merely nodded. If it was my loved one — Kade, Luke or Max — I wouldn't be able to keep out of it either. There was nothing worse than feeling helpless. "Just do your best. We'll do the same."

I remained rooted to my spot as he slowly slipped toward the tent opening. He was almost out before he turned back and stared at me. "Did I really create the cell?"

"Yes."

"Do you think ... do you think I'll end up there forever?"

"I know a bit about philosophy, and if there was ever the potential for a self-fulfilling prophecy it's probably inside your head. Your future isn't set in stone, though. You can still change what's going to happen."

"I only know one way to be."

"Then you'll die that way."

"Maybe that's for the best."

I never pictured him as a martyr, but I could see it now. "Good luck, Groove."

"Right back at you."

Once Groove left, Kade took the opportunity to pet me. He knew better than to do it in front of a potential enemy who disrespected women. Apparently he had no qualms of going full-on romance hero in front of Redmond, though.

"Tell me the truth, how much pain are you in?" He was gentle as he hugged me tight.

"I really am fine. It doesn't hurt all that much any longer." That was a bit of an exaggeration, but I had more important things on my mind. I flicked my eyes to Redmond. "Are you the only one from your family here?"

"Braden and Izzy are here. They're walking around so Izzy can read people. We didn't know what else to do."

"I'm not sure I do either, but I think we have to tear that cemetery apart after dark. That's the only thing I can think to do. There's a nest in there, even though I can't see how any of those mausoleums are big enough to house a bunch of banshees."

"The mausoleums probably aren't big enough," he acknowledged. "But not all them are what they appear to be. Some of them — including the Olivet one, which has been rebuilt a third time after we destroyed it twice — have basements."

"You're kidding." That seemed like an odd thing for a mausoleum, but my interest was officially piqued. "Why would someone build a basement in the middle of a cemetery?"

Redmond let loose a charming wink. "To do evil things, of course. Why else would you build a basement among thousands of dead people?"

I couldn't argue with his logic. "Good point. We're going to need your family. I have a plan. We can't do anything until after dark, though."

"You want to invade the cemetery again? We didn't find anything the other night."

"Wrong. We found a banshee."

"And you want to find another banshee? Do you think it will be Valentine?"

"No. I don't think whoever is doing this has had her long enough to turn her into a banshee. There's still time to save her."

"So ... how do we find her?"

"We cast a spell." I was grim. "We have a lot of magic between us. The dreamcatcher failed with the banshees — and we still don't know why, although I'm starting to develop a theory — but I think we can build a bigger and better spell with your help."

"My help?" He grinned. "What do you want me to do?"

"Act as a banshee lure."

His smile faded. "That doesn't sound fun."

"It won't be, but you'll have plenty of backup. Besides, we're going to add Izzy's magic into the mix. She's powerful. Between her, Raven, Nixie, Naida and me, there should be no stopping us."

"Okay. I'm willing to give it a try if you are. Do you really want to wait until after dark?"

"I don't see that we have much choice. If we start a war when there are people around, more of them could die … and that's on top of the potential exposure, which is a real fear for all of us. We can't risk that."

"Okay. Dusk it is. I'll have my family here."

"Good. We'll need them. I'll have my family here, too."

His smile was back. "Can you make the little hairy dude wear a dress? He cracks me up."

"No one makes Nellie do anything … but he'll definitely wear a dress. My guess is he'll crack out the evening wear."

"Sounds fun."

He would think that.

I SENT NOTICE OF MY PLAN TO MY co-workers via text message. They were aware I was deathly serious about what needed to be done, understood what I expected of them, and no one offered up a single word of dissent. We were running out of time. It was this or nothing, and nothing wasn't an option.

That meant there was essentially nothing to do but work and watch for the rest of the afternoon. I was too keyed up to focus on the problems of others, so I put Melissa in charge of my tent and spent the afternoon mingling with the crowd. I didn't expect to get a reading off any of them. Since the dreamcatcher wasn't working, though, it seemed my best option.

Kade decided to stick close, even though he thought I didn't notice, I kept catching him watching me from various spots between tents. Whenever I looked in his direction, he pretended he was talking to someone else or looking over some security issue only he could see. Instead of calling him on it, I decided to let him be. He was only doing it because he cared so very much. There were worse things in the world … and we were about to take one of them on.

"Can I have cotton candy?"

I swiveled at the voice, amused at the obvious wheedle. It was a little girl, golden pigtails perched on either side of her head, and she looked imploringly at the man who held her hand as they navigated the crowd.

"I don't know," the man replied, laughter in his voice. "I've seen you all sugared up before. It's never a good thing."

"I won't get sugared up."

"What do you think cotton candy is made of?"

"Angel hair. Angels are made of sugar."

"Well, you have a point."

There was something familiar about the man's voice, but his face didn't stir any memories. Still, I couldn't look away. The girl clearly knew her father was an easy mark, and she had every intention of getting that cotton candy. I had severe doubts her father could hold out much longer.

"I'll have to think about it," he said after a beat. "Your mother won't be happy if she knows I let you eat a bunch of junk."

"We could not tell her," the little girl suggested. "It could be our secret, like the time you got me a new doll after the lawnmower killed the first one."

The man snorted. "Yes, well ... I only did that to stop you from crying."

"It worked."

"It did."

"Cotton candy would keep me from crying."

"Good to know. I ... ." Slowly the man's eyes slid to me, as if he sensed me watching him. Even though I didn't recognize him, the same couldn't be said for him. His mouth dropped open when he saw me and awe crawled over his features. "Poet?"

"Who are you talking to?" The girl looked around until she found me. "Do you know her?"

The man kept a firm hold on her hand and waited until there was an opening in the crowd to cross.

"Is it you?" he asked when he was directly in front of me.

I was confused. "Do I know you?"

"You did a million years ago."

"A million, eh? I'll have you know I'm not a day over a thousand years old." I winked at the little girl to let her know I was joking, but she didn't seem impressed.

"We're going to get cotton candy," she announced, tugging on her father's hand. "We're going right now."

"Stop, Lacey," the man admonished, although his eyes never moved from my face. "I thought you were dead."

I remained confused. "I don't know you. At least I can't place you."

"No?" A slow smile spread across his face. "What if I tell you I had a dream last night and in it you were riding a purple unicorn?"

That's when the truth hit me straight across the face. "Hazy?" It wasn't possible. I'd heard he cleaned up his act and made it out. This guy didn't look anything like the man I remembered. Still, it fit.

He chuckled. "I haven't gone by that name in a long time. I'm Gary

Morgan. I own Morgan Automotive. It's about three blocks from here." He extended his hand as if we were meeting for the first time.

"Hello, Gary." My heart warmed at the sight of him. He looked as if he was doing really well, which was a relief. "I can't believe it's you."

"And I can't believe it's you. I thought you tore out of here twelve years ago."

"I did."

"You joined the circus." He smiled as he glanced around, pure joy emanating from his features. "You really did join the circus. Everyone thought I was making that up when I told them, but I was certain that's what you'd said."

"I did join the circus," I confirmed.

"You made it out."

"So did you."

"Only because I had nowhere to go but up." His smile was rueful. "I hit rock bottom when Junk died. I was right next to him. We went to sleep on top of the world, high as ... well ... kites. Oh, don't worry. My family knows about my past. I still go to meetings. You don't have to watch what you say in front of Lacey."

I smiled for the small girl's benefit ... and then something occurred to me. "Do you have a few minutes to talk?"

"I guess. But I did promise someone cotton candy."

"I can handle the cotton candy." I saluted Lacey. "I even have the perfect person to keep her entertained."

"Then let's talk."

I STATIONED KADE AND LACEY at a picnic table – a huge bag of cotton candy in front of them – and then motioned for Gary to sit with me across the way. He could keep an eye on his daughter without risking her over-hearing our conversation.

"You seem serious."

"I am." I launched into my tale, leaving out some of the more fantastical bits. He didn't need to know about the magic. I wanted him to know about the missing girls, and I wanted any insight he might have. He was former street, after all. He would understand how things went down without stretching his imagination.

"So you think there's a predator on the loose," he mused, rubbing his cheek and sipping from the malt Kade had purchased for him. "I can't say I'm surprised. I haven't really heard anything about it."

"You don't read the newspaper?"

"Not really. It's full of depressing news and I don't want to live in a depressed world."

"No. I'm sure you don't." I mustered a smile. "You've built a life for yourself ... and it's a great life. I'm so happy for you."

"It's nothing compared to the life you built for yourself."

"Yeah, but you had more to overcome. As for Junk, I'm sorry. I know you were close."

"We were," he agreed. "I wouldn't have made it out if he hadn't died. That was the catalyst I needed to become a better man."

"He would be happy to know what you've accomplished."

We beamed at each other for a long time, and then he sobered. "I don't know what to tell you about the missing girls. I'm sorry. I'm even sorry for Groove. I just don't keep my ear to the ground anymore. It seemed like a dangerous thing to do because I would be more likely to cross the line and go back if I kept a foot in that world."

That made sense. "It's okay. It was a long shot anyway."

"I'm still glad I got to see you. I often wondered what happened to you ... and there were times I was afraid. I even found the letters you gave me for Creek and Shadow a few years ago. They were in an old bag I carried at the time. I still have them — it seemed rude to throw them away — if you want them."

I was going to wave off the offer and then thought better of it. "I would like them back. I know it sounds weird, but I would like to deliver them."

"It doesn't sound weird. We all say our goodbyes in different ways. I can bring the letters by tomorrow."

"I really appreciate it."

He let loose a sigh. "If that's all, I promised Lacey some games."

"Just one thing." I had one more question to ask. "Do you remember Tawny?"

He scowled. "I remember her. She corrupted your friend Creek. I see Creek from time to time. I've helped her with her car more than once. She's doing okay. As for Tawny, she was bad news."

That was the most intense reaction I'd had to the Tawny question yet. "Do you know what happened to her?"

"Only what I heard. I mean, once you were gone, we never saw her. She went her own way and we went ours."

"What did you hear?"

"I heard she went west."

"That seems to be the general consensus." I was a bit disappointed. I'd hoped he would have more information.

"I think that was just a story she told to seem like a big shot," he added.

"Why is that?"

"Because I saw her after she supposedly left, and she didn't have a tan or anything."

I stilled. "You saw her? Where?"

"I was still on the street then, but not really. I was in treatment and trying to get a job. I had really cleaned up my act. She didn't even notice me because I'd cut my hair by then."

"Was she alone?"

"No."

"Who was she with?"

"I definitely remember because it seemed so weird to see her with him."

"Who? Was it Beacon?"

"No. It was your cop buddy. You probably don't know he's a cop. That Shadow guy we helped take care of? He turned out to be undercover."

It was as if the breath had been ripped from my lungs. "You saw Shadow with Tawny?"

"Yeah. They had their heads bent together and looked to be arguing. It wasn't pretty. She smacked him across the face and swore at him, said he betrayed her. It was all very *General Hospital*."

Well, well, well. "I need you to tell me everything you saw." I was grim. "It could be important."

"Sure. It won't take long because I don't know much of anything."

He knew more than he realized.

TWENTY-EIGHT

*C*ould it be?

I kept the conversation going with Gary until he finished his shake — mostly so I wouldn't look deranged when I tore off across the parking lot — but then I sent him on his way with free game passes for his daughter and a promise to clear time for him when he returned the letters. Lacey remained suspicious of me until I told her she could play as many games as she wanted for free. Then I was her hero.

The kid cracked me up.

I hugged Gary goodbye and promised to see him soon. He reiterated he would bring the letters the following day, promising he wouldn't forget. As much as I wanted to see them again, I had other things on my mind. Logan mainly.

"What are you going to do?" Kade asked when it was just the two of us. We stood between Nixie and Naida's tents so we could be out of the sun and enjoy a bit of privacy.

"Talk to him."

"Do you think that's wise? He's an FBI agent."

"So?"

"So ... he could arrest you."

The laugh that escaped was low and bitter. "Not if I don't let him ... and I have no intention of letting him."

"But ... what are you going to do?" Kade looked pained, as if he wanted to shackle me to his side so I couldn't run off half-cocked. I had news for him, I wasn't going to be shuttered away from the action, not when things were finally starting to heat up.

"I'm going to get him here," I replied without hesitation. "Then I'm going to ask him a few questions."

"And how do you plan to do that? He's not just going to fall victim to your mind control. I mean ... he knows you can do something. If he's truly paranormal – or in cahoots with someone paranormal – he'll have ways to block you. If he is involved in this — and it's obvious you think that — then he's dangerous. We need to come up with a plan to take him out."

"First, we have no proof he's involved in this," I reminded him. "We have a hazy memory from a guy who used to smoke so much pot Willie Nelson would've bowed down. I don't know what the truth is."

"Then why are you so wound up?"

"It doesn't make sense. Shadow used to warn us away from Tawny. He said she was a bad influence. Why would he do that if he was partnering with her?"

"You're back to calling him Shadow?" Kade was exasperated. "Have you considered that Agent Stone didn't want you hanging around her because he knew how dangerous she was? Maybe he was aware of something you weren't back then and he was desperate to keep you safe because he felt as if he owed you."

"If she's recruiting young women, why not us?"

"You said it yourself. You saved him, Poet. He might not be a good man, but he obviously respects you. He would've died without your intervention. I think, no matter what, he's obviously fond of you ... and not in the way I worried when I first saw you together."

"Oh, geez." I pinched the bridge of my nose. "I can't deal with this conversation now."

"Well, we're going to have it." He was firm. "I was jealous when I saw you with him that day. I remembered what you told me, and I couldn't help feeling a twinge at the way your face lit up when you talked to him. I thought I only wanted your face to light up that way for me. It turns out I was wrong."

"You were wrong?"

"Oh, you're loving this." He gave me a sloppy grin. "I was wrong. I want you happy no matter what. Even if, for some reason, your happiness isn't tied to me one day, I want you to always be laughing and smiling. That's what happens when you love someone. You want the best for them no matter what."

The emotion was naked on his face and I couldn't help being touched. "That's sweet." I patted his hand. "But I can't be happy without you. I've already come to that conclusion."

"Thank God." He pulled me into his arms, causing me to chuckle.

"You played that really smooth." I tipped my head back to stare into his eyes. "I don't love Logan the way I love you. I will always remember the things he did for us. If those memories are tainted now ... well ... I won't be happy, but I will get through it."

"I know you will." He kissed the tip of my nose. "I'll stand by you no matter what. How are you going to lure him to the fairgrounds?"

I had no doubt I could get him here. And I knew exactly how to do it.

THE SAME POLICE OFFICER WAS sitting in the same unmarked car around the corner when I snuck up behind him. I was already weaving my magic when he caught sight of me in the rear-view mirror. Before he even opened his mouth, he was under my spell.

I instructed him to call Logan with a tip that I was acting strange and had disappeared into the cemetery. Then, I waited near the mausoleums for Logan. I knew it was only a matter of time ... and I wasn't disappointed.

"What are you doing here?" he asked when he caught me sitting on the bench in front of the Grimlock mausoleum.

"Thinking about the meaning to life," I answered without hesitation.

"Have you come up with any answers?" He slid into the open spot next to me. He didn't seem agitated as much as curious.

"Maybe." I rolled my neck. "This is Lily Grimlock's final resting place."

"I see that. Did you know her?"

I shook my head. "No. But I've met her children. Well, I still haven't met Aidan, but apparently he's preparing for his wedding. I've met her other four children."

"I'm assuming the guy who was with you the other night was one of them. I remember the name."

"Yup."

"He's not your buddy Raven's boyfriend."

"Nope."

He shifted on the bench and studied my profile. "You seem agitated. Do you want to tell me what's going on?"

That was a loaded question if ever I heard one. "What was your relationship with Tawny?"

Whatever question he was expecting, that wasn't it. Logan's mouth dropped open as he incredulously stared. "What? Why would you ask that?"

"Because I know that before she supposedly left the area — and I know for a fact she didn't really leave — that she was meeting with you." Technically I only knew of the one meeting, but he didn't need to know that. "You warned us against hanging around with her, but you were having secret meetings."

His gaze hardened. "It sounds like you're accusing me."

"I am."

"I see." His tone was cold. "I thought you and I trusted each other. Granted, I knew there were still secrets — you're the only circus I've ever seen that carries around empty animal cages — but I figured we were good on the big stuff."

Now it was my turn to be flabbergasted. "You ... we ... what?"

We glared at one another, the atmosphere practically sparking.

"Perhaps we should start over," he hedged, backing down first. "I didn't mean to upset you. I just meant ... well ... I know you're not a normal circus."

This so wasn't what I was expecting. "I don't want to talk about the circus. I want to talk about Tawny."

"And I don't want to talk about Tawny. I guess we're at a standstill."

"We have to talk about Tawny."

"Why? She's been gone for years."

"No, she hasn't." The fury that had been slowly slipping away returned with a vengeance. "She's here. I saw her the night we arrived. She was directly outside this cemetery watching us. She has something to do with the banshees. I haven't figured it all out yet, but she's definitely involved."

"I don't ... banshees?" Logan's forehead wrinkled. "I don't even know what I'm supposed to say to that. I feel as if I'm on one of those hidden video programs and Ashton Kutcher is going to hop out at any second and tell me I've been punked."

Wow. His television references were dating him. It was unpleasant.

"You're so old," I complained, rubbing my forehead. "I need to know what your relationship was with Tawny. I need to know why you're working with her. Most importantly, I need to know what she's doing to those girls to turn them into banshees. She's got another new one, Groove's sister. There's still a chance to save her."

Logan stared at me for a long time, his eyes cloudy and unreadable. Finally, he shook his head. "I think we need to start at the beginning because you're not making any sense. Tell me why you think I have anything to do with Tawny."

There was no way I would turn on Gary. He'd built a wonderful life for himself. I wouldn't risk that. "Suffice it to say that someone saw you with her years after I left but before she fled. You were arguing and she said you betrayed her."

Logan's face turned a mottled shade of red. "Somebody heard that discussion?"

I felt sick to my stomach. "You've been protecting her all this time. Why? She's been dangerous for years. I mean ... she attacked Creek, for crying out loud. I know you didn't know the others enough to care about them, but there was a time you cared about Creek."

"Hey! I cared about both of you." His eyes flashed with annoyance. "As for Tawny, I don't know what it is you want to hear. I wasn't having an affair with her, if that's what has you so worked up."

"Oh, yes, that's it. I'm jealous. I had a crush on you when I was eighteen and I'm still harboring it today. I'm a silly female. All I can do is pine for you." My tone was withering.

"That's not what I'm saying."

"Then what are you saying?"

"I ... ." He trailed off and shook his head. "I can't tell you what was happening with Tawny. I literally cannot tell you. I'll be betraying my badge if I do."

He said it with such certainty it gave me pause ... and an opening. "Fine." I wedged myself in his head with little preamble, freezing him in place so I could look around without having to worry about him freaking out. It didn't take long to find what I was looking for, and when I was finished, I felt like an idiot.

"Oh, geez." I slid out of his mind and rubbed my forehead, watching as he returned to reality. He seemed dazed. That was normal, given the invasive mind probe I'd put on him. "Tawny was your confidential informant. She was passing you information on the street because you were going to take down Groove."

Logan's eyes went wide. "How can you possibly know that?"

"I'm a world-famous mind reader. Don't you know?"

"But ... that's not real."

"Oh, it's real." I felt shaky and queasy as I stretched my legs and stared at my feet. "Tawny was sharing information with you about Groove. In exchange, you were going to get her into a program and off the street. She was pregnant."

"She was," Logan confirmed. "I don't know how you know all of this, but ...

whatever. She was pregnant and wanted a way to save her child. This ... arrangement ... was all I could come up with."

"You didn't, though, did you? Save her child, I mean."

"No." He looked sad as he shook his head. "Groove was the baby's father. He found out that she was funneling information to me. I still don't know how it happened. I only told one person and that's because I needed help protecting her.

"She was angry when she realized she would be removed from the street right away," he continued. "She thought she had a few more weeks. I told her it was over, that she was going into the program, but she slipped out of the hotel I put her up in and went back to the street one last time."

"Did you ever find her?"

"No. I figured Groove killed her and hid her body so well that we'll never find it."

I thought about my trip through Groove's head. "Are you sure he was the father?"

"Why would she lie?"

"Why does anybody lie? The thing is, Groove never showed any interest in her. I'm not saying he's a good guy — not by a long shot — but I don't think he killed Tawny."

Logan looked interested. "Why do you say that?"

"Because he has protective instincts and I think he would've taken care of his own kid. That makes me think he wasn't sleeping with Tawny. If he caught her and decided to off her, she would've used the kid as a bargaining chip to save her life ... and he would've at least waited. He might've killed her after the fact, but he would've saved the child."

"So ... what are you saying?"

"I saw Tawny," I reminded him. "She was standing outside this cemetery, staring."

"She's dead, Poet. I would've seen her between now and then if she was still alive. She wasn't the sharpest tool in the kit. She couldn't keep hidden for years."

"She could if she was no longer human." I was grim. "I'm about to tell you something you may not like, but it's important. It's also the truth."

"Is this about why you don't have animals in your cages? I already know about shifters."

"You do?"

"Yeah. We know about paranormal creatures. I'm guessing you're one. I always had a feeling it was possible."

"I am," I agreed. "Before you ask, I don't know what I am ... other than psychic and capable of controlling people's minds. I did it to Groove earlier. That's how I saw what goes through his mind. He's already living in a prison of his own making. There was no hint of Tawny in there."

"So ... you don't think he killed her?" Logan rubbed his chin as he stared into the distance. "If he didn't, then she was lying to me. You mentioned a banshee. I don't know what that is."

I gave him a brief rundown, leaving nothing out but not going into great detail either. When I finished he didn't look happy, but he seemed to understand what I was saying.

"You don't think there's any chance of saving Tawny even if she's still alive," he surmised.

"She's long gone," I acknowledged. "She was probably turned not long after you last saw her. She was taken and tortured ... battered and beaten ... and who knows what else over the next few days, maybe even weeks. But not by Groove. We need to figure out who took her because that's the person we're looking for. That's the person creating the banshees and unleashing them on the street."

"Look at it from a law enforcement perspective," he prodded. "What are these banshees trying to do?"

"They're collecting souls. As far as I can tell, that's all they're doing."

"What can you do with a soul?"

"You can ingest it and prolong life. Wraiths do it."

"Can you do anything else?"

"Not that I'm aware of."

"Then ... maybe it's not the souls. Maybe that's just a byproduct. Maybe it's something else."

"Like what?"

"The souls that are being taken, are they mostly street people?"

I thought back to what Redmond had told me. "As a matter of fact, yeah. Why do you think that matters?"

"Because, from the start, I've always assumed we had a cleaner working. People are dying, girls are going missing. All the while, the street is getting cleaner. It will never be completely clean, but that doesn't matter to a mission-oriented killer like this."

He seemed to know his stuff. Something occurred to me. "You said there was one person you told about Tawny's status to help you keep her safe. Who was that?"

"Beacon. He agreed to give her a place to stay occasionally."

My heart plummeted to my stomach. "Beacon?"

"Yeah. Why?"

"Right before you became my prime suspect, I was focusing on him."

"But ... why?"

"There's something wrong with him. There always has been."

"He helps kids," Logan argued. "He's a good guy who helps kids."

"No, he's a guy who wears a mask," I corrected, my mind busy. "He doesn't help anyone but himself ... and that's what he's been doing all along. He's been helping himself."

"If he's so bad, why haven't you crawled into his head to look around?"

"Because he shutters." It wasn't hard to come up with an answer. "He shutters, and I never really wanted to see inside his head as a kid because I assumed there was nothing good there. When I returned as an adult, I kept my distance out of instinct. It's him."

"You can't take him down on an instinct," Logan warned. "That's what you're planning to do, isn't it?"

"Yes. I'm going to take him down ... and maybe save at least one girl in the process. The odds of saving the other banshees aren't great, but I'm going to try. Either way, they're all going down tonight."

"And how do you plan to do that? You can't simply control people and force them to do what you want them to do."

"Watch me."

TWENTY-NINE

y the time the Grimlocks arrived, I had a plan. Redmond stayed the entire day, lending a hand wherever he could manage. By the time we cleared everyone out, jobs had been assigned and everyone knew what was expected of them.

"We're going to need you with us," I told Izzy. "The extra magic you can funnel into the spell will help."

"No problem." Izzy bobbed her head. "I guess I'm just confused. You said that you used magic to keep the banshees out but it didn't really work. How do you know this spell will?"

I'd given this a great deal of thought. "The dreamcatcher failed because they're not really banshees. I mean ... they are in the truest sense of the word. They were tortured to death, amassed more human suffering than should be imaginable, but they didn't turn themselves into banshees. Beacon did that."

"I'm still behind the curve here," Logan volunteered from the back. He and Griffin had been eyeing each other with suspicion since being introduced. I was somewhat worried the police detective would find himself the subject of an investigation at some point, but I couldn't dwell on that now. Besides, Cormack seemed the sort of man who had a lot of pull. He would protect Griffin. "How is Beacon behind this?"

"He was never what he pretended to be. I'm pretty sure he's a warlock."

"Why do you think that?" Max asked, his face twisted with concentration. "I mean ... wouldn't you have picked up on that when you were a teenager?"

"I think I did. I was the only one who never trusted him. Everyone else thought he was a great guy. Even Logan thought he was trustworthy."

"You haven't told me anything that suggests he isn't trustworthy," Logan countered. "He helped me when Tawny was undercover. He helped protect her."

"Unless he didn't. She told you she was sleeping with Groove for information. I don't believe that. Groove wouldn't touch her. He's all about the street cred. There's no street cred in banging Tawny ... and he would've taken care of his kid if he'd knocked her up. That's simply who he is."

"He's a thug," Logan countered. "He's always been a thug."

"I'm not arguing with that assessment. He's simply not a thug who would've slept with Tawny. I bet, once you really go back over her statements, she didn't give you anything she got from Groove. She gave you information that Beacon filtered through her."

"Why would Beacon have sex with her?" Logan asked. "I mean ... what's his motivation?"

"He's a man," Luke answered for me. "If there's sex to be had, most men will have it. They're not picky."

"Poet just said Groove was picky."

"Groove didn't need to swim in Tawny's pond. He had his own pond. All gangs have groupies. He didn't need to seek anyone out. They came to him."

"I guess." Logan stroked his chin. "If you knew he was evil, why didn't you say something years ago? I could've taken care of him."

"I didn't understand what was going on with me. I knew I could do things others couldn't — and was very careful to keep that to myself — but I didn't know how far I could take it. Max taught me about controlling it. Back then, I only knew that Beacon's mind was a blank slate. That always made me uncomfortable. I hated the nights it was so cold I had no choice but to try to get a bed at his place. I didn't know about shuttering then. He shuttered around me because he realized what I was."

"Or, if he didn't realize what you were entirely, he got a hit off you," Max added. "I believe you. You must have more to go on than just a hunch, though."

"I do. He was the only person who knew that Tawny was working for Logan. He would've known what Logan was even back then. I never got a pervy vibe off him because he was careful not to show his true face. Why do you think he did that?"

"Because of Logan," Aisling perfunctorily answered. "He knew Logan was a cop and didn't want to risk the law falling on him. He stayed away from you and groomed others."

"Yeah. I always thought he just didn't like me. He clearly feared me."

"And with good reason." Kade moved his hand to my back. "I still don't understand what's going on with the banshees. Why can they slide over the dreamcatcher?"

"I think he's been over here sniffing it out, but he stayed on the other side. You haven't seen him on our turf have you?"

"No."

"That's because he realized what we have going on here and stayed away. These aren't normal banshees. We've already figured that out. What he's done is hollow them out. They could cross the dreamcatcher because they didn't have evil intentions. They were programmed to follow their master. There's no evil intent in blindly following orders."

"Ah." Realization dawned on Max's face and he became more animated. "That makes sense. When you created the dreamcatcher, you wanted to make sure it drew in evil beings. You didn't want to kill just for the sake of killing. If a paranormal wasn't dangerous, you were fine letting it be."

"So the banshees don't mean to do evil, they're simply fed orders and don't know right from wrong," Raven mused. "It's an ingenious plan. But how did it start? I mean ... how did he know he could do it?"

"I've been thinking about that. I don't think he's been doing this from the start. I think he was evil, used street kids for nefarious means, and hid his magic for a specific reason. I think Tawny was his first. That's why she looked different to Creek. She had red eyes when she attacked Creek. The banshees we've seen haven't had red eyes."

"You think he's been experimenting," Izzy deduced. "I get what you're saying. Tawny was his first. He made strides with her, but she's not perfect."

"I think she's a lieutenant of sorts," I said, chewing on my bottom lip. "She hasn't crossed the dreamcatcher either. That's because she still has a sense of being. She knows who she is, probably remembers on some level what she was."

"How did he turn her?" Logan asked. "I mean ... how did he do it in the first place?"

"My guess is he took her captive somewhere in the cemetery," I replied. "According to the Grimlocks, half the old mausoleums have basements underneath them. That means the older crew in Detroit was probably up to some funky stuff."

"I would agree with that," Cormack said. "I happen to know quite a few families that dabbled in dark arts. It was en vogue at the turn of the century. That would be 1900, not 2000."

"I bet Beacon is tied to one of those families."

"He is," Griffin volunteered. He had Aisling pinned close to his side. He didn't look happy about her being included in the raiding party, but he was a wise man, and a wise man never tells his tempestuous wife what she can and can't do. The baby was home with his sister and the mysterious Jerry, who I was really starting to wish I'd been able to meet. The rest of the clan was in for the fight.

"You know who he's related to?" I asked, surprised. "How did you figure it out?"

"It wasn't hard. The shelter is registered in his real name: Rick Baxter. I ran the name and came up with something interesting. His father had the same name ... but there's no mother listed on the birth certificate. The same thing happened with the grandfather. One son birthed, but no mother."

"And there it is," I said, shaking my head. "He's been alive for a long time ... and he's been changing his name to cover for it."

"I'm sure it was easier before the computer era," Griffin noted. "I very much doubt he'll be able to get away with that again."

"Then he'll move on to another location. It might even be in Detroit. It just won't be where anyone could recognize him. Is there a Baxter mausoleum?"

"Yep."

"Is it near the Grimlock mausoleum?"

"Right around the corner."

"Then that's where we're going."

IT WAS A MOTLEY CREW OF MAGICAL individuals who made their way into the cemetery. I put sentries on each exit. They had specific instructions. When the banshees fled — which was inevitable — they were to dispatch them. The banshees were beyond saving. If we could find Valentine alive, then we could do something. Otherwise ... the girls were lost causes.

It was a hard reality to swallow, but there was no other option.

The second part of the equation was more difficult. I had to ensure that Beacon would be in the cemetery. To pull that off, I needed Michelob and Cotton to run their mouths. They were still confused about the magic — probably would be for a very long time — but they were eager to help.

They weren't alone when they returned to the shelter. I couldn't risk that. I went with them. Because I could glamour myself, I made it look as if I was another young teenage runaway. We talked about how crazy the circus folk were, their plans to search all the mausoleums after dark, and made sure Beacon was within hearing distance. I knew he took the bait. Seth was watching the back cemetery entrance from the shadows and reported when he went inside.

Everything was in place.

Griffin led the way to the mausoleum. He'd printed out a cemetery map. I recognized the building as soon as I saw it. One of the banshees had been hiding near it right before attacking. She most certainly had been sent out as a distraction.

"Are we ready?" I looked to Kade for confirmation.

"Ready," Nellie confirmed, ax in hand. "We'll handle the stragglers."

"Try not to make it hurt," I admonished. "These girls are victims."

"This ax is for the big guy."

"I'll be handling the big guy." I was firm. "We have history. He's mine."

"If you say so."

Max remained outside with Nellie, Dolph and most of the Grimlocks. Aisling whined about not being allowed inside to witness the action, but she didn't have the required magic to meet the threshold. Raven, Nixie, Naida, Izzy and I headed inside. The mausoleum wouldn't be big enough for a larger group to spread out and protect itself.

"This is exciting," Izzy enthused as she watched me use my magic to pick the lock. "I love a good fight."

I smiled. She had an infectious aura. "I don't know about exciting, but I want it over. I can't leave knowing these girls are still at risk."

"We'll handle it." She patted my arm. "After, I would love for you to tell me my fortune. I have a few ideas and I want to know if they'll come true."

I'd seen a glimpse of her future upon our first meeting. "It's better not knowing," I offered. "If you spend too much time trying to avoid the bad stuff that you know is coming you might inadvertently mess with the good stuff. I guarantee you don't want to screw up the good stuff."

"Really?" She cast a curious gaze over her shoulder, to where Braden stood with his father. He'd been the loudest voice of dissent when it was announced not everyone could enter the mausoleum.

"Really," I confirmed, grinning. "Don't worry about him. He'll be fine."

"I can't help but worry."

"I'm sure he feels the same way." The lock tumbled with little complaint and I glanced between the other women before pushing open the door.

It was time.

. . .

THE MAUSOLEUM APPEARED EMPTY. I wasn't surprised. Beacon wouldn't stand in the middle of it and greet us with open arms. He would strike from a place of strength, wait until our backs were turned, and then attack when he thought we were most vulnerable. He had no idea that our backs would never be exposed.

"Where do we think the steps are?" Raven asked, glancing around. She looked like a normal woman with extraordinary hair in the muted light — someone had left a lantern burning — but I knew better. She was gearing up for a fight.

"They can't be far." I narrowed my eyes as I glanced around the room, extending my magic as I searched for a void. I found what I was looking for a few seconds later. "This way."

The east wall had open space behind it. Once I figured that out, it was only a matter of time before I found a button to press. When I did, the wall slid open to reveal stairs that led downward.

"It's like *Scooby-Doo*." Nixie's eyes sparkled. "That's kind of fun."

Nothing about this was going to be fun, but I didn't want to be the downer of the group and say it out loud. If she wanted to find joy in the attack, more power to her.

"I'll go first." I was insistent, even when Naida offered to send a tornado down in our stead. "No." I firmly shook my head. "I need to see him with my own eyes. He won't be able to hide from all of us."

"He won't," Raven agreed. "Go. I'll be right behind you."

True to her word, Raven remained close. Izzy was in the middle of the group, delight practically wafting off her. Nixie and Naida brought up the rear. Naida was a bit pouty because she couldn't use a killer tornado on our enemy, but once the bodies started flying, she would get over it.

We were quiet as we descended. It didn't matter. Beacon was well aware the moment we breached his inner sanctum, and the look on his face when we hit the bottom of the stairs was murderous.

"You just couldn't leave well enough alone, could you?" he complained, fury etched across his face, eyes gleaming with onyx fire. In the atmospheric light, the lines on his face looked deep and entrenched. He barely looked human. "Why didn't you stay away?"

"Why did you do this?" I challenged, gesturing toward the banshees flanking him on either side. "What made you even think it was okay to do this?"

"I'm doing important work," he replied, his tone icy. "I'm ridding the street of the vermin. I deserve a medal for it, not condemnation."

I expected him to justify his actions. That's who he was. "Tawny was your first?" My eyes fell on the woman in the corner. She'd stopped aging years ago, which was why I so easily recognized her. She was a creature of the darkness now, a black hole where her soul should be, and there was no getting her back. "I'm sorry for whatever happened to you," I offered. "I ... don't know what else to say."

She didn't respond, only bared her teeth.

"What happened to the baby?" I asked Beacon. "Your baby."

"Oh, please." He rolled his eyes. "I'm not father material and we both know it. I couldn't believe it when she told me. I mean ... what the hell? I can't believe she thought I would be happy about it. She assumed I would want her to stay with me rather than leave with that stupid FBI agent. She was wrong."

Things slid into place. "Logan was going to take her away. You were okay with that because you were only using her anyway. She didn't understand what you are, that you're incapable of love. She thought you would want your child. She thought you would want to create a family with her."

"She was trying to trap me. She got pregnant on purpose."

I had no idea if that was true. It hardly mattered. "You tortured her, experimented on her." I glanced around the room. It was filled with ancient equipment, a multitude of torture devices I'd only read about in books and hoped never to see with my own eyes. "You did it here."

"This is my laboratory. I've done a lot of experiments here."

"I bet you have." The banshees didn't move, only stared, awaiting instruction. They truly were empty vessels. The only other person alive in the room was Valentine, and she was a sobbing mess as she huddled in the corner. "How many girls have you killed over the years?"

"Enough."

"And why do you have them collecting souls? Is that because your light is starting to fade?"

Surprise, lightning fast, whipped across his face. "What are you talking about? I'm as strong as ever."

"No, you're not." This was the part of the puzzle I hadn't quite worked out until now. It had been touched on, but I'd dismissed it. I shouldn't have. "You're fading. I can see the veins pulsing under your skin. You've lived a long time. I don't know if this is the natural end to your cycle or if you're dying for another reason, but you're not long for this world. You've been ingesting the souls they've been stealing to prolong your life. Not enough to become a wraith, but enough to buy time.

"That's why you've stepped up your efforts," I continued. "I couldn't figure that part out before. If you created your first banshee with Tawny, why not create more right away? My guess is that it wasn't as easy to perfect the process as you originally thought. So, what? Did you keep her around as a pet? Make her do your bidding for years?"

"I don't have to answer your questions," he shot back.

I ignored the sass. "You had to create more the past few months because your light is fading and you need them to bring you souls more often. You got greedy. You were flying under the radar at first, but you couldn't sustain it. You needed more and more souls to survive ... so you created more and more banshees. You ingested their souls as they died and turned them into your vessels. You benefitted twice from each kill."

"They were wastes of space anyway," Beacon shot back. "They had nothing to contribute to society. They were never going to grow up, pay taxes and become so-called productive members of society. I was doing this world a favor by eradicating them. Then I was doing the world a greater favor by pointing them toward a cause."

"You aimed them at street kids and the homeless because you thought they wouldn't be missed. But they were. Logan missed them. Griffin Taylor missed them. They were on the hunt."

"I'm not afraid of them."

"You are afraid of me. Don't bother denying it. I know what you see when you look at me."

"An aberration of nature, just like me. I knew from the moment I saw you thirteen years ago. I knew long before you."

"I don't doubt it. I grew to understand, and now I'm stronger than you."

"You're not. I may be weaker than I used to be, but I can still take you."

"Can you take all of us?" I gestured as those with me fanned out to take fighting stances. Izzy almost made me laugh despite the serious situation, because she looked like an extra from a kung-fu movie the way she held her hands. I didn't laugh, though. It wasn't funny. It was ... depressing. It was altogether sad. And what happened in this place would haunt me forever.

It was time.

"I'm not afraid of little girls playing at magic," he seethed. "You're not strong enough to stop me. You'll never be strong enough."

"Let's see."

Our magic joined at the same time. Izzy's extra fire added a pretty purple punch. Beacon's eyes widened at the display, his gaze going to the lanterns on the walls as the flames flickered.

"I'm not afraid of you," he repeated. "You can't take me."

"If you believe that, you're dumber than you look," Raven snapped. "Good grief. Look around. It's over."

"No!" He roared the answer, raising his own hands in defiance. Red flames — probably like the red Creek saw in Tawny's eyes the day of the attack — arced out as the banshees flew in our direction. They moved at once, an army of the soulless with only one thing on their minds: killing. He probably thought he could use them as a distraction. I wouldn't allow that.

"Raven!" I yelled. She was already moving.

"I've got it." She withdrew a series of silver stars from her pocket and dispatched them throughout the room, muttering a spell under her breath. The stars flew true, each embedding into the chest of a banshee. Within an instant, the banshees turned to dust, five of them disappearing in a breath.

"No!" Beacon's fury only grew. He was alone now. He still had Tawny, but she didn't look all that interested in joining the fight. Instead, she merely stared at where the women had been standing moments before, despair lurking behind her eyes ... which had started to glow red. "Do something," he barked at Tawny. "Kill them. Do what I created you to do."

Tawny didn't move.

"She's done following your orders," I snapped. "She still has a sense of self, even if her soul is gone. She can fight you. That's the real reason you kept experimenting. You knew your first attempt was ultimately a failure."

"She was definitely a failed effort," he agreed, frowning when I took a menacing step toward him. "What is it you think you're doing?"

"Ending you." I raised my hands. Nixie and Izzy were on either side of me. I didn't need their magic, but they were holding firm. "When you're gone, no one will remember you."

"The kids will remember me." Even in death, he was defiant. "My legacy will live forever."

"No. You'll be replaced by someone good, someone who really wants to help. Your name won't even be a whisper on the wind in a few weeks."

"You can't beat me," he howled. "I won't let you."

"It's already too late for that." I raised my hands until they were stretched above my head. Izzy's fingers sparked as she added her magic to mine. The excitement never left her face. "Goodbye, Beacon. I hope no one has mercy on your soul wherever it goes."

I released the magic with a flourish, watching without emotion as it swallowed him whole. He screamed — I knew he would — but it didn't last long. He was gone within seconds, leaving only Tawny to deal with ... and a sobbing Valentine curled in a ball on the floor. Just like the banshees he created out of hate and fear, he dissolved into dust.

When I turned to Tawny she looked almost happy. I very much doubted she'd ever been able to embrace happiness — even before she came across Beacon — but there was a certain giddiness about her smile.

"We can't let you live." I was apologetic. "I'm sorry, but we have to wipe this place clean."

"It's fine." Tawny's voice rasped as she used the wall to keep herself upright. She was weak, failing just like Beacon. She wouldn't have lasted much longer. "I'm ready to go. I've been ready for a long time."

"I'm still sorry."

"You can't control everything, girl." Her lips curved into the sad approximation of a grin. "I never thought you would be the one to end this."

"Yeah, well ... it had to be someone."

"Just make it fast." She closed her eyes. "Do you think I'll go somewhere?"

I had no idea. "I hope so." I hesitated for a moment when raising my hand, but Raven caught my wrist before I could unleash my magic again.

"I've got it," she whispered. "You don't have to do this one."

"I can."

"You don't have to. Not everything is your responsibility."

In my heart, I knew that. It was nice to be reminded.

30

THIRTY

*C*leanup was easy. We had only one body to deal with. Tawny didn't dissolve like the others, but she decayed fast. Nellie and Dolph handled it. They'd been cut out of the fighting — everyone had because Beacon insisted on using the banshees as cannon fodder to protect himself — and no one was happy. Even the Grimlocks looked a bit disappointed.

"Are you okay?" Braden swooped toward Izzy when we slid outside.

She nodded, a giggle escaping. "It was nothing. I didn't even work up a sweat."

"If you want to work up a sweat, I have a few ideas for that."

"You always do."

I smiled as I watched them leave, shaking my head when Kade moved in to hug me. I accepted the embrace. It felt good to be held. It would feel better when I could shower and put the day behind me. For now, though, this was enough.

"How are you?" His voice was a whisper against my ear.

"I'm okay. I was wrong about the souls. He was eating them to stay alive. He was sick. It was his last desperate attempt to remain in this world. He didn't care that he was removing others in the process."

"Well, then we won't care that he's gone." He swayed back and forth, resting his chin on the top of my head. "I think we should get out of here. You need some sleep."

"I need a shower more."

"We can make both happen."

"Yeah." I held on a moment longer and then focused on the Grimlocks. The boys were obviously disappointed. Even Aisling looked down. Cormack, though, seemed happy. I wondered if that would last after I asked a favor of him. "Um ... before you go." I disengaged from Kade and moved toward him. "I have something to ask you. I know it's a lot, but you're the only person I know who can get it done."

He spared a glance for Valentine as Seth and Luke helped her from the mausoleum. She was in rough shape and needed to be transported to the hospital.

"Let me handle that," Logan offered, hurrying to the girl's side. "It's the least I can do. You guys have done the heavy lifting."

"Thanks." I smiled at him. "Make sure you call Groove."

"I'd rather not."

"He's her brother and she's going to want him. Besides, you won't have to worry about him much longer."

"No?" Logan's face lit with intrigue. "Why is that?"

"It's better if you don't know."

"I guess I'll just have to take your word for it." He hugged me. "I'm glad you found your happiness," he whispered. "These people, the things you do, it's important. You're important. But don't look back on this life. You're better off putting as much distance between you and this place as possible."

I didn't believe that. "This is just a place."

"It's not your home."

"No. My home is with them." I gestured toward Kade and Max as I pulled away. "Home isn't a street ... or four walls and a roof. It's love and people."

"And me," Luke added, pinning me with a pointed look. "Don't forget about me."

"I could never forget about you." I blew him a kiss and turned my eyes back to Logan. "You should probably look toward your future, too." I'd seen a glimpse of it during the hug. "You have something blonde coming your way."

"Hmm?" He looked puzzled. "I don't understand."

"You will. Eventually."

"Well ... as long as she's normal — or relatively normal — I should be fine."

He was in for a rude awakening. It wasn't good for him to dwell on that now, though. He had other things on his plate. "Watch Groove, but you don't need to move on him. It won't be long."

"You seem awfully sure of yourself."

"I am. His future is written, which is something I can rarely say. Let him spend time with his sister. Not because he needs it, but because she does. Then help her move past this life."

"Okay." He gave me another brief hug. "Will I ever see you again? You can see the future."

I smirked. "Never say never." I watched him go for what felt like a long time. Once he was clear of the area, I turned my attention to Cormack. "I don't want to take too much of your time, but I need to ask a big favor. You don't have to say yes, but know I'll cry if you say no."

He snorted. "Did Aisling tell you that's the way to get me to do things?"

"No, but I've seen her in action. I like to think I'm a quick learner."

"Then lay it on me. I would love to hear what you have in mind."

THE CIRCUS CLOSED AT FIVE the next day. Usually I would've been in the thick of the cleanup, but Kade and Max had urged me to run the few errands I had left. We would leave early the next morning, and there were two things I had to do.

I met Cormack at a Coney restaurant near Creek's house. He didn't as much as raise an eyebrow when he saw the dingy interior of the restaurant. Instead, he headed straight for me and slid in across the booth.

"This place smells divine," he noted. "It reminds me of my childhood."

I laughed. "It reminds me of the same thing. Did you do as I asked?"

"And hello to you, too," he drawled, shaking his head.

"I'm sorry." I held up my hands in contrition. "I didn't mean to come off so rude. I just ... I'm a little antsy. I'm going to visit an old friend." I pulled two envelopes out of my coat pocket. They were old and showing signs of age. "I wrote these before I left. One for Logan and one for Creek. They never got them. The guy I gave them to found them a few years ago and didn't have the heart to toss them. I have a second chance to deliver them and I'm anxious."

"It's closure," he noted. "You need it."

"Yeah. I ... did you do what I asked?" I was a bucket of nerves.

He laughed. "You remind me of my children. You even look enough like a few of them to pass from afar. Yes, I did as you asked. I now own the Beacon Shelter. It will be under new management within the week and I will be expanding services."

I exhaled heavily, relieved. "Thank you. I know that's probably more than you want to take on, but that shelter is important."

"It's not more than I want to take on. It's simply different than my usual endeavors. I'm thinking of putting Redmond in charge. I think he needs a little culture in his life."

I laughed, as he'd probably intended. "Thank you so much. I don't know that I'll ever be able to repay you. It had to be a lot of money."

"Money doesn't matter in the grand scheme of things ... and I've got plenty of it. You can't put a price on helping those most at risk. I will make sure that happens going forward. You can rest easy."

"Thank you." I rubbed my forehead. One task down. "I just ... thank you so much."

He reached across the table and rested his hand on top of my free hand. "You've done a wonderful thing here. You won't be remembered for it by anyone other than those who were there, but you'll be remembered fondly by us."

Tears pricked the back of my eyes. "Aisling said you were the best father ever. I guess she was right."

"She's always been my favorite child."

"You should probably give her a seafood bar for dinner tonight."

"I like the way you think." He leaned over the table and pressed a kiss to my forehead. That was enough to get the tears flowing freely. "I know your parents are gone."

I was surprised by the statement. "Did you reap their souls?"

"No." He was solemn as he shook his head. "I looked up the records last night. My wife reaped them. I don't know if they said anything to her. I don't know if they were afraid for you, but I'd bet they were. All I know is that they went to a good place. If you're worried about that, you shouldn't be."

I found, upon reflection, that I never worried they went to a bad place. "Thank you for that. For the other stuff, too."

"You mean your friend Noble? I checked on him. He'll be reburied with full military honors, and there will be a garden planted in his honor at the shelter. I've already started the ball rolling."

The man was fast. "You're a miracle worker."

"I am," he agreed. "I also have a home for your little urchins. I believe their names are Michelob and Cotton. They'll be going to a reaper family for the next year and a half. The individual in question is well aware of their background and that you'll be in constant contact. They'll be safe and well cared for."

And I thought Santa Claus was the best gift giver. "How did you get all of this accomplished so quickly?"

"I'm a good multi-tasker."

There was no doubt about that. "Well ... then I owe you about ten more thank-yous." I let out a shaky breath. "You didn't have to do all this for me. What I asked of you was too much. You not only came through, you went above and beyond. You're ... amazing."

Tears flowed freely now, and Cormack's finger was gentle as he brushed it against my cheek. "As I said, I didn't know your parents," he started. "I wish I had. As a parent, I feel as if I can speak for them. Wherever they are — and I'm betting they're only biding time until they see you again — they're watching you with a great amount of pride."

I choked on a sob.

"You're changing the world in the most important ways imaginable," he continued. "You have a family that isn't much different from mine. This might not have been their ultimate plan for you, but they can't be unhappy with the outcome."

"Yup. You're definitely a good dad." I could barely speak around the tears.

"With that in mind, I have one more surprise for you." He reached into the inside pocket of his suitcoat and retrieved an envelope. "I had Cillian conduct a little research for me. Your friend Creek has been going to school to become a paralegal. She'll be done with the coursework in two weeks. She has a job waiting for her at a law firm with a guaranteed salary and health benefits for her daughter."

An overwhelming flow of love washed over me. "What?"

"You heard me." His grin widened. "I won't allow her to be forgotten either."

"But ... that's going above and beyond."

"Is it? She's important to you. You helped us rid the street of a terror. On our own, we could've been hurt trying to take him out. You didn't allow that to happen. From where I stand, this is a paltry repayment."

"But ... ." I was overwhelmed.

"Your FBI friend was right about one thing yesterday. You shouldn't spend all your time looking back. Don't spend all of it looking forward either. Enjoy the present. You have a man who loves you, another who thinks you're his platonic life mate and yet another who thinks of himself as your father. You need to embrace all three."

"I have." I swiped the back of my hand over a tear-streaked cheek.

"Then keep it up." He patted my shoulder and then slid out of the booth. "If you return to the area, you know how to find us. Our door will always be open."

"Will the stuffy butler be on the other side of it?"

"Very likely."

"Well, it still might be worth a visit." I beamed at him and clutched the envelope he'd given me for Creek close to my chest. "I'll never forget any of you."

"Of course you won't." He winked. "We're unforgettable."

And, with those words he swept out of the restaurant. For a long time, I stared at the employment offer he'd given me. Then I exited the restaurant. I had two stops left — Logan and Creek — and the letters would mean different things to both of them.

Cormack was right. The past had to be put away. There was too much life left to live, and I couldn't live it if I was constantly looking over my shoulder.

It was time to say goodbye to the people I'd known and allow them to move forward to be the people they were meant to be.

It was time.